Lafcadio's Legacy

LINDA LINDHOLM

GLUE POT PRESS
NEW ORLEANS, LOUISIANA

Copyright © 2024 Linda Lindholm

All rights reserved. No part of this publication may be reproduced, distributed, or transmitted in any form or by any means, including photocopying, recording, or other electronic or mechanical methods, without the prior written permission of the author, except in the case of brief quotations embodied in reviews and certain other noncommercial uses permitted by copyright law.

All rights reserved by Linda Lindholm

Cover and interior design: Max Marbles & Linda Lindholm Publisher: Glue Pot Press
New Orleans, Louisiana

Printed in U.S.A.

ISBN: 978-0-9831616-6-0

To my friend Yuri with love
Takis

DEDICATION

To my mentor, inspiration, and friend

TAKIS EFSTATHIOU

INTRODUCTION

Patrick Lafcadio Hearn (1850-1904) wrote twenty-nine books in varied genres. His studies of American, Caribbean, and Japanese societies have been an inspiration, influence, and model for over a century. But none of his sensational writings can compare with this international man of letters' own life story. He is the most interesting subject of all.

Patrick Lafcadio Hearn was born June 27, 1850 on the Greek Ionian island of Lefkada (then Agia Maura, Santa Maura). He was the second child of the romantic but ill-fated union of Rosa Antoniou Cassimati, a Hellenic woman of noble Kythera lineage, and Charles Bush Hearn, a British Army medical officer of Anglo-Irish descent. Four months before his birth, his father was reassigned to duty in the West Indies and left the young family in Lefkada until he could send them to live with his parents in Ireland. In 1852, Rosa and Patrick journeyed to Dublin to live with the extended Hearn family. Illness and the cold, strange environment drove Rosa back to her homeland in Greece. His parents divorced and both remarried others and started new families. His father was reassigned by the military to India. Patrick never saw either his mother or father again. The boy was abandoned in Ireland and raised by his widowed, paternal great-aunt Sarah Holmes Brenane in a well-to-do, strict Dublin home. Although she was fond of little

Patrick, her house rules were formal, and foreboding. The bright and curious lad found comfort and escape from his sorrows in her library collection. It was among these dusty book stacks where he developed a love of the written word and art, which he called a 'personal rebirth'.

In 1863 Patrick went away to a Jesuit boarding school in Yvetot, France and then to St. Cuthbert's College, Ushaw, a Catholic seminary at what is now the University of Durham, England. A freak playground accident resulted in loss of sight in his left eye at age sixteen. His deformed eye was coated in white scar tissue and the other was red and bulging from overwork. Afterward, he became introverted, deeply self-conscious and insecure about his appearance. He long believed himself a misfit. Had this physical disability not been an issue, he may have felt more connected to the world he later floated through like a wandering ghost.

He found himself in strained financial circumstances when his entire inheritance, due to pass to him from his great-aunt, fell into bankruptcy and was lost. Patrick was forced to leave school. He spent a miserable, lonely, and bitter time in London East End at the home of a former maid. He generally lived a rootless, aimless existence. He educated himself by visiting the British Museum and libraries.

Hearn wandered the streets and spent time in workhouses to survive. He recoiled in disgust at encounters with British industrial and empire building society. Crestfallen in his expectations and alienated from the country and religion in which he was raised, he was forced in 1869 to immigrate to the United States, alone, at nineteen years old. As he entered the United States, he decided to register and use his middle name, Lafcadio, to honor his Greece heritage and break with his Irish Catholic background.

America was still recovering from its brutal Civil War and cultural divisions. Young Hearn made his way from New York to Cincinnati, Ohio. He survived grinding poverty, homelessness, and near starvation until Henry

Watkin, a reclusive Scottish printer, helped him find a career in journalism. Thanks to the Cincinnati Public Library he was able to read voraciously and develop an appreciation for French romantic writers.

Lafcadio paid his scrivener's dues with over fifteen years of writing for various news sources and translating French writers such as Gautier, Loti, Maupassant and Flaubert. His career as an American writer included enormous volumes of ground-breaking journalism magazine articles and as a newspaper reporter at the *Cincinnati Inquirer* and *Commercial*. His notoriety stemmed mostly from reports detailing the city's darker side, with shocking descriptions of morbid crime scenes. He spent years (1870-1877) in Cincinnati learning his craft as a creative storyteller.

Lafcadio's own down-and-out experiences deepened his sympathies for the common people, reminding his readers of what lay beneath society's veneer of respectability. He became known for his sensationist newspaper articles, chiefly featuring the exploited working class, criminals, psychologically and socially marginal people. Throughout his writing career, he showed profound respect for minorities, non-Western cultures, and those on the fringes of society.

In late 1877, he boarded a paddle-wheeler bound for New Orleans, Louisiana. Lafcadio immediately loved this Crescent City in a bend of the Mississippi River for its tropical warmth, multi-cultural history, sights, and sounds. After a difficult period of unemployment, illness, and poverty during the post-Civil War Reconstruction era, he went to work for the New Orleans *Item* (1878-1881) and then *Times-Democrat* (1881-1887). He became a local literary legend.

It was said that Lafcadio Hearn "invented New Orleans" with his reports on the mystique and frivolity of the French Quarter, Creole culture and music, voodoo, Cajun food, and the city's unique Southern character. His writings about New Orleans conjured up an exotic, mysterious, romantic city vision that attracted creative minds well into the next century and helped fuel a cultural renaissance. Reporting on the 1884 World Industrial Exposition in New Orleans connected Hearn to a national audience. The Expo Japan pavilion exhibit kindled his keen interest in the Orient.

LAFCADIO'S LEGACY

He was a prolific, regular contributor to popular publications of the day - *Harper's Magazine* and *Bazaar, Scribner's, Cosmopolitan, The Atlantic,* and *Century* magazines. Wanting to break with the daily drudgery of newspaper work and indulge his wanderlust, Lafcadio lived on the island of Martinique in the West Indies for two years (1887-1888), where he wrote about Caribbean people, legends, and folkways. During his time among the islanders, he completed two novels, *Chita* and *Youma*. *Harper's* magazine consolidated his travel writings and pictures from St. Pierre, Martinique into a book, *Two Years in the French West Indies*.

In an 1887 article, "The Recent Movement of Southern Literature", Lafcadio Hearn was listed among great writers such as Mark Twain, Robert Lewis Stevenson, and George Washington Cable, assuring his acceptance into the competitive American writing scene. Publishers and literary circles in New York City competed for this introverted, half-blind writer's works and sought after his attendance at public events and private salon gatherings. The complex, artificial, and hectic pace of New York confused and frustrated him to an unbelievable degree. Yet he went to the dreaded metropolis to seek national recognition for his three latest books *Chita: A Memory of Last Island; Youma: The Story of a West Indian Slave;* and *Two Years in the French West Indies*. He wanted to find sponsors for future, independent novel projects and leave newspaper reporting behind forever.

With his passion for exotic travel fired up from his time in the Caribbean West Indies, he quickly accepted an offer from the Canadian Pacific Railroad Company to write about a train trip across Canada as well as a ship journey to Japan. Artist, C.D. Weldon would accompany him to illustrate his narratives, adding a great deal to reader appeal. *Harper's* editor Henry Alden wrote to Hearn's Japan trip sponsors, "There is no writer of English so capable as he of fully appreciating and of adequately portraying with the utmost charm and felicity every shade, however quaint and subtle, of the life of strange people. The result of close studies by him in Japan will be a revelation to all readers."

Lafcadio took off to his new destination with too much trust and too little money in his pockets. On March 8th, 1890, when he crossed over the Canadian border headed toward the Land of the Rising Sun, Lafcadio Hearn's American days were over. He would never return from Japan.

Lafcadio, forever the itinerate journalist, was determined to observe and vividly report on the real life of the people of Japan as if his readers were living the daily existence and thinking with the thoughts of ordinary commoners. Readers clamored for any information on the country and people of Japan. The far east nation of Japan had been completely closed for centuries, under threat of death to any foreigner entering, or native leaving, the island.

Once Commodore Perry's U.S. Naval Fleet forced opened the ports for international trade, Japan began a dramatic shift to modernization. A continuing theme in Lafcadio's work was the quest for pure, authentic cultures uncorrupted by contact with the larger currents of change. Fortune handed Lafcadio a plum of an assignment in 1890 - to capture the fading vestiges of old Japan in the last moments before the country made its great transition into a new century of industrialization.

He is widely credited with being among the first to bring Japanese literature, culture, religion, customs, folktales, and interpretations to the Western world's attention. Knowing the historic changes occurring helps to understand why his observations and collections of ancient literature were so important to the preservation of Japan's heritage for future generations.

This Greek-born, wandering Anglo-Irishman traveled to Japan and became the West's foremost interpreter of all things Japanese, searching for some middle ground of human understanding between two disparate cultures. His author's junket turned into a pilgrimage, an odyssey.

He served as a bridge between the East and West. When he died in 1904, as Japanese citizen Koizumi Yakumo, he was acclaimed as the most influential authority of his generation on what is essential and lasting in Japanese culture. He was eulogized as an honored national writer/poet laureate, the one European author who could see into the Japanese soul. Japanese schoolchildren are assigned Koizumi Yakumo's books to learn English and about their own heritage through his folktales, legends, and ghost stories.

The majority of his books featured his beloved adopted home Japan, personal growth, and social consciousness. His humanitarian messages teach readers to be more empathetic, tolerant, and respectful toward other people, regardless of their race, national origin, or religion.

Although Lafcadio Hearn died over a century ago, his writings, both from the United States and Japan, remain valid, speaking clearly and directly to today's world and issues. Reading Hearn can seem like skimming the latest headlines. He binds together people of different cultures and distant epochs to break the barriers of time and place - proof that the written word can work magic. His writing speaks to the emotions as well as to the intellect. He thoughtfully observed, recorded, and published events of his era, but additionally possessed the prophetic vision of a seer, predicting future scientific, economic, educational, and social advances that have occurred.

The life journey that brought Lafcadio to Japan was arduous and chaotic. It was fraught with abrupt departures, dire financial straits, struggles with prevailing social conventions, shattered emotional connections, and finally international recognition for his literary genius.

This civilized nomad traveled the world and wrote about the strikingly exotic things and people he encountered. But the most unusual and interesting subject was the man himself. His unconventional life and eccentric personality make Lafcadio's biography and visionary books relevant in today's world. *Lafcadio's Legacy* is an in-depth story specifically about his life in Japan (1890-1904) and the continued impact of his works and philosophy.

LAFCADIO'S LEGACY

CHAPTER 1

Lafcadio Hearn stuffed all his worldly possessions into two enormous bags. Staggering under their weight and bulk, on March 8, 1890 he boarded a train for Montreal, Canada. The image of him from behind with the bulging suitcases was the first illustration artist C.D. Weldon recorded of their journey to Japan.

Lafcadio and Weldon traveled north from New York to Montreal, the gray limestone city, with streets covered in late winter snow. He described his impressions of his arrival, "As I step from the railroad depot, not upon Canadian soil, but on Canadian ice. Ice, many inches thick, sheets the pavement: and lines of sleighs, instead of lines of hacks, wait before the station for passengers. No wheeled vehicles are visible, except one hotel omnibus, only sleighs are passing... It is quite cold, but beautifully clear. Over the frozen white miles of St. Lawrence River sleighs are moving – so far away that it looks like a crawling of beetles."

Their trip from New York to Montreal to Vancouver, British Columbia by train, then a steamship for Yokohama, Japan was financed by the President of Canadian Pacific Railway (CPRR), the legendary Sir William Van Horne. He wanted favorable articles about experiences on CPRR trains and ships to encourage future travelers. Construction of the 1865-mile, transcontinental route was completed only four years earlier in 1886. In Montreal, Hearn and Weldon collected their (CPRR) train and ship tickets along with a $250 stipend from Van Horne and set out on their daring journey.

Eight thousand miles of land and sea lay ahead. Although he still longed for Caribbean island tropics where he'd lived for two years, Lafcadio felt the pull of new horizons westward toward Japan, 'the most eastern East'.

They crossed the North American continent aboard a Canadian Pacific train, passing Lake Superior, Winnipeg, and the Prairies. Much of the scenery was covered by spring snow and the blanketing whiteness strained his one good eye. Temperatures dropped to twenty-five below zero. Lafcadio was constantly cold, but found the Rocky Mountains breathtaking.

He wrote, "One mountain we pass has three jagged summits with vast clefts between. We are nearly five thousand three hundred feet above sea…we descend…the train rocking like a ship as we rush through canyons and gorges and valleys…And it is here, in these canyons and above these charms, that for the first time one obtains a full sense of the human effort which spanned the northern continent with this wonderful highway of steel, a full comprehension of the enormity of the labour involved." He wrote of the enormous challenges and dangers of railway construction in the Rockies such as "avalanches which rush down one slope with such fury that the impetus carries them up the opposite slope."

With his railroad publicity assignment in mind, he produced a bundle of travel notes. His trip observations were published in a *Harper's Magazine* 1890 article "A Winter Journey to Japan." From his sleeper train interestingly named *Yokohama*, he noted, "There is not one buffalo now upon the Buffalo Plains; all have been murdered for their hides…The wanton destruction of the buffalo was the extermination also of a human race. And I have been reading on the train in some Canadian paper, of Indians frenzied by hunger."

As they approached the west coast Province of British Columbia, he wrote, "We passed great ranges in the night and are now steaming through canyons of the Fraser River. Above us the wooded mountains still lift their snows to the sun. Below us the river runs like a black ribbon edged with white, it is iced along its edges."

Lafcadio predicted that the small town of Vancouver, sitting in an immense wilderness at the edge of the world was "destined to be a mighty city" in the future. The first European to explore this northwestern corner of North America was Ioannis Fokas, a Greek pilot, better known by his hispanized name of Juan de Fuca, who served Philip II of Spain. The straits between Vancouver Island, British Columbia and the Olympic Peninsula of Washington state were named after him.

At Vancouver, British Columbia, on March 17, 1890, Hearn and Weldon boarded the *S. S. Abyssinia*, a sturdy steamship, to cross the Pacific Ocean toward Yokohama in the Country of Eight Islands. The ship could carry up to two hundred first-class passengers and one thousand in steerage. It had a speed of 13 knots or 15 miles per hour.

The seventeen-day crossing was dismal and disappointing. Most days were filled with rain, sleet, and snow, relived occasionally by a dull sun and heavy green seas. There was never another ship or remote point of land to be seen on the dreary ocean. Lafcadio could only stay on deck for a few minutes at a time due to icy headwinds.

Onboard, he described ship travel, "…and always an immense rhythmical groaning and crackling of timbers, as the steamer, rocking like a cradle, forges her way through the enormous billowing at thirteen knots an hour."

He couldn't read or work in his poorly lit cabin, where the sparse light coming through the porthole was often blotted out by waves crashing against the hull. Most of his time was spent in a tiny smoking room where the captain would stop in to give him updates on the weather and share his pessimistic fear of uprising among the Chinese crew and steerage passengers. Lafcadio once visited the steerage section to observe the Chinamen in their cramped quarters. There were a hundred or so alive and sixty dead in the hold being transported home for burial. A silent game of fan-tan was in progress. Due to his heightened sense of smell, the scented candle wax, unwashed bodies, and opium smoke drove him away.

As the sun rose on April 4th, 1890 (the 23rd Meiji by Japanese reckoning) Lafcadio and Weldon went on deck in the cold, fresh air, eager for their first view of Japan. The sea was a waste of black ink, and jagged mountains rose blue against the horizon slowly filling with sunrise's rosy flame. Stars were still faintly burning. He could not yet spot the sacred Mt. Fuji.

A ship's officer laughed and told him, "You are looking too low. Higher up, much higher!" He looked up into the heart of the sky, and suddenly, where he had seen nothing, the snowy top of Mt. Fijiyama hung above the dark shore. The foothills beneath were still wrapped in gray fog. Fiji stood austerely pure and beautiful, like a vision of unattainable virtue. The wondrous spectacle struck him dumb.

Lafcadio later wrote about his first sighting of Mt. Fuji, "There with a delicious shock of surprise I see something for which I had been looking,---far exceeding all anticipation---but so ghostly, so dream white against the morning blue, that I did not observe it at the first glance: an exquisite snowy cone towering above all other visible things---Fujiyama...I see...only the perfect crown, seeming to hang in the sky like a delicate film,---a phantom."

After a long silent pause Lafcadio whispered, "I want to die here!"

The more matter-of-fact Weldon, leaning on the wooden rail next to him, exclaimed, "I don't. I want to live here!"

They watched strange little boats rushing out from Yokohama to meet their steamer until it was time for them to disembark. Whenever Lafcadio went some place for the first time, he was overcome with childlike joy, excitement, and curiosity. His imagination whirled.

That night Lafcadio, Weldon, and some fellow passengers attended a geisha performance. They watched a dance where each performer had to give up an article of clothing whenever she made a mistake in step or gesture. Just like when he attended quadroon balls in New Orleans, he was too enthralled with the dark-skinned ladies to leave. When his friends were ready to return to their quarters, he refused to go with them.

Weldon and Hearn decided that each would go his own way once they went ashore. Lafcadio Hearn had always preferred to work alone, so they agreed to consult occasionally. As soon as Lafcadio completed an article, he would contact Weldon to supply illustrations suitable for the piece.

Lafcadio arrived in Japan at a time of disruptive social, political, and economic change. Japan had just won the Sino-Japanese War against China and was rapidly modernizing. The old traditional society of simplicity and charm were under threat. He had his reporting work cut out for him.

Lafcadio found a reasonable waterfront hotel, Carey's, 93 Yamashita-cho. He described the manager, Carey, an American mulatto, as "a kind, and a good man to the bones of him." The small hotel was frequented by sailors. He described it as "an atmosphere of sailors and sealers and mates and masters of small craft…a salty medium of water-dogs."

It was an island of refuge in a swirl of city and port activities. Lafcadio was uncomfortable in the more sedate, respectable places that tourists frequented. He liked Carey's because he could slip in and out without notice. He always got along better with rough men who weren't too drunk, than he did with businessmen and socialites. Carey's hotel would be a good base for his explorations.

CHAPTER 2

One of Lafcadio's first actions was to seek out Professor Basil Hall Chamberlain to present a letter of introduction from William Patten, *Harper's* Art Editor and fellow collector of Japanese books and oddities. Chamberlain was a British Professor of Philosophy and Japanese language at Tokyo Imperial University. Chamberlain had lived in the country since 1873 and was fluent in several dialects of Japanese. He was a distinguished writer of Japanese life and literature, producing some of the earliest translations of *haiku* poetry into English. He was a pioneering scholar of the Ainu and Ryukyuan languages and became famous for his excellent and amusing encyclopedia, *Things Japanese*.

Lafcadio was impressed by Chamberlain's works he'd read among Patten's library books. Henry Alden, an editor at *Harper's*, previously sent the professor a copy of Lafcadio's *Some Chinese Ghosts*, so the two authors were remotely familiar with one another.

"If you really want to understand Japanese culture and beliefs, you must know about their history, especially the national policy of isolationism, *sakoku*, for over 250 years and how it has altered dramatically recently," the knowledgeable professor advised when they first met.

With Chamberlain's help and by reading all he could find by other scholarly observers, Lafcadio pieced together an overview of the radical changes and sweeping transformations during Meiji Restoration. Like the journalist and ethnographer he was, he wanted to learn everything he could about the country and the revolutionary times he was entering. He studied past history and the country's recent opening of trade with the West. In addition to Lafcadio's own research, Professor Chamberlain, in his university lecturing way, told him:

"In the 17th century, after a century of brutal warfare, the Tokugawa Ieyasu government founded a ruling system focused on establishing social, political, and international affairs. The political structure bound all powerful feudal lords (*daimyos*) to the hereditary military dictator (*shogunate*) and limited individuals from acquiring too much power or territory. Shogun commanders were technically appointed by the emperor; however, control of the military became control of the country."

"What did this new Japanese government call itself? How was it organized?" asked Lafcadio, anxious to learn all he could from an expert.

"The old shogunate military government was called the *bakufu*. Social castes were ranked with samurai warriors at the top, followed by farmers, artisans, and merchants. Through the establishment of rigid social hierarchy, Japan experienced an era of internal peace, stability, and economic growth.

The Tokugawa regime, which ruled from 1603 until 1868---called the Edo period, attempted to seal Japan off from the outside world to prevent change. The foreign relations policy of isolation (*sakoku*) was strictly imposed and enforced to prevent any threat to the stability of the shogunate and to maintain peace in the archipelago of Japan. For about 250 years, *sakoku* laws prescribed the death penalty for foreigners entering or Japanese nationals leaving the country."

"That seems rather extreme," said Lafcadio.

"Just remember that due to its isolation, Japan was never a colony. The strict *sakoku*, closed country policy of the shogun Tokugawa Ieyasu, who banned all Christian missionaries and Western foreigners from the insular empire, helped Japan escape the curse of Western imperialism."

"I thought I read where there were some Dutch allowed to bring in Chinese goods like porcelain and sandalwood."

"In 1635 the national isolation policy was altered slightly to allow Chinese and Dutch traders limited to a tiny artificial island Dejima in the bay of Nagasaki. In 1844 the Dutch sent a diplomatic mission urging the *bakufu* military government to open the country, but restrictions on foreign trade remained. That same year, the Dutch King William II sent a letter urging Japan to end their isolation policies before the Western world imposed it by force. The letter was ignored."

"Dutch, British, and French ships continued to visit the islands to request commercial relations. The Japanese response was to fortify coastal defenses and add gun emplacements in preparation for potential attacks. In 1846 Commander James Biddle of the American East Indian fleet sailed two warships into Uraga Harbor near Yokohama and met with bakufu representatives about allowing foreign traders to enter its ports. Because of increased incursions of foreign ships into Japanese waters, the feudal lords and samurai were internally debating and divided between seclusion and expulsion of Westerners versus opening the country to trade and international intercourse. Therefore, no resolution was reached at that time. Between 1790 and 1853, at least twenty-seven U.S. ships visited Japan, only to be rudely turned away."

"What eventually broke the blockade of foreign trade?"

"The United States needed ports in Japan for provisions and fuel for Pacific merchants, whaling ships, and military. The Japanese learned that Commodore Perry had sailed to Japan with 'full and discretionary powers', including the possible use of force if the Japanese treated him as badly as they had Commodore Biddle. When Perry called on the Ryukyu Islands in May, 1853, he threatened local authorities with attack by hundreds of well-armed troops if he were not allowed trading rights and supplies. His every action was reported to authorities in the Edo capital.

"Finally, the cooperation of Japan was unilaterally forced by massive naval strength when the Commodore, under orders from President Millard Fillmore, entered Edo Bay on July 8, 1853 with a squadron of U.S. warships firing their powerful cannons. The Japanese called them black ships (*kurofune*) because of their billowing black smoke. They booted down the door to Japan because they wanted supplies like coal, whale oil and water. The goals of Perry's expedition were to explore, survey, establish diplomatic relations and negotiate trade agreements. Americans also believed in the concept of manifest destiny and the desire to introduce the Christian religion and the benefits of western civilization on what they perceived as backward Asian countries," Professor Chamberlain continued.

"Perry presented the Japanese government a letter from President Fillmore with the American demands. Shogun Tokugawa Ieyoshi had recently died and was succeeded by a sickly son Tokugawa Iesada, leaving administration of the country in the hands of the Council of Elders. Extensive debate occurred in shogunal court and Council. They knew the country's defenses were totally inadequate to repel the American military by force. So they decided to accept virtually all the demands in Fillmore's letter. Still weeks of negotiations ensued, accompanied by diplomatic gestures such as the exchange of gifts, cultural displays, and performances. The *bakufu* shogun, in spite of opposition from supporters of the emperor in Kyoto, finally signed the Treaty of Kanagawa or Perry Convention on March 31, 1854, and later the Harris Treaty 1858. Perry's intimidating gunboat diplomacy had forced an end to Japan's 220-year-old policy of isolation. Japan accepted US demands and opened its doors for the first time in two centuries."

"Didn't the other shogun warlords resist this threat to their power and control?" Lafcadio asked.

"Shoguns' claims of loyalty to the throne and roles as subduers of barbarians were questioned when they supported allowing foreign trade. Firmly xenophobic activists chanted "*Sonno joi*", "Revere the emperor! Expel the barbarians!" Dissatisfied with the shogun Council of Elders' management of national affairs, samurai warriors used their swords against the hated westerners and all who sided with them. Western military advances were too powerful a force against ancient weapons. Additionally, the uprising exacted a heavy toll on samurai political enemies. Anti-foreign aggression provoked stern countermeasures by the Americans, such as the bombardment of Kagoshima and Shimonoseki and other devastating diplomatic sanctions. Expelling foreigners by force would prove impossible."

"It sounds like a bloody internal civil war was fought over the issue," said Lafcadio.

"You are right," answered Chamberlain. "Military coups and shogunal armies continued internally battling each other for control. When British minister Sir Harry Parkes arrived in 1865, he decided not to negotiate with all the various regional *bakufu* governments and went directly to the imperial court in Kyoto. A group of Japanese noble counselors secretly went to England and their focus became national unity - to overthrow Japan's feudal system and create a new government headed by the emperor."

"How was the emperor going to change hundreds of years of regional strongholds in power?"

"The emperor's grand plan was to consolidate his power by commanding a modern army that would supplant the samurai caste that had served the shogun warlords for centuries. The shogunal samurai were defeated by organized militia units that used Western arms and training methods. The new imperial army advanced on Edo and the city surrendered without a battle. In January 1868 the principal *daimyo* leaders were summoned to Kyoto and forced to accept the restoration of imperial rule. The young Meiji emperor moved to the Tokugawa castle in Edo and renamed the city Tokyo, meaning Eastern Capital. With the emperor and his national supporters now in control, the modernization of Japan began."

"How did the new leadership plan to replace such an old deeply entrenched system?"

"The Meiji government was convinced that Japan needed a constitution for unified national government, industrialization to gain commercial strength, and a well-trained and armed military for national security to protect independence and achieve equality with the West. Leaders of the Meiji Restoration, as their revolution came to be known, announced that the Emperor of Japan would henceforth exercise supreme authority in all internal and external affairs of the country.

"Japanese people and the former Tokugawa regime shoguns were convincingly told that radical changes such as restoration of imperial rule would protect Japan against the threat of being colonized by Western forces like other parts of the world. 'If we take the initiative, we can dominate; if we do not, we will be dominated,' leaders like Shimazu Nariakira concluded."

"I can't believe all the powerful warlords and samurai gave up so easily."

"Not all shoguns were onboard with the changes in government and so holdouts started the Boshin War. Some shogunate forces escaped to Hokkaido in the north and attempted to establish a separate Republic of Ezo. However, the ex-shogun armies were defeated by forces loyal to the Emperor. All Tokugawa lands were seized and put under imperial control. Japan's 280 domains were turned into 72 prefectures, each under the control of a state-appointed governor. Many daimyos who cooperated with the new regime were given positions with the new Meiji government."

"What does *meiji* mean?" asked Lafcadio.

"The word "*Meiji*" meant 'enlightened rule'. The goal of the reformists was to combine modern advances with traditional eastern values. The Meiji slogans were "*Fokoku kyohei*---Enrich the country, strengthen the military" and "*Bunmeikaika*---Civilization and Enlightenment." The Emperor's 1868 Charter Oath goals declared that "Knowledge shall be sought all over the world, and thereby the foundations of imperial rule shall be strengthened."

"Yes, they had a pavilion at the 1885 New Orleans World Fair Exposition. I was reporting on the event for my newspaper. It was my favorite display."

"Groups of government officials and students went on missions to Europe and the United States to seek information and the goodwill essential for growth and revision of early unequal treaties. Opening the ports for worldwide trade, Japanese citizens moving to western countries for education purposes, and the immigration of foreign teachers, specialists, and advisors all contributed to expanding the people of Japan's knowledge of western customs, technology, and institutions. In order to become a great nation, it was deemed essential for Japan to modernize based on western models and to acquire a western spirit. Since it was a forced encounter with European modernity, the Japanese internalized certain aspects by deliberately imitating and selectively adapting to the West."

"From the little I have observed, it appears to me that Japan imported reforms from the West, adopting only hybrid modern ways. One could call it an imitative modernity," said Lafcadio.

"Japan 'self-colonized' so that they could protect their country and culture from imperialist foreign power plays and takeovers," Chamberlain explained.

"What happened to the old shogun regime leaders, their armies, and followers?"

"During the restoration, political power moved from the Tokugawa shogunate to an oligarchy of prominent Japanese intellectual leaders mostly from Satsuma and Choshu provinces. Their belief in the more traditional practice of imperial rule, left the sixteen-year-old emperor serving mostly as a titular head, the country's spiritual authority while his ministers assumed governance of the nation in his name. To consolidate their power against remnants of the Edo period regime, the Meiji government changed from being a feudal society to having a market economy. One of the first reforms initiated was to abolish the social hierarchy of four class divisions (samurai warriors at the top, followed by farmers, artisans, and merchants). The old class system was replaced by three orders. Feudal lords and court nobles became 'peers-*kazoku*' or became former 'samurai-*shizoku*'. All other people were classified as 'commoners-*heimin*'."

Chamberlain continued, "Throughout Japan there were approximately two million samurai, plus their retainers. The elite samurai were originally paid annual fixed stipends. First, the newly formed Imperial government taxed their payments, then made it compulsory that they convert the stipends into lump-sum, nonconvertible government bonds. Lacking business experience and because of inflation, many soon lost their wealth. Other symbolic class distinctions such as the privilege of wearing swords and long hair topknots were abolished, which deprived the samurai of their status. However, the more educated found employment as government officials, policemen, teachers, and military officers."

"It would be a natural progression to use the samurai caste in military and administrative positions," Lafcadio agreed.

"Yes, but as part of the military reform, a national conscription system was instituted mandating that every male upon turning 21 would serve for four years in the armed forces. The samurai monopoly on military service and ancient privilege of bearing arms was suddenly extended to all men in the nation. The mixing of recruits from around the country and the strict discipline of military life led to the breakdown of many discriminatory, cultural, and religious customs.

"The military was the first to modernize clothing, food, housing, technology, training, and hiring of foreign consultants. Military needs led to the development of nationwide communication and transportation systems, heavy industry like shipbuilding, iron smelters, spinning mills concrete, stone and brick buildings, organizational professionals, certifications, conferences, accounting, and other innovations that soon spread into the private business sector. With this, industrial zones rapidly grew and the population migrated from the rural countryside to work in industrial centers. With the open ports, Japan became consumers not only of goods, but of Western technology, and applied their new knowledge to produce items to be sold around the world."

"How were the vast holdings of the shoguns handled?"

"After abolition of the class divisions, the new Japanese government turned its attention to land reform. Land became private property and therefore capable of being transferred. A centralized land tax system, supplemented by paper money, was initiated to finance national programs. A 3% tax on the land value forced poor farmers to sell their property and become tenants. This led to migration to the cities and other countries overseas.

"The Meiji government invested tax revenues into industry and education as part of their policy of 'enriching the nation'. Guild monopolies were banned, and freedom of commerce allowed all citizens to engage in trade. Corporations, limited liability, and joint stock companies were introduced, along with measures to promote new technology and raise business and agricultural outputs. Foreign specialists such as naval or civil engineers were hired on two or three-years contracts, long enough for the Japanese to learn their skills. Japan's government subsidized and invested in infrastructure such as railways, ports, shipping, telegraphs, roads, post offices, banks, universities, and other commercial ventures."

"What about those who didn't like or follow the new systems and rules?" Lafcadio wanted to know.

"To win foreign approval, a national legal system and administrative system were adopted. A criminal code based on the Napoleonic model and a commercial code under German influence contributed to the modernization of Japanese society. The civil code overturned feudal obligations and established individual rights and property ownership. A People's Constitution was drawn up as a way to provide national unity and strength through deliberative assemblies and public discussion. Elections were held and the initial Diet (*Kokkai*) met in 1890."

"How did they get the common people on board with all the changes and prepare them for industrialization and modernization of their country?"

"Education of the populous was a key element in the modernization movement, providing skilled workers and literate citizens. The Japanese government established a national system of free public schools that was compulsory for all, regardless of gender or previous class distinction. In addition to mathematics, reading, writing and other utilitarian subjects, the students were instructed in 'moral training' - traditional values of filial piety and loyalty to reinforce their duty to the national state and the emperor. The school system became an effective instrument of national policy. Schools have employed over 3,000 foreign teachers to instruct students in international subjects and Western ideas. Tokyo and Kyoto Universities were founded. The study of law became a way into government service, based on merit instead of social rank."

"What other ways did the new government educate the public and the world at large?"

"Other important areas of modernization were publications and arts. The printing press replaced wood block printing. Western literature and ideas were distributed through books, newspapers, translations, and magazines. This year, 1890, we have 716 newspapers in print in Japan. Western curiosity and appreciation of traditional Japanese arts and styles was the rage throughout the Western world. Trade with Japan led to a popular cultural trend of *Japonisme* when many aspects of Japanese culture influenced art in America and Europe. Van Gogh even organized an exhibit of Japanese prints in Arles."

"Just walking or riding around I see lots of modern influence."

"Yes, Ironically, the Japanese have been exchanging ceremonial robes for western clothing, wearing short haircuts, hats, woolen clothes, and carrying umbrellas and pocket watches. Housing has gone from paper on wooden frames to brick and concrete. Kerosene, gas and electric lighting replaced rapeseed lamps. Eating and drinking habits of the West have grown in popularity. To break from their feudal past era of shoguns and to westernize and modernize, the government ordered the destruction of a majority of Japanese castles. Thousands of Japanese Buddhist and Shinto religious idols, temples, and shrines were smashed and destroyed. Destruction of cultural heritage was accompanied by outlawing of many traditional practices. Some feel that under the threat of foreign invasion, the country 'self-colonialized' to stay independent. Japan changed more in the four and a half decades since the arrival of Commodore Perry than in the prior three centuries."

In conclusion, Basil Hall Chamberlain said, "To have lived through the transition stage of modern Japan makes a man feel preternaturally old; for here he is in modern times…and yet he can himself distinctively remember the Middle Ages."

Learning about the history and changes that were taking place in Japan were invaluable lessons for Lafcadio or anyone trying to understand and report about the country and people. Professor Chamberlain became a valued mentor and friend.

CHAPTER 3

Lafcadio had been drawn to Japan for years. He remembered the delight and wonder he'd experienced as an eight-year-old viewing the bric-a-brac in the sea captain's cottage in Carnarvon, Wales when on vacation with his great aunt Sarah. He returned time after time to the Japanese pavilion at the New Orleans 1884 World Exposition and wrote several enthusiastic articles about the breathtaking displays.

He wrote his old friend Watkin, "Have also wild theories regarding Japan. Splendid field for study in Japan...Climate just like England,---perhaps a little milder." He devoured Loti's travel novels about the Far East; Proclaimed Sir Edwin Arnold's *Light of Asia* profound; and Bonded with William Patten, *Harper's* Art Editor, over Japanese art and his vast collection of books about Japan.

One day when browsing in a used bookstore in Philadelphia, he came upon Percival Lowell's *The Soul of the Far East*. Lowell had spent significant time in Japan, writing on Japanese religion, psychology, and behavior. His texts were filled with observations and academic discussions of various aspect of Japanese life. In essence, Lowell postulated that human progress is a function of the qualities of individuality and imagination. Lafcadio insisted his friends read every word, calling it a "marvelous, colossal, splendid, god-like book of books...the finest book on the East ever written." He soon found that one could read a thousand descriptions, but it wouldn't be real until seen in person. Now he was in Japan and it was so much more intriguing than he ever imagined it would be.

Already thinking he might overstay his assignment time in Japan, he wrote to Professor Chamberlain about his research and writing purpose in Japan.

"I want to stay in Japan longer than anticipated and need some means of support. I would be willing to teach or act as an English tutor. In New Orleans I made the acquaintance of Ichizo Hattori, the Japanese Minister of Agriculture and Commerce at the Japanese exposition during the 1884 New Orleans Exposition. He might have a kind memory of me and our time together."

服部一三 (1851-1929)

The kingdom, still in a state of cultural, military, and industrial transformation, was lacking qualified instructors for the hundreds of thousands of schoolboys studying English. Spurred by the Meiji Renovation and Japan's need for modernization and catching up to the West by learning English from a native speaker, Lafcadio was in the right place at the right time. Fortunately for him, by 1890 Hattori was a bureau director, the Vice-Minister of Education. Hattori Ishizo and Tokyo University Professor Chamberlain's connections and introductions would prove instrumental in getting Lafcadio a teaching job in Japan.

Chamberlain responded to Lafcadio's letter at once. Correspondence went back and forth between Yokohama and Tokyo, full of questions, answers, and a wide range of intellectual matters. Chamberlain agreed to help him find employment to supplement his journalism.

When Lafcadio first went up to Tokyo and met the professor, he immediately liked him. Chamberlain was a small, decisive man, about the same age as Hearn, but certainly in a more settled position. He was linguistically gifted and orthodox. He was a famous Japanologist, author, and had lived in Japan since 1873. Once again, Lafcadio found a mentor to look up to, admire, and to depend on. The child in him always had a crying inner need for someone or something to believe in.

At their first meeting, Chamberlain advised Lafcadio, "Do not fail to write down your first impressions as soon as possible. They are evanescent, you know; they will never come to you again, once they have faded out; and yet of all the strange sensations you may receive in this country, you will feel none so charming as these."

Lafcadio hired a rickshaw (*jinrikisha*) and runner (*kuruma*) named Cha to take him out of the European quarter and through the native sections of Yokohama. At the hotel he'd asked the word for temple (*tera*) and calling out "*tera*" over and over, had Cha take him from one sacred place to another, long into darkness of the evening. His runner's smile was so gentle that as they passed the natives everyone smiled in return in kindness, wishing them well. Lafcadio, a receptive sightseer as dark-skinned and small as the locals, was moved to smile back. Cha, like a tireless horse, trotting around town roused Lafcadio's compassion and gratitude so much that he paid his guide double.

He wrote in "My First Day in the Orient":
"It is with delicious surprise of the first journey through Japanese streets---unable to make one's *kuruma*-runner understand anything but gestures, frantic gestures to roll on anywhere, everywhere, since all is unspeakably pleasurable and new---that one receives the real sensation of being in the Orient, in this Far East so much read of, so long dreamed of, yet, as the eyes bear witness, heretofore all unknown."

"There is a romance even in the first full consciousness of this rather commonplace fact; but for me this consciousness is transfigured inexpressibly by the divine beauty of the day. There is some charm unutterable in the morning air, cool with the coolness of Japanese spring and wind-waves from the snowy cone of Fuji; a charm perhaps due rather to softest lucidity than to any positive tone,---an atmospheric limpidity extraordinary, with only a suggestion of blue in it, through which the most distant objects appear focused with amazing sharpness. The sun is only pleasantly warm; the *jinrikisha*, or *kuruma*, is the most cosy little vehicle imaginable; and the street-vistas, as seen above the dancing white mushroom-shaped hat of my sandaled runner, have an allurement of which I fancy that I could never weary.

"Elfish everything seems; for everything as well as everybody is small and queer, and mysterious: the little houses under their blue roofs, the little shop-fronts hung with blue, and the smiling little people in the blue costumes. The illusion is only broken by the occasional passing of a tall foreigner, and by divers shop-signs bearing announcements in absurd attempts at English. Nevertheless such discords only serve to emphasize reality; they never materially lessen the fascination of the funny little streets...

"And perhaps the supremely pleasurable impression of this morning is that produced by the singular gentleness of popular scrutiny. Everybody looks at you curiously; but there is never anything disagreeable, much less hostile in the gaze: most commonly, it is accompanied by a smile or half-smile. And the ultimate consequence of all these kindly curious looks and smiles is that the stranger finds himself thinking of fairyland. Hackneyed to the degree of provocation this statement no doubt is... suddenly in a world where everything is upon a smaller and daintier scale than with us, a world of lesser and seemingly kindlier beings,---a world where all movement is slow and soft, and voices are hushed,---a world where land, life, and sky are unlike all that one has known elsewhere,---this is surely the realization, for imaginations nourished with English folklore, of the old dream of a World of Elves..."

Lafcadio's practiced reporter's eye was drawn to the contrasts between Eastern and Western objects - "the line of telegraph poles.... a shop of American sewing-machines next to a shop of a maker of Buddhist images; the establishment of a photographer beside the establishment of a manufacturer of straw sandals." He would eventually study these incongruities, but as he wrote, "On the first day, at least, the old alone is new for the stranger, and suffices to absorb his attention."

CHAPTER 4

Lafcadio's runner pulled the rickshaw up a hill, halted suddenly and exclaimed, "*Tera*-temple." He pointed to an immense flight of broad stone steps. The cart shafts were lowered to the ground so he could dismount. Most temples in Japan were built on hilltops or cliffs, with long flights of stairs leading up to either ornate gates or starkly simple *torii*. A *torii* gate is two lofty columns, like gate pillars, supporting two horizontal cross beams, the lower and lighter beams are fitted a little distance below the summit; and the upper larger beam is supported on top of the columns and project well beyond them to the right and left. The *torii* is a Shinto symbol at the (*miya*) shrine of the gods of a more ancient faith of the land.

Whether made of stone, wood, or metal, the construction of a torii varies little in design. When you see a majestic one, it appears as some beautiful Japanese letter towering against the sky, with bold angles and curves made with four sweeps of a master's brush.

As Lafcadio ascended, he came upon a broad terrace in front of a gate with dragons entwined in the frieze above the door. The coiling dragons appeared to ungulate with a swarming motion. He passed through the carved portal and up more steps to a second gate. Most Buddhist temple gates are watched over by two guardians on either side called *Nio*. They protect the temple from evil spirits and humans with malicious intentions. The left guardian is called *Misshaku* or *Ungyo* and is blue representing water. The right guardian, *Naraen Kongo* or *Agyo*, is red, representing fire. Together they symbolize the alpha and omega, birth and death, beginning and end of all things.

With aching muscles, he arrived and passed through this entrance to a courtyard where graceful votive lanterns of stone stood like monuments. A pair of stone lions of Buddha, male and female, guarded a long, low building topped with a gabled roof of blue tiles. This was the temple.

Lafcadio took off his shoes and left them on the simple wooden steps. A young man slid thin white paper screens aside and bowed to him in a gracious welcome. He was surrounded with an unfamiliar sweet smell of Japanese incense. Matting, thick as bedding, was soft under his feet. After the blazing sun, the filtered light inside was like moonlight. As his sight adjusted, he was drawn to enormous colored paper flowers, symbolic lotus-blossoms with bright green leaves curling below and gilded on the upper surface. At the end of the dark room, facing the entrance sat the altar of Buddha. But there was no statue.

The young man who ushered him into the temple approached. To Lafcadio's great surprise he said in perfect English, "That is the shrine of Buddha."

"I would like to make an offering to Buddha," Lafcadio responded.

"It is not necessary," he said with a polite smile. But when Lafcadio insisted the guide placed the little offering upon the altar and then invited him to visit his room in a wing of the building.

Lafcadio and the young man sat on the beautifully matted floor and talked. It turned out his name was Akira Manabe. He was in his last week of studies at the temple. He'd learned English at the Imperial University of Tokyo.

Finally, the student asked, "Are you a Christian?"

"Lafcadio answered truthfully, "No."

"Are you a Buddhist?" the young man asked.

"Not exactly."

"Then why do you make offerings if you do not believe in Buddha?"

"I revere the beauty of his teachings, and the faith of those who follow it," replied Lafcadio.

"Are there Buddhists in England and America?"

"There are. At least a great many interested in Buddhist philosophy. Why are there no images of Buddha in your temple?"

"There is a small one in the shrine on the altar, but the shrine is closed. The large images of Buddha are not exposed every day, only on festival days and some only once or twice a year."

Akira reached into an alcove and took out a copy of Olcott's *Buddhist Catechism*. "Take this to study. Give me your address and I will call on you when I finish my training here," he said, presenting it with both hands.

Lafcadio could see others ascending the steps and gracefully kneeling to pray before the entrance of the temple. They would clap their hands slowly and loudly three times, bow, pray silently, and depart. He turned to Akira and asked him, "Why do they clap their hands three times before praying?"

"Three times for the Sansei, the Three Powers: Heaven, Earth and Man. The clapping represents awakening from the dream of the long night."

"What dream? What night?"

"The Buddha said: 'All beings are only dreaming in this fleeting world of unhappiness.'"

"Then the clapping signifies that in prayer the soul awakens?"

"Yes. Buddhists believe the soul always was, always will be."

As Lafcadio and Akira talked, the elderly Chief Priest of the temple entered, accompanied by two young priests. They were introduced and everyone bowed three times, showing the glossy crowns of their smoothly shaven heads. They sat down on the floor. Their unsmiling faces were as stony and impassive as the faces of images, but their eyes observed him very closely.

Akira interpreted as Lafcadio haltingly tried to discuss translations of the Sutras he'd read in their Sacred Books of the East and ask questions. The grave younger priests listened without change of countenance and uttered no words in response. But the wise old priest answered each inquiry in turn through the interpreter. He carefully took a few treasures out of a polished chest, dusted them off, and showed them to Lafcadio, the reverent pilgrim stranger.

Then the old, white-robed priest bowed and held out a bowl into which Lafcadio dropped a few coins. He saw that it was filled with hot water. Having no tea to serve his guest, the priest had been offering the best he had. Lafcadio's face turned bright red with embarrassment. No change came over the host's wrinkled features. He just carried the bowl away and returned with another and a little sugar cake-*kashi* stamped with a Swastika, the ancient Indian symbol of the Wheel of Law. The priest, between continuous coughs, courteously motioned for him to eat and drink.

Afterward, at the threshold Lafcadio bowed his goodbyes. The others bowed very low, only Akira smiled. As he departed Lafcadio heard a series of hollow, rattling coughs from behind the paper screen, so persistent that he believed if he returned another time, he would be asking for the elder priest in vain.

When Lafcadio descended the mount, Cha waiting below asked if he wanted to see more temples, "*Tera?*" His passenger nodded yes and resumed his seat in the rickshaw (*jinrikisha*) because he'd not yet seen Buddha. They halted again at the foot of another hill and lofty flight of stairs. Standing before him was a great gateway, a *torii* of enigmatic beauty.

At the top of the summit, Lafcadio found himself in a park with a small temple at the right. It was disappointingly closed, but he wandered into a grove of cherry trees covered in a dazzling array of snowy blossoms. The ground below the trees and the path before him were white with thick, soft, perfumed petals.

Cha told him, "The trees have been so long domesticated and caressed by man that they have acquired souls." He translated a sign, obviously meant for crude heartless foreigners, and read, "It is forbidden to injure the trees."

After a day of exploring the streets and temples, Cha stopped at one last temple. Through smoky incense Lafcadio spotted a colossal bronze lamp with snarling dragons coiled about its stem. In the dimness of the inner sanctuary, a priest pulled back screen after screen for him to view gilded brasses and sacred inscriptions. When he looked for the image of a deity or the temple's presiding spirit in the last opening, he saw only a round, pale disk of polished metal - a mirror reflecting his own face. The mockery of the mirror stayed with him. He wondered if he'd ever discover what he sought outside of himself, outside of his imagination?

The sun was setting when he left the temple. Cha stopped to light a paper lantern to see his way back to the hotel. Lafcadio sat back in the rickshaw dazed and confused by the interminable maze of mysterious signs. He felt the coming of a drowsiness that, for him, always followed enchantment.

In one of Lafcadio's first descriptions of his reaction to Japan he wrote, "The country is, however full of the strangest charm. Artistically it is one vast museum. Socially and naturally it is really a fairyland. The first impression produced by the Japanese themselves is that of being among the kindest of kind fairies. The religion seized my emotions at once, and absorbed them. I am steeped in Buddhism, a Buddhism totally unlike that of books - something infinitely tender, touching, naif, beautiful.

"I mingle with the crowds of pilgrims to the great shrines; I ring the great bells; and burn incense rods before the great smiling gods. My study is confined to the popular religion so far, and its relation to popular character and art. There are phases of this art surprisingly Greek, and legends amazing in their similarity to Hellenic myths - especially the myths of Hades. From the Greek kingdoms of India some Greek art is thought to have been filtered through China and Korea into antique Japan."

He discovered a place for himself that he'd unknowingly longed for. He and the Greeks worshipped beauty and aesthetics, and so did the Japanese. He noted the extraordinary, picturesque charm and considered it a utopia. His escape from the ugly commonplace of the West was complete. He'd found his way home. Japan offered a new life, along with escape from unwanted relationships, unbearable tedium, and lost illusions.

CHAPTER 5

The next week, true to his promise, Akira Manabe stood in his long kimono, bowing and smiling, at the door to Lafcadio's hotel room.

"I am here to offer my humble services. I can take you to interesting places in Yokohama or perhaps we could discuss Buddhism. In exchange will you, Hearn-san, be so kind as to tell me some things I want to know about America. I will be available to help you until October, when I am going to the Buddhist holy city of Kyoto to edit a magazine."

After a week on his own and studying Chamberlain's *Handbook of Colloquial Japanese*, Lafcadio realized he desperately needed help with language. He immediately hired Akira, the young Buddhist, to be his interpreter and guide. It was a windfall to have such a delightful companion to provide invaluable assistance in studying Japanese language, philosophy, and life. Akira's knowledge and insights were the basis for Lafcadio's original letters and articles about the Land of the Rising Sun.

He wrote Henry Watkin, "Here I am in the land of dreams, surrounded by strange Gods. I seem to have known and loved them before somewhere."

In a letter to fellow journalist and world-traveler Elizabeth Bisland, he said in fever-pitched enthusiasm, "I feel indescribably toward Japan. Of course, Nature here is not Nature of the tropics, which is so splendid and savage and omnipotently beautiful that I feel at this very moment of writing the same pain in my heart I felt when leaving Martinique. This is a domesticated Nature, which loves man and makes itself beautiful for him in a quiet grey-and-blue way like the Japanese women; and the trees know what people say about them - seem to have little souls. What I love about Japan is the Japanese, - the poor simple humanity of the country. It is divine.

"And I believe that their art is as far in advance of our art as old Greek art was superior to that of the earliest European art-gropings...There is nothing in this world approaching the naïve natural charm of them. No book ever written has reflected it. I think there is more art in a print by Hokuai or those who came after him than in a $10,000 painting---no, a $100,000 painting. We are barbarians! I do not merely think these things; I am sure of them as death. I only wish I could be reincarnated in some little Japanese baby, so that I could see and feel the world as beautifully as a Japanese brain does."

He agreed with Percival Lowell's observations and remarked to his new mentor, Basil Chamberlain that "the Japanese people are the happiest people in the world, is superlatively true. It is the old Greek soul again. To escape out of Western civilization into Japanese life is like escaping from a pressure of ten atmospheres into a perfectly normal medium."

Lafcadio found the charms of Japan intangible and volatile like perfume. After living two weeks in this 'medium' he had no desire to leave his land of dreams. He'd spent most of his life on the move, but in Japan he found a home for his restless, floating spirit. There were times in America when he was so broken that he considered suicide. In Japan, the culture gave him reasons to live.

CHAPTER 6

In Lafcadio's first days in Japan he thrived in a whirlwind of discovery, affirmations, and inquiry, the "same kind of madness as the first love of a boy." He was in love with a new place. If the Japanese spring had remained mild his initial enchantment might have lasted longer. But it began to rain and rained for weeks without a break. He could not get out to see the places and people he wanted to write about. Unable to gather notes, his "blue devils" of depression set in and he began to fret. An enforced isolation and idleness gave him time to worry and brood, not a good thing for Lafcadio.

There he sat thousands of miles from the United States, weather bound, practically friendless, and low on funds again. He flashed back on the days he'd been homeless and starving in London, Cincinnati, New Orleans, and St. Pierre. The cost of living in Japan was more than he expected and his meager savings were dwindling rapidly. Lafcadio had moved to Japan, as always, with an empty purse. He wrote to Dr. Gould, who he stayed with for several months in Philadelphia, to get his library from *Harper's* editor Henry Alden, sell it, or keep it and send him what money he could. He wrote another letter to Alden to release the library to Gould, since he was under a greater debt to the doctor, and he had nothing else to pay him with.

He felt like a fool for letting Patten and Alden reassure him that he could support himself by writing about the Far East. He had no head for business and when he found things were not as he expected, he unfairly blamed *Harper's* for his trip to Japan without committing to accept a word he wrote.

He was angry with his travel companion Weldon for trying to hurry him along with his writing so that *Scribner's* magazine would not release their series of articles on Japan first. He'd resented Weldon's aggressive, take-charge attitude from the time they'd left New York. He'd told Alden that the desire to utilize him "simply to illustrate the idiocies of a sign-painter; rather overreached the plan." He resented that the illustrator was being paid more per page than he was for writing text.

As he sat fuming, he received another letter from Alden inquiring about his instructions to give Gould the books and papers. It also contained certain directions about his collaboration with Weldon. That note was the last straw to the overwrought writer. His discontent was magnified by paranoia. In an unreasoning rage, Lafcadio grabbed his pen and wrote a furious tirade against Alden.

In a fit of characteristic pique, he accused Alden of forcing him to make a will in his favor, treating him outrageously, abandoning him in the middle of an epidemic, and trying to starve him to death while he was in the West Indies and that he was doing it again. Whenever Lafcadio was angry, he was rude; When infuriated, he became blasphemous.

Lafcadio wrote that his former literary patron, "broke the promises which you voluntarily made; you lied to me in every possible manner for the purpose of duping me into the power of your brutal firm, which deals in books precisely as they might deal in pork or hay…What do I care about your vulgar Magazine anyhow? What inducements have I ever had to allow my work to be spoiled in it? Your firm is a hundred years behind; ignorant, brutal, mean, absurdly ignorant, incredibly ignorant of what art is, what literature is, what good taste is. But it makes money like pork-packeries and butcheries and loan-offices make money."

Lafcadio's nervous apprehensions got the best of him as he reread his contract letter with *Harper's*. The contract clearly stated that they were not obligated to accept his work at all. His anger not yet appeased, he shot off a letter to J. Henry Harper accusing him of fraud and being selfish to the marrow. In it he pointed out that since *Harper's* was under no contractual obligation to accept his materials, he said, "As there is no obligation on one side, I suppose there is none on the other - as the law holds." He also told J. Henry Harper to "go to the devil." He enclosed his contracts for *Youma* and *Chita* in the envelope and said he wished nothing more to do with *Harper's*.

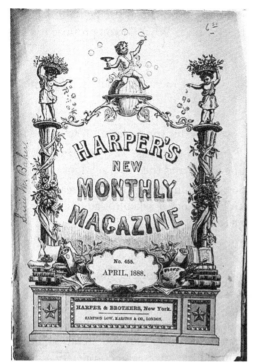

In Lafcadio's irate letters to *Harper's Magazine*, he swore like the sailors at Carey's hotel in his tirade about the publication's staff: "Lying clerks and hypocritical, thieving editors…artists whose artistic ability consists in farting sixty-seven times to the minute---scallywags, scoundrels, swindlers, sons of bitches. Pisspots-with-the-handles-broken-off-and-the-bottom-knocked-out - Ignoramuses with the souls of slime composed of seventeen different kinds of shit." He called them "miserable, beggarly, buggerly, cowardly, rascally, boorish, brutal sons of bitches."

He concluded with, "Please understand that your resentment has for me less than the value of a bottled fart, and your bank account less consequence than a wooden shit-house struck by lightning."

Lafcadio saw illustrator Weldon by chance on May 7th, as he returned from the wharves. They'd only come across each other a few times since arrival. He told him triumphantly what he'd done.

"I've made a clean break with *Harper's*. I wrote to Harry Harper and Henry Alden and told them what I thought of them and their horrid publications," he boasted.

"You haven't sent the letters yet have you?" asked a concerned Weldon.

"Lafcadio waved toward a steamer just sailing out of the Yokohama harbor and replied, "Yes, they are on that ship." He then went into his mad monologue tirade against Harper Bros.

Weldon inquired, "What about Van Horne at Canadian Pacific Railroad who advanced us the money and free passage? What do you propose to do about that obligation?"

"Well, they can look to Harper Bros. for settlement or I could send them a new article."

Lafcadio had written the article he owed for his trip to Japan. It was published in the November 1890 *Harper's Magazine* as "A Winter Journey to Japan". Van Horne of CPRR saw the article and tried to reach him to tell him that he found it "one of the most charming things I've ever read...I am more than pleased - delighted." Van Horne never asked for anything else, nor did Canadian Pacific reprint the story.

Lafcadio received an answer from Henry Alden with decorous attempts to defend his and the company's actions. It was a kindly, dignified letter such as a father would write to an errant son.

He began: "Personally, I have tried to be your friend, expressing to you most freely my sympathetic appreciation of your genius and literary ability, sharing your enthusiasm with undisguised frankness, and co-operating with you in every way I could, always wishing for you the best success. I have become sufficiently attached to you to feel all the pain which a friend can feel to find that his friendship has been wholly and from the first, not only misunderstood but construed with hostility...Caring still enough for you to wish you to understand me, I remain sincerely your friend, H. M. Alden."

The patient, generous letter from Alden had no lasting effect on Lafcadio. He felt no twinge of remorse. He lashed out at Henry Alden's letter with vigorous Irish profanity. He wrote to a friend the next year still complaining about Alden as, "the arch-hypocrite who edits, or pretends to be the editor, of their magazine, is the only one against whom I feel any special resentment. He is the most astounding liar and trickster I ever met..." He maintained that the Harper Bros. cheated him out of $37 dollars for supplements he compiled just before he left New York.

Lafcadio wrote a torrent of abusive denunciations to Harper's Bros. In spite of his insulting letters, they sent him a check for $150 in payment for his article "A Winter Journey to Japan" and provided him with a statement of account with references to sales of his books and royalties on the same.

They responded in part, "The Messrs. Harper prefer to ignore your recent letters to them if it is in any way possible for them to make an appeal from the writer of these to the Mr. Hearn they thought they knew, the author of *Chita* whom they have always endeavored to treat with proper consideration and with that frankness and courtesy which should characterize the relations between publisher and author." Contrary to false rumors, for years Hearn did receive and accept royalty checks for *Chita, Youma,* and *Two Years in the French West Indies* from Harpers Bros. through their London agents.

Lafcadio's tantrums and destructive actions were not out of character. He had a history of arguing with editors and friends over perceived wrongs, and making a bad habit of wearing out his welcome. He certainly had the art of creating enemies.

He stopped writing to *Harper's* and never sent them any more articles. One by one he'd severed his ties with the United States. Although there was no misunderstanding, he never again wrote to Dr. Rudolph Matas, a dear friend in New Orleans whom he'd loved like a brother. Page Baker, his *Times Democrat* newspaper editor, received a few letters, until Lafcadio didn't complete a contract Baker had arranged for him. Correspondence with his motherly landlady Mrs. Courtney in New Orleans ceased, due to her failing health. His friendships with journalist Krehbiel and longtime correspondent George Gould had practically ended before he'd left New York.

Dr. Gould received Hearn's library from Alden, but never sold or sent Lafcadio any money for them. Lafcadio told another friend Ellwood Hendrick, "From Japan I wrote to him to do so (get the books from Alden), only after he had already done it without my knowledge. On application for some of them by mail he wrote that our correspondence was over, sending me a volume for which he charged postage. And he never returned my notes, in lieu of which I had asked him to take the books and settle the debt - trusting his honor. So I paid dearly for that patronage. 'Bitter,' saith the Italian proverb, 'is another man's bread.'"

Gould, used Lafcadio's unpublished notes and papers, to publish reports about the effects of his nearsightedness on his literary output. Gould would write such things about him like: "To have character is to control circumstances; Hearn was always its slave. Except in one particular circumstance, the pursuit of literary excellence, Hearn had no character whatsoever. He was a perfect chameleon, always a mirror of the friend of the instant." Dr. Gould said that Hearn's intellect and aesthetics were wholly a produce of the morbidities of his defective vision. Hurtful personal comments were the coup-de-grace to totally finish that relationship.

Lafcadio ended his American friendships, with the exceptions of occasional correspondences with his father-figure Cincinnati printer Henry Watkin, fellow writer Elizabeth Bisland, and his reliable New York pal Ellwood Hendrick.

Fate struck hard on his side of the world, leaving Lafcadio without a publisher or friends or a source of income. Weldon warned him that all his negative thoughts and actions did not protect him; they just made him smaller. After his break with *Harper's* he had to sit down to a banquet of consequences caused by his rash actions.

Being in crisis, without friends and money in strange new places, seemed to be a repetitive, predictable, and self-made pattern in his life. But he refused to accept that he might end up a vagabond like he'd been in London, New York, Cincinnati, and New Orleans.

"I shall get along somehow," he wrote to Elizabeth Bisland. "I am so very tired of being hard-pushed, and ignored, and starved,---and obliged to undergo moral humiliations which are worse than hunger and cold, that I have ceased to be ashamed to ask you to say a good word for me where you can." He confided in a letter "It will be better to be a Japanese school teacher than to work for *Harper's* at $500 a year. Still, it seems to me for the first time that my life is really a failure."

CHAPTER 7

A massive general destruction of his connections to America was perhaps in some way necessary and typical for Lafcadio Hearn. Yet in doing so, he was left alone, ill with anger in a strange land where he could not speak the language. He had destroyed key professional connections that might have provided him financial security. Once again, he needed to rebuild his life in a new location.

He began looking about for ways to support himself. He'd brought two letters of introduction with him---to Professor Basil Hall Chamberlain and Mitchell McDonald, the Paymaster of the United States Navy in Yokohama. He had contacted Chamberlain and next went to meet McDonald.

Mitchell McDonald was an American naval officer that journalist Elizabeth Bisland met during her trip around the world. Gallant, good-natured Lieutenant McDonald was her Tokyo escort. He was also a principal owner and promoter of the Grand Hotel of Yokohama. Lafcadio and McDonald shared no literary interests, but Lafcadio found him an honest, cheerful, good fellow, something of a far-eastern counterpart of kindhearted Ellwood Hendrick. Additionally, McDonald was a competent businessman, at home in the mysteries of finance.

McDonald began to help Lafcadio immediately. During his quarrel with *Harper's*, Lafcadio had rashly returned an unopened royalty check that he badly needed. McDonald went to the postal authorities of Yokohama, got the check back and convinced him to accept the money and loans during his crisis.

Lafcadio got along equally well with Chamberlain the scholar and McDonald the businessman. They both set out to see if they could find him a job in Japan. In the meantime, his funds were drying up. He needed to find something to do at once. One day he just walked into the English Victoria Public School headmaster's office. The man was impressed by Lafcadio Hearn's list of published books and gave him a job as a tutor.

Edward Clarke, a crippled fifteen-year-old of mixed Japanese and Western parentage, was Lafcadio's student for several hours per week. He was introduced to the short, broad-shouldered foreigner as "a literary gentleman" who would tutor him in English. At first the blind eye startled the young man, but he checked himself remembering his own twisted foot. Clarke recalled Hearn as the main teacher who awakened his passion for learning. He advised the teenaged Clarke never to go into writing unless he had either genius or an income. He used a trick with his student - first to offer glowing praise, then correct with equally crushing criticism.

The enjoyment and success at tutoring led Lafcadio to write to Basil Chamberlain, "If I have a chance, I think I shall be able to make myself valuable." He was thinking of his writing, but now considered teaching. "An English teacher whom I met here, has given me some information about Japanese schools; and from what I could learn through him, I think I should be very glad to serve as an English teacher in a public school. I should not be at all particular as to what part of Japan I might be sent, nor how long a period my services might be required."

The Japanese government, in its formidable attempt to compete with the West, had made English language a required subject in Japanese high schools and universities. They'd expressed an extraordinary willingness to hire foreigners and compensate them well.

Chamberlain, with the help of Hattori, the Minister of Education, found a teaching opportunity for Lafcadio right away. The vacancy was in Matsue, a city in Shimane Prefecture, 450 miles southwest of Tokyo, across Honshu on the Japan Sea. They arranged an interview with Governor Koteda of

Shimane Prefecture who happened to be in Tokyo. Koteda was a man of strong paternalistic interest in what happened in his province.

Governor Koteda and Lafcadio met and enjoyed mutual respect, so he was hired. A contract provided that he would teach English in two schools in Matsue, the Normal School and the Middle School, starting in September. He would receive a monthly salary of $100 U. S. dollars. But that amount was worth double in such a remote place as Shimane Province. The governor advanced Lafcadio eighty yen to relocate.

Lafcadio found the appointment especially attractive because it was in one of the island's oldest provinces, dating back to the legendary Kamiyo era. The "province of the ancient Shinto gods" was virtually untouched by encroaching Western influences. Lafcadio saw nineteenth-century civilization invading the loveliness of the Far East and he abhorred the effects. He declared from what he'd observed so far that the pragmatic, militant New Japan's heart was "as hollow and bitter as a dried lemon", and he wanted no part of it. He wrote, "The traveler who enters suddenly into a period of social change---especially change from a feudal past to a democratic present---is likely to regret the decay of things beautiful and the ugliness of things new."

In 1868 the anti-Western shogun was overthrown and a year later a modern constitution was adopted. Meiji New Order realized it could either be subservient to the West or make a concerted all-out effort to modernize and industrialize Japan. The country leaders chose to adopt Westernization of their traditions and culture. By 1890 (Meiji 23) there was a surge of imperialist expansion and an "Open Door" policy in the Far East, enforced by the American "Great White Fleet".

Before starting his post in Matsue, Lafcadio and his guide Akira wanted to explore more of Yokohama and the east coast of Japan. The pair punctuated their hectic weeks of sightseeing with days of swimming at the beaches. One day they took a train through narrow valleys to the once great city of Kamakura. A belfry in one of the temples held a bell six-hundred and fifty years old. Lafcadio was allowed to swing a great wooden beam to sound the bell.

He described the ancient bell tone as, "a sound deep as thunder, rich as the bass of a mighty organ,---a sound enormous, extraordinary, yet beautiful,--- rolls over the hills and away. Then swiftly follows another and lesser and sweeter billow of tone; then another; then an eddying of waves of echoes.

Only once was it struck, the astounding bell; yet it continues to sob and moan for at least ten minutes!"

Lafcadio saw pictures of Daibutsu, with eyes of peace, "the half-closed eyes that seem to watch you through their eyelids of bronze as gently as those of a child…" And in contrast, the King of Death, Enma, with "eyes of nightmare." An amazing range of feelings and thoughts quivered through him.

Lafcadio continuously asked Akira to tell him stories and myths. The ancient tales, jokes, and history he teased out of his guide permeated Lafcadio's first written sketches of Japan. An example of this was when he asked:

"Akira, do the Japanese always keep their vows to the gods?"

Akira smiled a sweet smile and answered, "There was a man who promised to build a *torii*, a sacred gate of good metal if his prayers were granted. And he obtained all that he desired. And then he built a *torii* with three exceedingly small needles."

Whether alone or accompanied by Akira, Lafcadio continued to wander about and make copious notes on everything he saw and felt. He wrote to Elizabeth, "I love their gods, their customs, their dress, their bird-like quavering songs, their houses, their superstitions, their faults…Now as for myself - I am going to become a country schoolmaster in Japan, probably for several long years. The language is unspeakably difficult to learn; I believe it can only be learned by ear. Teaching will help me to learn it; and before learning it, to write anything enduring upon Japan would be absurdly impossible. Literary work will not support one here…What I wish to do, what I want to do for its own sake; and so intend to settle, if possible, in this country, among a people who seem to me the most lovable in the world."

CHAPTER 8

With Akira Manabe by his side as interpreter and guide, Lafcadio Hearn left the bustling port city of Yokohama. Their destination was the town of Matsue in the Izumo district of Shimane, on the other side of Honshu Island, almost four hundred miles away. They were embarking on a strenuous journey that included a train to Okayama, then several days in rickshaws over the mountains from the Pacific side to the Sea of Japan, and finally a small ship from Yonago to Matsue.

The train traveled along the rocky coast. Mountains massed in waves at the right as far as the eye could see. Lafcadio took out his small telescope to glimpse at the sea between the hills. The small valleys between the mountains were filled with garden-like tea terraces and rice patties. Hour after dulling hour they passed cities, rivers, canals, and farms. In Osaka and the port of Kobe, he saw islands of the Inland Sea marked with ships and sails. Their rail travel ended in Okayama, the Chugoku region capital and home of the 16th century Black Crow Castle.

Akira arranged with strong runners to pull their *kurama* rickshaws over the mountains to Izumo, the land of Kamiyo, and the ancient gods. It was a rough, four-day journey. Lafcadio wrote a description of what he saw as he braced himself in the lightweight cart, and rode along the bumpy roads:

"Through the valleys most of the long route lies, valleys always open to higher valleys, while the road ascends, valley between mountains with ricefields ascending their slopes by successions of diked terraces which look like enormous green flights of steps. Above them are shadowing somber forest of cedar and pine; and above these wooded summits loom indigo shapes of farther hill overtopped by peaked silhouettes of vapory gray."

In Yokohama and Kamakura, Lafcadio had been just another curious tourist. But on this journey west he began to take part in the real life of Japan. He saw and deeply felt the common humanity of the Japanese. One night in a village near the Sea of Japan, he was entranced by the Bon-Festival of the Dead ceremony of farewell. Each home in the town had made small boats of closely woven barley straw and loaded them with dainty food, tiny lanterns, and messages of love to their departed ancestors. They launched the boats of the blessed ghosts on waterways, hoping their phantom fleets would go all the way to the sea. Lafcadio described how the waters sparkled to the horizon with the lights of the dead, and the sea wind was fragrant with incense.

He observed dancers at a Bon-Odori festival. The vibrating music and the dancers' pulsating motions mesmerized him. He watched many types of dancing, some performed by outcast women and others by the *miko* or Shinto priestesses, certainly worthy of all respect. Men danced as well as women, and all children danced. He wrote, "The fine forms of Oriental dancing are really dramatic performances, - silent monologues of a most artistic kind."

Describing the Bon-Odori dance, "All together glide the right foot forward one pace, without lifting the sandal from the ground, and extend both hands to the right, with a strange floating motion and a smiling, mysterious obeisance. Then the right foot is drawn back with a repetition of the waving of both hands and the mysterious bow."

More than just the music, he found a universal, familiar emotion - "something not of only one place or time, but vibrant to all common joy or pain of being, under the universal sun."

At a marketplace they visited, Lafcadio was startled by a shrill static stream of noise, like leaking steam. Akira laughed at him and explained that the sound was only insects in boxes. The loud hum was made by scores of huge green crickets, each in tiny bamboo cages. "They are sold as pets for children to play with. They feed them melon and eggplant rind." Beautiful, netted cages of fireflies could also be purchased for five cents.

In the next stage of the journey Lafcadio and Akira took a small vessel along the coast from Yonago into the open Sea of Japan. When they got to Izumo on the west coast, Lafcadio decided that before he began teaching that he wanted to do more swimming. Some of Izumo's finest beaches were at Kizuki, twenty-five miles from Matsue, so they broke up the trip and stayed for a few days.

The village atmosphere was quiet and unhurried, and the beach ideal. Lafcadio was among people who'd never seen a European before, so the natives asked Akira all manner of questions about the foreigner, then apologized for their curiosity with smiles and humble bows.

When the travelers arrived in the town, their accommodations looked like a faded print from an old picture book. An aged innkeeper graciously welcomed them to his weather-beaten medieval hotel. Even myopic Lafcadio was aware of the aesthetics and exquisite attention to detail. Items from the ancient, uncontaminated past, like the iron kettle decorated with dragon and cloud designs, flowered lacquer ware, porcelain wine cups, and bronze teacup holders, earned his admiration.

"Akira, I can assure you that anything ugly or commonplace in this island empire is the results of foreign influence!"

"Curiosities and dainty objects bewilder you by their very multitude; on either side of you, wherever you turn your eyes, are countless wonderful things as yet incomprehensible. There comes to mind something said by a practical American on hearing of a great fire in Japan: "Oh! those people can afford fires; their houses are so cheaply built." It is true that the frail wooden house of the common people can be cheaply and quickly replaced; but that which was within them to make them beautiful cannot,---and every fire is an art tragedy. For this is the land of infinite hand-made variety; machinery has not yet been able to introduce sameness and utilitarian ugliness in cheap production (except in response to foreign demand for bad taste to suit vulgar markets), and each object made by the artist or artisan differs still from all others, even of his own making. And each time something beautiful perishes by fire, it is a something representing an individual idea," Lafcadio wrote.

"Happily, the art impulse itself, in this country of conflagrations, has a vitality which survives each generation of artists, and defies the flame that changes their labour to ashes or melts it to shapelessness. The idea whose symbol has perished will reappear again in other creations. Every artist is a ghostly worker. His art is an inheritance. His fingers are guided by the dead in the delineation of a flying bird, of the vapours of mountains, of the colours of the morning and the evening, of the shape of branches and the spring burst of flowers…Wherefore, one coloured print by a Hokusai or Hiroshige, originally sold for less than a cent, may have more real art in it than many a Western painting valued at more than the worth of a whole Japanese street."

On his journey west with Akira, Lafcadio wanted to visit one of the oldest and holiest Shinto shrines - the great *Izumo-taisha* temple that he'd read about. There was no record of the date of its establishment. Lafcadio was disappointed to learn that foreigners were never allowed in the temple, and only a few were given permission to visit its extensive grounds. He was appeased when a town official and priest from the temple invited him to a banquet. The priest told him legends of the local deities and let him inspect valuable manuscripts.

Lafcadio, ready to see his new home base, took a small boat through an island lagoon, up a clear river between mountains and marshy fields, and at last into the center of Matsue. Anchorage was in the shadow of an arching white bridge where the Ohashi River flowed out of Shinji Lake, through the town, and onward to the Sea of Japan.

Matsue was a delightful surprise. For a population of forty thousand, it was remarkably clean, bright, and contained. Matsue had been a feudal stronghold until the violent revolutions of 1871. During the early feudal days remote places like Matsue were considered outposts suitable for offenders too strong in fluence or position to be treated like criminals. In olden days there was little tolerance in religion or in politics, so broad-minded monks or progressive thinkers at court were sent to desolate locations where their ambitions would be permanently crushed. Distinct pre-Meiji cultural tones and customs were preserved by the people and governor of Matsue. Nothing of the Western European or American world had taken root. The merchants, priests, samurai, and common people were far removed from the influence of foreigners.

CHAPTER 9

On August 30, 1890, Lafcadio Hearn spent his first night in the city of Matsue, the government center of Shimane Prefecture, Izumo, "land of the gods". He and Akira Manabe checked into the Tomitaya Inn on Zaimoku Street. Akira could only stay a short while to get Lafcadio settled in before he had to return to Kyoto for work as editor of a Buddhist journal.

Lafcadio's room balcony overhung the Ohashi River with its swift current coming out of the lower end of Lake Shinji. He could see the wharf anchorage of his arrival boat and other steamers that served various ports of the coast of the Japan Sea. The city of Matsue sat in the middle of a network laced with moats and canals. Only a generation before, these waterways formed defenses for a massive castle on a hill in the city center.

The castle town was originally established by Horio Yoshiharu, lord of the Matsue clan, between 1607-1611 as the stronghold of the Matsudaira feudal lords' family. It served as the base of Naomasa, a blood relative of the great ruler Ieyasu, and after several generations the home of a lord named Fumaiko. The city was the seat of the Matsue domain under the Tokugawa shogun until the Meiji restoration. Despite the city being in an isolated region, it retained its noble aesthetic atmosphere.

When Lafcadio arrived, the castle, in the midst of great walls and pine forest, stood empty. The rulers' medieval authority and function were forbidden by edict. Japan was trying to move out of the Middle Ages into the modern world.

So far removed from Western influence, Matsue was living in a distinctly pre-Meiji world of its own. "The city can be definitely divided into three architectural quarters: District for the merchants and shopkeepers in the heart of the settlement, where all the houses are two stories high; the district of the temples in the southeastern part of town; and the district of the shizoku, formerly called samurai, comprising a vast number of large roomy, garden-girt, one-story dwellings. From these elegant homes, in feudal days, could be summoned at a moment's notice five thousand 'two-sworded men' with their armed retainers, making a fighting total for the city alone of probably not less than thirteen thousand warriors. More than one-third of all the buildings were samurai homes; for Matsue was the military center of the most ancient province of Japan."

The knightly caste of warriors mustered most thickly about the centuries-old Castle Oshiroyama, on its citadel mound. Lafcadio described the castle as a "vast, iron-grey dragon" on its hilltop perch overlooking the city.

There were indications in everyday life of samurai traditions and the older Shinto religion in community rituals, ceremonies, and festivals. The governor, Mr. Koteda, was quite earnest about reviving the national spirit of former days so people of past generations could relive the days of their youth. He supported old-fashioned horse races and sword and spear contests. Like a feudal lord, he had the discipline of chivalry of the old warrior class. He was very skillful in the art of fencing. The mayor received Lafcadio warmly and invited the new teacher to the town's historical events.

From his perch at the inn and walks around the town, Lafcadio was following Chamberlain's advice and recording his first impressions. He watched and listened intensely to write "Pulse of the Land in The Chief City in the Province of the Gods". He described the first noises of the city's wakening life made by "the pondering pestle of the rice cleaners"; "the boom of the great bell of Tokoji, the Zenshu temple, shaking over the town"; "cries of the earliest itinerant vendors"; "Buddhist hour of morning prayer"; and one, two, three, four clapping salutes to the rising sun, bird songs, and "continuing louder and louder the pattering of geta (wooden sandals) over the Ohashi bridge...rapid, merry, musical, like the sound of an enormous dance."

He painted visual and spiritual pictures of the waterfront, sky, and Mt. Daisen, the Fuji of Izumo, overlooking the city. He walked his readers through the street scenes and temples of the city. Watching the people as best he could with his limited sight, he told of children's games, wrestlers' contests, dancers, marching troops, flower arranging festivals, and pilgrims. Of his observations, he writes:

"I myself have become so accustomed to surprises, to interesting or extraordinary sights, that when a day happens to pass during which nothing remarkable has been heard or seen I feel vaguely discontented. But such blank days are rare: they occur in my own case when the weather is too detestable to permit going out-of-doors. For with ever so little money one can always obtain the pleasure of looking at curious things."

Lafcadio told of the grim castle's legend of a maiden interred alive under the walls of the castle at the time of its erection as a sacrifice to some forgotten gods. Her name was not recorded but everyone remembered that she was very beautiful and loved to dance. Afterwards, a law had to be passed forbidding any girl to dance in the streets of Matsue, or the hill would shudder and the great castle quiver from basement to summit.

On Lafcadio's way home one night he watched a woman standing on the bridge tossing tiny papers into the current with a picture of a divinity named Jizo and the *kaimyo* soul-name of her deceased child. He learned that on the forty-ninth day after the burial, she went to this place of running water to drop the little papers in one-by-one while repeating the holy invocation, "*Namu Jizo, Dai Bosatsu*" to pray for his soul. As a new light rose from behind the mountain peaks, others along the waterfront start clapping to salute the coming of the White Moon, Lady O-Tsuki-San.

At night he heard the voices of the city, the great temple bells rolling their soft Buddhist thunder across the dark; songs of night-walkers merry with wine; and chanting cries of peddlers making their last rounds, selling buckwheat cakes, sweet amber syrup for children, fortune-telling, and divining or love papers written in invisible ink. Lafcadio listened, felt, and recorded his first days in Matsue.

He took Pierre Loti's approach to descriptive writing, taking note of every fresh and powerful impression. Early writings had a tendency toward over-ripeness, but he'd begun to return to a clearer descriptive approach like he'd used as a journalist. He executed his works with technical control, strength of form, and depth of perception. He described his evolving style in terms of "lucidity, sharpness, firm hard outline" and of the "supreme artistic quality, self-restraint," with attendant qualities of "concentration, simplicity, and power". His adopted picturesque writing customs began deepening and expanding. By the time he arrived in Matsue, he was fusing pure description with folklore, legends, and his own instructive, attentive, and enthusiastic voice. This expository combination would enable him to become the ideal interpreter of Japan to the West.

CHAPTER 10

Lafcadio reported to Governor Yasusada Koteda at the prefectural office first. The campuses of the government primary, elementary, middle, and normal schools were across the street from the Izumo gubernatorial offices. After his formal greeting to the authority that hired him, he and Akira proceeded to the nearby Middle School to meet the dean, Sentaro Nishida.

Lafcadio immediately liked Nishida, a frail little man who would serve as his mentor and friend. He explained, "You will be teaching four hours a week in the normal school or Shihan-Gakko and the remainder of time dedicated to the twelve to sixteen-year-old boy students at the middle school or Jinjo Chugakko. You have been hired to teach dictation, reading, composition, and conversation, a total of twelve classes."

After explaining his assigned duties and methods of instruction, Nishida showed him around the campus buildings, took him to meet his teaching colleagues, and back to the governor's office. When he entered the governor's suites, he spotted a group of officials assembled there in rich-colored silk ceremonial robes. Before he had time to feel self-conscious about his simple Western garb, the governor greeted him warmly. Lafcadio felt the "placid force and kindness of a Buddha" in the tall governor. They chatted like old acquaintances through an interpreter.

When he left the gathering, told Akira, "I am twice blessed to be working for men like Sentaro Nishida and Yasusada Koteda."

Nishida and Lafcadio liked each other from the beginning. He found the kind dean of the professors to be clever, learned, brave, amiable, and not a flatterer. He said, "He points out my escapes; he tells me all; he is a real man, an amiable man." Unfortunately, Nishida was in failing health. "He is always ill. How bad God is! I am angry. This is a very cruel world that so good a man can be so ill. Why cannot the bad men have all the diseases?"

On September 2nd Lafcadio Hearn began his new career as a teacher. Nishida, also an English teacher, introduced him to his class. The young men in their formal school uniforms were curious about this new foreign instructor. They stared at the forty-year-old man who was as dark complexioned as many Japanese and small statured as them. His five-foot-three-inch height ceased to worry him, since he was taller than most of his colleagues. The small Japanese houses and miniature gardens seemed designed on his scale.

Japanese students were accustomed to obeying and revering their teachers, so in quiet decorum they watched their new instructor and listened closely when he spoke to them in clear, short English sentences with his low, gentle musical voice. They certainly noticed his uneven eyes, one marbled, sunken, and blind, and the other protruding and myopic. In politeness, no one paid undue attention or commented about his strange look.

Boys of middle and normal schools were products of severe military training and took on their burden of academic studies with the same discipline. When Lafcadio and Nishida entered the room, the students all rose and bowed in unison. Yet he was pleased to find that this respect was not based on fear or because they had faced the cruel severity of schoolmasters, like young Lafcadio had experienced in England.

Nishida had prepared the day's lesson plan. He stayed in the classroom for a while to help Lafcadio, who they called *Herun-san*, to establish a routine and call roll. In normal school the bowing and answering roll call was done under the sharp command of a class captain. All cadet-students were required to greet teachers with a sharp military salute, but Lafcadio ask them to call him Sensei Teacher, rather than Sir. When he pronounced names, sometimes after laborious difficulty, or asked questions, the loud resonant prompt answers would startle him. Earnest faces looked up to him for instructions to begin.

After his first day, Lafcadio hurried back to the inn to tell Akira about his classes and the difficulty he'd had in pronouncing roll call names. He related how most of them were docile and patient about his stumbling efforts. By law they'd been studying English since childhood but couldn't understand everything he said verbally. However, they understood when he wrote difficult or important words on the blackboard in his beautiful script. He confided in his loyal friend "I anticipate no difficulties, especially with Nishida nearby to help."

Lafcadio was soon in a routine of his five hours of teaching at the school. Confusion and awkwardness gradually disappeared. He fostered flowing communication with clear and consistent methods. The sheltered young men of Matsue were in awe of his worldliness and life experiences. He caught their imaginations and entertained them with his stories from Arthurian legends and Greek mythology. He was a diligent teacher giving the students subjects for composition that they had to write in his presence. When he assigned short essays to write in English, he challenged them to not only use new words and phrases but to think and be honest in their statements. For most, it was the first time they'd examined their daily living habits, ideas, and thoughts about their own feelings.

He encouraged them to be proud of their national customs, traditions, and gods. Many previous teachers were missionaries who berated them for being heathens and tried to convert them to Christianity. He asserted, "The missionaries everywhere represent the edge---the *acies*, to use the Roman word---of Occidental aggression." Lafcadio was a rare Western observer of Japan who did not take superiority of Western Christian civilization as an act of faith. He was convinced that, for ordinary citizens of the lower strata of society, their fundamental human rights were better safeguarded in Japanese slums than in European or American great cities he'd known.

Privately he remarked, "I am practically a traitor to England and a renegade. But in the eternal order of things, I know I am right." About the same time, Robert Stevenson was writing from Samoa declaring that the changes of the natives' habits, instigated by missionaries as a result of conversions, were "bloodier than a bombardment."

Hearn wrote, "It has been wisely observed by the greatest of modern thinkers that mankind has progressed more rapidly in every other respect than in morality."

In addition to completely dissimilar English and the regular courses taught, all the students had to learn the written and spoken forms of their own language, a huge alphabet of ideographs. The strain was hard on their young bodies and minds, especially since their diets of boiled rice and bean curd did not build and support physical or mental welfare. This saddened him. Otherwise, he found no fault or cause for complaint against the administration, instructors, or students of the Matsue education system.

Teachers at the middle school and normal school were provided a lounge where they could gather to eat, rest, smoke, or work on their lesson plans. Lafcadio was assigned a desk right next to Sentaro Nishida's desk. It was equipped with a small blue and white charcoal brazier hibachi for lighting pipes and dumping ashes. Tea was served at regular intervals. Lafcadio preferred the less pretentious, more cheerful lounge at the middle school. There were a few instructors who spoke English so he could join in chats when he wanted to.

The governor and education administrators were honored to have a scholar and published author teaching in their schools. In Japan he felt he had escaped past social scandals, public opinion, and the real or imagined enemies in the English and American churches. Lafcadio was becoming confident in his abilities and performance as an instructor. He soon became a prominent citizen in the appreciative community of Matsue and began participating in the general life of the community.

Lafcadio was invited to the governor's home and shown his art collection. The governor's daughter presented a caged songbird, an *uguisu*, to him. It had a remarkable voice and one of its repeated phrases was a Buddhist prayer. With Lafcadio's renewed interest in how Buddhism penetrated everyday life, this was a charming gift.

The humbleness, hospitality, and interest of Matsue's people pleased him. He said, "I must also confess that the very absence of Individuality essentially characteristic of the Occidental is one of the charms of Japanese social life for me: here the individual does not strive to expand his own individuality at the expense of everyone else."

Astounding even himself, he agreed to give a public presentation. He wrote to Basil Chamberlain in October:

"I had to make a speech before the educational association of Izumo the other day and in citing the labours of Darwin, Lubbock, Huxley, and others, I quoted also Taylor's delightful little book on Anthropology. My speech was the 'Value of the Imagination as a Factor in Education'. Hearn felt that Japanese education attached too much importance to rote memorization and did not cultivate the imagination. The Governor ordered the talk to be translated and printed;---so I am being for the moment perhaps much more highly considered than I ought to be."

Lafcadio was fortunate that Western ideas currently popular in Japan were the same as those that shaped his thinking in science and philosophy. His colleagues had admiration for the social applications of evolution. With his up-to-date Western ideas and his respect for Japanese customs, Lafcadio became a celebrity in Matsue. This man of letters was considered a great person in an unindustrialized corner of the world. He was both proud and flustered by the attention

CHAPTER 11

As they talked one day in the teachers' lounge, Nishida discovered that Lafcadio was denied entrance to the Kizuki temple. It turned out that Nashida was a personal friend of Takanori Senke, *Guji*, the high priest of the temple. The Senke family had been responsible for the holy place for eighty-two generations. Within three days Lafcadio received an invitation to visit the Shinto shrine the following weekend. The *Guji* was making an exception to his ancestors' prohibition against foreigners because he thought a Western writer could help the world learn about the revered Shinto home.

On September 14, Lafcadio and Akira excitedly set out for the village of Kizuki, the home of the ancient shrine of Izumo-Taisha, the oldest sacred place of Shinto. The first stage of their journey was to transverse Lake Shinji on a small steamer. He sat cross-legged on the roof of the cabin, using his telescope to view the mountains and horizon. Then they took *jinrikishas*- rickshaws over several miles of plains crisscrossed by several streams. It was getting dark by the time they rolled into town. Shopkeepers were shuttering their stores and going home for the night.

Inabaya Inn gave the weary travelers a warm reception. They accepted Lafcadio without fuss, like any other pilgrim. He was impressed by the clean, elegant accommodations. After they had eaten and rested, the innkeeper suggested a nocturnal visit to the shrine grounds.

Men scurried ahead of them with paper lanterns to light the moonless way. They followed bronze *torii* and an avenue of ancient trees to the foot of the mountain. A massive gate opened onto an outer courtyard. He and other pilgrims with their lanterns looked like giant fireflies flitting about in the nighttime. In the second courtyard, the Hall of Prayer's imposing façade loomed up through the darkness. Soft hand-clapping prayers echoed from inside the temple, but pilgrims had to content themselves with bowing and praying some distance from the edifice.

The next morning, as Lafcadio and Akira finished their breakfast, a young Shinto priest in blue ceremonial dress came to escort them to the temple. The priest insisted Akira must wear ceremonial trousers or he would not be admitted. Their innkeeper rescued the panic-stricken fellow with a loan of the proper attire. Lafcadio tidied up his own appearance by putting on a clean white collar and new tie.

He enjoyed seeing the village and long path leading up to the shrine in the daylight. The grounds surrounding the temple Taisha had been considered holy for three thousand years. The very trees, soil, and rocks were sacred. Their visit fell on one of the numerous Shinto festival days. Hundreds of reverent kimonoed pilgrims massed in the generous, graveled courtyards. Young priestesses, called the daughters of the gods, gracefully danced through the visitors to flutes and drums played by priests. The crowd circled the grounds counterclockwise. Worshipers approached the doorway of the Hall of Prayer, dropped coins or handfuls of rice in the entryway box, clapped their hands four times, and bowed in brief prayer. Masses of people clapping sounded like the continued rushing of a waterfall.

Lafcadio passed beyond the blowing curtains in the Hall of Prayer into the innermost court. He stared in awe at the structure held up by great pillars and massive beams, set before the memory of man. A broad flight of ironbound stairs took them in among a double line of solemn motionless priests clad in purple and gold robes with high headgear. All eyes followed the first Occidental allowed inside the temple.

Following his guide and Akira's examples he removed his shoes, bowed, and did a ritualistic hand washing. Attendant guides in billowing silk robes signaled them to join in at the rear of a procession. Lafcadio felt like a barbarian in his clothes and graceless movements. He was conducted to an immense hall at the end of the temple. Gold brocade curtains were drawn aside to reveal a regal bearded figure seated on the matted floor. His white robes were spread out in undulating, sculptured folds. This commanding figure was the hereditary *Guji* of Taisha, high priest of the Shinto shrine. Lafcadio's small party knelt before him and bowed their heads to the floor.

Lafcadio peeked out to see that the *Guji* and his attendants all had aquiline, aristocratic features quite unlike the commoners they served. Their demeanor was more military than priestly. As Akira began translating, he soon found his stern host, Takanori Senke, surprisingly gracious and kind. He told them about the temple's history, customs, and legends. A collection of relics had been laid out in advance for the guests. Lafcadio was allowed to inspect the display of fine swords, a jade flute, antiques helmets, a bundle of long arrows with double pointed heads, onyx and jasper jewels, and a metal mirror.

A white-robed young woman came in to perform a sacred *Miko* dance. Afterward, the *Guji* and his chief priest took Lafcadio on a tour of the buildings, pointing out thousand-year-old paintings, Shinto curios, and the temple library. As a final honor, Senke took Lafcadio to his own quarters where he opened a locked chest and let him examine manuscripts written by ancient poets, warlords, and emperors. Since Shinto had no great body of literature or profound philosophy like the Buddhists, Western theologians belittled Shinto religion as an indigenous natural religion, merely ancestor and emperor worship.

On Sunday night as Lafcadio traveled back to Matsue, he felt that while some aspects of Shinto seemed childish and crude, the visit to Kizuki gave him a glimpse into the whole soul of a people. He wondered if this nationalistic faith might hold something more heroic and loyal. He began to realize how sustaining an instinctive and inherent devotion could be. Shinto, the ancient nature religion, seemed to him an "occult force…part of the Soul of the Race." It resonated with his own belief in ghostly presences and the world of the dead governing the world of the living.

He remarked, "When we become conscious that we owe whatever is wise or good or strong or beautiful in each one of us, not to one particular inner individuality, but to the struggles and sufferings and experiences of the whole unknown chain of human lives behind us, reaching back into mystery unthinkable,---the worship of ancestors seems an extremely righteous thing to do."

During his friendships with Buddhists Nishida and Akira, he learned that there should be more sincerity and heart in human relations and more silence and simplicity in their interactions.

With his head filled with the reverence and awe of this shrine visit, he wrote to Professor Chamberlain, "I have just returned from my first really great Japanese experience. It might have impressed even a more unbelieving mind than my own."

After his first visit to Kitzuki, he returned often. Lafcadio would leave early on Saturday, his day off, and return Sunday night. He enjoyed Kitzuki immensely. He could visit the shrine for wonder; explore small curiosity shops; received warm hospitality at the inn; and swim through the curved bay out to offshore rocks at a nearby beach. He admired the ancient village with its customs and rituals.

Although thousands of pilgrims from around the Empire visited the great Izumo shrine, the small, half-blind teacher from Matsue became well known in the town and an honored guest at the inn. The maids came to adore him. He would talk to each of them in his baby kind of Japanese. They felt protective of their odd foreigner.

One seventeen-year-old maid named O-sani Yasuda would accompany him to the shrine, carry the lantern when he took late night strolls under the old pine trees, and go with him down to the beach for his swim. She learned not to be afraid when he swam out beyond her sight or floated on his back. He'd laugh at her concern and assure her, "My body never sinks." All her life she remembered the day when he bought her a costly tortoise shell hairpin with a seabird and waves design.

Lafcadio spent every Sunday and holiday visiting legendary places and temples around the province. It pleased him when he learned that classical Izumo was the oldest of the provinces. Seeing the great shrine at Kitsuki and in the little shrines of Matsue, he realized how natural but important the "way of the gods" was in the everyday life of the people. Based on his experiences in this part of Japan, he wrote in his first book:

"Buddhism has a voluminous theology, a profound philosophy, a literature vast as the sea. Shinto has no philosophy, no code of ethics, no metaphysics; and yet, by its very immateriality, it can resist the invasion of Occidental religious thoughts as no other Orient faith can. Shinto extends a welcome to Western science, but remains the irresistible opponent of Western religion; and the foreign zealots who would strive against it are astounded to find the power that foils their uttermost efforts indefinable as magnetism and invulnerable as air." He felt too much philosophy or religion would clip even an angel's wings.

Lafcadio was impressed with the Japanese ability to take in the new while not giving up the old. They could greedily absorb and use whatever was learned from other cultures while maintaining their own distinct identity. The decency of daily common existence in the small towns isolated from the rest of Japan provided him hints into the mystery of Japanese life. He was enchanted by how a powerful state of devotion could be generated by rituals, myths, and loyalty to the past.

CHAPTER 12

Lafcadio's honor of having an audience with the high priest at Kitsuki Shinto temple distinguished him in the eyes of Matsue's people. After his daily teaching duties were over, he would set out to explore saying, "I must make divers pilgrimages, for all about the city, beyond the waters or beyond the hills, lie holy places immemorially old."

For example, North of Matsue, along the coast to Kaka, there was an enormous cavern by the sea. It was guarded by a famous stone Jizo, a statue of a Buddhist Bodhisattva, dedicated to the divine protection of children. Legend said that each night ghosts of little children piled up stacks of pebbles and rocks before the statue. The next days, faint but noticeable tiny fresh footprints were left in the sand. Lafcadio arranged a journey by boat to this site. He brought a traditional pilgrim's gift of small straw sandals, children's zori, and left them inside the cave, hoping to keep the infant ghosts from cutting their feet on the sharp rocks.

After Akira Manabe left Matsue to start his job in Kyoto as a journal editor, Lafcadio had no one to come home to, share meals with, and accompany him on adventures. It made him more aware of being a foreigner and newcomer. By the end of October, he decided to move out of the Tomitaya Inn into a rented house of his own. Most changes and progress in Lafcadio's life were accompanied with a quarrel of some sort, and this was no exception.

Lafcadio was morally offended by the conduct of the innkeeper, not toward him as a guest, but in the host's treatment of his daughter. The proprietor of the inn had a little girl with a disfiguring disease of the eyes. She needed immediate medical attention and Lafcadio, who was particularly sensitive to any trouble with vision, repeatedly tried to get the father to take her to the hospital. When he realized the father had no intention of spending his money to save the girl's sight, Lafcadio paid the fees for the necessary treatments and her eyes were saved. He could not stay under the roof of such a heartless parent, so in a hot rage moved away from the inn.

He rented a small two-story dwelling from the merchant Orihara on Sueji Honmachi Street, with a garden pavilion. It sat on the edge of Shinjiko Lake just above a many-pillared white bridge spanning Ohashi River. He called it the "bird-cage house" because of its size and frailness. It was in a prime location to observe and hear the daily comings and goings of the town's people. With his telescope he could see the surrounding mountain peaks, each with its own divine story attached to it.

Lafcadio decided to adopt the Japanese lifestyle, writing, "I think it is only by this way, in the course of years, that I can get at the soul or *kokoro* of the common people,---which is my aim."

He began living less and less like a foreigner. When he came home from teaching, he would immediately take off his hard leather shoes, stiff collared shirts and binding coat to put on his loose-fitting kimono robe, obi sash, and tabi footwear. He slept on a Japanese futon padded bed with its tiny wooden pillows on a matted floor. On pleasant days he would push open the *shoji*-room dividers made of translucent paper sheets on a lattice frame to let in fresh air and sunlight. He sat on his zabuton cushion and smoked tobacco in a carved, long-stemmed Japanese pipe.

For the first year he ate only local Japanese food. Later he confessed to reverting to occasional gluttonous servings of beefsteak, sausages, bread and ale - "the fault of my ancestors…the ferocious, wolfish hereditary instincts and tendencies of boreal mankind. The sins of the father, etc."

Now that he had his own abode, Sentaro Nishida, his younger colleague at the middle school, would stop by his house to talk. National differences and age barriers were broken down and they quickly became best friends. Men in his past, of unusual intelligence like Krehbiel, Matas, Crosby, and Hendrick were necessary to Lafcadio. He needed friends with whom he could relax, talk freely of his thoughts and concerns, drink too much, read poetry, and be ambitious.

Lafcadio's students also visited their esteemed professor to ask questions and bask in his presence. They approached and softly knocked, "*Tano-mo-o,*

I ask to enter." He later wrote, "Sometimes they scarcely speak at all, but appear to sink into a sort of happy reverie. What they come for really is the quiet pleasure of sympathy. Not an intellectual sympathy, but the sympathy of pure good-will: the simple pleasure of being quite comfortable with a friend."

Another Western teacher before Lafcadio was a thick-skinned, obtuse missionary who tried to convert them to Christianity and berated their Japanese beliefs and customs. This new master Herun-san was different. He was not arrogant and did not look down on the Japanese. On the contrary, Lafcadio was adamant in telling his students to think about themselves as never before and to be more Japanese. He knew Plato was right when he said, "Nothing taught by force stays in the soul."

People with open minds are more empathetic as they seek to understand a culture. Rather than judge others, they try to understand how culture, history, religion, and character influence actions. An open-minded person allows for human differences. The visiting young men found their new instructor receptive to listening to their problems, joys, and dreams.

Lafcadio Hearn personified the *sensei*-teacher who had qualities they could admire and respect. Before the Meiji era, instructors were reverently respected due to ancient custom. Wisdom was voluntarily sought, while that of the West was thrust upon Japan by violence. His pupils still followed the Chinese code which ordained that 'even the shadow of a teacher must not be trodden on.'

Herun-san's students thought him a heroic figure because he sometimes wore an eye patch when teaching. They speculated that he must have lost his eye in a duel or battle. Lafcadio stood a little over five feet tall and was not necessarily a handsome man by Western standards, but few in remote Matsue knew how foreigners were supposed to look, so they never commented on his person. Everyone remained discrete about his appearance and impaired eyesight.

In turn, Lafcadio surprisingly found that he enjoyed the professor-student relationship and was satisfied in the job overall. He disliked monotonous drill work, grading examination papers, and he often grew impatient with long teaching hours that took time away from his writing. He was learning more about Japan from his students than any other source. At times student assigned compositions and talks were the basis for subject matter as he prepared his first book, *Glimpses of Unfamiliar Japan*.

Lafcadio found himself in a quandary. He wanted to write about pre-Meiji Japan. Matsue, a remote city still not served by a railroad, where the old ways were still powerful, was a resource for him. Yet, the central government anxiously scrutinized every aspect of education. The schools were set up to act as agents of change for the Meiji government. They wanted to modernize the country and adopt new international ways. In order to compete on equal terms with the Western world, they insisted on that one essential tool, English - the very language that Lafcadio taught. He was afraid that he was contributing to the changes he dreaded.

Keenly interested in other schools than his own, he found that the kindergarten allowed young children to learn while playing in light attractive rooms. It reminded him of Spencer's theories in which the needs of the emotions and needs of the body took precedence over the needs of pure intellect. But the schools were also teaching science and logic, so he wondered what would happen to faith and traditional ways when these children grew up.

In this case, two of his greatest enthusiasms, science and tradition, were in seemingly irreconcilable conflict. Matsue represented the Old Japan he'd been yearning for. He'd found Tokyo and Yokohama already contaminated by the West. Lafcadio hated to see Japan lose its ancient ways and become industrialized and homogenized like the rest of the world

CHAPTER 13

When the gloomy cold rains of an early winter set in, Lafcadio only had the Japanese style, porcelain, charcoal burning hibachi in his paper-thin birdcage house. Even with its winter adaptation, the *kotatsu* devise for conserving heat of the coals by covering both the hibachi and legs of those huddled around it with a comforter or quilt, Lafcadio was constantly cold.

That first winter, icy winds blew from Asia across the Sea of Japan, piling snow drifts against his fragile house. His walls were as cold as outdoors. The locals called the alternating rain with sun, and chilly winds "mad weather". The temperature could change three or four times in twenty-four hours. Matsue was covered in record-breaking snow over five feet deep that winter. If his "province of the gods" enchantment had a flaw, severe cold was it. He could not get warm at home or at school.

Within a few weeks, he was ill with a debilitating respiratory infection and had to take leave from teaching and go to bed. He was worried and lonely. In January of 1891, he wrote to Professor Chamberlain:

"I myself am very sick. I boasted too soon about my immunity from cold. I have been severely touched where I thought myself strongest---in my lungs---and have passed some weeks in bed. My first serious discouragement came with this check to my enthusiasm; I fear a few more winters of this kind will put me underground. But this has been a very exceptional winter, they say. The first snowstorm piled five feet of snow about my house, which faces the lake, looking at Kitsuki. All the mountains are white, and the country is smothered with snow, and the wind is very severe. I never saw a heavier snowfall in the United States or Canada. The thermometer does not go so low as you might suppose, not more than twelve degrees above zero; but the houses are cold as cattle barns, and the *hibachi* and the *kotatsu* are mere shadows of heat---ghosts, illusions. But I have the blues now; perhaps tomorrow everything will be cheerful again. The authorities are astonishingly kind to me. If they were not, I do not know what I should do."

Lafcadio lay in his sick bed and dreamed of warmer climates like tropical Martinique and considered traveling on to the Philippines. He wondered how anyone could cultivate Buddhist sentiments when they were freezing. He wrote, "Cold compels painful notions of solidity; cold sharpens the delusion of personality; cold quickens egotism; cold numbs thought, and shrivels up the little wings of dreams."

As the rain and snows continued, a wave of pneumonia swept through Matsue. Sentaro Nishida fell dangerously ill. Lafcadio was greatly relieved when his friend recovered enough to visit the birdcage again. Sentaro observed how Lafcadio suffered with illness in his comfortless home. It was obvious that he could not take care of himself alone. Soon after, he came to Lafcadio with a simple solution to his plight – the answer would be marriage to a young Japanese girl. He listened quietly. He'd considered himself a man of high romance, but knew he dreamed in vain. He'd always said the best he could hope for was the gratitude of some meek young creature who might feel attached to him because of his kindness.

Likewise, he said to a friend in New Orleans Julia Baker years before, that he "would not care for intellectual companionship in a wife, but if he ever married he would choose some simple quiet person who would stay in her domestic sphere, be content with his affection, and stay meekly outside his realm of thought". He'd also written, "There is one type of ideal woman very seldom described in poetry---the old maid, the woman whom sorrow or misfortune prevents from fulfilling her natural destiny."

Much of the time, he had not supposed he would ever marry. But now he was being offered the chance to give his prophetic words a life - a marriage of convenience and companionship for a lifelong worshipper of Venus. Would he marry an old maid, a simple quiet person who stay in her homemaker realm and let him work?

Somehow, at that moment, Nishida's suggestion that he marry someone who would order his affairs, provide for his domestic needs in his new country, and keep him warmer than the *kotatsu*, seemed like the most natural things in the world to agree to. Lafcadio found Japanese women dainty and appealing. Plus, a native wife would not interfere with his work and let him come and go as he pleased. His friend had just the woman in mind.

Setsu or Setsuko (b. 1868), meaning true or virtuous, was the twenty-two-year-old daughter of the Koizumi family of Matsue. Koizumi was an honorable name. The family had belonged to the samurai swordsmen rank of the *daimio* prince. The revolution to overthrow the Shoguns and restore the Mikado emperor to power had broken the feudal structure of Japanese society. With the downfall of the *daimyos*, the lesser nobility samurai also collapsed. Many of those once great warriors lost their positions and sank onto great poverty.

Previously the leader of a powerful samurai caste, her grandfather and his descendants had survived the social revolution of 1868 with their principles and manners intact, but now were functionless and impoverished. Their income from the feudal lord was cut off and they had no training in trades or commerce.

In Japanese society the nucleus of the family was the child-parent relationship, not the husband-wife bond. Marriage ties did not have the same religious significance given to them in Occidental culture. By marrying, Setsu would be helping her family to whom she owed her first duty. She would marry a foreign stranger if her elders agreed to it because she'd been trained in obedience and deference from childhood. In old Japanese culture, women were taught to restrain and bury their own ideas and feelings (*enryo*) in everyday interactions and to do what was expected by society and the family.

Through Sentaro Nashida's mediation the marriage between Lafcadio Hearn and Setsu Koizumi was arranged. An alliance with a white foreigner would have been considered a disgrace under ordinary circumstances; but the Koizumi family needed the union for survival. The reconstructive changes from feudalism to imperial rule reduced families of rank to poverty and obscurity. House and land went first, then article by article, all things not necessary to exist passed cheaply to the rich, whose wealth was called "the money of tears" (*namida no kane*). In desperation, some kin opened the graves of their ancestors to remove their precious samurai swords and sheaths and replace them with common ones in case the deceased warrior might need them. Occasionally young girls were sold to train as geishas, but not Setsuko, who earned money for her family by weaving and housekeeping for others.

Sentaro Nishida was sure Setsu would be a quiet, dutiful wife, grateful for the protection and kindness of the foreign teacher. He'd explained to his new friend Lafcadio that marrying her would be an act of compassion on his part because he would take on financial responsibility for the family as well. He felt Lafcadio would also honor any responsibilities he assumed. The forty-year-old Lafcadio calmly thought it over and told Nishida to go ahead with the proposal.

Professor Nishida made sure the proposal was managed in a traditional, respectable fashion by an estimable go-between, Professor Nishida himself. It was a bond contracted for the betterment of both parties. He believed both his friends would benefit from the arrangement. When Nishida met with the parents of Setsuko Koizumi, they said they'd heard of Lafcadio Hearn. According to the local paper *San'in Shimbun*, the American writer was too talented for such an isolated place and his salary was second only to the prefectural Governor's. The newspaper reported that the governor had honored him with invitations to horse races, tournaments, performances, and gatherings in the official residence.

Lafcadio discovered right away that "the foreigner's every act is a subject for comment. There is no such thing in Japan as privacy. There are no secrets. Every earthly thing a man does is known to everybody, and life is extravagantly, astoundingly frank. The moral effect is, in my opinion, extremely good."

Setsu's family were assured Lafcadio Hearn was not like other foreigners and was highly respected by fellow teachers and students. They thought *Herun-san* would be kind to Setsu and be a good son-in-law. They accepted the proposal of marriage.

Setsu was not particularly pretty, but she had the charm of gentle grace about her. In fact, she'd been married at a very early age to Tameji Inagaki, son of a formerly well-to-do gentry family. Unable to endure the shame of hopeless poverty of his own family and of the deposed samurai Koizumi family, her alcoholic husband deserted her and disappeared. She and her family followed procedures at the city hall for dissolving the marriage to Tameji and reregistered her name under the house of Koizumi. As a rejected divorced woman, she may never have remarried at all.

Setsu might have been secretly a little sad that she couldn't wait for a more romantic youthful union. The age difference between her and Lafcadio was 18 years; she was 22 and he was 40. She held vague fears of the unknown, such as a general belief among people that Europeans had feet like horse's hoof, because they wore leather bags on their feet instead of sandals. One of the old-fashioned names for foreigners was 'one-toed fellows.' She may have been a little fearful about marrying Nishida's one-eyed older friend, especially knowing nothing of foreign customs and traditions.

But Setsu was a pious daughter and would do as she was told. There was a large household to feed, and dignity and honor do not fill empty rice bowls. It was a bonus that she'd have a home of her own with no husband's family to serve. In-laws could be cruel if they wished. She found out that she'd also been chosen because she was more mature and could read and write in Japanese. Both were strange requests for a foreigner.

"Do you speak any English? she was asked by Nashida in the arrangement interview.

Setsu rattled off, 'Thank you, please, yes, no, good, bad, hello, goodbye, sorry, man, woman, big, and small", her entire vocabulary.

"Does he speak Japanese? How will we communicate?"

"He knows about the same few words in Japanese, plus '*miya*' for the temples he likes to visit. Like others, you can talk by drawing pictures, pointing, and playacting. It was easier when the Imperial University man Akira was in town. If it is important, one of the students from the normal school can come over and translate."

"He's been in Japan for five months. Is he a slow learner?" she laughed.

"Don't be insulting. There are others who would want this position. But he likes the idea of being with the daughter of a great samurai."

"Typical foreigner," she scoffed, unable to hide her prejudice.

When Lafcadio and Setsu first met, she stood with lowered eyes. She'd been loaned her foster mother's best silk brocade formal kimono, the only one that had not been sold. Lafcadio appraised her with his right eye through his thick handheld magnifying disc. She was glad she'd been told of his blind eye and tried to think of the covering whiteness as storm clouds before summer rains.

Lafcadio wore his heavy seaman's overcoat over a padded kimono, Western suit trousers, leather gloves, a knitted scarf around his neck, and his usual wide brimmed hat. She would have thought him rude or addled if Nishida had not mentioned Lafcadio's sensitivity to the cold and that he'd been sick for weeks with fever and a rasping cough.

In January, 1891, the twenty-fourth year of Meiji, Lafcadio and Setsu were married in a civil ceremony. They celebrated their nuptials with an exchange of rice wine in front of members of her family and his friends from Matsue. The local authorities recorded their marriage contract. Lafcadio now was unofficially part of a pre-existing family that was willing to accept him as one of their own. Under Japanese law the only way for a foreigner to marry a Japanese woman was to be adopted into her family and become a Japanese citizen. Nonetheless, Lafcadio considered himself "morally, and according to public opinion, fast married."

Lafcadio Hearn and his Wife.

CHAPTER 14

Lafcacio's friends abroad were surprised that he entered into an arranged marriage with such a traditional, plain, non-English speaking woman. And that he took on responsibility for her family members as well. However, when Lafcadio made the commitment, he had every intention of remaining with Setsu and raising a family in the Japanese tradition. Often foreign men would marry and un-marry as easily as renting a house and giving it up. Lafcadio was bound by his own private standard. He would not be deserting his foreign bride after a while like the amoral Pierre Loti or *Madame Butterfly*'s Lieutenant Pinkerton or his own father.

Nothing in the background of either of them could have prepared them for the complications they were about to face. However, two disparate people from completely different cultures were both committed to work on a solid, permanent relationship. Setsu's mother had said the same words every mother of a bride says, "Go forth bravely to your new life, just as a soldier goes to battle. Look in the mirror every day, for if selfishness or pride are in the heart, they will grow into the lines of the face. Watch closely. Be strong like the pine, yield in gentle obedience like the swaying bamboo, and yet, like the fragrant plum blossoming beneath the snow, never lose the gentle perseverance of loyal womanhood. It will bring you peace."

Her mother reminded Setsu that the life of a samurai, man or woman, is the same: loyalty to the overlord husband and bravery in defense of his honor. Setsu was a refined woman, trained never to show anger, grief, or jealousy even under circumstances compelling all three. She was expected to use pure sweetness to correct any faults of her husband, and never wound his feelings. A wife was to be outwardly the ideal of perfect selflessness.

All the circumstances were strange to the new bride. When she moved into the birdcage house on the lake, she found that Lafcadio had only the basic minimum - one futon, one table and chair, one suit of clothes, one kimono, and a few books. She began to bring order into his life. She cleaned the house top-to-bottom and brought in necessary items for daily life. She ordered new bedding quilts and padded kimonos for him. The weather was too wet and cold to wash and properly dry the old worn ones he had. She could have a maid, but enjoyed doing much of the housework herself in a rush of proprietary zeal. They were settling into a life of living together.

First the language barrier had to be addressed. Setsu's English was non-existent and Lafcadio's Japanese extremely rudimental. He applied himself to learning Japanese. He did not press her to learn English because he preferred that she remain a true daughter of Japan, not contaminated with Western ideas and influences. By not reading or speaking a word of English, she was certain to stay out of his intellectual world.

They used pantomime and interpreters at first. Then with the diligent use of dictionaries, they gradually developed a language of their own for everyday communications. They called their pidgin Japanese, *Herun-San kotoba* - Hearn's dialect, a combination of Japanese-English baby talk that only they could understand. Much of it came from Lafcadio's misuse and clumsy pronunciation of words. He knew some Japanese, but it was not quite enough to converse or read.

In *Herun-san* language, 'not enough' and 'hunger' were the same word. Setsu's grandfather used to say, "*Herun-san* speaks Japanese like a drunk lady poet," as he mimicked his words in a high voice and using speech only women used. Lafcadio's Japanese echoed his wife's voice because she taught him.

In the matters of household affairs, Lafcadio respectfully gave her control and let her use her own judgment. He would tell her, "I know how to teach and write, and that is all. You know better about other things. It will please me most if you do as you like."

As a proper Japanese wife, it was her duty to manage and conserve their income. When the Shoguns were overthrown in revolution and the Mikado emperor restored to power, the feudal structure of society was destroyed. The samurai, like the monarchist noble *emigres* (immigrants) after the French Revolution, sank into great poverty when the Meiji government cut support. The Koizumi family's rank and fortune were lost. In a short period, they became impoverished ex-elite. Men of samurai rank had a code of ethics that taught them utter contempt for money, and they knew nothing about business. It had always been considered a disgrace for them to handle finances, so the management of business affairs and earning a living was left to their faithful women. Setsu had painstakingly supported her family by weaving and sewing. Her entire life, Setsu Koizumi had counted every coin twice.

From the beginning, Lafcadio's carelessness about money alarmed her. She found him shockingly extravagant. If they went shopping and she saw a kimono she liked, he might try to buy five or six for her. "But they are so cheap," he'd explain when she protested. If she liked a piece of art, he'd overpay the artist to protect him from being cheated. He continued to use his pocket money to give the family and household little gifts. She reminded herself that these acts "rose from the kindness of his heart" and offset them with her own careful, rigid management.

She learned to avert some of his extravagances by indirection. He quickly realized that she was a better manager than he ever was and placed his finances in her hands. His personal needs, like tobacco and books, were relatively few and simple, so she was able to deposit a large portion of his salary in the bank each month. If her frugal decisions ran counter to his wishes, he stood by her choices. "*Gomen*, I'm sorry. Little Setsu is right!" She was silently happy about his un-Japanese openness of pride in her as his wife and partner.

At home Setsu was a very traditional, submissive housewife. Every morning she would hand him his clothes, garment by garment, as she was trained to do. When they went out together, she'd walk several paces behind him. If he worked late, she'd try to stay awake or apologize, "Pardon me for being the first to sleep." Every samurai girl was taught never to lose control of mind or body, even in sleep. When she said goodnight, she'd settle herself into *kinoji* the proper sleeping position for a woman. Men might stretch themselves out carelessly, but women must curve into the modest, dignified character *kinoji*, which means 'spirit of control'.

Setsu soon realized that nothing was to interfere with Lafcadio's work. She quickly learned to manage the household so that their paper-walled house would remain absolutely quiet when he was at home. Even sweeping or opening a drawer might "break his beautiful soap bubble" of concentration. Thinking of his inviolable sphere that way made his requirements seem more reasonable.

He may not have been obsessed or in love erotically like he had been with his first love Mattie Foley in Cincinnati or others, but he admired Setsu's sensible ways and grew to cherish and depend on her completely. He admired her time-honored virtues of modesty and selflessness. He soon found that beauty was not in the face, but was a light in the heart. Also that the most ordinary things could be extraordinary, simply by doing them with the right person.

Even when he became melancholy or depressed, he made the decision to stay put. He confessed to his New York friend Ellwood Hendrick, "My household relations have been extremely happy. The only trouble is that they begin to take the shape of something unbreakable, and to bind me fast here at the very time I was beginning to feel like going away."

Later he wrote about how marriage had transformed his life, "Marriage seems to me the certain destruction of all that emotion and suffering,---so that one afterwards looks back at the old times with wonder. One cannot dream or desire anything more, after love is transmuted into the friendship of marriage. It is like a haven from which you can see the dangerous sea currents, running like violent bands beyond you out of sight."

Lafcadio wrote to Chamberlain, "But how sweet the Japanese woman is! All the possibilities of the race for goodness seem to be concentrated in her. It shakes one's faith in some Occidental doctrines. If this is the result of suppression and oppression, then these are not altogether bad. On the other hand, how diamond hard the character of the American woman becomes under the idolatry of which she is the subject."

Lafcadio always had deep feelings for his intellectual sister, Elizabeth Bisland, but he was also disturbed by the cold, calculating, ambitious aspects of her personality. He maintained, "Only nature and Woman are unspeakably sweet." Society women were seen by him as corrupted, those who had fallen from grace.

Setsu could dismiss many of Lafcadio's idiosyncrasies to his artistic temperament. But she was alarmed and frightened by his outbursts and emotional extremes. Unlike Japanese men, he had no patience with people over minor infractions and was unable to disguise his anger. He was elated or irritated to an abnormal degree.

She could hear him in his study, weeping uncontrollably or laughing until tears ran down his face. He'd appear in a trance, his face white and drawn, or moaning as his pen flew over his yellow paper. He was busy studying and writing all the time. His mind was never at rest. Sometimes he would get lost in his work for days, unconscious of his surroundings.

One night she found his study dense from smoke from the oil lamp and Lafcadio almost suffocated. Although he had a very sensitive nose for odors, he'd noticed nothing in his writing frenzy. He became reckless about his own health and wasted himself in his creative sprees. She was hesitant but eventually took her fears to Professor Nishida.

"Do you think my husband is losing his mind? Has he lost one of his souls? Good men can have up to nine souls, but with his depressions and lack of patience I am afraid that he is losing his. What can I do to help him?"

"Hearn-San is only behaving as other writers do. He is a very nervous and sensitive man, and too deeply interested in writing. That is all. It would be better if he didn't work so hard, had more pleasures, and saw his friends oftener."

Taking Nishida's advice, she tried to draw Lafcadio out to art exhibits or wrestling matches they both enjoyed. But when she suggested he was working too much, his reply was always the same, "I'm only happy when I'm working. I never get tired when I have something to write. You can make me happy by telling me all the legends you know and anything interesting you see or hear."

Setsu gradually adjusted to his moods and strange habits as a writer. She came to admire and feel deep affection for the eccentric *gakusha*-scholar she had married. She took pride in her honored position as the wife of a foreign author and teacher.

Under the watchful eye of Setsu, they saved two hundred dollars and were receiving occasional royalty checks for books like *Chita, Youma,* and *Two Years in the French West Indies*. She pointed out to Lafcadio that while the little garden house served his bachelor requirements, now that he was a man of consequence and position in Matuse, they should live accordingly. He saw no reason to change, but accepted her advice and they went house hunting.

Setsue finally found a samurai estate in the shadow of the ancient castle spires. There was a river running by the impressive gate and a mountainous hill overlooking the garden. He would miss the sunsets on the lake, but Setsu would not miss the noisy Ohashi Bridge. In June, 1891, Lafcadio, Setsu, a maid and an adopted street cat moved into a more secluded and spacious ex-samurai house-*yashiki* called Kitabori. The rent was four dollars a month. In their beautiful home, the fourteen rooms contained hanging pictures painted on silk kakemono, and vases in the alcoves, and a hibachi encircled by plush kneeling cushions.

Every room had sliding panels that opened onto one of three gardens surrounding the *yashiki* house. A fulltime gardener attended the trees, shrubs, plants and flowers, lotus ponds, and raked gravel plots. The garden master spent hours teaching Lafcadio the Japanese names of every creature and object in his exquisite, cultivated world.

Lafcadio describes the scene "In a Japanese Garden": "I have already become too fond of my dwelling-place. Each day after returning from my college duties and exchanging my teacher's uniform for the infinitely more comfortable Japanese robe, I find more than compensation for the weariness of five class-hours in the simple pleasure of squatting on the shaded veranda overlooking the gardens."

"Those antique garden walls, high-mossed below their ruined coping of tiles, seem to shut out even the murmur of the city's life. There are no sounds but the voices of birds, the shrilling of semi cicadae, or, at long, lazy interval, the solitary splash of a diving frog. Nay, those walls seclude me from much more than city streets. Outside them hums the changed Japan of telegraphs and newspapers and steamships; within dwell the all-reposing peace of nature and the dreams of the sixteenth century. There is a charm of quaintness in the very air, a faint sense of something viewless and sweet all about one; perhaps the gentle haunting of dead ladies who looked like the ladies of the old picture-books, and who lived here when all this was new. Even in the summer light---touching the strange gray shapes of stone, thrilling through the foliage of the long-loved trees---there is a tenderness of a phantom caress. These are the gardens of the past. The future will know them only as dreams, creations of a forgotten art, whose charm no genius may reproduce."

Lafcadio was sensitive to people, birds, flowers, trees---Not because they were his, but because he was awake to the extraordinary beauty of things.

CHAPTER 15

Lafcadio lived a comfortable life in Matsue. He was different from the harassed and homeless man in cities like Cincinnati and New Orleans. The angry man he was in Yokohama was calmer and more adaptable. He moved about his new life in an aura of substantial dignity and importance.

Kitabori, the ancient samurai's house, was the center of his world of marriage, teaching, and writing. It symbolized everything good he had found in remote Matsue. He discovered that home could be another person or family unit. He had never really belonged to a family in any way that could count, so he was delighted with the acquisition of Setsu's mother, father, grandfather and grandmother, and family servants. He never balked at the support, duties, obligations and benefits which having a family entailed.

Moving to the spacious samurai house by the castle's northern moat made room under one roof for the whole extended family he inherited through marriage. Setsu's grandfather was his favorite relative. He spent hours with the interesting elderly man who represented the old Japan that Lafcadio had fallen in love with. Grandfather devoted his days to reading, to memories, and trying to avoid or adjust to unwelcome ideas of progressive reform. He believed that to have forced the god-descended emperor from his palace of holiness and peace and plunge him into a material world of sordid duties, was sacrilege. And that the loss of shogun and samurai power was a sorrowful thing for Japan. On certain holidays he would dress in his worn cloth garments with closed sleeves and bloomer like skirt, over which rattled a lacquered-scaled breastplate crossed stitched with his shogun's crest. There were no weapons or horses to ride, so he bowed before the family altar and said his prayers. Grandfather always sat very straight with samurai dignity. He still had an undaunted air and a slight left shoulder droop like one who once wore two swords. Lafcadio loved the old hero's traditions and stories.

The arranged marriage to Setsu worked out better than her family or Lafcadio's friends had hoped for them. He was getting older and found himself dissatisfied with temporary relationships with women. He consciously resolved to exorcise his curse and delusion of the "Eternal Feminine, the woman thou shalt never know." He was tired of living alone and was anxious to have children. At thirty-five he'd confessed to a friend, "No man died so utterly as the man without children."

Each one changed the other as they settled into married life. There were some bumps in the road. Setsu was publicly embarrassed many times when Lafcadio lost his temper or became impatient with anything he disliked. He never acted like a proper Japanese husband in that he included her in conversation with company and praised her to others more than was decorous. They were often heard laughing together. It was unseemly to joke and giggle with a wife - laughter with geishas was customary, but not with one's spouse.

He found that he could not get close to Japanese men, as it was considered terribly vulgar to pat someone on the back or shoulder and say hello. He had to maintain a certain distance even from his best friends. Setsu's strict adherence to old-fashioned etiquette helped Lafcadio learn and adapt to Japanese social and family life.

His comfort and peacefulness in the *Kitabori* house were possible because of his modest prosperity from teaching salaries and royalties earned with his pen. For the first time in his life, he was not stressed about money matters. His earnings allowed them to live in the former samurai's house in the shadow of the ruined Daimyo's castle. Its design, making utility elegant, was a kind of beauty new to him. A polished framework of bare wood, clean straw-matted floors, and sliding walls and windows that unfolded room-to-room for spaciousness and opened the house to various views of the natural garden spaces within the compound walls.

Most days he and Setsu strolled about the gardens, enjoying their private domain with pride. She taught him how to say the names of flowers, insects, and animals they encountered. He was entertained by the antics of all the small creatures. He made a pet of a snake that lived on the edge of a lotus pond, sometimes feeding it bits of his meal. Setsu was horrified, but he reassured her, "Snakes don't mean to be harmful. They are not bad and won't hurt you if you leave them alone. I give him food so that he will not eat the frogs," he said to calm her.

She admired him even more for his delicate and sensitive side. For a child who had been teased by malicious people until he cried, the keenness of his sensibility was astonishing. Love and understanding permeated his solitude. Time with Setsu was one of the happiest portions of his life.

One afternoon as Lafcadio walked through his garden, he stopped to contemplate the irises and moss-covered rocks around his lotus pond and listen to the birds singing in on the cherry tree branch. He went to his desk and put pen to paper and wrote a melancholy prophecy:

"Already a multitude of gardens, more spacious and more beautiful than mine, have been converted into rice fields or bamboos groves. And the quaint Izumo city, touched at last by some long-projected railway line…will swell, and change, and grow commonplace, and demand these grounds for the building of factories and mills. Not from here alone, but from all the land the ancient peace and the ancient charm seem doomed to pass away. For impermanency is the nature of all things, more particularly in Japan."

Lafcadio found it exhilarating to look at the world in a new and curious manner - of taking his body and mind, trained in Western competitive ways, and conforming them to a slower pace. He aligned himself in many ways with native customs. This discipline was a lifestyle adjustment he'd never had to make elsewhere. He passionately dedicated himself to an attuning of his whole being.

Under Setsu's regime of practical management of their finances and home, Lafcadio relaxed in quiet satisfaction. She took care of all the details and daily complications and petty annoyances that might distract him or keep him from his work. He delegated such affairs to her so he could concentrate on his teaching and writing. He settled into a productive pace, without the frustrations and lunges of despair that plagued him in the past. He felt that Japan promised him many books.

Lafcadio would sometimes look up from his writing desk to see one or two of his students standing wordlessly in the doorway or on the veranda, hoping for his attention. He remembered a fellow Greek philosopher Aristole, who taught that educating the student's mind without educating his heart was no education at all.

Frequent visitors included Otani-Masanobu, Adzukizawa, Ishihara, Ando Ryu, Shida, and others. He observed his students and described some of them in his essay *From the Diary of a Teacher*.

"Masanobu visits me seldom and always comes alone. A slender, handsome lad, with rather feminine features, reserved and perfectly self-possessed in manner, refined. He is somewhat serious, does not often smile; and I never heard him laugh. He has risen to the head of his class and appears to remain there without any extraordinary effort. Much of his leisure time he devotes to botany---collecting and classifying plants. He is a musician, like all the male members of his family. He plays a variety of instruments never seen or heard in the West…When Masanobu comes to the house, it is usually in order to invite me to attend some Buddhist or Shinto festival matsuri which he knows will interest me."

"Adzukizawa bears so little resemblance to Masanobu that one might suppose the two belong to totally different races. Adzukizawa is large, raw-boned, heavy-looking, with a face singularly like that of a North American Indian. His people are not rich; he can afford few pleasures which cost money, except one, buying books. Even to do this he works in his leisure hours to earn money. He is a perfect bookworm, a natural-born researcher, a collector of curious documents, a haunter of all the queer second-hand stores in Teramachi and other streets where old manuscripts or prints are on sale as wastepaper. He is an omnivorous reader, and a perpetual borrower of volumes, which he always returns in perfect condition after having copied what he deemed most valuable to him. Happily, he is so strong that no amount of study is likely to injure his health, and his nerves are tough as wire. It is Japanese custom to set cakes and tea before visitors. I always have both in readiness. Adzukizawa alone refuses to taste cakes or confectionery of any kind, saying: "As I am the youngest brother, I must begin to earn my own living soon. I shall have to endure much hardship. And if I allow myself to like dainties now, I shall only suffer more later on."

When students came to call, Lafcadio would push aside his papers and talk with them. Many became devoted to their Western teacher. He was good company for the idealistic and impressionable young men who wanted to go beyond their limited schooling in Matsue and learn something of the greater world from which *Herun-san* had come to them. He would tell them stories of Europe and America or explain Occidental ideas and thoughts that were difficult for their Oriental minds to grasp. His interpretive genius, intuitive nature, and sympathetic responses were what made him a successful teacher. While he instructed them in English, he was also putting Western culture into examples and terms they could understand.

Many of the young men brought family heirlooms with them - a book, scroll, or carving to share. In turn, Lafcadio might show them the beginnings of his long-stemmed, carved pipe collection. He was proud of his unique pipes with all sorts of figures carved on the bowls - faces of gods, demons, goblins, humans, birds, insects, and flowers. It characterized him, showing his zeal in preserving the unusual and picturesque of old Japan. A fine pipe becomes an heirloom. The careful loading, smoking, cleaning and putting away of the pipe had elements of ceremony, like the preparation and serving of tea. He also appeared occasionally at their celebrations and festivals. He spent New Year's Eve of 1891 at Omani Masanobu's home.

Among his students he could capture the opinions, emotions, manners, reactions, and thoughts that added to his knowledge of Japan. This collection of information was given specific personal color, rather than a general cast. He never forgot that he was going to turn his newly acquired stories, observations, and personal notes into publishable books and articles. Lafcadio became a collector of miscellany, countless bits of information on old Japan that was fast being discarded by the Japanese themselves, and a transcriber of quaint local lore.

His favorite guest was always Professor Nishida. He found his colleague's virtues of kindness and intelligence an admirable combination. Other instructors from the middle school would come to visit and talk. With Setsu's encouragement, occasionally he would invite a few of his colleagues for dinner. From the other rooms, she could hear the guests entertaining Lafcadio with spirited singing of popular Japanese songs or telling him local history, myths, and tales. He attempted to be an active member of the faculty and community as much as his solitary nature would allow.

He was particularly attracted to Japanese folklore because cultural heritage was being threatened by a scientific civilization that he had grown to despise. He loved the ordinary life, the daily life of the Japanese, possibly because he found it superior in many ways to the industrialized West. To show his opposition to modernization, he aligned himself any way he could with native customs.

He adopted Setsu's strict ways of Japanese home life. He only sat in a chair when he wrote, wore kimonos except when teaching, and his diet of native food was so complete that he refused to eat bread. Although, he would secretly slip off at times to Kamata Saiji's Occidental restaurant for a roast beef dinner. He never told Setsu or Nishida, because after the local newspaper made such a fuss over how commendable his preference for

Japanese food was, he felt compelled to maintain the appearance of eating local fare only.

In early summer, his Japanese diet disagreed with him so violently that he fell alarmingly ill. In desperation, Setsu's father prepared to pledge himself to a year of semi-starvation if the gods would heal his son-in-law. Rising weakly from his sick bed, Lafcadio threw such a fit of anger over the sacrifice that his father-in-law proposed, that he was convinced to find a more rational way to appease his deities. Setsu hired a cook who could prepare Western foods that contained more protein, dairy, and vitamins. By incorporating variety into his diet, he recovered, regained his strength, and even put on a few pounds.

CHAPTER 16

Lafcadio's friends and students collected Japanese history, legends, and folklore for him, but his favorite storyteller was his wife Setsu. After most of the household had gone to bed, she began their nighttime ritual of stories. It was the ghost stories he loved the most.

At first, the telling was slow because she had to constantly refer to the dictionary. Translation halted the tale since she needed to pause, find, and consider the right word and context. Often by the time she got to the end of the story, he'd forgotten the beginning. She had to repeat herself several times. He liked it boiled down to the rough essence of the plot and the pearl of the story, except when he asked questions about details or exactly what the characters said to each other. Key elements he found interesting would be noted on his yellow tablet.

At times, Setsu would lower the lantern's light and their room filled with shadows. Lafcadio listened to his wife's tales as if they were part of the action in a haunted house or temple. He liked the way she'd act out the dramatic or terrifying parts until it made him shiver. He'd get so eager that his face and eyes burned with excitement. While working on writing a story, they would go into adjoining rooms and role-play, calling out the characters' dialogue back and forth. This was how Lafcadio became absorbed in the story and wrote it through his own emotions and well-chosen words.

He put the best of her stories into English. He had an instinct for finding the permanent archetypes of human experience in each tale that contained the secret power to move the reader. He knew which elements to emphasize and put them into words the western mind could relate to.

If she read a story to him, he'd say, "There is no use of your reading it from the book. I prefer your own words and phrases, all from your own thought. Otherwise, it won't do." So she had to study and memorize stories on her own before telling them. Sometimes the horrible texts and scenes gave her terrible nightmares she'd have to stop talking about such things for a while.

Fellow teachers told him stories of the brave samurai battles and deeds. But Setsu included the women's side of the story, tales considered gossip not worth a man's breath. One night she confided her own mother Shiomi Chie's story to Lafcadio. Setsu began:

"My mother survived two husbands. On the cusp of thirteen, Shiomi Chie was betrothed to the first son of a samurai house whose family was no longer said aloud now. When her husband failed to appear in their sleeping chamber on their first night of matrimony, she fell asleep waiting for him. She awoke to the muffled sounds of her new husband and Yuki a young maid, who had only hours before swept clean the very courtyard where they both lay, publicly declaring their love. Chie found him leaning against a stone lantern with his belly slashed and his throat cut. The chambermaid was lying at the foot of a pine tree, her head almost completely severed. The blood was fresh and bright red, pouring from her neck and his stomach. Shiomi Chie looked down at her husband's face and then at the maid's. 'So, this is true love', she thought. She then alerted the guards at the front gate that they had slept through a murder-suicide, and she returned to the sleeping chamber to await her widow's fate.

"Soon the samurai house was a river of tears, mostly shed by the maids who had long known of the love affair between the young Master and Yuki. Shiomi Chie shed no tears. She showed humility and deference toward her deceased husband's family, careful never to utter his name or his deeds in the days to come. The maid's own name was erased from the story even before her body grew cold. By morning, the news of the lovers' deaths had swept through Matsue, and Shiomi Chie was being praised in the houses in the shadows of Matsue Castle as a female worthy of the Shiomi name. Among the maids in these same houses, Shiomi Chie became known as the Ice Bride. Among the maids in the house of her deceased husband, she was known as the Blood Bride. Just the year before, Shiomi Chie's own father Masuemon reportedly committed ritual suicide (*seppuku*) in Edo in remonstration against his lord. His dramatic remonstration death (*kanshi*) became the basis for a kabuki theater play."

Lafcadio gasped when he heard the story, but related to it. "My mother Rosa was like Shiomi Chie," he said. He later shortened Shoimi Chie in their *Herun-san* language to Chie, to refer to a woman of noble birth, beautiful, and brave, whose tragic story and end was implied.

To compose a ghost story, or a legend, or a romance, Lafcadio studied numerous oral and written versions of a work. But he relied greatly on Setsu's reenactments, which allowed him to personally experience and be possessed by it. He could be seen pacing around rooms, moaning and crying as a story affected him. Then using the literary model of Hans Christian Andersen, he'd simplify, amplify, clarify, rearrange, and transform it before putting it on paper. He admired the great art of Andersen, with his magical simplicity, and astounding force of compression.

An example of emulating this style is found in Hearn's Japanese tale of *Oshidori* of a grown-up duckling, and its ultimate sacrifice. In summary: A falconer and hunter named Sonjo saw a pair of *oshidori* mandarin ducks swimming together in the river at a place called Akanuma. To kill *oshidori* is bad luck, but Sonjo was very hungry. He shot at the pair. The female escaped into the rushes, but the male was killed. The hunter had his victim for dinner.

Later that night he dreamed a dreary dream where a beautiful woman came into his room and began to weep so bitterly that Sonjo felt his heart was being torn out.

"Why did you kill him?---of what was he guilty? We were so happy together. What harm did he ever do you? Do you even know what a cruel wicked thing you have done? Me too you have killed, for I will not live without my husband!"

She sobbed out the words of a poem: "At the coming of twilight I invited him to return with me - Now to sleep alone in the shadow of the rushes of Akanuma - ah! What misery unspeakable! Tomorrow you will see", so saying and weeping very piteously she went away.

When Sonjo woke up the dream was so vivid that he was greatly troubled. He resolved to go to Akanuma to learn if his dream was anything more than a bad dream. There near the riverbank he saw the female *oshidori* swimming alone. Instead of trying to escape she swam straight toward him, staring in a strange, fixed way. Then with her beak, she suddenly tore open her own body, and died before the hunter's eyes. Sonjo shaved his head and became a priest.

Another Andersen-like, condensed story was told by Lafcadio in *The Dream of a Summer Day*:

"Long, long ago there lived somewhere among the mountains a poor woodcutter and his wife. They were very old and had no children. Every day the husband went alone to the forest to cut wood, while the wife sat weaving at home.

"One day the old man went further into the forest than was his custom to seek a certain kind of wood; and he suddenly found himself at the edge of a little spring he had never seen before. The water was strangely clear and cold, and he was thirsty; for the day was hot, and he had been working hard. So he doffed his great straw hat, knelt down, and took a long drink. That water seemed to refresh him in a most extraordinary way. Then he caught sight of his own face in the spring and started back. It was certainly his own face, but not at all as he was accustomed to see it in the old mirror at home. It was the face of a very young man! He could not believe his eyes. He put up both hands to his head, which had been quite bald only a moment before. It was covered with thick black hair. And his face had become smooth as a boy's; every wrinkle was gone. At the same moment he discovered himself full of new strength. He stared in astonishment at the limbs that had been so long withered by age; they were now shapely and hard with dense young muscle. Unknowingly he had drunk at the Fountain of Youth; and that draught had transformed him.

"First, he leaped high and shouted for joy; then he ran home faster than he'd ever run before in his life. When he entered his house, his wife was frightened, because she took him for a stranger; and when he told her the wonder, she could not at once believe him. But after a long time he was able to convince her that the young man she now saw before her was really her husband; and he told her where the spring was and asked her to go there with him.

Then she said: "You have become so handsome and so young that you cannot continue to love an old woman; so I must drink some of that water immediately. But it will never do for both of us to be away from the house at the same time. You wait here while I go.' And she ran to the woods all by herself. She found the spring, knelt down and began to drink. Oh! How cool and sweet that water was! She drank and drank and drank, and stopped for breath only to begin to drink again.

"Her husband waited for her impatiently; he expected to see her come back changed into a pretty, slim girl. But she did not come back at all. He got anxious, shut up the house, and went to look for her. When he reached the spring he could not see her. He was just on the point of returning when he heard a little wail in the high grass near the spring. He searched there and discovered his wife's clothes and a baby - a very small baby, perhaps six months old!

"For the old woman had drunk too deeply of the magical water; she had drunk herself back beyond the time of youth into the period of speechless infancy. He took up the child in his arms. It looked at him in a sad, wondering way. He carried it home, murmuring to it, thinking strange, melancholy thoughts."

Lafcadio Hearn felt strongly about the value of the supernatural in fiction; it went to the heart of his major works. He explained to his student how the old Anglo-Saxons spoke of a man's ghost, instead of speaking of his spirit or soul. Everything relating to the supernatural or religion - even God himself, the giver of life, is always called the Holy Ghost. Lafcadio thought of the mystery of the universe as a ghostly mystery and every human having a shadow soul.

He taught his students to touch men's souls; and that souls can be made to feel by words. But writers must do more than read to create the thrill. They must feel the emotional or imaginative experiences they encounter, as in their dreams. Religion and superstition can enhance waking dreams and dream truths. He was a living example of using the artistic elements of terror and romance to furnish the world with classic epics through his poetry and literature.

CHAPTER 17

Lafcadio gathered stories from every bridge crossing, every street, every temple, and every encounter with his family and acquaintances. On his long walks along the lower shores of the lake, he discovered a caste of people who were excluded from the carefully regulated Japanese society. They did the jobs no one else would take on, with a monopoly on the rag and wastepaper business. They were buyers of refuse, from old bottles to broken-down machinery, making some prosperous.

Nevertheless, public prejudice against them was almost as strong as in former years and with ancient laws. Under no circumstances could they get employment as servants or a common laborer unless they went to a distant city and hope to conceal their origin. But if found out, they chanced being killed by fellow laborers. Centuries of isolation and prejudice had fixed and molded the manners of the class in recognizable ways. Even its language had a special and curious dialect. They had to preserve their literature orally because they could not read or write. Discrimination had kept their children from the new educational opportunities that the era of Meiji had bestowed on the masses.

He finally convinced his friend Nishida to go with him to the nearby village of outcasts, *yama-no-mono*, who lived completely apart from other Japanese. His instincts as an investigative reporter kicked in like they had in Cincinnati, New Orleans, and Martinique, where he often found his best material on the fringes of society. The keenness of his observation was honed working for the newspapers, but the deep empathy he had for discarded people was his own personal quality.

He described his experience: "The settlement is at the southern end of Matsue, in a tiny valley, or rather hollow among the *yama* hills which form a half-circle behind the southern end of the city. Few Japanese of the better classes have ever visited such a village; and even the poorest of the common people shun the place as they would shun a center of contagion; for the idea of defilement, both moral and physical, is still attached to the very name of the inhabitants. Thus, although the settlement is within half an hour's walk from the heart of the city, probably not half a dozen of the forty thousand residents of Matsue have visited it...

"I was anxious to see something of a class so singularly situated and specialized; and I had the good fortune to meet a Japanese gentleman who, although belonging to the highest class of Matsue, was kind enough to agree to accompany me to their village, where he had never been himself. On the way thither he told me many curious things about the *yama-no-mono*. In feudal times these people had been kindly treated by the samurai; and they were often allowed or invited to enter the courts of the samurai dwellings to sing and dance, for which performances they were paid... Their song and dance represented their highest comprehension of aesthetic and emotional matters.

"I was extremely surprised at the aspect of the place; for I had expected to see a great deal of ugliness and filth. On the contrary, I saw a multitude of neat dwellings, with pretty gardens about them, and pictures on the walls of the rooms...The village was picturesque, green with trees and plants. It had its own Shinto temple and large public bathhouse.

"A crowd soon gathered to look at the strangers who had come to their village,---a rare event for them. The faces looked like the faces of Matsue." The one or two sinister faces made Lafcadio recall faces of gypsies. "There were no exchanges of civilities, as upon meeting a *heimin*, a Japanese of the better class would no sooner think of taking off his hat to a *yama-no-mono* as a West Indian planter would think of bowing to a negro."

After the town tour was finished, performers danced and sung ballads for which their people were known. He felt sorry when the visit was over. He had sympathy for the young singers, victims of prejudice so ancient that its origins were no longer known. Lafcadio, who never learned proper prejudice, talked to the outcasts, listened to their music, watched their dances, and wrote down copious notes. Later he sent a letter about his observations to the *Japan Mail*, an English language newspaper and saw it published in June, 1891. He used this same material for a talk at the Asiatic Society of Japan and in his later book *Kokoro*.

Everywhere he went he learned more about attitudes, histories, myths, beliefs, and customs. For example, in Japan it was offensive to pass unwrapped money from hand to hand, so it was always slipped between papers. Even the most regular transactions and routines seemed to be ruled by ritual and courtesies.

When Lafcadio was out and about, he often took his wife Setsu with him as a translator and manager of funds. They used the summer months to travel and explore. In July they hired a boat to take them along the Iron Coast, Izumo's forbidding edge of the Sea of Japan. It was full of labyrinths of caves and precipices, broken only by fishing villages hidden in small inlets. Wedged between the cliffs and the sea, the houses seemed painfully compressed. Many gave the impression they were created out of wrecks of junks.

Lafcadio and Setsu headed for Kaka-ura to revisit the cave of the children's ghosts. They were fortunate to be on the wild western coast on a rare windless day, because it was forbidden to go to the caverns if there was "enough breeze to move three hairs". The boat's crew consisted of an old man in the stern wearing only a cloth about his loins and an old woman in the bow fully dressed, with an immense straw, mushroom-shaped hat. He and Setsu squatted on a mat in the center of the boat.

Being a strong and avid swimmer, Lafcadio slipped out of his clothes and into the smooth deep sea to swim alongside the boat. He amazed the couple with his various styles and swimming strokes. Swelling waves made him stop and climb back aboard. Although the wind seemed to hold its breath that day, white breakers reached far up the cliffs and dashed their foam over the splintered crags towering from the sea skyward. Massive rock formations of nightmarish shapes rose from the depths. For two long hours they toiled along the jagged coast.

They cross a large bay to enter the mouth of a wonderful cavern, lofty and full of light. The water was clear as air, so one was able to see rocks twenty feet down. As they entered the great cavern, Lafcadio was about to reenter the water for a swim, but the boatman fearfully screamed in protest at him. Setsu told him they were afraid of sharks in the water, but the reality was that they were afraid of disturbing the ghosts who swam in the sacred waters and invited certain death.

As they advanced, the boatman took a stone from the bottom of the boat and began to rap heavily on the bow. Hollow echoes thundered all through the cave. Many seamen did this when passing through perilous places or places believed to be haunted by goblins, similar to a man walking on a lonely road in the dark of night singing at the top of his lungs.

The small craft glided through a second and third entrance to the Kukedo shrine sacred to both the Shinto and Buddhist faiths. A slow stream dripped off the projecting white rock roof, the flow seeming as white as the rock itself. This was the legendary Fountain of Jizo, a constant fountain of 'milk' at which the souls of dead children drink. In the dim cave Lafcadio looked up at the smiling face of the Jizo statue.

The boat grounded on a gravely shore so passengers could disembark to visit the little pebble cairns which the children were said to stack up each night. Lafcadio replaced his shoes with a pair of straw sandals to keep him from slipping on the wet rocks. The piles of rocks were so tightly packed he knocked over a few in passing. The boatwoman told him to follow her on the path, because if he knocked over the little towers the ghost children would cry. To atone, he built up double what he destroyed. The pale stone image of Jizo, the protecting god, silently watched over the small party. Lafcadio was intrigued with the hunt for small footprints in the sand and the myths behind them. He spotted three distinct prints of tiny naked feet. He was told the children only come from their watery realm to work on rock cairns at night when the sun and humans are away.

Lafcadio and Setsu made several other journeys from Matsue to explore the area. Of course, his presence generated curiosity of the locals. One night as they sat waiting for dinner in the village inn, a silent crowd gathered to watch them. The innkeeper, wishing to shield his guests, closed the shoji sliding windows. The excluded spectators were told they might look at the foreigner when he returned to his boat.

Despite the innkeeper's reprimands, and dissatisfied about being shut out, the curious multitude began to tear small holes in the *shoji* opaque paper windowpanes in several places. Lafcadio could see eyes gleaming at every opening. To amuse himself, he got up and pushed a pear slice through the hole. After a hesitant moment a small hand reached up to snatch away the offering. He continued with pieces of radish and pear, which were accepted with charming little bursts of laughter. Not all encounters with the Japanese were so pleasant because when the country folk were full of sake, they tended to be mischievous. Lafcadio and Setsu stayed in the town of Yabase for a few days to enjoy the swimming. Hearing of a special dance performance in the nearby village of Otsuka, they went with a throng of locals to attend. Though he wore Japanese dress and spoke some of their language, he attracted negative attention. As they left the dance, bad-mannered natives threw mud and sand at him. Setsu was outraged and made vigorous protests as the couple retreated to Yabase.

The hostility he experienced gave him an unpleasant realization that he would always be considered an alien. He wrote to Basil Chamberlain saying that "the pelting was not as savage as it would have been in Europe, ... a Western crowd would have thrown rotten eggs or stones." He also wrote to him about stones when he rhetorically asked "But why, oh why did the Japanese prefer bathing resorts where the bottom was all jagged rocks and stones instead of velvety stretches of sand? Was it because of their rare artistic perception of the beauty of stones? I have been a convert to this religion of stones;---but stones under water, unseen, sharp-edged, brutal, only remind one of the shores of the Lake of Blood in the Buddhist kakemono paintings on silk."

Sometimes Lafcadio traveled with his best friend Sentaro Nishida to view ceremonies, art or calligraphy exhibits, or swim for a week or so. In July when they went to Kizuki, he grew so lonesome for Setsu that he sent for her to join them at Hotel Inabaya near the Otorii great gate for Izumi Taisha shrine. Setsu's former mother-in-law Tomi Inagaki had been raised by the important family of Takahama-ke a Shinto priest. She gathered the family in Kizuki to openly announce that Setsu had become the wife of Lafcadio Hearn. The high priest, Takanori Senke, hosted the three Matsue visitors for a dinner at his residence. In the lantern-lit courtyard afterward, two hundred brightly costumed natives presented a private performance of a harvest dance he had been wishing to see.

In addition, the *Guji*-high priest gave him some curios and manuscripts written expressly for him and pictures of the *Miko* dance he saw at the temple on a previous visit. On one visit Lafcadio received a replica of the simple wood fire drill with which the sacred fire was kindled. Through Chamberlain he donated it to the British Museum in London.

Lafcadio learned to behave with the expected courtesy of the Japanese. Like a chameleon he could take on the coloration of his surroundings. With his active curiosity and keen intellect, he enjoyed and appreciated all he observed. He was accepted in places where no or few Westerners had ever gone, such as being received at Shinto's fountainhead Taisha Temple.

One of his great disappointments that August was when he took Setsu back to Shimoichi, the village where he first saw the *bon-odori* dance at the Feast of All Souls to honor the dead, and they learned the police had forbidden the dance. He was annoyed and proclaimed, "The police are worthless! The old customs of Japan, very interesting customs, are discarded. It is the Christians who are to blame; they cast aside all the Japanese ways and try to imitate Western things." But Setsu heard two other reasons - that large gatherings were forbidden due to cholera, and that to have a foreigner present on the one night the ancestors return from the unseen world was an unforgiveable offense. The pair later found the *bon-odori* dances in other villages along the coast.

Near the conclusion of their summer travel outings, Lafcadio discovered Mionoseki, a semi-circular fishing village near the tip of Cape Miho. The only things of interest were a famous group of pines on the cape ridge, the fishing, and a shrine to the god *Koto-shiro-mushi-no-Kami*. The inn where they stayed had balconies cantilevered above the harbor. He was seen diving from the balcony into the deep water for his morning swim. He complained that he could not get eggs for breakfast because the local god Mionoseki hated eggs. But, even this inconvenience was beguiling. He hoped the little lost village would never change.

He wrote to Ellwood Hendrick that he'd been "traveling alone with my little wife, who translates my 'Hearnian dialect' into Japanese. I am the only man who ever attempted to learn the people seriously; and I think I shall succeed." He also sent similarly enthusiastic letters to Elizabeth Bisland, Captain Mitchell McDonald, and Basil Hall Chamberlain. Lafcadio was now the seasoned dweller among the remote Japanese on the coast of the Japan Sea. Chamberlain, who was editing his new edition of *Murray's Guide to Japan*, entrusted the section on Shimane Prefecture to him for revisions.

To help with the updated guide, he traveled to the countryside when he was not teaching or ensconced in his writing. As a chronicler of life in Japan, he had the advantage of living among the people and living a local lifestyle within a Japanese family. With Setsu's input he could write with authority about Japanese women, household customs, rituals, shrines, foods, and more. But he understood that, in spite of his admiration of Japanese ways, he could never become Japanese himself or be fully accepted among its people. He was immutably a Westerner.

CHAPTER 18

Although Lafcadio Hearn fit in well as a citizen, teacher, and writer in Matsue, the dread of another freezing winter in Matsue brought on vague feelings of uneasiness. As in the past, Lafcadio's restlessness would eventually work its way into imperative flight.

During the previous severe winter, he found it necessary to wear his heavy overcoat even in the classroom and his home. He was chilled to the bone all the time. He was plagued with coughs and lung congestion and found that, at forty-one, he did not recuperate quickly.

As the seasons changed and days grew cooler, he discussed his anxiety with his physician and Nishida. They both agreed that extreme Izumo weather was too rigorous for his constitution and advised him to search for a teaching post in a warmer part of the country.

He wrote to his friend Professor Chamberlain to ask him to use his influence with the government officials to find him another position, preferably at a higher salary and in one of the southern provinces. Although Chamberlain had retired from the University, he consulted with the proper officials in the bureaus of the Education Department and soon found Lafcadio a position in southern Japan that paid twice his current salary. Though teaching hours would be a bit longer, he immediately accepted.

The new post was that of English instructor in a government college in Kumamoto, in the province of Kyushu. With no need to worry about his health or finances, his future looked bright. But he also fretted. Would the Kumamoto College have such dedicated students as Otani, Tanabe, Asakichi or Ochiai? He could never expect to find such an intelligent loyal friend as Nishida. Would the staff have quality teachers like Sato, Nakamura, Katayama, and the happy Tamura? His thoughts lingered on this chapter of his life, wondering if he would ever know such a long, unbroken experience of human kindness. He loved the honesty of the Matsue people, who were in awe of nature and spirit.

Thoughts of leaving his friends, students, and beloved gardens in the shadows of Matsue Castle made Lafcadio poignantly sad. As the master of the household, he had to set an example for his wife and servants who were also facing a new outside world for the first time. He was responsible for more than just himself. Following Japanese tradition of caring for family, he now was the sole support of seven people. The moral burden was greater than the financial one in Japan. Royalties from the United States were dwindling. Taking on a family had changed his style of life. He also needed more money to assemble his book of impressions. He hoped that new experiences in Kyushu and other parts of Japan would restore his "pen of fire" – the motivation to produce other books.

Past experiences had taught Lafcadio that for him moving and separations had turned out to be forever. There was no need to persuade his wife. His decision to move from Matsue was fine with Setsu. His destiny and destinations were now also hers. She never imagined life on the island of Kyushu, in the large city of Kumamoto, just as she'd never thought she'd be married to an Occidental professor. The promise of new adventure overrode any fear she may have had.

Setsu felt none of Lafcadio's romantic attachment for this old, feudal town. She'd suffered from poverty and discrimination growing up in her birth city, so she was ready to move on. Her parents preferred to remain, so the couple assured them they'd get back for visits occasionally. He already felt a foretaste of nostalgia for Izumo and Matsue. His stay in traditional Matsue had been formative, even though it was only a little over a year. It was there he had found what he wanted in life - a devoted wife and extended family, teaching, a sense of home, and countless topics for writing. It was in Matsue that he began to discover who he was.

Preparations to move disrupted Lafcadio's peaceful home life and work schedule. Setsu convinced the maid, cook, and their *kurumaya* rickshaw man to accompany them to Kumamoto. The house, including all Lafcadio's books and papers, was packed up for the move.

Nishda was suddenly taken quite ill and bedridden with his recurring lung ailment. Lafcadio and Setsu had noticed droplets of blood on his handkerchief when he coughed at their last outing. The condition became so severe that no one was allowed to visit him.

Lafcadio was lonely without his best friend. He sent over the study lamp from his workstation with a note, "It isn't much, but it burns well and will serve as a souvenir." He also made a gift of his treasured *uguisu* holy bird that the Governor's daughter had given him his first weeks in Matsue. *Ho-ke-ko* was the prayer song it sang in sweet meditative warbling.

During the last days of October, while he waited for his passport, he was honored with a farewell assembly at the middle school, highlighted by a touching address in English by his student Otani. His students presented him with a daimyo feudal lord's sword and teaching colleagues gifted the family a pair of ancient Izumo vases. Cadets of the Normal school gave a banquet and escorted him home in military formation. They shouted hearty farewells and swore to march him to the steamer when he left. They were unable to keep their promise because the next day Asian cholera broke out in the school and within two days several cadets and teachers were dead.

When departure day, November 15, 1891, arrived, Lafcadio begged the principle to forbid any gathering on his behalf. But as he left his home an hour after sunrise, hundreds of citizens, students, and instructors stood at his gate and escorted him through the city to the steamer at the wharf. Nishida-san was not among the throng, but the headmaster's aged father brought a farewell note, penned from his sickbed. Lafcadio put the letter in his coat pocket next to his heart. His throat tightened as he looked back at the large assembly, the long white bridge, lake, and distant mountain.

Lafcadio boarded the little steamship, climbed to the tiny deck cabin roof, waved his floppy hat, and shouted in English "Goodbye, Goodbye!" until they were out of sight.

Shouts came back to him, "*Banzai, banzai!* Ten thousand years of long life to you! Ten thousand years!"

The voices, the white bridge over the river, and the faces faded to a memory. More than the ceremonial and formal leave-taking events, the informal cheering and waving of caps was the farewell Lafcadio recalled for the rest of his life.

CHAPTER 19

After the emotional goodbyes at the wharf in Matsue, the steamer crossed Lake Shinji and left the passengers on the opposite shore. Lafcadio engaged vehicles to carry his party of five to Kumamoto. He had his own rickshaw man to pull one of the fragile vehicles over the backbone of Honshu's mountains to the south. After several jolting days, with stops at night in inns unused to foreigners, at last they came to the port of Hiroshima. Here the little group took an Inland Sea steamer along the Honshu coast for a day and a half.

The next leg of the journey was another one hundred and twenty miles in two trains across the interior of the island. They looked out the windows at volcanic landscapes and lush valleys of rice crops. When the train pulled into the large, modern Kumamoto station, Lafcadio was not alone in wondering about the different world they were about to enter. This new city was far from Matsue, a thousand miles south of Tokyo, and still farther from Dublin, New York, Cincinnati, and New Orleans.

Kyushu was the southernmost and third largest of Japan's main islands. It faced the Chinese coast and Formosa. The large island was known for its active volcanoes like Mt. Aso, natural hot springs, and beaches. Kyushu was noted for various types of porcelain - Arita, Imari, Satsuma and Karatsu.

As they entered Kumamoto, he was unimpressed with the "straggling, dull, unsightly" half-Europeanized city. The 1877 Saigo Rebellion destroyed most of the old town. Much was burned to ashes when Japan was trying to convert from a feudal to a modern state. Swept by fire during the civil war, the rebuilding seemed to consist of hastily erected, flimsy shelters and antiseptic, red brick buildings. Lafcadio hated the big city at first sight because it was so modernized, had no temples, priests, or curious customs, and it appeared "devilishly ugly and commonplace...a disgusting blank."

The town was dominated by the ruins of the gigantic Kumamoto Castle, an ancient fortress now occupied by a garrison brimming with soldiers.

It depressed Lafcadio. He said Kumamoto was "the most uninteresting city I was ever in in Japan…there is nothing beautiful here" when he couldn't find any pretty streets, or great temples, or any parks or gardens. He missed Matsue and "the life of the tiny villages - that is the real Japan I love. Somehow or other, Kumamoto doesn't seem to me Japan at all. I hate it." In Kumamoto Lafcadio complained not only about the modernization, but also his perceived savageness of the city's lower classes and peasants. He increasingly found fault with many things in Japan that were not true to his idyllic image.

Lafcadio thought Kumamoto, Yokohama, and Tokyo already contaminated by the West and no longer the Japan he'd hoped to find. He would now have to "suffer the sorrows of the nineteenth century." He considered the Old Japanese culture superior in many ways to the industrialized West. He was seeing the fourteenth century turn swiftly, amazingly, into the twentieth - one of the great births of history - and he would eventually write about it. He was not yet aware of the importance and magnitude of the task he had been set to do.

At the time, he blamed the city in transition for his spiritual discomfort. But there was no time for retrospection or regrets about leaving his enchanted abode in the north. He was there to do a job and support his family.

Within a few days Setsu located a house as spacious as their former home in Matsue, but the gardens were ordinary, stunted versions of his precious *yashiki*. The first thing they did was make renovations to his writing space. Paper window and wall shutters in his study were replaced by glass. The hibachi was removed to make space for an unsightly but efficient Franklin stove, allowing him to write in comfort.

"My folks say I have never said a cross word since I had a warm room. Heat thus appears as a moral force. Just think how holy I should be could I live forever under the equator."

The entire household struggled with the unfamiliar city and in making their Izumo dialect understood. The fact that they all felt as alien in Kumamoto as Lafcadio, made the whole relocated group feel closer. He and Setsu made sure the maids took free time to explore the city. They enjoyed the bright lights and shops filled with all kinds of exotic goods. Setsu was in a mix of constant confusion and amazement over the new customs and sights.

One morning Setsu rushed into the house, "*Shoji* goblin!" she cried out. "In the garden next door." Lafcadio, not knowing if he understood the word correctly, hurried to look over the neighbor's bamboo fence. There was a goat bleating and chewing on the bushes. Setsu had never seen a goat, or a pig, or a goose before. There was a lot for her and the staff to discover in their new environment.

One of the members of their relocating group, the *kurumaya*- rickshaw runner, was returned home almost immediately after arrival. When Lafcadio learned that he'd lied and forsaken his wife in Matsue to come with him, he was sent back. An older runner was hired to replace the errant husband. The new *kurumaya* delighted Lafcadio with stories of fox superstitions.

Lafcadio began work at the government college, Higher Middle School, also called the Fifth National College of Kumamoto in Kyushu. The school was outside the city proper to the northeast, two miles from his home. Inside the great stone and brick buildings, the walls were thick, the halls long and cold - very disappointing to Lafcadio, who felt as if the structures were shutting out life itself.

He found out that the director had hesitated to hire him, a foreigner and only non-Japanese teacher. There was a definite coolness toward him from the administration and staff. He felt it was because, "the last teacher was a missionary and a fraud, as many missionaries are. I was astonished to find none of the boys had been trained by him to compose or to talk. He had simply wasted their time. The condition of his appointment had rendered proselytism impossible; he left in disgust. I have to struggle against the unpopularity of my predecessor."

Nevertheless, Lafcadio liked his director, Mr. Kano. "He had told me to teach as I please for the present; and having discarded the readers adopted for the three upper classes, I am filling up the time with conversation, and some slight instruction about English literature. The choice of the readers was disgraceful."

Over a year later in 1893 he was still teaching without books, only word of mouth and chalk. He had to draw the substance of his lessons from his own experiences and imagination. The main thing was to teach them to express themselves in English without books to help them. The students were poorly prepared in English and at first did not understand him at all. At least his salary of two hundred American dollars allowed him and Setsu to live comfortably and save money.

Even that security was threatened when a political struggle in the Tokyo Diet government erupted. There was debate whether the school itself would exist any longer and whether the teachers would receive their monthly wages. Lafcadio took the threat of delays in payment as a personal affront. He wrote worried letters to Chamberlain in Tokyo asking him to find out the fate of the school. The Diet reconsidered closing the school, and salaries were paid.

He found his teaching colleagues brisk, impersonal and a bit crass. "They preferred beer and cigars to sake and pipes. Their brains seem to have shriveled up like kernels in roasted nuts." A few spoke English or French, but they exchanged little more than formal 'Good morning' or 'Good evening' salutations. After his first month there, he'd formed no friendships. He only saw his fellow teachers during school hours and the students rarely called on him. At times he felt lonely and disheartened. Without his old friend and principal Nishida to guide him, he was sure he was making etiquette and language mistakes.

He taught students for twenty-seven hours a week. He first found them unpleasant, unresponsive and unprepared as academics. There was no old-fashioned respectfulness or eagerness to learn that bonded teachers and pupils like he had in Matsue. The atmosphere in Kumamoto was harsh, without mannered old traditions. He worried that modern science might be taking away their faith or even erasing the memory of Buddha's words from the mind of the Japanese.

By the time students reached the Higher School level, education became a competition for their place in life. College was five years of classes plus three years for preparation for the great universities. During their college years, Japanese intellectuals took part in a game with too many players and too few prizes. Students were cruelly overworked. Lafcadio wondered if the education system of New Japan was wrong. "Competition is the law of the jungle, but cooperation is the law of civilization." His advice about not abandoning the old ways fell on deaf ears.

Most of his students were older and had gone through mandatory military training. Kumamoto was a center of conservative feelings where the martial arts and samurai spirit lived on.

Lafcadio describes the samurai personality of one of his students: "Ishihara is a samurai a very influential lad in his class because of his uncommon force of character. Compared with others, he has a somewhat brusque, independent manner, pleasing, however, by its honest manliness. He says everything he thinks, and precisely in the tone that he thinks it, even to the degree of being a little embarrassing sometimes. He does not hesitate, for example, to find fault with a teacher's method of explanation, and to insist upon a more lucid one. He has criticized me more than once; but I never found that he was wrong."

This militaristic "Spirit of New Japan" prepared students to stand ready as a corps of iron soldiers if a national emergency arose. Lafcadio respected their fighting prowess and reconciled with it due to the similarity to traditional Greek Spartan spirit.

His students could be excellent workers, but at times were extremely hard-hearted and hard-headed. Kyushu men prided themselves on directness and stoicism. They were beginning to treat rationalism and science as gods to be worshipped. Nishida consoled and advised him to respect the elder virtues of this stern and militant part of the Empire. Lafcadio grew to understand, but not really like, the Kyushu strong will in the face of suffering, and action in the face of provocation.

Lafcadio did admire Mr. Akizuki, the Chinese Classics professor, as one who represented the respectful warrior traditions and ideals of all that was noble and true. He extolled him as *Kami-Sama*, an eminent superior, a divine soul who advocated filial piety.

At the beginning there was a lapse of respect and good manners among his students. When he entered the classroom, indifferent and expressionless faces greeted him. Since he was so nearsighted, they took advantage to sleep, work on other subjects and amuse themselves at the back of the room. Not understanding the teacher's English, they didn't even try. But soon, even the unfriendly ones were learning English through Lafcadio's natural ability.

He explained his method, "Sometimes I would write familiar stories for the class, all in simple sentences, and in words of one syllable. I would suggest themes to write upon, of which the nature almost compelled simple treatment."

As they learned to follow his spoken word, they began asking him for stories. He entranced them with tales from Greek myths, Arthurian legends, from Hawthorne, from their own Japanese folk stories. He also offered them friendly personal advice on their readings, finances, and studies.

When they confessed to being discouraged and asked, "what should I do?" Lafcadio would say, "Encourage others."

Lafcadio would turn away educated, modernized, wealthy Japanese who came calling. He considered them "a soft reflection of Latin types, without the Latin force and brilliancy and passion - somewhat as in dreams the memory of people we have known become smilingly aerial and imponderable." He attributed nobility to Old Japan and vulgarity to New Japan. The followers of the West seemed materialistic and soulless to him compared to the spiritual East.

Government College campus consisted of large brick buildings scattered over rolling grounds. The pure utilitarian architecture with many windows was so modern that he felt it could be situated in Europe or the United States. Getting to the teachers' lounge took Lafcadio over ten minutes, not enough time to visit and relax between classes, so he rarely went there. When he did, he sat alone in a corner and smoked his pipe. He had no friends except Professor Hikogoro Shimizu with whom he had conversations about dear old Matsue and Kijuki. He missed the friendly banter and intellectual conversations at his schools in Matsue.

Instead of trekking to the instructors' retreat, and to escape the tumultuous life of the college campus, he'd take his one-hour lunch break in a different setting. Lafcadio picked his way through tall grass and stones up the ridge of the hill behind the college to an ancient village cemetery. He'd sit on the pedestal of a stone Buddha and eat his lunch of fried fish, rice, pickles, and beans. Beyond the school the landscape before him looked like old Japanese color-prints found in picture books. The Plain of Higo appeared banded and seamed by all tones of green, intercrossed as if laid on by an artist's long brush strokes. In his article "The Stone Buddha", he discussed the differences between Western and Asian art, especially the use of shadows. This writing was based on his observations from the ridge above the school.

Lafcadio continued to correspond with his friends and students Otani, Tanabe, and Adzukizawa in Matsue. He often asked them specific questions about Shinto, myths, customs and such. He moved beyond casual questioning and offered them payment and aid in going on to higher schools if they would do research for him. To Aszukizawa he wrote, "I want to know what is done every day in Izumo. It's no use to send me anything out of books…If I ask you to translate something, please never try to translate a Japanese idiom by an English idiom. Simply translate the words exactly, however funny it seems." Lafcadio wanted to get as bone-close to customs and words as he could to be able to understand Japanese thinking and feeling through his students and fellow instructors.

One Kumamoto teacher was Kano Jigoro Shihan (1960-1938), a smaller man than Lafcadio, started *jiu-jitsu* fighting system to develop his strength. Kano was the founder of Judo, one of the first martial arts to gain international recognition and become an official Olympic sport. The use of black and white belts and dan rankings to show relative proficiency levels is attributed to Kano. His well-known mottos include: "good use of energy" and "mutual welfare and benefit".

On his deathbed Kano asked to be buried in a white belt instead of a black belt because he wanted to be remembered as a learner, not a master. Kano Jigoro taught "Assume that your opponent will be bigger, stronger and faster than you. Learn to rely on technique, timing, and leverage rather than brute strength."

The concept of judo was explained as, "resisting a more powerful opponent will result in your defeat, while adjusting to and evading your opponent's attack will cause him to lose his balance, his power will be reduced, and you will defeat him".

The concept of maximum efficiency with minimum effort used in *jiu-jitsu* and *kodokan judo* made a deep impression on Lafcadio. Also, his father-in-law, the former samurai would chant "Zen seven, ken three" as he went through his martial arts exercises each day. It stood for the proportional ability of the sword (ken) or any other weapon as only 30 percent responsible for a person's failure or success. The 70 percent factor (the Zen of the chant) in any battle or in solving a problem is found within a person. Inner training must be devoted to cultivating that inner power.

Lafcadio reminded his students that their attitudes and efforts were two things they could control in life. He explored the transcendental nature of martial arts as a creative discipline that could develop a man physically, spiritually, and mentally.

He commented: "What Western brain could have elaborated this strange teaching, never to oppose force by force, but only direct and utilize the power of attack; to overthrow the enemy solely through his own strength, to vanquish him by his sole efforts? Surely none! The Western mind appears to work in straight lines; the Oriental, in wonderful curves and circles."

Lafcadio, impressed by Kano's philosophy and knowledge of martial arts, wrote an article on judo, calling it jiujutsu. His article introduced and popularized the sport techniques in the Americas and Europe. Soon after, there was a cartoon of a small female suffragette tossing a beefy policeman to the ground during a women's Right to Vote rally.

He compared Japan's modernization as a Judo-like use of power of one's opponent to beat them. Japan had adopted nothing out of mere imitative reasons, she had copied Western civilization to increase her strength.

Japan never completely accepted cultures, philosophical traditions, or systems of governance formed in other countries. The Japanese possess an amazing power of cultural synthesis, whose excellence lies in taking in foreign cultures as they are and transforming them. It was the ability to coexist, rather than replace one with the other, that defined its national character.

CHAPTER 20

Lafcadio's disappointments with teaching at the Fifth Higher School and the city of Kumamoto were tempered by his home life. The job paid enough money to give him the freedom to write and support his sizable family who relied on him for protection, food, housing, clothing, and guidance.

In a letter to Ellwood Hendrick he noted, "I have nine lives depending on my work---wife, wife's mother, wife's father, wife's adopted mother, wife's father's father, and then servants, and a Buddhist student. How would you like that? It wouldn't do in America. But here it is nothing, no appreciable burden. The moral burden is heavy enough. You can't let a little world grow up around you, to depend on you, and then break it all up---not if you are a respectable person. And I indulge in the luxury of "filial piety", a virtue of which the good and evil results are only known to us Orientals." He learned that the greatness in a man is in his integrity and ability to affect those around him positively.

"I have at home a little world, to whom I am Love and Light and Food. It is a very gentle world. It is only happy when I am happy. If I even look tired, it is silent, and walks on tiptoe. It is a moral force. I dare not fret about anything when I can help it---for others would fret more. So I try to keep it right."

At his home refuge he found a world of the old ways, old thoughts, and old courtesies. It was so peaceful and gentle that sometimes he was afraid it might vanish. Other than Setsu, her eighty-four-year-old grandfather soon became Lafcadio's beloved favorite among the relatives. In her grandfather's mind, he was still living in the pre-Meiji times, working as a tutor to the daimyo powerful feudal lord's son. He maintained disciplined samurai habits and beautiful manners. Once when he'd forgotten his tobacco, with military sternness he ordered a transfer boat around. In deference to his authority and age, the captain complied.

The old man was a library of thoughts, ideas, and traditional ways from past generations. An old saying captured the exchange, "With the crown of snow, there cometh wisdom." Lafcadio spent precious hours with him, coaxing stories out of him about his life, old legends, and the history of Japan at the time of his youth. In Japanese fashion, the honored patriarch relinquished his responsibilities and duties to his children and lived a life of contemplation and delight. Lafcadio lovingly called him Grandfather and he called his grandson-in-law 'Hellum' and called Setsu 'Chi-yo', an alternative name that Lafcadio never used for her.

The eccentric, hard-of-hearing grandfather was prone to wander the streets of Kumamoto. He steered himself by the sun or the smoke of nearby Mt. Aso to the east. When the absent-minded elder got lost, he'd find a hospitable spot to sit down, smoke his pipe, and wait for one of the servants or his grandson-in-law to find him and take him safely home. When he arrived home, he'd entertain the worried family with his day's adventures. Comic little misfortunes often befell him. Lafcadio found the grandfather's yawn amusing. It was "very peculiar, languid and long drawn out (and catching), somewhat sad-sounding, but could be heard from every room of the house. Ah, that tired-of-the-world yawn of his again," he smiled.

According to Lafcadio, like the other elder men of Japan, grandfather was "divine…I do not know any other word to express what they are." He believed that the older Japanese were closer to the answers of the enigmas of life because they still recognized moral beauty as greater than intellectual beauty.

Lafcadio was comfortable in his family relations and responsibilities. He thrived on the regularity and security in his life. In October of 1893 he wrote to Chamberlain about one typical day of his life. He detailed how he rose at 6 am, made prayers and offerings, ate a light breakfast and headed to school to teach. He wrote of the rituals upon his return home and how the household entertained and occupied their time…rest, bath hour, supper, guests, reading, stories, writing, and then to bed.

Lafcadio lived the life of a thoroughly traditional Japanese husband since his marriage to Setsu. The exception was having substantial Western meals in the mornings and evenings (beefsteak and beer) to maintain his now excellent health. Setsu was pleased when his kimonos began to fit a bit tighter. He sometimes felt that his two meals of Western food, glass box of a study, and the Franklin stove was admitting defeat. But living totally native might mean dying before he could accomplish any credible works.

At times Lafcadio longed for American or European companionship. At one point he invited Joseph Tunison, a writer in New York, to come to Japan, but nothing came of the offer. When the Kyushu winter turned treacherously cold, Lafcadio yearned wishfully for the warmth of the tropics in Martinique. But he couldn't imagine going back to those worlds now that his new life was so appealing and satisfying. If his memories or thoughts kept him awake at night, he'd go into his office and write at his custom-built high desk and chair.

During his first two years in Japan, two articles had been published in America in the *Atlantic Monthly*. The magazine's new editor, Horace Elisha Scudder, had an avid interest in the traditional cultures of the Far East, so he gave Lafcadio the freedom to write about anything and everything he wished. True to form, he churned out impressive studies and beguiling pieces on the land of the rising sun. Between 1890 and 1896, *The Atlantic* would publish almost two dozen of Lafcadio's chronicles of Japanese life.

Some of his short pieces were glimpses of everyday life, such as writing down ditties of the day sung in the streets by washermen, carpenters, smiths, rice-cleaners, and bamboo weavers. Japanese folk songs he called *hayri-uta*, were mostly love songs, corresponding to the natural stages of emotional experiences. Lafcadio enjoyed a lifelong attraction to working class people and their music. In it he found a sense of universal brotherhood - that people were the same, in all places and times. He wanted to get this message out to the world.

Out of the blue, Lafcadio contacted Page Baker, his editor at the *Times Democrat* newspaper in New Orleans. "You seem to be the best friend I've got outside of Japan. You really do things for a fellow," he wrote. Together they worked out a syndication of articles that hastily appeared in the *Times Democrat* and other publications in February 1892. Lafcadio was grateful for the extra income so he could continue to work on shaping his first book about Japan.

Chamberlain, on his way to England, received a letter from Lafcadio: "Perhaps you may see on your way some newspapers containing fragments of mine. They are not the best, and please don't judge me by them. But as I was offered the sum of $800 for four MSS (which I must recast later) by a syndicate (English, American, and Australian) I accepted."

While reconnecting to some of his friends in the United States, he received letters from family in England that he'd never met or known. His half-sisters, from his father Charles' marriage to Alicia Goslin Crawford, the pretty golden-haired lady in Dublin, had read about him or seen his picture in a magazine or newspaper and reached out. Both his father and the second wife were dead, but their daughters Elizabeth Sarah Maude, Minnie Charlotte, and Posey Gertrude led sheltered lives in England since their births in India. Minnie married John Buckley Atkinson and had three children. Posey married a Mr. Brown. The unmarried sister, Elizabeth Sarah Maude, nicknamed Lillah, had once visited Lafcadio's full brother Daniel James Hearn in America.

Lafcadio received letters from all three of his half-sisters, but he only answered Minnie Atkinson's gentle note that included a photograph. He responded: "The more I see of your face in photos, the more I feel drawn toward you…But imagining won't do always. I would like to know more of you than a photograph or a rare letter can tell. I don't know, remember, anything at all about you. I do not know where you were born, where you were educated, - anything of your life; or what is much more, infinitely more important, I don't know your emotions and thoughts and feelings and experiences of the past. What you are now, I can guess. But what were you, long ago? What memories haunt you…"

The correspondence with his sister Minnie only lasted three or four years. Lafcadio stopped writing suddenly. Hearing from this distant half-sister was too great an expense of emotion. He could never quiet forgive them for their mother's actions that cost his own mother so dearly. He told Chamberlain that letters from relatives in England made him "indigo" blue. Lafcadio's life in Kumamoto centered about his family and his writing.

Lafcadio's articles printed in *The Atlantic Monthly* were enormously popular when they appeared in the American magazine and were syndicated to a number of newspapers. More praise followed when his stories were consolidated and published in two volumes as *Glimpses of Unfamiliar Japan* (1894).

In January, 1893, he finished the last chapter of his first book on Japan, *Glimpses of Unfamiliar Japan*. The publisher Houghton Mifflin Company of Boston had to be persuaded to accept and print the expansive manuscript. He was constantly sending more materials for them to include, like the Japanese ballads and other data Nishida collected for him. As they lost patience, he sent what he had.

The manuscript was much larger than the company had originally stipulated. He argued that the most important thing was to make the book as comprehensive as possible. He even offered to forego payment for the additional materials. After hesitating, they agreed to publish it in two volumes. Lafcadio spent his summer months correcting and revising the large bundles of proofs shipped in ten installments to Kumamoto from Boston.

He sent certain pages to Chamberlain in Tokyo for comments and gratefully made the minor changes he suggested. But when the professor, like the editor of *The Atlantic*, objected to an overuse of Japanese words, Lafcadio defended his position. He felt words were like people, though unintelligible, they impressed by exotic appearance and foreign air. He argued that Japanese words were interesting precisely because they were unintelligible.

He stood firm on his use of Japanese words: "Is there any reason why we should not try to make people hear, to make them see, to make them feel? Surely one who has never heard Wagner, cannot appreciate Wagner without study. Why should the people not be forcibly introduced to foreign words, as they were introduced to tea and coffee and tobacco?"

Chamberlain answered as a friend: "Because they won't buy your book, and you won't make any money."

And Lafcadio replied, "Surely, I have never yet made, and never expect to make any money. Neither do I expect to write ever for the multitude. I write for beloved friends who can see color in words, can smell the perfume of syllables in blossom, can be shocked with the fine elfish electricity of words. And in the eternal order of things, words will eventually have their rights recognized by the people."

Glimpses of Unfamiliar Japan was dedicated to both Lieutenant McDonald and Professor Chamberlain. In *Glimpses*, Lafcadio wrote extensively about local superstitions and myths, especially about how to deal with tricky fox spirits. One such story advises:

"When a *Ninko* (Human-fox) comes to your house at night and knocks, there is a peculiar, muffled sound about the knocking by which you can tell that the visitor is a fox---if you have experienced ears. For a fox knocks at doors with its tail. If you open, then you will see a man, or perhaps a beautiful girl, who will talk to you only in fragments of words, but nevertheless in such a way that you can perfectly understand. A fox cannot pronounce a whole word, but a part only... Then, if you are a friend of foxes, the visitor will present you with a little gift of some sort, and a once vanish away into the darkness. Whatever the gift may be, it will seem much larger that night than in the morning. Only a part of a fox gift is real.

"A Matsue samurai going home one night saw a fox running for its life pursued by dogs. He beat the dogs off with his umbrella, thus giving the fox a chance to escape. On the following evening he heard someone knock at his door...and on opening saw a very pretty girl standing there, who said to him: "Last night I should have died but for your august kindness. I know not how to thank you enough: this is only a pitiable little present." And she laid a small bundle at his feet and went away. He opened the bundle and found two beautiful ducks and two pieces of silver money, each worth ten or twelve dollars, such as are now eagerly sought for by collectors of antique things. After a little while, one of the coins changed before his eyes into a piece of grass; the other was always good."

Much of what Lafcadio had previously written were his first impressions of Japan, words on paper with the fresh eyes of an impressionist painter. He wrote it in a sympathetic and entertaining style to appeal to the modern readers' mood. To him, the frame of mind he had at arrival seemed to be treasured memories, illusions that were forever over and belonged to the past. By the time the *Glimpses* book was published he had moved on to a new concept and opinion of Japan and its people.

Just as he would do in his subsequent works, Lafcadio stressed that his writings about Japan were based on his interests in the common people. His journalism articles in Cincinnati often featured the world of the negro levee quarter and society's underdogs. In New Orleans and Martinique, he immersed himself in the Creole culture and doomed anti-bellum South. Sometimes his identification with the lower classes and contrasting the superiority of the unsophisticated to the bourgeois, led him to adopt patronizing attitudes. But he was never patronizing toward the Japanese.

The New Order's upper-class Japanese were quick to criticize: "Lafcadio Hearn gives an unworthy picture of Japan. He writes of matters in which the modern Japanese are no longer interested," they declared. Considering the source of this thinly veiled antagonism helped him to neutralize its sting. Public opinion eventually would elevate him to the position of Japan's most revered Western writer.

CHAPTER 21

Basil Chamberlain recommended W.B. Mason to Hearn. Mason, from Yokohama, was Professor Chamberlain's guidebook collaborator and a Tokyo college instructor. Lafcadio and Mason both had Japanese wives and were stuck in dull civil service and government jobs, frustrated by unfulfilled ambitions. Hearn was instructed to send Mason materials to include in *Murray's Guide to Japan* revisions.

Lafcadio began an easy correspondence with Mason. "You write the most delightful letters, but I haven't the faintest ghost of an idea who you are. I don't know whether I ought even to try to find out. It is charming to know one's friends as amiable ghosts thus." They wrote of insights, self-doubts, introspections, discomforts, and disillusions about Japan. Once again Lafcadio had a friend to share his innermost thoughts and dreams with.

He told Mason, "My whole study must be the heart of the commonest people." He was exploring the inner rather than the outer life of Japan. His third book would be titled *Kokoro*, heart things. The Japanese word character "signifies also mind, in the emotional sense; spirit; courage; resolve; sentiment; affection; and inner meaning, - Just as we say in English, 'the heart of things'."

With *Images* off his writing desk, while collecting data for new books, he and Setsu took excursions out of Kumamoto. "To please Chamberlain", who was preparing a Japanese guidebook, "and also to please myself", Lafcadio took Setsu with him to Kyoto, Kobe, Nara, and the unknown Oki Islands on the north coast.

Oki-no-kuni or the Land of Oki, consisted of two groups of small islands in the Sea of Japan about one hundred miles from the Izumo coast. Travel between the west coast of Japan and Oki was very dangerous during the winter months, as it ceased communications with the mainland. These mountainous islands had only small areas for cultivation. The chief source of income came from their fisheries.

Setsu was not eager to visit the isolated islands because she'd heard that the natives were barbarously crude. That was the very reason they appealed to Lafcadio, who felt sure such primitive places would provide valuable notes. He'd read old legends and imaginative stories of Oki, plus the fact that the islands were *terra incognita*. None of his Japanese acquaintances could give him any information about Oki, beyond the fact that in ancient times it had been a place of banishment for emperors dethroned by military usurpers. Few Japanese from the main island and no Westerners, except seamen from lost ships, ever went to Oki Islands.

A former fellow teacher who had been to the islands told him that although simple, the people were civilized, honest, and extremely kind to strangers. The locals' boast was that of having kept their race unchanged since the time of the first Japanese---the Age of the Gods. Lafcadio was determined to visit Oki.

To get there, Lafcadio and Setsu had to board a steamship, *joki* to sail all the way around Honshu through the Straights of Shimonoseki to the little port of Sakai. They next sailed out into the Japan Sea on a dangerous squabby little boat full of melons, baskets of squirming eels, and unhappy chickens. The couple sat on coiled ropes on the cabin roof, thinking they might have some chance to live during a catastrophe. The couple visited Saigo, Beppu, Ura-no-go, and Hishiura. The shorelines were a procession of broken shapes, separated by little bays with fishing hamlets hidden within. When the boat came into the harbor of Mionoseki, immediately passengers stood, turned to the island shrine torii gate, and clapped their hands in Shinto prayer.

"Are they praying that nothing horrible happens to this boat?" he asked Setsu.

"More likely they are praying for good fortune. Although there is a saying that the gods only laugh when men pray to them for wealth."

"Is that why some of the glazed earthenware I saw has the laughing face of a god on it?"

"That represents the saying, 'Whenever the happy laugh, the God rejoices.'"

One of the last islands they visited had beautiful, dramatic mountain shapes and small villages with no connecting roads. The couple spent almost a month exploring the various islands and their settlements. As his impressions during his first days in Japan, the houses, temples, narrow streets, and people fascinated him. He paid closer attention to the inhabitants than their habitats.

He wrote descriptions of the charming landscapes and the extraordinary colors: "…phantom-color, delicate, elfish, indescribable, ---created by the wonderful atmosphere. Vapors enchant the distances, bathing peaks in bewitchments of blue and gray of a hundred tones, transforming cliffs to amethyst, stretching spectral gauzes across the topazine morning, magnifying the splendor of noon, filling the evening with the smoke of gold, bronzing the waters, banding the sundown with ghostly purple and green of nacre. The old Japanese artists who made the marvelous *ehon* picture books tried to fix the sensation of these enchantments in color, and they were successful in their backgrounds to a degree almost miraculous."

Lafcadio found a strange, wild beauty in Japanese landscapes, a beauty that was not easily defined, though he filled notebooks with new ideas, old stories, and impressions. He found the people he met courteous and overly generous. One young physician with whom he dined at his charming home, tried to send him away loaded with costly presents. When Lafcadio attempted to decline to take anything, the fellow secretly sent them to the hotel, which Japanese etiquette made it impossible to return. Another teacher, having heard of Hearn's interest in the islands, brought two fine maps that he'd made himself. A third visitor, while they squatted to smoke pipes together, saw that Lafcadio admired his carved black coral pipe case. He severed the case from his tobacco pouch and presented it to him as a gift. Once that was done it would have been rude in the extreme to refuse. After that experience, Lafcadio was careful to never again admire anything in the presence of the owner.

Japan had been closed for centuries and natives on the islands had never seen "foreign devils" before. In the village of Urago, curiosity got out of control when a jostling, shouting crowd swarmed their inn from ground to roof to get a glimpse of them. When they filled the balcony of a house across the way, the weight of the onlookers collapsed the balcony. Fortunately, no one was killed, but police had to be called to remove the injured and restore order.

The natives' insatiable, unfriendly behavior did not improve. Wherever Lafcadio went, a pressing mob surrounded him. He drew the population after him with the pattering of geta wooden shoes like the sound of surf. Except for that particular sound, there was absolute silence, not a word was spoken. There was no rudeness or roughness in their curiosity, yet he was forced to take his notebooks and nervous wife to more worldly communities. He was bone-tired but never bored. Setsu did not find the trip as entertaining or relish the adventure as much as her husband. But soon even Lafcadio grew tired of the bad roads and foul smells. Homeward bound, there arose a sadness mixed with love for Oki---chiefly because it was there that he felt, as nowhere else in Japan, the full joy of escape from the far-reaching influences of high-pressure, artificial civilization.

Before they left the Oki Islands, Setsu and Lafcadio met and fell in love with a little samurai boy, Masayoshi, whose noble family had fled Izumo when the shogunate hereditary military dictatorship was overthrown. They were victims of the cruel sudden changes forced upon the Japanese civilization and samurai by the Christian bayonets for their holy motive of gain. The boy's old warrior caste family knew only the arts of courtesy and the arts of war. Kumagae Masayoshi worked in the hotel as a servant. Lafcadio found him so intelligent that he couldn't stand to leave him in his current situation.

Masayoshi accepted the offer to leave the island with his new benefactors to live with them and go to school in Kumamoto. Setsu supervised his care. Although it complicated her responsibilities, it made her happy to have this bright new addition to their household. The young student also helped interpret and performed useful task for them.

Their friend Nishida-san joined them in Mionoseki for a week's happy reunion. They talked away the days and evenings. When Nishida returned to Matsue, Lafcadio wrote to him: "We felt quite lonesome after you went away, and especially at supper-time when there were only two mats instead of three, laid upon the *suzumi-dai*, overlooking the bay." Since Mionoseki had a religious ban on eggs, Nishida sent a carton of eggs from Matsue so Lafcadio's diet would stay familiar.

Lafcadio wrote to W. B. Mason about his trips and feelings: "Professor Chamberlain spoke to me about the variability of one's feelings toward Japan being like the oscillation of a pendulum: one day swinging toward pessimism and the next to optimism. I have this feeling very often, and I suppose you must have had it many times. But the pessimistic feeling is generally coincident with some experience of New Japan, and the optimistic with something of Old Japan. But with what hideous rapidity Japan is modernizing, after all!---not in costume or architecture, or habit, but in heart and manner. The emotional nature of the race is changing. Will it ever be beautiful again? It is a very very hard thing to study the Japanese soul…But who - not a madman - should try to write a book for Japanese to read, after having acquired some knowledge of things? Buddhism alone gives us any consolatory ideas on the subject; but it is now vulgar to mention Buddhism to the Japanese."

Nurtured by a nature-worshipping environment, Shintoism evolved, followed by a uniquely Japanese form of synchronized Shinto-Buddhism ever since the seventh century. It broke Lafcadio's heart to see it rejected in favor of Western religious cults and modernism.

Lafcadio and Setsu were ready to return to Kumamoto and the comforts of their own home. They missed the ship that would have taken them by water around Honshu and were forced to make the journey overland by rickshaw. Torrential rains had washed out roads and the going was rough. The farm country guesthouses for travelers were few and shabby. For three days they struggled across the mountains to catch the train back to the city.

After weeks of such stimulation and discomfort, they arrived in Kumamoto and returned to their routines of household duties and teaching. At the Fifth Higher School there was a different crop of students to train. A new headmaster, Mr. Sakurai, a very young and silent man, replaced the amiable Mr. Kano. After more than a year, Lafcadio still had no intimate friends among his colleagues, no mental company other than books. He felt the others disliked him for some unknown reason but considered that perhaps the trouble lay in his inability to understand the Kyushu people.

He told Hendrick about spending his lunch hours alone on the hillside above the school with the Buddha statue that looked down on him through its half-closed eyelids of stone. Lafcadio commented, "He never answers me, but he looks very sad, - smiles like one who has received an injury which he cannot return, and you know that is the most pathetic of smiles. And the snakes twist before my feet as I descend to the sound of the bell. There is my only companion for you! But I like him better than those who look like him waiting for me in the classroom."

When Lafcadio wandered into certain sections of Kumamoto, hisses of hatred followed him. They called after him, "*Ijin*" or "*Tojin*" or "*Ke-tojin*", the last of which means 'hairy foreigner' and was not intended as a compliment. He wrote to Chamberlain, "Although I don't go out alone, the changing feeling of even the adult population toward a foreigner wandering through their streets was strongly visible. A sadness, such as I never felt before in Japan, came over me…how utterly dead Old Japan is, and how ugly New Japan is becoming."

Lafcadio felt the mocking, surges of xenophobia were merely national awakenings to the dangers of Occidental influences, so tried not to take it personally. But it foreshadowed a certain amount of insecurity about his employment. Many foreign instructors were being dismissed and he feared his contract might not be renewed. He told Nishida "The school here is getting rather disagreeable. I think they are trying to get rid of me."

He coped with irritations in public and at the school, but discouragement over the government's educational policies increased. Several times a year he found that some of his most brilliant students had committed suicide. They left confessions saying they felt like failures at keeping up with the heavy workload and overly competitive exam environment.

During elementary school years, the students had been taught to internalize their own feelings and go with what society expected in daily interactions. Particular importance was given to compromise to avoid conflicts and development of empathy for others. Dissention produced negative consequences. Traditionally, Lafcadio's students accepted relationships of hierarchy and domination in exchange for protection. They believed in the concept that Japanese society was a large family, with an emperor of divine origin at the apex. He was their guardian throughout history, protecting his subjects in exchange for obedience and hard work. But with the rise in modernization and Western ways, the social structure fabric began to tear. The cultural and religious changes gave rise to social Darwinism resulting in bullying (*ijime*), deaths and suicides related to overworking and stress (*karoshi*), and severe societal withdrawal and reclusion (*hikikomori*).

Additionally, Japan went to war with China while he was in Kumamoto. The war spirit manifested itself in a painful way at his school when many students killed themselves when they were denied a chance of military service, in duty to their beloved Emperor. Delicate souls were dying in the New Japan and the rougher ones were triumphing. Lafcadio did not fit in with the progressive movement toward modernization, militarization, and westernization of the country. But he dared not leave the government education system until he found employment elsewhere.

Another unhappy aspect of living in Kumamoto was the frequent earthquakes. Lafcadio developed a disgusting fear of earthquakes. During severe tremors, the entire household ran out of the house to spend the night in uncomfortable bamboo fields. It deeply disturbed him that the dreadful power of nature could destroy his home and everyone under its roof. Another disappointment was that by winter young Masayoshi from the Oki Islands had become defiant, disruptive, and composed taunting songs. Lafcadio admitted that "my little boy turned out badly" and sent him back to his people.

In December 1892, Lafcadio and his extended family moved to a new house at 35 Nishihiribata, Tsuboi. It had a more interesting and impressive garden. He described it as "a pretty house with a pretty garden - surrounded by cemeteries and images of the gods."

The garden was designed to look wild, with fifteen boulders brought up from the Shirakawa River. He enjoyed the beauty of ancient surfaces affected by wind, water, and time. Unlike art manufactured by humans, these pieces were neutral and pure. He told Setsu, "I believe I was born Japanese, but accidentally appeared in the wrong place, but now I have found my way home."

With the move, they were able to conserve money. By July, 1893, he reported to Hendrick that, "My little wife and I have saved nearly $3500 thousand Japanese dollars between us." Lafcadio's goal was to be financial safe enough to leave teaching and devote all his time to writing.

Although household money was painstakingly guarded by everyone but Hearn, the members of the household would occasionally venture out to attend the theater, call on friends, or go shopping. He tried to keep everyone away from European and American goods and direct them to Japanese objects as "twice as pretty and durable".

As always, Lafcadio invested in books. He'd started a second library collection composed of modern and classic works, rather than the exotic items of the library he considered lost to Dr. George Gould, with whom he stayed several months in Philadelphia, USA. He enjoyed the odor of books' leather, cloth, and paper pages, inhaling their aroma as if they were incense. He indulged in reading and re-reading several authors. Thinking of writing a series of Japanese short stories, he reviewed the best short stories from around the world.

He revisited his beloved French school of romantic literature. The Romantic Movement was all about the senses, but Lafcadio now found that the love and worship of beauty alone was not enough. Realism was needed.

Following the teachings of Herbert Spencer, he believed that "morality, pure and simple, has nothing to do with the matter. It is a question of force, self-balance, self-control, intellectual power of a certain order."

Lafcadio wanted his writing art to be aspirational, to achieve something meaningful as well. He aimed to reach the heart of the people but realized with a freezing skepticism how little he knew Japan and its people. He wrote to Chamberlain:

"The illusions are forever over; but the memory of many unpleasant things remains. I know much more about the Japanese than I did a year ago; and still I am far from understanding them as well. Even my own little wife is somewhat mysterious still to me, though always in a lovable way."

Lafcadio studied people around him every day, but discovered how little one could know about their thoughts and feelings. As an example, he wrote about his household cook who seemed to be the happiest of mortals. He laughed invariably when spoken to, looked delighted when working, and appeared to know nothing of the small troubles of life.

"My cook wears a smiling, healthy, rather pleasant face. He is a good-looking young man. Whenever I used to think of him I thought of the smile, I saw a mask before me merry as one of those little masks of *Oho-kumi-nushi-no-kami* they sell at Mionoseki. One day I looked through a little hole in the *shoji* and saw him alone. The face was not the same face. It was thin and drawn and showed queer lines worn by pain, anger, and old hardship. I thought, 'He will look just like that when he is dead.' I coughed gently to announce my presence and went in, and the man was all changed, young and happy again. At once the face smoothed, softened, lighted up as by a miracle of rejuvenation. Miracle indeed, of perpetual unselfish self-control. I have never seen that look of trouble in his face since. But I know when he is alone he wears it. He never shows his real face to me; he wears the mask of happiness as an etiquette."

Lafcadio became interested in reality - the real face of the cook, the real face of Japan. He began to write less about general impressions and landscapes and focused on particulars about people and feelings.

CHAPTER 22

During the summer of 1893 there were no arduous trips to gather notes. Setsu was pregnant with their first child, due in autumn. Lafcadio concentrated intense energy on her rather than matters outside their home. It was the most important thing ever to happen in his life, so he was terrified and joyful all at once. Her family all took part in the preparations.

In July he took a week to visit Nagasaki. He stayed in an ugly Western hotel that he couldn't leave soon enough. The summer heat was sultry. He used his discomfort of the intolerable summer weather as a framework for a story, "The Dream of a Summer Day", retelling of the Japanese fairytale of Urashima: "Fourteen hundred and sixteen years ago, the fisher-boy Urashima Taro left the shore of Suminoye in his boat. Summer days were then as now…".

In Japan there was a custom for the expectant family to borrow a baby so they could get used to handling a child and having one among them. Lafcadio hardly touched the infant, but studied him carefully. The child smiled, went to sleep when he was supposed to, and never cried. He was impressed by the Buddha-like calm nature of the baby and could only hope for one so agreeable.

Lafcadio wrote to Ellwood Hendrick, "There is universal joy because of the birth in prospect, and I am accused of not seeming joyful enough. I am not sorry. But I hope that my little one will never have to face life in the West, but may always dwell in the Buddhist atmosphere…I only have anxiety for her: still she is so strong that I trust the gods will be kind to us."

Inside their home compound the family's happiness and optimism helped calm Lafcadio's forebodings. They felt since he was dark featured and small, that the baby would probably look more Japanese than a usual mixed marriage child.

The first week of November Lafcadio's anxiety turned to fear and he contacted the chief surgeon at the government garrison and asked if he would attend Setsu. The doctor advised him to trust Mrs. Hearn to the native midwives who had been handling such things for thousands of years. In the unlikely event anything serious happened he could call on him. Setsu preferred the customary midwives. When her labor started Setsu's mother summoned two midwives. Lafcadio disliked them on sight since they rudely pushed him aside to begin their work.

He insisted on remaining at her bedside to reassure her. As her labor progressed and her suffering intensified, he became panicked with fear and pity. He realized how sacred maternity was in the life cycle. His thoughts went dark at the possibility that men could be cruel to women who bore their children.

Over and over, Lafcadio pleaded with Destiny, "Come into the world gently! Be healthy! Come into the world with good eyes, have good eyes!"

He felt totally helpless. Eventually Setsu, the grandmother, and midwives forcefully told him it would be best for him to leave and go back to his work. But he was unable to read or write. He went out into the garden. The house looked like a giant paper-sided lantern, a magic-lantern. He watched the shadows flicker across the closed paper shoji screens of Setsu's room.

At one o'clock on the morning of November 17, 1893, in the city of Kumamoto, Lafcadio was electrified by the shrill, thin cry of a newborn infant. As he rose to go into the house, Grandfather rushed out shouting, "Hellum! Great treasure child is born!" Setsu had given birth to a son. When he entered her room and looked at his child he could not speak. He held his breath as one might do to stop time when something wonderful has touched them.

Later he wrote, "The most strangely beautiful creature on earth lay before him." Setsu had given birth to Leopold Kazuo Koizumi, a child with perfect eyes. Lafcadio felt humble and grateful to the unknowable powers that had treated them so kindly.

The next day Lafcadio wrote letters to his friends Nishida, Chamberlain, Hendrick, Mason, and several others announcing his son's birth. He said to Hendrick: "Last night my child was born,---a very strong boy, with large black eyes; he looks more like a Japanese, however, than a foreign boy. He had my nose, but his mother's features in some other respects, curiously blended with mine. There is no fault with him; and the physicians say, from the form of his little bones, that he promises to become very tall. A cross between European and Japanese is nearly always an improvement when both parents are in good condition; and happily the old military caste to which my wife belongs is a strong one...The little man will wear sandals and dress like a Japanese, and become a good little Buddhist. He will not have to go to church, and listen to stupid sermons, and be perpetually tormented by absurd conventions.

"If ever you become a father, I think the strongest and strangest sensation of your life will be hearing for the first time the thin cry of your own child. For a moment you have the strange feeling of being double; but there is something more, quite impossible to analyze---perhaps the echo in a man's heart of all sensations felt by all the gathers and mothers of his race at a similar instant in the past. It is a very tender, but also very ghostly feeling...No man can possibly know what life means, what the world means, what anything means, until he has a child and loves it. And then the whole universe changes---and nothing will ever again seem exactly as it seemed before."

The child thrived. Like his father, his first name was dropped and the middle name Kazuo, meaning "the first of the excellent---the best of the peerless" was used from the beginning. Lafcadio nicknamed him Kajii-wo or Kajio. Kajio's hair was chestnut and wavy and soon looked more European than Japanese. Lafcadio doted over him and always put his son's security and future before his own.

When Professor Chamberlain sent congratulations, he wrote, "This little being needs my whole life, time, strength, care---everything I can give before going to the *hakabe* graveyard; I shall hardly be able to freight and supply the ship for its voyage. No more life-ships shall be launched! I am rather proud however of this one and not much afraid to the future therefor."

The Hearn home revolved around the plump, round-faced Kajio. A nurse was added to the household staff, and everyone found themselves busy day and night with the infant. Lafcadio confessed himself "greatly fallen into oblivion" and was happy being just a fond spectator. Setsu was shocked at how Lafcadio "set him going in life" with lavish purchases of silk kimonos and toys. He bought a gleaming baby carriage from Yokohama that caused a neighborhood event when they took outings.

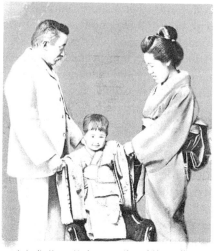
Lafcadio Hearn, his Japanese wife, and his son, Kazuo

The love of the child was another unbreakable bond. Lafcadio was the center of a family unit. He was relieved of the feelings of being an outcast, the burden of separateness he'd carried all his life until then. He wrote to friends about being "Life and Food and other things" to nearly twelve people in his home. "However intolerable anything else is, at home I enter into my little smiling world of old ways and thoughts and courtesies; where all is soft and gentle as something seen in sleep. It is so soft, so intangibly gentle, and lovable and artless that sometimes it seems a dream only; and then a fear comes that it might vanish away. It has become me."

Chamberlain and Mason corresponded and discussed the baby like two conscientious godfathers and sent their ideas and conclusions to Lafcadio. One bit of advice was to protect the child from fear of darkness. After the terrors of his own childhood, he definitely concurred. His two friends asked what he had decided to do about his son's citizenship. If the family resumed world travels, what would be the best status for Kazuo? The issue of travel aside, at Lafcadio's age he was considering what would happen to his family if he died. He wrote:

"Leaving the moral question aside altogether---though it is a stronger one than any---there comes the consideration of the facts, thus: The Japanese are still the best people in the world to live among; therefore, why wish ever to live elsewhere? No one will, or ever could, love me any more than those about me now love me; and that is the most precious consideration in life aside from the mere capacity to live. The ugly questions are death and the lack of employment. The latter is quite possible. The former is important. In either event, it was better that mother and son were able to live in the interior, and own their own homestead, and have a little revenue, and take care of each other until better times."

Although he announced his marriage to friends and family in the United States, there was no American embassy in Japan to formally register his union with Setsu, nor had he legally registered his marriage in Japan.

Even though many considered Lafcadio Hearn an American expatriate writer, he was actually a British citizen. He was a British subject as his father was British and he was born on a Greek island that was British controlled. He never thought of becoming USA citizen, yet wrote to a friend, "I had eighteen years of American life, and so got out of touch with Europe and think of America when I make comparisons. I had to work at literature through their vehicles." He thought of himself as an American writer.

If he became a Japanese citizen, he would lose his foreign status that granted him a much higher salary than a Japanese professor would earn. He worried that by naturalizing that his salary and benefits received by foreigners would be reduced to a Japanese employee level. He summarized:

"I don't quite see the morality of the reduction, for services should be paid according to the market value at least; ---but there is no doubt it would be made. Being a Japanese citizen would, of course, make no difference whatever as to my relations in any civilized countries abroad. It would only make some difference in an uncivilized country, ---such as revolutionary South America, where English or French, or American protection is a good thing to have. But the long and short of the matter is that I am anxious about Setsu's and the boy's interests: my own being concerned only at that point where their injury would be Setsu's injury."

Conversely, English citizenship would be worse than useless to his family. If Setsu and their son became English citizens, they would lose all native property rights and be forced to live only in restricted Open Port cities. They could not purchase even the smallest parcel of land or choose where to call home. Setsu would never feel at home in the Europeanized life of the open ports. They'd dreamed of someday going back to Matsue and buying the samurai house they had loved there.

He wanted to have Setsu legally registered as his wife, but the Japanese bureaucracy would not register a marriage between a Japanese and a non-Japanese on a family register. There was no law of naturalization except by adoption. Additionally, Japan had passed new inter-racial marriage laws under which his marriage would no longer be legal. He was told that for his son to preserve his Japanese nationality, his birth had to be registered under Setsu's name only. Lafcadio would have to be adopted into his wife's father's Koizumi family as "incoming husband". If Lafcadio put Kazuo under his name, his son became a foreigner, with all the incumbent restrictions.

If Lafcadio died without settling the matter of citizenship, his estate and royalties would be outside the bounds of Japanese or British law, and everything would pass to his family overseas. At that time there were unequal treaties - to become a naturalized Japanese subject was the only means by which a Westerner could leave his inheritance to his Japanese family without any legal troubles with his Western relatives. Lafcadio was extremely careful about the matter of inheritance since he always thought that he'd been robbed of his own inheritance from his great-aunt Sarah Brenane. If he did not become a Japanese citizen, the house of Koizumi would inherit nothing but sorrow and loss. The solution that was best for his family seemed clear. He needed to give up his British citizenship. Britain did not allow it subjects to have dual citizenship. Even though it could reduce his earning power, Lafcadio Hearn decided to become a Japanese national to legitimize Setsu and Kazuo's status as his wife and son.

To become a Japanese subject, Lafcadio had to be adopted by his Japanese family and listed a family member in the existing Koizumi family register. After the death, disappearance, and resignation of her three brothers, a branch of the Koizumi family was founded with Setsu as its head on August 27, 1895. Registers did not permit separate family names so he would assume their name Koizumi, meaning "little spring".

After great consideration, Lafcadio, together with Setsu's parents, chose a first name, Yakumo, which meant "Eight Clouds". Lafcadio said he chose this naturalization name because Yakumo was the first word in the "most ancient poem extant in the Japanese language", as well as a second designation for the old province name for the Matsue area, Izumo, "my beloved province the Place of the Issuing of Clouds".

Setsu, with the help of attorney Masujima Rokuichio who studied law in Britain, drew up a request for Lafcadio's application for an "alien incoming husband marriage" to become a subject of Japan through adoption in November 1895. Government officials called Setsu to their city offices and later came to their home and asked endless questions. Afterward bureaucratic silence followed, and they waited. The prefectural governor's request for Lafcadio's oath of allegiance to the Emperor of Japan, which implied a renunciation of allegiance to the British Crown, was dealt with by the British consul in January 1896.

After typical procedural delays, on February 10, 1896, the government informed Lafcadio Hearn/Koizumi Yakumo that he was officially a naturalized Japanese citizen. He replaced Setsu as the family head on February 13 and the next day Kazuo, who had been registered as her 'privately born son' in the old family registry, was moved to the new Koizumi family branch as their legitimate child.

Lafcadio is said to be the very first person to legally acquire Japanese nationality via naturalization under the Empire of Japan's first constitution Article 18. From that point forward he signed documents and many of his letters Y. Koizumi.

For a man who, for his entire life, had rebelled against religious and societal conventions, he was now a legal subject of one of the least individualistic countries in the world. A famous Japanese proverb that illustrated this says, "The nail that sticks out shall be hammered down." The despotism of collective opinion forced conformity on all its subjects. Even poor manners were considered an indignity. The expression in Japan for an unceremonious, rude, or bad-mannered person is "another than expected person". It explained the tradition that an individual does not do anything unexpected, that all is arranged by rule and order.

Lafcadio understood and wrote "unselfish and frank qualities of man are necessary to the preservation of society and its development." But he also believed that "inflexible subservience to an enforced social consensus would lead to social, psychological, and moral stagnation, mediocrity, impersonal dependence, as well as to madness."

He admired the men of the old Japan because they represented the virtues of their society, one he felt was morally better than that of the West. Better in kindness, benevolence, courtesy, heroism, simple faith, self-sacrifice, loyalty, self-control, filial piety, and the in the capacity to be content with a little. Old Japanese society cultivated those qualities, but at the cost of the individual. Western society cultivated the individual by a competition in intellectual power, calculating and action. In the struggle for existence in the new world, the strong and clever succeed. He knew that to compete with the West in industry, commerce, and finance, that the people needed to adopt the methods of the West and learn a more rational morality.

As he walked about in Japan, people would call out *gaijin*, 'foreigner' behind his back. He understood the hecklers' reason for anger. Sometimes they'd mistake him for an *ainoku*, half-Japanese, which pleased him greatly. He realistically knew that he would never be treated as a genuine Japanese because of his Caucasian face and his limited ability to speak Japanese. They did not realize he was in fact, Yakima Koizumi, a Japanese citizen and proud patriot. From the beginning, Lafcadio had felt the ideological pull of a quest for preservation of Japanese traditions, high moral ideals, and national self-respect.

At home, Lafcadio and his household would sing patriotic songs like *Kampira, fune, fune* and the Japanese national anthem *Kimigayo*, which literally means 'You are the World'.

"You see, I have nothing Western about me," he boasted to Setsu.

"But look at your nose!" she remarked back.

"Oh, pity me because of my nose, for I, Koizumi Yakumo, truly love Japan more than any Japanese."

He wrote to his half-sister Minnie in defense of the Japanese military during the war with Russia, which he called "a struggle for national existence." He felt it was a contest between David from the East and Goliath from the West and he did not favor the Occidental giants. He prophetically wrote:

"Japan is doing well without us (Occidental West) and we have not been kind enough to her to win her love. We have persecuted her with hordes of fanatical missionaries, robbed her by unjust treaties, forced her to pay monstrous indemnities for trifling wrongs. We have forced her to become strong, and she is going to do without us presently the future is dark."

In Lafcadio's estimation Meiji Japan - small, new, and overshadowed by great world powers struggling for empires, was fighting to stay alive. Ironically, he understood that Japan had to modernize not as a matter of choice, but of national survival. He saw Japan threatened by the military forces of Russia and China, but also the financial might of America and England. The whole country, the Japanese race itself, fought for national independence.

Just like in Cincinnati, New Orleans, and New York, he saw Japan quickly setting aside old traditions and values to modernize and being swept away in crass and soulless materialism. It was the poor people *en masse* that he described as, "moral, the goodness of ten thousand years is in the marrow of their bones." To the end, he would assert the same sentiment, "The veritable strength of Japan still lies in the moral nature of her common people---her farmers and fishers, artisans and laborers---the patient quiet folk one sees toiling in the rice-fields or occupied with the humblest of crafts and callings in city by-ways."

Lafcadio's quest for a place or culture that was pure and uncorrupted by change was a continuing theme in his work. He sided with Old Japan and grieved over encroachment of the New Japan. He wrote, "The new Japan will be richer and stronger in many ways, but it will neither be so happy nor so kindly as the old." As in all his lofty ideals, he found inevitable disappointment.

CHAPTER 23

With war emptying the national coffers, the future of government employees was even more uncertain. Increased anti-foreign sentiments left Lafcadio feeling increasingly insecure about his teaching position in Kumamoto. His colleague Sakuma frankly warned him:

"Old Japan was far from good, uncivilized…there was poverty, sexism, and superstition. To me and others your idealization of Old Japan is romanticism that rapidly modernizing Japan can ill afford. We need to become a powerful modern state and combat colonization by world powers. Hearn, we have no time to participate in your Japanologist hobby!"

Lafcadio countered quickly, "Japan was 'civilized' well before the Westerners arrived. Surely you know the difference between backward-looking nostalgia and recording of genuine tradition. Pushing the old wisdom and ways under the rug will ruin the sensibility that has been formed over Japan's long history. She would be rootless and unstable if modernization destroyed the traditional way of living."

Sakura just shrugged at the eccentric foreign teacher and walked away. Right before Lafcadio's eyes people were being corrupted and adopting Western ways. "The old courtesy, the old faith, the old kindness are vanishing like snow in the sun," he complained.

Lafcadio's sense of uncertainty and persecution drove him to write a letter to Basil Chamberlain regarding making a change. He told his friend that with earthquakes, his home being robbed, and thunderstorms, Kumamoto had become his idea of "a prison in the bottom of hell."

He was weary of working under the government's educational policies and shadow boxing with the school's cold instructors and authorities. With bitter sarcasm, he described to Chamberlain what the Japanese administration expected of him: "Never ask any questions regarding business; Never ask why; Never criticize even when requested; Never speak favorably or unfavorably of officials, students or employees; Favorable criticism may prove much more objectionable than the other; Give no direct refusal under any circumstances, but only say it is difficult for the moment or certainly, but take care to forget about it; Direct refusals are not forgiven, the other devices are respected and admired; Do not imagine the question of application, efficiency, or conduct in relation to students is of any official importance. The points required from the foreigner are simply 2: (1) Keep the clams in good humor. (2) Pass everybody." He told Chamberlain he'd work anywhere else for half the pay if he could have only fifty percent more peace of mind.

Over the past three years Lafcadio's contract had been renewed each March, but by June there was no word from the college director of the Fifth Higher School. Frustrated, Lafcadio abruptly dismissed his class, went home early, and wrote a harsh letter of resignation. Thankfully, he realized in time that with family obligations he could not afford such ruthless satisfaction. He tore up the letter and made an appointment to see the college headmaster Sakurai in person.

Since Sakurai only spoke Japanese and French, they had an awkward conversation in the second language for both. The headmaster listened politely to Lafcadio's complaints about the rudeness and conspiracies of other teachers and the lack of his contract renewal. He was assured that he would receive a contract immediately because it was just an administrative oversight. He told Hearn-san he was generally liked by his colleagues, and their coldness was only due to cultural restraint. The absence of comprehension and sympathy was a veritable torture for him. Lafcadio agreed to remain the last three weeks of that school term but would not commit himself further.

During school break, Lafcadio took Setsu, her mother, and the boy on a four-day pilgrimage to Kompira Shrine on the small island of Shikoku. The weather was good and sights entertaining. The small family group was accepted as one belonging to the scene, all passing as Japanese. A small incident marred the trip when the grandmother fell while ascending the temple steps carrying the baby. Kazuo was not hurt, but Lafcadio was uneasy until they were all safely back at home. He wrote a charming letter about the happy trip to Chamberlain, calling it "The Adventures of Kajio."

Setsu preferred not to travel during the hottest summer months. Lafcadio decided to use the remaining school vacation time to go alone to look after some long-neglected business matters in Tokyo and Yokohama. Chamberlain was going to be in the mountains of Hakone with his family so offered him the use of his home while in the capital. Nishida planned to meet him there. It also turned out that Mason and his family would be in Yokohama for the summer.

Lafcadio had been isolated in the interior with no masculine Western companions with whom to speak with in his own language and thought patterns. Although a bit frightened, he took off for the cities. The weeklong trip by boat and train was the first time in four years that he'd left his virtual seclusion in remote Matsue and Kumamoto. After meeting and talking to Americans and Europeans he met along the way, his isolated life seemed lonely and dull, except for thoughts of his beloved family.

Upon arriving in Yokohama in summer of 1895, he observed, "The foreign concession of an open port offers a striking contrast to its far-Eastern environment. In the well-ordered ugliness of its streets, one finds suggestions of places not on this side of the world - just as though fragments of the Occident had been magically brought overseas: bits of Liverpool, of Marseilles, of New York, of New Orleans, and bits of tropical towns in colonies twelve or fifteen thousand miles away. The mercantile buildings, immense by comparison with the low light Japanese shops, seem to utter the menace of financial power....The dominant element is English and American, - English being in the majority. All the faults and some of the finer qualities of the masterful races can be studied here."

Lafcadio feared he'd landed in Scandinavia instead of Yokohama because the town was filled with 'giants', so many tall, blonde, hawk-nosed Englishmen. They talked with loud voices and smoked large, foul-smelling cigars. Women laughed with their mouths open and wore western style dresses and short hair. His first question was, "Are they all widows?" because it had been a Japanese custom for a widow to cut off her hair at the neck and bury half of it with her husband, the other half to be kept until her own death. Lafcadio found out the hairstyle was only another fashion copied in the desire to imitate Westerners. Nothing seemed refined or delicate in Yokohama, only coarse and big, which repelled his artistic soul.

In one moment Lafcadio would exclaim how there was no limit to the greatness of the West...Mozart, Shakespeare, Bach, and Beethoven. Then next he'd express his hatred of the West. His love-hate relationship with the West was intermingled with his love and hate relationship with Japan. When he missed the West, he disliked Japan. Next, as he hated the arrogance of the West, he loved Japan.

In his writings, Lafcadio was preoccupied with expressing his vision of Japan with whose culture he developed an extraordinary empathy. He wanted to explain Japanese life and beliefs to his Western audience, but also used Japan as a mirror to show the West its moral inadequacy.

When he and the green-eyed, red-bearded Mason connected in person they felt like they'd known each other forever. They could commensurate on how toxic it was to be enslaved in daily drudgery of government work, Lafcadio at the Fifth Higher School and Mason seventeen years with the Department of Posts and Telegraphs.

Lafcadio liked the man as well as his letters and called him a "beautiful soul". They had family gatherings at Mason's home and swam together for hours at sun-drenched beaches. Lafcadio was blissful. In turn, Mason was astonished by his friend's ability to quote long passages from books and the obscure tales he related. He called Lafcadio a "giant of thought expression" and "emperor in the realm of words". They passed the days, as Lafcadio said, "in debaucheries of beefsteak, whisky and lemonade, gin and ginger ale and beer."

Lafcadio continued reports to Chamberlain: "But I fear all these experiences will demoralize me. After rescue, a castaway enjoys too much the food offered; a physician stands by to prevent him eating enough. My ghostly part was really too hungry for such an experience and feels longings not wholesome for it; sympathy is the supreme delight of life. I ought now to meet some horribly disagreeable foreigners, so as to have my pleasure checked a little. Besides, I am much too happy to write essays and sketches." He had a misguided belief that kindness or pleasure made him dumb and lethargic, and that his best writing came only out of unhappiness.

Through Mason, Lafcadio met Nobushige Amenomori, an accomplished writer in both English and Japanese. Amenomori impressed him with his profound mind and his offer to assemble the Buddhist materials he needed. Lafcadio when asking questions about Buddhism, added, "Don't imagine that I know anything. I have read as many sutras as I could find in English or French, ---that's all...Nothing valuable is ever lost upon me,---even your least word containing a new thought, and your letter was more than valuable."

He wrote to Amenomori, "You understand, of course, how difficult it is for a foreigner to convey to Western minds the feeling of these things as they impress him. On the other hand, he cannot convey the feeling of the Japanese mind, because he has not experienced it...I must tell you also that your frank encouragement, as a representative Japanese thinker, gave me the principal stimulus." He dedicated his book *Kokoro* to Amenomori, his Japanese writer friend.

Lafcadio was convinced Amenomori was the best intellectual among Japanese scholars and poets. The two would read or send each other their manuscripts before publication. Lafadio appreciated an honest, friendly, well-meant criticism from someone he respected. Quoting a letter from him, "Your last letter, just received, completely smashes me, and I rather enjoy being smashed. As for wanting to know, I should like to sit down at your feet for two or three years and learn one ten-thousandth part of the strange and beautiful things which you know. Of course, the changes shall be made as you indicate." He continued, "My obligation to you is not small. With this MS, I can very easily finish my sketch. The MS itself puts me, however, rather in awe of you. I shall feel quite shaky about your judgment of my forthcoming book, you will find so many errors in it."

Amenomori also relayed incidences of how Lafcadio set less value on his own abilities than their actual worth and resented what he considered undue praise. Once a journalist was in Japan and introduced himself, "Mr. Hearn, I have visited Japan several times, and I may say that I have read everything of interest touching her people and her history that I could find, and I wish to say that in my opinion you have written the most interesting and valuable work on Japan that the world possesses today. I merely want to shake your hand thank you for your splendid achievement." Rather than being happy about the recognition, "Lafcadio blushed like a girl, stammered his thanks, and turned away with a diffidence which he could not control."

Lafcadio was modest and when another author sent him a letter complimenting him on his books, he told Amenomori, "I had a letter from him full of such fulsome and offensive compliments that I supposed he was trying to be sarcastic, saying I thought him a fine master of sarcasm, and I have not heard from him since."

In contrast, one time in way of an answer to Lafcadio's questions on Buddhism, Amenomori sent him a copy of a manuscript he's prepared on the same subjects as to those to which his questions related, telling him he could make use of whatever he liked of it and at the same time he asked Lafcadio's opinion about it. The response read, "To be quite brief, then ---

the MS. won't do at all; and I can only advise you to burn it at once." The manuscript was promptly thrown into the fire and they had a hearty laugh over it when they met a few days later.

To his friend and benefactor Basil Chamberlain he wrote, "My love of Buddhism..." and goes on to tell him, "If it were possible for me to adopt a faith, I should adopt it." Two years later he wrote the professor, "If I ever get in a good place for it, I must begin serious Buddhism studies. I have a splendid idea for a popular book on the subject." He confessed to his New York friend Ellwood Hendrick that his "project to study Buddhism is indefinitely delayed by the language barrier" and joked that the "deeper mysteries of Buddhism cannot be explained in the Hearnian dialect."

Lafcadio's enjoyment of his time away continued when he went to Tokyo on July 17th. Illness prevented Nishida from joining him in Tokyo as planned, but nothing marred his experiences. He took up residence at Chamberlain's house at 19 Akasaka Daimachi. Servants provided him with a mosquito netted bed and excellent meals. The most intoxicating aspect of the home was Chamberlain's richly stocked library. He spent hours browsing hundreds of books on innumerable topics. After savoring them, he replaced each tome to its proper place. He read voraciously. There were shelves full of books on Japanese language, history, and folklore.

Regarding the books on Japan, he confessed to Chamberlain, "I really had no idea until now how much had been done in certain lines; and feeling that all I could do would be only to add a few bricks to the great Babel, I have become properly humble,---I hope."

Lafcadio was able to slip away to Yokohama to see Mason a few more times and a side trip to the Hakone Highlands to visit with Chamberlain for two days at the Hotel Fujiya in Miyanoshita. In spite of himself, he was becoming spoiled by the kind of luxury most Westerners enjoyed in Japan.

Lafcadio did not forget that the main purpose of his trip was to arrange for publication of his works. His business negotiations went smoothly. Lafcadio, who once declared, "Publishers are enemies", had learned how to deal with them. Before he left Tokyo, he had a tentative agreement with Takejiro Hasegawa, a leading Japanese publisher of books in English, for the publication of a series of finely bound fairy tales. Lafcadio was pleased that his own initiative produced a solid outlet for his writings, one that continued for years.

The company was respected for printing fine, hand-sewn books printed in color from woodblocks on double leaves of crepe paper. Hasegawa pioneered the production of attractive Japanese publications in English intended for export to European and American markets. He paired established *ukiyo-e* artists with prominent expatriates in Tokyo like Lafcadio to produce successful series.

Lafcadio Hearn's reputation as a writer was growing. The *Atlantic Monthly* was publishing his essays and stories with some regularity; three to five sketches appeared each year. A story published in July 1894, entitled "Red Bride", about the double suicide of a couple not allowed to marry, garnered praise from even the hard-to-please Chamberlain. Writing about contemporary life was a successful new direction. He began to explore other employment opportunities.

Lafcadio headed home full of confidence about his writing, but with no firm decision regarding his teaching position in Kumamoto. He arrived home to a warm welcome on July 31st. He doted on his wife and child and handed out gifts to everyone in the household. Lafcadio was more affectionate and demonstrative than society would have found polite. Setsu knew that her European husband showed his feelings without shame, whereas convention chained Japanese men. To maintain dignity and good form, men pulled a mask over their face and close their lips to avoid showing any affection or respect toward a wife in public. Lafcadio respected cultural formalities, but in his home, all knew how deep his feelings were for his family. Despite the stimulating sights and company on his eastern vacation, it was good to be inside his garden walls again.

Within days, the city trembled in waves of earthquakes. In the middle of the night a violent shock split the house walls and his family had to flee into the garden until morning.

He dreaded the imminent opening of the school and his return to the demoralizing system of education. He wrote to Amenomori, "I am hoping to leave the government service…it is uncertain to the degree of terror, ---a sword of Damocles."

Many of Lafcadio's students were being called into military service after the imperial declaration of war on China. Troops poured into Kumamoto. He worried as many of his students were already on being drawn into the gathering cyclones of death. Amid this chaos, it was no wonder that when an offer of a full-time job at an English newspaper in Kobe came to him, he immediately accepted.

CHAPTER 24

Leaving the financial security of teaching at the Fifth Higher School was frightening. He was giving up the certainty of a government job without knowing how the Kobe newspaper venture would turn out. He did not want to betray the responsibility and trust his family relied upon. He hoped his writing would make up the salary difference. He told headmaster Sakurai he was giving up teaching because of his health and resigned his position. It seemed a good time to leave as on September 22nd he'd sent off his second completed book on Japan for publication.

The Koizumi family members were all tired of Kumamoto. They never felt at home in Kyushu. Great-grandfather wanted them to return to Matsue, but when reminded of how the winters were too hazardous for Hellum's constitution, he and another Izumo male relative went back to their native province alone to live out their final years. Setsu was excited to be moving to one of the great cities of Honshu. Lafcadio wrote, "There is a nomad restlessness in this race...Even the sweetest Japanese woman has something of this Tartar soul...she is ready tomorrow to pull up the pegs and travel a thousand ri."

In the second week of October 1894, Lafcadio, wife Setsu, son Kajio, father and mother-in-law, two female servants, and the remaining male relative left Kumamoto. They traveled by railroad and steamer to the port city of Kobe on the Inland Sea. Although Kobe was many hours of train travel away, it put Lafcadio a little closer to his friends in Yokohama and Tokyo. And Buddhist shrines in Kyoto were only fifty miles away.

Kobe was one of the two greatest ports in Japan. A confusion of ships from all over the world crowded the harbor. Half the people seen on the streets were tall, fair-haired merchants or seamen. Foreign colonies thrived and prospered under the special protection of treaty rights forced upon the country at the opening of the Empire. Houses in the foreign section were Western style, but beyond that quarter there was not as much evidence of the West.

The surrounding environs were beautiful and city layout pleasing. Three thousand-foot peaks of the steep, wooded Rokko Range sheltered the city on the north. The hills were green with pine, home to innumerable butterflies, fireflies, and dragonflies. The city was on a hillside that sloped gently toward the deep wide bay. City avenues ran parallel to the mountain range, each one terracing upward to allow a view of the water from any street. Lafcadio wanted to live in a place where everything was kind, gentle, neat, artistic, and spotlessly clean - the reverse of what was happening as the West vexed the continent, with the monstrous and hideous multiplying daily.

Kobe *Chronicle* editor Robert Young and his wife were at the station to welcome the Hearn/Koizumi family. Lafcadio and Setsu liked the black-bearded Scot and his English wife from the start. That first day he deposited his family and went straight to the *Chronicle* office to get acquainted with the job and meet the staff. Robert Young knew his news business. He'd had experience on the *English Saturday Review*. Lafcadio felt Young's views were liberal---meaning practical, scientific, and not pressured by the missionaries. He thought being a general assistant under such an open-minded man might prove interesting.

The Young family helped Setsu find a house with hillside gardens in the rear and a second story balcony that overlooked street shops and the bay. The household settled in within weeks. Lafcadio found the house rather nondescript - foreign upstairs and Japanese downstairs. But it would do until he could build a fine home for them in the spring.

In spite of his previous vow never to work again as a newspaper journalist, Lafcadio was a fulltime editorial writer for the English-language Kobe *Chronicle*. For a monthly salary of 100 yen, he was responsible for writing daily editorials on matters that supposedly interested the foreign merchants, consular employees, bankers, military personnel, shippers, and visitors to Japan. They were mostly bland commentaries on topics like: Japanese Emigration to the West Indies; Patriotism and Education; Are Englishmen Angels?; and The Labor Problem in America.

He also wrote editorials about more controversial things that interested him personally, but these were not as highly charged or as barbed as he would have wished them. They included titles: "Japanese Educational Policy"; "The Race Problem in America"; "Earthquakes and National Character"; "The Kurumaya Question"; "The Question of Male and Female Equality"; and "A New Chance for Buddhism".

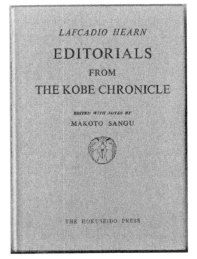

He wasted no literary efforts on his Kobe readers, but did address current problems like dishonest rickshaw runners' dealings with foreigners, pathetic prostitution in the port, the need for better government pay to postal and telegraph employees, and current laws which prohibited a Japanese woman married to a foreigner from owning and inheriting property. All were personal topics at the top of his mind. He sent a year's free subscription to Nishida so his friend could follow his writings.

On a typical day, Lafcadio and Young would meet and set the subject for the day's editorial. Young recalled the way Hearn worked:

"It was remarkable with what ease he could turn out an article. As soon as the subject was decided upon he would go to his own room, where he had a specially high desk to suit his defective eyesight, and sitting there with his nose not more than an inch from the paper he would write industriously for an hour until the article was finished."

His years in journalism in Cincinnati and New Orleans taught him to take observations and turn them into articles. The Japanese form of *zuihitsu*, a genre of literature consisting of loosely connecting fragmented ideas and personal essays, suited him. The "running brush" where the text moves from one idea to another but then is pulled together with associative interacting parts, was the vehicle he used for ideas and impressions.

The *zuihitsu* change of style in his work was demonstrated in "Bits of Life and Death", a collection of his observations of domestic and village life. He learned how to shock with simple words. For example, he describes the calmness of two murderers after they'd hacked a helpless victim to death with swords: "Ichiro and O-Noto sit down by the lantern to take breath, for the work was hard."

Lafcadio was determined to save his journalist job, so he could not be too critical about the modernization of Japan, or the sacrifices the Japanese masses were making for the war efforts, or the steady move toward one vast industrial federation of commerce. However, he still wrote about his abhorred natural enemy - the Christian missionaries. He admitted to himself that his hatred of Christian dogma resulted from childhood experiences. He was annoyed to be condemned by the Church, especially when it threatened his newspaper's business. But he would not stop his war on the dogmatic missionary standard bearers who were chipping away at the centuries-old faith of the people. He would provoke the missionaries with questions like, "What has been the moral value of Christianity to mankind?" Or "Why is Western civilization still in slavery to religious hypocrisy?"

Christianity was changing Japan's national identity, worldview, society, and culture. Recent conversions were based on self-interest or fear and had shallow roots compared to the nature-based beliefs over the centuries. He'd taught his pupils "to respect their own beautiful faith, and the gods of their fathers."

He talked to his student Ochiai about the distinction of Christianity as a religion versus as a sect. "A religion is a moral belief which causes men to live honestly and to be kind and good to each other. A sect is made by differences of belief as to what is true religious teaching. Truth is what makes a religion, moral truth; sects are made by differences of opinion about the meaning of sacred texts."

"When someone tells you that refusing to bow before the portrait of the Emperor is Christianity, that person is not a Christian, but a bigot...To refuse to pay respect to another country's customs and religions is ignorant and vulgar. If I go into a Christian church, although I am not a Christian, I must take off my hat. If I go into a Mohammedan mosque, I must take off my shoes. Such tokens of respect are purely social. Again, when a funeral goes by, we take off our hats. That means, 'Although none of my friends have died, I sympathize with your sorrow.' It is curious and right...Respect has nothing to do with your faith; it is a question of social politeness and gentlemanliness. Religion ought to be of the heart...A true gentleman respects all religions."

Lafcadio, a journalist with twenty years of experience, responded in print quickly to report the natural catastrophe when a giant wave that killed more than 20,000 people in North Japan. In his story "A Living God", he was the first to use the now common word *tsunami*. As in his book *Chita*, about a storm that swept away an island and swallowed up all its inhabitants, he dramatized the miraculous moment of survival. New Orleans even credits him with creating the word 'zombie". He was adept at turning journalistic realism into legendary myth. He contributed some employment inquiry letters to the McClure Syndicate and there was talk about an expedition to the Philippines, but that research project was never realized.

The Youngs would invite Lafcadio and his family to their home for Sunday dinners. He was pleased how they admired and fussed over Setsu. Having been surrounded by native women for five years, Lafcadio would forget and consistently speak to Mrs. Young in his dialectic and labored Japanese. Setsu pleaded with him to teach her English, but he told her, "English is ugly coming from the mouth of a Japanese woman". He liked the way she spoke breathlessly, softly, as if she were telling secrets. So Setsu's social world remained confined, centered around him and home.

Robert Young tried to introduce Lafcadio to the English-speaking community and include him in their activities, but he was generally unresponsive to such opportunities. His dislike of open port city life misled people into regarding him as eccentric or a recluse. He mingled very little with the foreign population, keeping as much as possible to himself. His mind tended toward judgment and separation from superficial people. He'd say, "You see how absurd I have become...I avoid everything which does not help me to make the best of myself - small as it may be. Time is the most precious of all things conceivable. I can't waste it by going out to hear people talk nonsense."

He'd occasionally accept invitations when other guests were present, but his years of isolation made him uncomfortable in the give-and-take of general conversation. If a guest disagreed with him, he'd shrug his shoulders, and leave both the table and the house. Lafcadio Hearn was a curiosity. Yet when Young could entice him to join some of his acquaintances for a meal or discussion, he could be charming. Young wrote, "In the company of a few friends, however, he would thaw out, and, having a wonderful memory, was an excellent raconteur, and would illuminate from his wide reading any subject under discussion."

Glimpses of Unfamiliar Japan was published in America, England, France, and Germany. He dedicated it, in a token of affection and gratitude, "To the Friends, Paymaster Mitchell McDonald, U.S.N. and Basil Hall Chamberlain, Esq., Emeritus Professor of Philology and Japanese in the Imperial

University of Tokyo". It was a book that took travelers to hidden places and provided insights into the lives of everyday Japanese. Observations of traditions, superstitions, and lifestyles were journalistic, yet romantically sympathetic to the culture of his adopted country. His stories and essays were written in English for English-speaking readers. When he wrote "we", he meant "we Westerners". Lafcadio did not think of himself as Irish, Greek, English, American, or even Japanese - he was a 'Westerner' because he had claim to each nationality, but not a full claim to any one country. He was a citizen of the world, a cosmopolitan fully at home in no nation.

When his first book on Japan arrived in Kobe, Lafcadio found flaws and fault in his original naïve sentiments, but acknowledged that they reflected his honest convictions at the time of writing. He expected his second book *Out of the East* to be a more realistic and credible work. While others had written about Japan from the scholar and tourist point of view, Lafcadio's books had the mark of authenticity of inside experiences and taking part in the daily existence of the common people. He did not treat the Japanese as interesting curios, but a people shaped by different traditions important enough to challenge the Western ones. His own view was, "The difference between myself and other writers on Japan, is simply that I have become practically Japanese." In his daily existence he was a resident, citizen, teacher, and family man. *Out of the East* was dedicated: "To Nishida Sentaro - In Dear Remembrance of Izumo Days".

The reviews and comments from the Western world about *Glimpses* were mostly favorable. His reports on Japan struck a chord with many Europeans and Americans at the time who were also questioning Western traditions and values. Even the negative comments created attention that helped sell his books. One critic in the *London Athenaeum* dismissed Lafcadio Hearn because "he associated himself with the Japanese, and the Japanese were savages lacking in Western morality."

Praise and bias against his book stoked enthusiasm for the Orient. Stefan Zweig, in a translation introduction said, "one no longer perceives Hearn's books as written with the pen, but rather drawn with the paint brush of the Japanese." Lafcadio's articles and essays were being serialized on a regular basis in the *Atlantic Monthly*.

He wrote to his old mentor Henry Watkin: "Dear Old Dad: How often I have thought of you, and wondered about you, and wished I could pass with you more of the old-fashioned evenings, reading ancient volumes of the *Atlantic Monthly*,---so much better a magazine in those days than in these, when I am regularly advertised as one of its contributors.

"I often wonder now at your infinite patience with the extraordinary, superhuman foolishness and wickedness of the worst pet you ever had in your life. When I think of all the naughty, mean, absurd, detestable things I did to vex you and to scandalize you, I can't for the life of me understand why you didn't want to kill me,---as a sacrifice to the Gods. What an idiot I was! And how could you be so good?---and why do men change so? I think of my old self as of something which ought not to have been allowed to exist on the face of the earth, and yet, in my present self, I sometimes feel ghostly reminders that the old self was very real indeed. Well, I wish I were near you to love you and make up for all old troubles....

"My book will be out by the time you get this letter, that is, my first book on Japan. Effie can read bits of it to you. And I figure in the *Atlantic* every few months. Cheap fame;---the amazing fortune I once expected doesn't turn up at all. I have been obliged to learn the fact that I am not a genius, and that I must be content with the crumbs from the table...

"I wish I could tell you about the ideas of Western civilization which are produced by a long sojourn in the Orient. How pleasant to read to you strange stories and theories from the Far East! Still I have become so accustomed to Japanese life that a return to Western ways would not be altogether easy...Love to you always and believe me ever, Your extremely bad and ungrateful Grey-headed boy, Lafcadio Hearn."

CHAPTER 25

In December, only three months into Lafcadio's job at the Kobe *Chronicle*, his right eye became severely inflamed from peripheral neuritis. The doctor insisted he rest in a darkened room if he ever intended to work again. Frenetic work as a journalist and past fits of poverty had ruined his overall health.

Lafcadio wrote Ellwood Hendrick: "My eyes, or eye, giving out. You dear old fellow, I've been through some trouble. Indeed, I broke down, and had to remain three weeks with compresses over my eyes in a dark room. I am now over it and able to write and read for a short time every day, but have been warned to leave routine newspaper work alone. Which I must do."

The crisis in his physical health was accompanied by a crisis in his mental health. His eyesight recovered more quickly than his emotions. To him his prospects appeared as dark as the room in which he lay bedridden. Under the threat of total blindness, he became immobilized by the idea of letting down his dependent family.

To Chamberlain he wrote: "I feel just now empty and useless and a dead failure." He lay in idle disillusionment, beating himself up over perceived failures in teaching, journalism, and for experiencing a writing block. He felt he was grinding, grinding all the time but was drained on sensations, dreams and glimpses that he'd always relied upon to write. Before he'd believed that since he had only half the eyesight of ordinary folks, that he was gifted with genius and the ability to see not only the visible world, but a spiritual and immaterial world as well. Now he was in doubt of his abilities.

He also told Chamberlain: "My conclusion is that the charm of Japanese life is largely the charm of childhood, and that the most beautiful of all race childhoods is passing into an adolescence which threatens to prove repulsive." In a second letter he continued his rant, "It seems as if everything had quite suddenly come clear to me, and utterly void of emotional interest. I felt as if I hated Japan unspeakably, and the whole world seemed not worth living in…"

Lafcadio believed that childlike mystery was what connected him to the processes of imagination and creativity, so he fell into depression when he matured into his adolescence of writing. This matured phase was the end of his romance with the fairytale of Japan. He was dissatisfied and unable to look at his former work.

He fantasized about escaping the winter cold and sailing to the South Pacific. In early times he would have done just that, but he had Setsu, his son, and a family who loved him. Setsu was also pregnant with their second child. He would not be like his father who abandoned wife and children. He willed himself to remain where he was and confront reality. His work would be his path out of a dark place, his way of dealing with the world. He took refuge in his study from the storms of doubts and his own anxious mind.

One day two women came to Lafcadio's house selling ballads. They sang their songs to a gathering of people and moved them to tears with its intensity and emotional dimension. He could see and feel the pathos and haunting beauty of things. Afterward he listened to their sad life story, realizing that he could still be intrigued by human nature, with all its good, bad, ugly and beautiful. The encounter made him believe that he still had his vocation and ability to write about things vividly. The music brought back memories.

As a child in Ireland he enjoyed listening to Irish folk songs, often sung by wandering gypsies. In Cincinnati he frequented dance halls, bars, and docks where the African Americans played and sang their blues and gospel music. They projected sadness, happiness, humor, and bawdiness. He recorded the lyrics and included them in a few of his newspaper articles. He was an early ethnographer and folklorist, writing about the music of ordinary people.

When Lafcadio lived in New Orleans fifteen years before jazz was born, he would wander the streets to collect musical scores and lyrics of Creole music to send to his New York City music critic friend Henry Krehbiel. He wrote a letter asking, "Did you ever hear negros play the piano by ear? There are several curiosities here, Creole negroes. Sometimes we pay them a bottle of wine to come here and play for us. They use the piano exactly like a banjo." He liked the African-influenced Creole music and spoke of it favorably, "It hath a most sweet sound to me; and to the ethnologist a most fascinating interest. Verily, I would rather listen to it, than hear a symphony of Beethoven!"

Hearn wrote to Professor Chamberlain about the blind singer, "I have always been much impressed and charmed by primitive music." He especially enjoyed the Japanese Bon Odori songs and dances of Shimoichi village, Tottori Prefecture. He refuted Chamberlain's claim that Japanese music was just noise. Lafcadio knew Westerners felt that only classical music was regarded as proper. But after hearing the Japanese street musicians and observing the New Orleans ragtime music culture, his ear was keen and without prejudice. He even enjoyed the chirping of insects, considering it to be musical.

After months of illness and stagnation, he wrote another more hopeful letter to Chamberlain:

"...I must do better some day with something or acknowledge myself dead failure. I really think I have stored away in me somewhere powers larger than those I have yet been able to use. Of course I don't mean that I have hidden wisdom, or anything of that sort; but I believe I have some power to reach the public emotionally, if conditions allow.

"One little story which would never die, might suffice - or a volume of little stories...I might write an essay on some topic of which I am now quite ignorant by studying the subject for the necessary time. But a story cannot be written by the help of study at all...It must be a sensation in one's own life---and not peculiar to any place and time."

Lafcadio recovered from his illness, depression, and grew in confidence enough to start writing again. He began to realize that excellence was as much about attitude as skill. It was a matter of recreating himself through trial and error, pain and suffering, and the ability to conquer his own fears. He walked about in the city and watched people. Emotions threaded through all his stories. This period was busy and fruitful enough for him to live on writing income without working for wages.

He confided to Chamberlain, "My first work was awfully florid. Self-control was the hardest thing to learn...After years of studying poetical prose, I am forced now to study simplicity. After attempting my utmost at ornamentation, I am converted by my own mistakes. The great point is to touch with simple words." He also admitted, "I should like now to go through many paragraphs written years ago and sober them down."

"It is true I am not satisfied and already unable to look at my former work. But the moment a man can feel satisfied with himself, progress stops...And I feel my style is not yet fixed,---too artificial. By another year of study or two I think I shall be able to do better...Composition becomes difficult only when it becomes work, that is literary labor without a strong inspirational impulse or an emotional feeling behind it." He blamed newspaper work for encouraging the former weaker side of his writing but appreciated it for teaching him habits of industry.

When Lafcadio lived in Martinique for two years and wrote about the Caribbean tropics, his writing style was an explosive sensory overload of colors, vegetation, scents, topography, and characters. He felt at home in a society of mixed races. Writing detailed portraits of the lifestyle of the French West Indies people included other-worldly descriptions of the sky, sea, and exotic, volcanic island landscapes. He wrote in rebellious and sensual tones, declaring that the island nature itself was "nude, warm, savage and amorous". As always, his words were a journey as much within the interior dreamscapes of his mind.

Chamberlain, in praising one of Hearn's early works, said, "Of course the style is too ornamental for everyday use. The impression - the taste left in my mouth by your wonderful descriptions is like that of some luscious fruit or triumph of confectionery, which, though one could not live on it altogether, appropriately graces a royal or a wedding table."

Lafcadio eventually abandoned the richness of his earlier writing style and aimed more for simplicity. The shadowy, transparent stories he wrote in Japan were completely different than the splendid flowery wording in his West Indies studies. The two styles were as opposite as a Gothic cathedral and a Shinto shrine.

Lafcadio's early method of writing evolved from the sensitive styles typical of his favorite poet, the florid Shelley; romantic Poe (he'd even called himself 'The Raven'); William Beckford, the gothic novelist; George Borrow who traveled with exotic gypsies; and Pierre Loti's picturesque travelogues. During his newspaper career, he was a masterly word-painter and the apostle of the exotic, while also producing editorials of the best journalistic type, followed with literary novels. After time in Japan, he instead began to emulate the magical simplicity of telling tales like Rudyard

Kipling and Hans Christian Andersen. Lafcadio learned from Japan itself the virtues of sparseness.

He described his new method of writing to Hendrick, "All the best work is done the way ants do things - little by little, in tiny, tireless, and regular additions."

He advised his New York friend on writing, "You must see interesting things, of course only in flashes and patches. But preserve in writing the memory of these. In a year you will be astounded to find them self-arranging, kaleidoscopically, into something symmetrical, and trying to live. Then play God, and breathe into the nostrils, and be astonished and pleased."

His method was to force himself to do the preliminary work and let the thought develop itself, the best results coming out of the unconscious. This method led to several rewrites and final versions. He could work for hours changing and rearranging words in a single paragraph.

He wrote to Chamberlain, "For me words have color, form, character. They have faces, ports, manners, gesticulations; ---they have moods, humours, eccentricities; ---they have tints, tones, personalities." And they had all these additional qualities even without reference to their meanings. Words were seen as magic spells that protected him against enemies, like David's pebbles against Goliath.

He labored to make himself an artist rather than a mere journalist. Newspapers and magazines complained about his use of exclamation points, or commas followed by dashes, or semi-colons. But Lafcadio followed his own punctuation guide to give voice to his work. He claimed to be writing for the ear, not the eye. He wanted the passage to sound exactly right when read aloud. Struggles over words were worth it when he found the perfect incantation.

Lafcadio and Amenomori were still exchanging manuscripts for honest opinions. He told his friend about his method of writing and editing, "I hope you will not think it preposterous for me to resist criticism until I find myself obliged to give in. That is really the duty of a writer under all ordinary circumstances, because he is supposed to do his best, and change of one word may affect the whole construction and quality (especially musical) of a sentence. But these circumstances are extraordinary, and it does seem a little cheeky not to accept your criticism at once, instead of trying to oppose them. But you know why,---so many other things are involved in change. Thank you for your kindness in criticizing: even if I kick against the pricks for a moment, I am not less grateful and delighted on that account."

If Lafcadio was very careful in making any changes in what he had written, he was more careful in the original writing of a piece. He never wrote on the spur of the moment. He took whatever time was necessary to make the work effective. He worked on several sketches or essays at once. He composed in parts and waited for the segments to build up into a whole.

Regarding the order of writing, he told his friend, "I never begin. It is too much trouble. I write down the easiest thing first, then something else,--- finally the forty or fifty fragments interlink somehow, and shape into a body." In certain cases, it took a long time for the fragments to shape into a body.

Simply having read, seen, or heard about a subject was not enough for Lafcadio to begin writing about it. He waited to feel them. His mind was in a state of restless suspension until the desired sensation came to him.

He wrote about his moods to Amenomori, "But somehow, working is against the grain. I get no thrill, no fission no sensation. I want new experiences...Perhaps the power to feel thrill dies with the approach of a man's fiftieth year...Must I die and be born again to feel the charm of the Far East; ---or will Nobushige Amenomori discover for me some unfamiliar blossom growing beside the Fountain of Immortality? Alas I don't know! He is largely absorbed by things awfully practical, ---guidebooks, hotels, silk-stocks, markets, and politics, I suppose," he teased about some of Amenomori's latest projects.

His friend said that once Lafcadio got his desired feeling back, "he was honest to himself and believed he had made at least an approach to truth. And in order to publish the truth he had thus found, he did all that lay in his power. Fame or profit did not form his main object. His principal aim was to get at truth, and once having secured it, he boldly gave it out; he did not mind what immediate consequences it might bring upon him, firmly believing that the truth he unfolded would win at length." Lafcadio used to say, "Literary work is nearly all sacrifice."

Lafcadio's 1895 year that began in illness, depression, and fear ended in confidence and success. One day while in Yokohama, he visited the small Buddhist temple he remembered from his first days in Japan. Many changes had taken place without and within. He asked about the old priest and found that he'd died the winter before. The old priest's replacement wrote a prayer down on paper for Lafcadio. He'd insightfully asked Buddha not for material wishes, but for the return of his lost illusions.

CHAPTER 26

On December 13, 1895, Lafcadio Hearn received a letter from Dr. M. Toyama, president of the College of Literature at the Tokyo Imperial University. The letter had been preceded by Basil Chamberlain talking to Lafcadio about the possibility of joining the faculty of the most influential schools in Japan.

Dr. Toyama, the supervisor of the study of English, asked Lafcadio to be the Chair of English Language and Literature at the University. Toyama had studied in Michigan, United States. He was impressed by Lafcadio's growing literary reputation and read his articles in the *Atlantic Journal*. The publication of *Glimpses of Unfamiliar Japan*, followed quickly in June 1895 by his second book *Out of the East*, bolstered his reputation not only in the United States and England, but also in Japan.

Toyama believed that the addition of an international author such as Hearn to the faculty would strengthen the English Department. Usually, professors would be appointed for two years, but he would ask the Diet to make the appointment three years. He assured Lafcadio, "In our college you shall not be troubled by such underlings as you seem to have been with in Kumamoto."

Lafcadio's first concern was that his salary would be reduced because of his adoption as a Japanese citizen, because Japanese professors were paid considerably less than foreign teachers. Toyama said he would make inquiries regarding wages. He assured Lafcadio that he'd have minimal teaching hours and wrote, "I have no doubt you will have plenty of time to carry on your literary work, and I hope your work will not suffer in quality by your coming into contact with the university people, as you will have a new field in the investigation of the character of the Japanese people."

Lafcadio was flattered by the offer but remained skeptical. He valued his newly found independence and time to research and read. Toyama sent him a preliminary contract to run from September 10, 1896 to July 31, 1899. He inquired about his citizenship. When Lafcadio answered that he was now Koizumi Yakumo, Toyama addressed all future correspondence to him as Yakumo Koizumi, using the English order for the name. He said the citizenship matter raised some concerns and he would let him know when they had been resolved. He doubted that the University would meet his salary demands, but if they did agree he would be tied to a new location and duties for at least three years.

Lafcadio liked Toyama and sent him a copy of his recently published third Japanese book *Kokoro: Hints and Echoes of Japanese Inner Life* (1896).

Using the excuse of recuperation from his recent illness, he began to travel around Japan. Lafcadio took Setsu and Kazuo home to visit Matsue in Izumo. An article, "Notes of a Trip to Izumo" appeared later in the *Atlantic Monthly* and gave insights into the emotions he felt returning to his first home. He walked the city alone or with his wife and child. After years of absence, experience and knowledge had inevitably changed his perspective. He visited his former house and middle school. The reunion with his old friend Nishida was joyful but also distressful, because his dear companion was visibly in the death grip of tuberculosis.

Lafcadio wrote, "After all, nobody can revisit with absolute impunity a place once loved and deserted…Was not the lost charm something that had evaporated out of my own life…" His article spoke of his anticipation and doubts at making major changes in his life: "For me the New Japan is waiting; the great capital so long dreaded, draws me to her vortex at last. And the question I now keep asking myself is whether in that New Japan I can be fortunate enough at happy moments to meet with something of the Old."

At the end of summer, Lafcadio received an offer he could accept from the College of Literature at Tokyo Imperial University. His teaching position would have moderate hours and considerable honor, at a monthly pay rate paid to foreign professors - four hundred dollars a month. He accepted and the family prepared to move to Tokyo.

To anyone else, becoming a professor at Japan's most prestigious university would be a lifetime accomplishment. But Lafcadio dreaded the prospect. He'd often shared his opinions that "There was no Japan in Tokyo...it was the most horrible place in Japan---only dirty shoes, absurd fashions, wickedly expensive living, airs, vanities, gossip." He disliked Tokyo as much as he disliked New York, for many the same reasons. "Working there is against the grain. I get no thrill, no frisson, no sensation. I want new experiences, perhaps, and Tokyo is no place for them," he fussed.

On the other hand, Setsu, his "simple sweet-hearted country girl", was overjoyed to be moving to the capital. Lafcadio remarked, "In spite of all I say, Setsu thinks of Tokyo just as a French lady thinks of Paris." On August 27, 1896 they moved from Kobe to Tokyo.

Imperial University provided living quarters near the campus for faculty members; but Lafcadio wanted to live as far away as practical. They settled in Ushigome, a suburb of Tokyo, two and a half miles from the University. Their new address was Number 21 Tomihisa-cho, Ushigome. It was a ten-room native house that the builders had just completed. Lafcadio felt the garden was small enough to be dismissed as no garden at all. In compensation, the building sat on a hill with a pleasant view.

The streets in front of their utilitarian house showed signs of the city's expansion. The roads were torn up and ditches were being dug for a new water pipe system. Lafcadio could overlook this disruption because behind the house there was a field that led up another hill dark with cedars. Birds, rabbits, and foxes made their home among the interlacing oak, pine, and cedar trees. Within walking distance were rice fields and bamboo groves. They were practically in the country and able to observe changing seasons.

Out exploring his new environment, Lafcadio discovered a Buddhist temple of the Tendai Sect hidden in the trees. Kobudera Temple was built in 1643 by a Daimyo prince as a place for family worship. The curious structure was constructed of peeled timbers of burled wood. All the pillars had knots left, the natural wood having been made without carpenter's planes. *Ji-sho-in* was the religious name of the temple. The weather-worn building contained centuries' worth of Buddhist sculpture and scripture.

The ancient temple's elderly abbot, Tatara, invited Lafcadio to visit the gardens, pine grove, cemetery, and ragged compound grounds whenever he wanted. The temple almost became an annex to his study. The household knew where to look for Lafcadio if he could not be found at home. The abbot allowed them to use the grounds to grow vegetables such as carrots, corn, radishes, pumpkins, and cucumbers. The products from the patch were sufficient to feed a family of five.

Lafcadio and Setsu walked to the temple compound almost every morning and evening. The peaceful quiet of Kobudera was solace to his dislike for life in a modern city. He said the Kobudera made his life bearable in the "dead waste and muddle of Tokyo".

Lafcadio asked Setsu, "Mamma-san, is it hard to get into a temple? Isn't there any way by which I could live in the temple?"

"You are not a priest Yakumo, so perhaps you cannot very well do so."

"I should prefer to be a priest, and how pleased I should be if I could be one. You could become a nun at the same time, and Kazuo a novice. How cute he would look! Every day we should read the scriptures and take care of the graves. That would be true happiness!"

"Pray that you may be born a priest in the next world!"

Lafcadio had a deep affinity with Buddhist thought and practice that he'd developed since his days in New Orleans. When his writing inspiration waned, he reflected, "I can imagine no means of consoling myself except by plunging into the study of Buddhism - evolution, dissolution, re-evolution, re-dissolution, forevermore? Really, Buddhism alone gives us any consolatory ideas on the subject; but it is now vulgar to mention Buddhism to the Japanese." In "A Conservative", he stated that "Buddhism strongly fortified by Western science will meet the future needs of the race."

Lafcadio wrote challenging articles about Buddhist doctrines and concepts like Karma, Nirvana, and the idea of preexistence. He was not trapped in dogma. He studied multilayered approaches to Eternal Truth that stands beyond dogma and the intellectual mind. Mainly he wanted to study how Buddhism expressed itself in the daily life of the Japanese - in their rituals, customs, proverbs, riddles, legends, toys, burials, festivals, and other charming oddities.

Through observations and studies, he found that Buddhism, on its ages-long journey from India to Japan, dropped most of its elements of terror. Or at least they were softened by the goodly company of jolly and helpful Shinto gods. The seven gods of fortune---Industry, Wealth, Wisdom, Strength, Beauty, Happiness, and Long Life were seen everywhere as they watch over the land with kindly helpful light. In Shintoism, even death is only a floating cloud through which one passes on their journey of nature's eternal life. There was no judging vengeful patriarch in the sky or brooding sorrow at the feet of the peasant priest of Nazareth hanging on a cross.

Lafcadio claimed, "At its core, the primal Japanese spirit sprang from ancestor worship which flowed directly from the fountainhead of Shinto. In primitive Japan, ancestor worship was the first form of belief. The guardian ghosts demanded of their living descendants that they should be good and brave in their own way." The complex and combined religions of Japan aroused his intellectual interest.

One of Lafcadio's favorite written tales was about a Buddhist monk named Kawashin Koji who owned a painting so detailed that it flowed with life. A samurai chieftain offered to buy it, but the monk wouldn't sell. The samurai had him killed. But when the painting was brought to the chieftain and unrolled, it was blank - nothing remained on the paper. Lafcadio suggested in many of his writings that "there are many stories to prove that really great pictures have souls."

Lafcadio's earlier extensive studies of Western psychologists, biologists, and philosophers like Spencer, Huxley, Wallace, and Schneider contributed to his deeper understanding of Buddhist philosophy. He admitted that he had three reasons for studying and writing about the basic principles of Buddhism: to eliminate the West's misunderstanding and condemnation of Buddhism as atheism; to differentiate philosophical beliefs from popular ones among the common people; and to promote its study among students of modern philosophy. He considered Buddhist texts and concepts in his collections of essays and stories produced in Japan.

His imagination was fired up over the differences between East-West concepts of the soul. For Buddhists the conventional soul does not exist. Nirvana is the state where the individual being is dissolved – "that state of mind in which the consciousness both of sensations and of ideas had wholly passed away into the light of formless omnipotence". Lafcadio warned that Western minds couldn't understand the concept of nirvana or absolute nothingness, nor accept that extinction does not mean soul death.

Buddhism sees all things as being in a constant state of transformation and transition. Lafcadio called Japan "the land of impermanence".

"Generally speaking, we construct for endurance, the Japanese for impermanency. Few things for common use are made in Japan with a view to durability. The straw sandals worn out and replaced at each stage of a journey; the robe consisting of a few simple widths loosely stitched together for wearing, and unstitched again for washing; the fresh chopsticks served to each new guest at a hotel; the light shoji frames serving at once for windows and walls, and repapered twice a year; the mattings renewed every autumn, - all these are but random examples of countless small things in daily life that illustrate the national contentment with impermanency.

"Even during the comparatively brief period of her written history, Japan has had more than sixty capitals, of which the greater number have completely disappeared. Fires, earthquakes, and many other causes particularly account for this. Every Japanese city is rebuilt within the time of a generation. Some temples and a few colossal fortresses offer exceptions…Every Shinto temple is necessarily rebuilt at more or less lengthy intervals; and the holiest, the shrine of Ise, in obedience to immemorial custom, must be demolished every twenty years, and its timbers cut into thousands of tiny charms, which are distributed to pilgrims.

"Houses are not built to last. The common people have no ancestral homes. The dearest spot to all is not the place of birth, but the place of burial. There is little that is permanent save the resting place of the dead and sites of the ancient shrines. The influence of Buddhism could in no lands impel minds to the love of material stability. The teaching is that all attachment to persons, place or to things must be fraught with sorrow. Doctrines of impermanency must, in course of time, have profoundly influenced national character…Nothing is more characteristic of that life than its extreme fluidity.

"To imagine that the emotional character of an Oriental race could be transformed by contact with Occidental ideas is absurd. Emotional life, which is older than intellectual life, and deeper, can no more be altered suddenly by a change of milieu than the surface of the mirror can be changed by passing reflections."

Lafcadio used his religious and philosophical writings to show how cultures overlapped and merged. Kipling wrote, "East is East and West is West, and never the twain shall meet." But Lafcadio tried to promote their interrelatedness and mutual understanding between the two worlds. He honestly attempted to correct the West's mistaken views of the Land of Sunrise, the result of superficial descriptions by travelers and missionaries.

He was a successful interpreter and expounder of Japanese inner life due to his keen insight, deep sympathy, and insatiable desire to learn. He described Japanese life and thought as no foreigner had ever done before. He did not sacrifice his own beliefs, it was just that so many of the country's ideas coincided with his and he took a spiritual interest in them, especially evolutionist ideas in the principles of psychology, biology, and ethics. He said, "Real science is very much in accord with Buddhism; and Huxley said that only a very shallow thinker could reject Buddhism as irrational."

He was never a fanatical believer of any religion. His study and writings on Buddhism were philosophical and practical. While he was positive toward Buddhist philosophy, he never formally adopted the religion. He did not accept all its beliefs, and always remained an observer. His beliefs were a multileveled approach to the Eternal Truth that stood beyond the shackles of a limited mind and dogma.

He wanted to understand and communicate the influence of religion on art, habits, and rituals of the Japanese people. The Buddhist teachings of the duty of kindness to all living creatures and awareness of suffering, had a powerful influence upon national customs and habits. Even the Shinto doctrine of conscience, the sense of right and wrong, was not denied, but Buddhist believed that the essential nature of Buddha existed in every human creature. Lafcadio's objective in the study of Japanese religions and philosophies was to broaden his own consciousness and the intellectual horizons of his readers.

He acted as an interpreter of the spirit of Japan. He discovered that the Buddhist teaching of kindness and pity for all sufferings transcended the intellectual boundaries of the scientific West and Eastern religions provided him with an inexhaustible source of interest. He favored Buddhism because he found it "a universal scientific creed nobler than any which has ever existed."

CHAPTER 27

Lafcadio Hearn began teaching English Literature classes at Tokyo Imperial University. Its students were known for being recalcitrant, unruly, and judgmental about teachers. They would disrupt or walk out of a class if they felt bored. University students were generally in their mid-twenties, many were former military, so couldn't be treated like children. The local system allowed first, second, and third-year men to attend the same classes. This arrangement prevented Lafcadio from first teaching simpler things and then moving on to more complex matters in successive years. It was his job to introduce classes to English literature and convince them of the potential power that intellect and emotion had in written works. He believed that great literature was the highest achievement of a life or an era.

Lafcadio complained about the absence of books and lack of preparation by the students. He used books from his own library and had Ellwood Hendrick ship others to him through an American dealer, paying for the supplies himself. A shift in his original assignment meant that he was to dedicate all his time to English literature. He was given the freedom to select the study materials and rearrange his classes.

Years after he settled in Japan, Lafcadio got a letter from the Philadelphia doctor George Gould asking if he wanted his books back. He did not answer the letter because he couldn't guess the purpose of it. He feared it might be a ruse and that an answer would give Gould evidence to support possession of his library of rare books. As a Professor of English literature, a complete collection of masterpieces, such he could not then afford to replace would have been of immense value to him. He wanted to clear up the matter, but when he didn't answer right away, Gould's wrath was stirred up to the point where he threatened to publish all sorts of scandals about Lafcadio.

In Gould's later book *Concerning Lafcadio Hearn*, he claimed that as a 'close friend', he knew Hearn was "deprived by nature, by the necessities of his life or by conscious intention, of religion, morality, scholarship, magnanimity, loyalty, character benevolence, and other constituents of personal greatness...except in pursuit of literary excellence, Hearn had no character whatever." Great controversy arose around the Gould book and numerous friends, including Mitchell McDonald, defended Lafcadio's honor and name in printed rebuttals. Gould then excused his refusal to return Lafcadio's library by saying that since there were no books on Japan in the library, Hearn probably did not want them anyway.

At first, students came to Lafcadio's lectures out of curiosity. They were skeptical of this odd-looking, unconventional new professor. Lafcadio was relieved when, out of Japanese courtesy, no one mentioned, or seemed to notice or be repelled by his blind eye. They'd found other foreign teachers indifferent and proud, and it was a contrast to see Lafcadio teaching. Soon they were not only attentive, but were inspired.

Eventually, whenever Lafcadio lectured, crowds up to one hundred and fifty would gather in filled classrooms. Students felt it was an honor and a privilege to attend. As he spoke quietly, his voice low and dreamful, the students sat in silent admiration. Some even described his effect on listeners as hypnotic.

Lafcadio's phenomenal memory allowed him to lecture without outlines, notes, or fully prepared remarks. A former student, Ryuji Tanabe, said, "He brought with him a tiny memorandum containing only names and dates. He used to make sketches on the board, should a description of anything exotic or unfamiliar to us occur in quotations." He taught this tedious way twelve hours a week. He began the school day by unwrapping the books he would need for the class from a blue or purple *furoshihiki* scarf in which Japanese carried things. Lafcadio described his lectures as "dictated out of my head."

Respecting that English was a second language for his students, he always spoke very slowly and distinctly, in the simplest and clearest possible English. He understood their difficulty, so took pains to speak clearly because many of his students had learned English by eye, not by ear. They could read newspapers or books, but if someone spoke rapidly, they would immediately become confused and understand nothing.

He would go to the chalkboard and write out any difficult word or unfamiliar name. He used Elizabeth Bisland's name as a typical woman's name in English. He would write it on the board and have the uniformed rows of students chant in chorus, E-liz-a-beth Bees-land. He always kept a picture of her in his study. Setsu felt his attachment to it was similar to religious veneration, so did not interfere.

Lafcadio's classes would sometimes vote on what they wanted to study. Different school terms they would study Tennyson, read miscellaneous texts from various Victorian authors, struggle through *Paradise Lost*, history of early English literature, and then modern fiction. Lafcadio would alternate his courses to please himself. He shared with friends that he'd be happier teaching French literature, but he chose works that were not attuned to his preferences or personality.

He told them many of the Greek myths, among which Oedipus and the Sphinx seemed to especially please them because of the hidden moral. Of the modern stories, they greatly liked Nathaniel Hawthorne's short gothic story "Rappacini's Daughter", "Monos and Daimonos" by Edward Bulwer, and "Silence" by Edgar Allan Poe. However, *Frankenstein* tales of horror of physical force like *Hercules* did not impress them. Stories like Sir Thomas Mallory's *Morte d'Arthur*, about knightly principles and idealism elicited unexpected comments. They said they found the supposed heroic actions contrary even to the principles of Christian religion, society, loyalty, love, and morals of all countries.

Lafcadio learned that the Western ideals of heroism, strength of purpose, and contempt of death did not appeal to Japanese youth. Japanese males regarded such qualities a matter of course, belonging to manhood and inseparable from it, rather than exceptional. Within their culture they saw the samurai as a total human being, whereas men like the knights of old, who were completely absorbed in their fighting skills, as having degenerated into a function - one spoke in a war machine wheel.

Many were able to record Lafcadio's lectures verbatim. One of his students, Ochiai, patiently took down his master's lectures in longhand and translated them into a book. Inspired by Lafcadio, he later also became a professor at the University of Tokyo.

Some of Lafcadio's opinions about various writers were recorded by various students: Kipling was simply "the greatest writer of short stories in English: he is all mind and eye...sensitiveness extraordinary."; William Blake was like a great Zen teacher who "suggested questions without giving answers; you; you must think of the answers for yourself"; Wordsworth was a poet who produced "an astonishing amount of nonsense" and had no sense of humor...but his love of children, family, country, and friends "found in his verse the most beautiful expression which English poetry can offer"; Coleridge "was able to influence the intellectual life of England in matters of religious feeling" and also "infused something ghostly and supernatural into poetry." Byron "infused the whole of European literature with the Satanic spirit which signified a vague recognition of another law than that of pure morality---the law of struggle, the law of battle, and the splendor of strength even in a bad or cruel cause."; Charlotte Bronte expressed "her own experiences of love, despair, and struggle, but this with the very highest art of the novel writer, with a skill of grouping incident and of communicating vividness to the least detail."; Sir Thomas Browne was "the first great English writer to create an original classic style"; and Wilkie Collins was "the greatest inventor of plots we ever had."

Lafcadio did not just teach English literature, he taught the love of that literature. He showed them the love of certain books, authors, pages, and perhaps certain verses. They learned how writers who died centuries ago could become friends, how books break the shackles of time. The important thing was to reveal the beauty of the written word, a beauty that could only be felt.

He encouraged his students to apply their new knowledge of English literature to the creation of a modern Japanese literature. He taught that the individual and the era shaped the production of literary works. One of his students wrote, "His lectures on English literature were revelations to us, at once poignant and lucid." A colleague came into the class one day and students were in tears over his reading a simple poem. It was a rare and even shameful thing for a Japanese man to be seen crying. Even a coolie would be ashamed of showing such emotion.

Lafcadio tried to adapt his lessons to the Japanese way of feeling and thinking. He wanted to inspire their intellectual, emotional, and moral consciousness by reading and writing about their own rich history, and culture, and thereby become aware of the changes taking place. He pleaded with them to preserve their ancient, time-honored customs. He loved the poetry and music of old Japan and was not at all pleased with the vision of New Japan. He planted seeds of enthusiasm and ambition in his pupils.

He told them, "Draw on your inspiration the primary source of almost everything that is beautiful in the literature which treats of what lies beyond mere daily experience." In his lectures he told his students that they should also understand the literary value of folklore. "To an unimaginative and dryly practical man such things are simply superstition, absurd rubbish. But to the true poet or dramatist or storyteller they are all, or nearly all, of priceless value. There is something ghostly in all art."

Lafcadio earned the admiration of his students by respecting and honoring their culture. He encouraged them to preserve the traditions and literature of their own country. Many foreign instructors considered Japan inferior to the West and displayed arrogance and superiority. On the other hand, Hearn-san, because of his open mind, demonstrated admiration for different races, religions, and traditions. He helped his students think about other people as fellow human beings and the importance of helping those in need where they could.

"Empathy for another is essential in life. You have to feel for one another if you are going to survive with dignity," he told them.

Lafcadio taught English Literature, but also good manners and what was considered proper and polite in Western society - how to treat people; speak openly; ask not command; and other such subtle differences. Although he taught literature and took issue with modernization, cultural loss and moral decline, he was realistic about the importance of science to the point of encouraging his students to study pragmatic subjects like engineering. He also promoted travel because he knew that the interactions his student would have as they went new places and met people would expand and sharpen their minds. He believed that there were inward and outward dispositions, and a person who lacked either one was incomplete. Every student was treated as if they had vast potential and were sacred, until the sacred in them remembered.

Lafcadio's students learned not only English language vocabulary and literature, but the culture behind the words. He never tried to convert or make foreigners out of his Japanese pupils. One of his greatest talents was his ability to encourage students to discover their own heritage and express their thoughts and feelings in the context of their writing. He taught ways for them to explain their culture, country, and themselves as Japanese to the

English-speaking world. This was the experience of Takahiko Tomoeda, a student of Hearn's from 1893-1894. Tomoeda diligently kept a notebook of Hearn's English class lectures in Kumamoto. The discovery of the notebook in the Tomoeda archives shed light on how he taught in his early educational career.

Boys from Matsue and Kumamoto were among the University students Lafcadio taught in Tokyo. They renewed old friendships and once again came to him asking for advice and comfort. Masanobu Otani, who delivered the Matsue middle-school pupils' farewell address, entered Tokyo Imperial University when Hearn-san began teaching there. Lafcadio covered Otani's expenses for his three-year university courses, making it possible for him to attend. He entered into an informal, but steady paid arrangement for Otani to gather information of assigned subjects and translate documents in his spare time for Lafcadio's research. He received twelve yen each month for his work. He dismissed him from working during exams and advised his young assistant, including lectures on taking care of his health. Adzukizawa and a few others assisted in the same way as Otani. Masanobu Otani became a teacher in Hiroshima and wrote, "Words really fail to express my gratitude to him. I shall never forget his extreme kindness…He is my ever-remembered benefactor."

Lafcadio personally helped numerous other students like Ochiai who studied medicine. Another favored student from Matsue, Ryuji Tanabe, enrolled in his classes and wrote down every lecture he attended, later to be printed.

There was a Japanese custom that allowed students to live in a person's house rent free while at university, asking only help with chores and care of children. There were customarily small rooms in most homes called student rooms. Setsu and Lafcadio thoroughly approved of this practice and since Kumamoto had students living with them. In Tokyo they always had one or two boys as part of their household. The young men tutored the children, went on vacation with them, and accompanied Lafcadio on his walks. They were not treated like servants, but members of an extended family.

Lafcadio had a way of reaching young students both intellectually and emotionally. In the classroom his musical voice was mesmerizing. One student said, "It often seemed to us as if we were actually leaning out from the bar of Heaven beside the Blessed Damozel or walking along the corridors of the Palace of Art, till the bell for the recess broke the spell." Lafcadio Hearn became more than admired; he was adored by his students. He was their role model, their hero.

The Japanese education system placed an emphasis on memorizing, yet Lafcadio stressed that imagination was just as important. At a lecture he delivered at a parents' meeting in Shinjuku Tokyo, he told the group that Japanese parents were too dependent on teachers in their children's education. He suggested that while basic education and discipline should take place in the home, he noted that some schools, systems of entrance examinations, and families pushed the students too hard. His observation from over a hundred years ago is still a major issue in Japan's educational system today.

Shortly after he took on the chair of English Literature at the Tokyo Imperial University, Nobushige Amenomori wrote him a letter addressed on the envelope to Professor Lafcadio Hearn.

He wrote back, "Perhaps it will seem strange to you, but I do feel a little uncomfortable at being addressed as Professor. I don't feel wise enough yet for that title, though I may have, according to the suggestions of the University folks, to let it appear on my next title page. But I am not even a graduate of any school, much less of a university. Please do not write 'Professor' on the envelope, to you I do not wish to be anything more than plain 'H' or 'K'."

Amenomori replied, "It is quite needless for you to feel uneasy about being called a professor, because you are a professor in a university" With regard to Lafcadio being a non-graduate, his friend cited the examples of J.S. Mills, H. Spencer, and others and said, "It is not from the machine-dug wells of universities alone that we get water of knowledge, but that there have been springs and fountains of truth, whence have gushed out living streams, giving new life to human thought; not to speak of such men as Socrates, Confucius, Jesus, and Sakya-muni, none of whom was the product of a university workshop."

CHAPTER 28

Lafcadio was not fond of or connected to his fellow university professors. He studied them as an interesting species that amused him.

The foreigner teachers on staff at the Tokyo Imperial University were never secure in their positions. Government and anti-foreign public sentiment could turn against them at any moment. He described it as "reposing upon the safety valve of a steam-boiler---much cracked, with many rivets loose, and the engineers studying how to be out of the way when the great whang-bang comes around."

This tension hung over the entire foreign element in the capital. He wrote to Ellwood Hendrick, "This is panic, pure and simple. But there is reason for it - considering the class of minds. We are all in Japan living over earthquakes. Nothing is stable. All Japanese officialdom is perpetually in flux, nothing but the throne is even temporarily fixed; and the direction of the current depends much on intrigue. They shift like currents in the sea, off a coast of tides. But the side currents penetrate everywhere, and *clapotent* rattle all comers, and swirl round the writing stool of the smallest clerk, whose pen trembles with continual fear for his wife's and babies' rice."

University professors drew and saved their wages in preparation for possible disaster. The threat of being fired or deported generated betrayal and scheming among them. Lafcadio learned to be wary of his colleagues. In the teachers' lounge he'd sit with a newspaper or book in hand, the international signal of wanting to be left alone. However, there developed an odd affinity among a small group of foreign teachers separate from the majority of native teachers. They would spend their free time on campus somewhat together.

They included a Russian professor of Philosophy from Heidelberg; German professor of Sanskrit and Philology from Leipzig; Professor of French Literature, a Jesuit from Lyons; American professor of Law; and Lafcadio, the professor of English Literature 'from the devil knows where'. He confessed to Hendrick, "Horror of horrors. I do believe I like the Jesuit best of all---yet I'm sure he would burn me!"

Lafcadio was a genius and inspired writer, but he was also capable of being self-centered, rude, difficult, condescending, dishonest, paranoid, stubbornly certain of his positions, and devious. He was not what one would call friend material in most situations or relationships. He made several enemies over the years.

"I wish there was some kindred soul here to exchange ideas with betimes and that soul yours," he wrote to Amenomori. "The Tokyo affections of culture are disgusting shams; I do not think there is one f----r in the capital capable even of stating correctly the position of the higher agnosticism, not one, even if you put all the books on the subject in his hands."

He pleaded with his friend to stay in touch with him, "However, if we cannot talk, or walk through some luminous street at night, we can surely write betimes. When you are not too busy, I hope you will write to me, and feel assured of a prompt reply."

Lafcadio and others honored one scholar in Tokyo, Ernest Fenollosa. When many treasured paintings, porcelains, sculptures, bronzes, and rolls of calligraphy were being carelessly sold or thrown away, Mr. and Mrs. Fenollosa embarrassed and cajoled the Japanese government into preserving its heritage. The couple shipped art objects to museums like the Museum of Fine Arts in Boston and collectors to save them. Fenollosas tried to get closer to Hearn, but he was embarrassed by their attention.

Lafcadio's physical distance from the university had its advantages. Since he lived two and a half miles from campus, over difficult to impassable roads, the others seldom visited his home or socialized with him outside of work. When he arrived at the university, he immediately went to his lecture room. He was very diligent and regular about his teaching schedule and was never absent unless he was sick. When he was not teaching, he'd walk about the campus garden or sit smoking. No one dared interrupt his meditation.

He had pleasant relations with two English-speaking teachers: Osman Edwards who dedicated his book, *Japanese Plays and Playfellows*, to Hearn; and

Earnest Foxwell, who admired and emulated Hearn's classroom style of teaching.

When Lafcadio first met Foxwell, the man was recovering from smallpox and his face was 'beetroot colored'. Having suffered rejections himself, based on his vision disability, he did not pay the slightest attention to Foxwell's appearance, which was greatly appreciated.

Foxwell encouraged Lafcadio not to write exclusively about the old Japan while ignoring the modern bustle of the New Japan. He told him to paint a portrait of the Japanese as they were currently. Only in his last book, *Japan: An Attempt at Interpretation*, did Lafcadio follow his friend's advice. Foxwell disagreed with him on some issues such as his excluding himself from the foreign colony groups and his extreme condemnation of the missionaries. In spite of their differences, their arguments stayed friendly, and they remained on good terms during their association.

Dr. Toyama was the only person Lafcadio cared for as a personal friend. He reminded him of Sentaro Nishida in his kindness and helpful ways. Toyama always believed in him and showed him special considerations. Occasionally Lafcadio could be lured to the Tokyo Club where he held his audiences spellbound for hours at a time, "talking in beauty as easily as the bird sings".

Lafcadio and Basil Chamberlain both lived in the same city and taught in different departments of the same university, but their once intimate friendship strangely lapsed. Even though he longed for Western companionship, Lafcadio no longer visited or wrote to Chamberlain for advice or intellectual stimulation.

Chamberlain had strongly advocated for Lafcadio's appointment to the university, but somehow Lafcadio had the feeling his friend had not been sympathetic early enough to his plight in Kumamoto. Additionally, even though he dedicated *Glimpses* to Chamberlain, he perceived the professor didn't like the book because he declined to review it.

Another theory about the split was more personal. Lafcadio wrote to Page Baker that his feelings were deeply hurt when Chamberlain said to him, "No, you'll never be a ladies' man". Lafcadio thought he was mocking his appearance. They did not have a fight but following the comment that he saw as an insult he did not write or answer any letters. It was Lafcadio's tragic loss, because after six years of lively correspondence, like his letters to Krehbiel in earlier years, no one ever filled those gaps in his intellectual life.

Lafcadio always spoke well of Chamberlain within the family but did not reach out to see him.

Chamberlain made attempts to reconcile or apologize for whatever upset the irascible Lafcadio, but he was only met with coldness and silence. Understanding his erratic temperament and disposition, Chamberlain accepted the rejection. Although disinherited by Lafcadio, he considered him among his life's truly revered friends till the last.

Chamberlain later wrote of their broken friendship: "Lafcadio's dropping of friends seemed to me to have its roots in that very quality which made the chief charm of his works. I mean his idealism. Friends, when he first made them, were for him more than mortal men, they stood endowed with every perfection. But he was not emotional merely; another side of his mind had the keen insight of a man of science. Thus, he soon came to see that his idols had clay feet, and, being so purely subjective in his judgments, he was indignant with them for having, as he thought, deceiving him. His disillusionment with a series of friends in whom he had once thought to find intellectual sympathy is seen to have been inevitable. Thus it was hardly possible for him to retain old ties of friendship. Lafcadio himself was the greater sufferer from all this than anyone else; for he possessed the affectionate disposition of a child, and suffered poignantly when sympathy was withdrawn, or what amounted to the same - when he himself withdrew it. He was much to be pitied - always wishing to love, and discovering each time that his love had been misplaced."

Chamberlain also recalled that Lafcadio "saw details very distinctly while incapable of understanding them as a whole. Not only was this the case mentally but also physically. Blind of one eye, he was extremely short-sighted of the other. On entering a room his habit was to grope all around, closely examining wallpaper, the backs of books, pictures, curios, and other ornaments. Of these he could have drawn up an exact catalogue: but he had never properly seen either the horizon or the stars." Later he wrote of Lafcadio more generously, "Never perhaps was scientific accuracy of detail married to such tender and exquisite brilliancy of style." Hearn constructed his own reality narratives of splits and lost friends.

Likewise, there was a break between Lafcadio and W. B. Mason. After his arrive in Tokyo, there were no more letters to Mason or mentions of visits with him in nearby Yokohama. Mason thought maybe Lafcadio couldn't get over one time when he'd entered his home without taking off his shoes. Lafcadio saw the oversight as an insult to his domain and to his wife. In his insecurity, he believed that greater offenses and rejections grew out of small ones - that criticism ripened into hatred. If a person overstepped on one occasion, that in time all bounds would be abused. Yet again, sometimes Lafcadio was just done with friends. Not mad or upset, just done. He would turn and simply walk away.

During a period of despondency Lafcadio wrote to his sister, Minnie Atkinson and asked her to be 'the friend at court' to drum up more attention for his literary works from leading English periodicals. Even though she tried never to say anything her erratic brother could find fault with or anger him, something in her answer offended him. When she received her next letter from Japan, the envelope contained only her own last letter. He shut her out along with so many others. At times it was Lafcadio's quick temper, irascibility, and lifelong propensity to utilize a sudden, scorched-earth policy that terminated friendships. But not in all cases.

Correspondence with his oldest and dearest friend, Cincinnati printer Henry Watkin ceased, not because of a falling out, but because Watkin had been ailing, bankrupt, and had entered the Old Men's Home. He had moved from the cozy shop where they spent precious time twenty-six years before, and took his packet of cherished letters, cards, and notes from Raven.

Dr. Matas, his doctor and dear friend in New Orleans, suggested that there was no apparent reason for Lafcadio's wholesale cessation of correspondence with many American friends, except that time, distance, and his complete absorption of all his thoughts and interests in his newly adopted country had the effect of diluting and vaporizing old friendships. He said, "When we consider Hearn's extraordinarily emotional and mercurial personality, and the tremendous fervor that he put into the production of his marvelous Japanese literature, and the depth of attachment to his Japanese wife and children - it is not necessary to interpret his seeming indifference to selfish or callous ingratitude, or suppositious grievances." Dr. Matas never ceased to believe that although he did not stay in touch, that Lafcadio frequently and kindly remembered him and other friends.

There always seemed to be a need to reinvent himself. First Patrick Lafcadio Hearn, the orphan became Paddy, a muckraking journalist from Ireland whose sensationalism rocked Cincinnati. Then he became a well-paid literary figure, the Greek romantic Lafcadio Hearn in New Orleans and New York. In the West Indies he was the intellectual observer reporting on the fascinating native Creole culture. In Japan he reversed himself and identified with the traditional common people and touted their superiority to the modern Western world. He was to become Koizumi Yakumo, an internationally acclaimed writer and national poet of Japan. Patrick Lafcadio Hearn's frenetic life was filled with seeming contradictions.

One friendship that he maintained was with U. S. Naval officer Mitchell McDonald, someone who never made demands upon him. The easy-going U.S. Navy paymaster and Yokohama Hotel owner would allow him freedom from responsibility and entertained him with good foods, talking, and lazy swims at Kamakura Beach. His letters and weekend visits broke up Lafcadio's seclusion.

McDonald came to visit Lafcadio and his family in Tokyo on Sundays. There was a rocking chair in the study saved just for him. Lafcadio had disciplined himself to act with reserve in Japanese society and at home, but when McDonald visited, the family could hear them laughing out loud. The casual manner of their friendship was a relief to Lafcadio, who was homesick for joking and talking about unimportant, ordinary Western facts, references, and fancies. McDonald wanted to pull Lafcadio out of his shell of morbid depression and lack of confidence. The writer admitted the visits energized him and sparked his ambition.

Lafcadio could talk to him about his work but warned McDonald not to overrate him. "Unless I can manage in the next three years to write something very extraordinary indeed, I fear you will be horribly disappointed some day." But then added, "Don't for a moment imagine me modest in literary matters." Whenever the businessman-naval officer praised his work, Lafcadio would tell him, "I can see bad execution where you would not see it unless I pointed it out to you." Lafcadio had once written to Amenomori, "What you call my modesty, is rather the fear of immodesty,---of appearing willing to figure, among my friends, as something bigger than I know myself to be."

He would lecture McDonald on bookish matters, but McDonald brusquely took the lead when he advised Lafcadio on money or personal concerns.

He trusted McDonald to look after his financial affairs and his family. He'd invested some of his savings into one of McDonald's business deals and made a tidy profit, though he had avoided putting his hard-earned money into ventures since the Hard Times Restaurant fiasco back in New Orleans.

Even after his venture into capitalism, he admitted, "The mere idea of business is a horror, a nightmare, a torture unspeakable. I would rather burn a five-hundred-dollar bill than invest it. The greatest favor you can ever do me is to take off my hands even the business I have---contracts and the like, so that I need never again to remember them." Lafcadio drew up a will naming his trusted friend McDonald as his executor.

One blustery winter day Lafcadio visited Yokohama. In his haste he'd left his overcoat behind in Tokyo. When McDonald met him at the rail station, he immediately took off his own coat and wrapped it around his shivering friend. Upon his return, Lafcadio wrote a letter of gratitude, "But what can one do with a man who deliberately takes off his own coat to cover his friend during a nine minutes' drive? I shall remember the feeling of that coat---warmth of friendship must also have been electrical in it---until I die."

CHAPTER 29

Lafcadio had a dear friend and confidant in Mitchell McDonald. However, his relationships with the university professors and students were restricted to campus. After his teaching and advisory obligations were finished, he hurried home to write.

His wife Setsu made sure the Ushigome household members and staff honored his need for quiet and privacy. They arranged their cleaning and other duties around his schedule. All visitors and vendors to the house were managed or sent away so Lafcadio could concentrate on his work behind closed doors. Excursions outside his home became rare, not just due to his temperament but to enable his writing.

To prepare the depth, substance, and heart of English literature to young men with Oriental mindsets, he needed to be free from petty intrusions and interruptions. Before his break with Chamberlain, he wrote an example of his interchange on how Easterners and Westerners thought differently about romance:

"Teacher," cry my students, "why are English novels all about love and marriage? That seems to us very strange."

"They say 'strange'. They think 'indecent'. Then I try to explain, "My dear lads, the world of the West is not as the world of the East. In the West, Society is not, as you know, constituted upon the same plan. A man must make his own family; the family does not make him. What you do not know, is that for the average educated man without money, life is a bitter and terrible fight, a battle in which no quarter is given. And what is the simplest and most natural thing of all in Japan, to get married, is in the West extremely difficult and dangerous. Yet all a man's life turns upon that effort. Without a wife he has no home. He seeks success, in order to be rich enough to get married. Success in life means success in marriage. And the obstacles are many and wonderful"...(I explain) "Therefore English novels treat love and marriage above all things; because these mean everything in life for the English middle classes at least; and the middle class like these books, and make men rich who write them well, because they sympathize with the imaginary sufferings of the lovers. Which you don't, because you can't. And I guess you are right on that score....

"Now the Japanese thinks it indecent even to talk about his wife, and at least impolite to talk about his children. This doesn't mean that he is without affection at all. The affection is all right but mere mention of it, he thinks, suggests other matters---unfortunate necessities of existence. He introduces his wife to a European, simply because he's heard it is the strange and barbarous Western custom to do such things; but otherwise his women live in shadows by themselves. They are used to it---would be unhappy or awkward if pulled out of it. He does not mention his marriage except to a few intimates invited to the wedding; and still more rarely after the birth of his child, for obvious reasons.

"An English novel would seem to him a morbid piece of nonsense ...There is a vast reserve of tenderness in even our roughest Western natures, that comes out only in the shocks of life, as fire from flint. By tenderness I don't mean simple woman-loving, sexual inclination, but something higher developed out of the primitive loving, etc.- sensibility, comprehension, readiness to do for the weak on impulse. I can't see this in the Orient except among the women. The Japanese woman preserved the purity and grace - the whole capacity of the race for goodness - all locked up within her."

Lafcadio's writings feature women often and prominently. He writes of them sympathetically, such as: his Cincinnati article about "Dolly: An Idyll of the Levee"; "The Death of Marie Laveau, the Voodoo Queen in New Orleans"; "Les Porteuses carriers of Martinique"; and "Of A Dancing Girl" story of a Japanese geisha. The main characters of his novels *Chita* and *Youma* were women, incorporating memories of his mother Rosa. Even his great-aunt Sarah Brenane in Ireland provided Lafcadio a role model for a woman of courage who defied strict social taboos and her Protestant family to marry outside her religion. His Irish nursemaid Kate Ronane not only fueled his love for fairy tales and ghost stories, but probably she and his landlady Mrs. Courtney in New Orleans also provided prototypes for later stories about ordinary working women.

Lafcadio's longing for the Eternal Feminine likely began after being separated from his beloved mother Rosa. Many of his stories centered around a theme of a hero in love with a dead woman or her ghost…just as he was in love with the memory of his mother who disappear from his life when he was young. In many cases, his writing wishfully turns separation into reunion.

In late 1896, Setsu gave birth to a second son, Iwao. He had a dark complexion and almond eyes. Lafcadio was overly concerned about her recovery from a difficult childbirth. Setsu's health had always been excellent, and though the doctors could find nothing particularly wrong, her strength was ebbing away. Afterward her health was a priority, something to be protected for the sake of the children. As he held her, faint with relief and gratitude, he told Setsu, "No matter what happens, you must always take care of your health, Mama-san. You don't belong to yourself anymore. You belong to the children. They'll need you for many, many years!"

The celebration of the birth of a healthy son was overshadowed by news that Lafcadio's most loved Japanese friend, Sentaro Nishida of Matsue, died on the fifteenth of March, in the thirtieth year of Meiji at thirty-four years old. The household fell into deep mourning. At first, he couldn't believe Nishida was dead. He saw someone walking on the street and stopped him mistakenly believing it was Nishida. He felt very kindly toward the stranger because of the resemblance.

He was told that just before he died Nishida woke up in the middle of the night, and called out, "Mother, have you heard from my friend? Is his son well?" and fell back into his final sleep. Lafcadio wept and berated the universe for being so cruel.

"How bad God is! I am angry. Nature seems strangely cruel in making such a life and destroying it before the time of ripeness. The good hearts and the fine brains pass to dust, while the coarse and the cunning survive all dangers," he raged.

One of Setsu's lifelong friends also died. Lafcadio described her as "all embroidery and soul". For weeks, grief filled the Hearn house. It took up space and seemed to suck out the air. The first forty-nine days when "the soul hovers near the eaves" were sad, but the curling incense of the shrine and constantly burning candles made the family feel the souls were near. Everyone in the household lovingly did things in the name of the dear ones to free them from the shackles of the world so they could go happily to the Land of Rest.

Setsu consoled him by explaining some of her beliefs, "No one you love is really lost. Although you can't hold them any more than you can hold moonlight, they are forever inside you and still yours. We will keep them in our hearts and honor them by living a good full life."

He wrote to Ellwood Hendrick about their bereavements: "Imagine beings who never in their lives, did anything which was not---I will not say 'right', that is commonplace---any single things which was not beautiful! Should I write this the world would, of course, call me a liar, as it has become accustomed to do. But I could not now even write of them except to you; the wounds are raw. I am thinking about the Velvet Souls in general, and all ever known by me in particular. Almost in every place where I lived long, it was given to me to meet a velvet soul or two, presences which with a word or look wrapped all your being around in a softness and warmth of emotional caress inexpressible. I have found such souls in Japan---but only Japanese souls. But they are melting into the night."

Ladcadio tried to ease his pain by visualizing Nashida walking along a pleasant forest path with many other pilgrims. They were all wearing the white robes, pilgrim hats, and straw sandals in which they were buried. Each day his friend was getting farther and farther away. As time passed, he settled back onto his old routines, but it seemed everyone and everything had somehow changed. The spirit of merriment was gone.

"What a world it is! We think of our absent friends and acquaintances always as we last saw them, and rarely think of the possibilities of change of conditions till we hear of them that such changes have occurred. The older I grow the more fragile and fugitive everything seems."

For Lafcadio's summer vacation, he couldn't face visiting Matsue with Nashida gone, so the family decided to go to Yaizu, a primitive fishing village. His friend Tamura found them four upper rooms behind a fish shop. Lafcadio was able to discard his professor uniform and set the pen aside for a few weeks of relaxation. He took long walks and swam daily in the quiet waters of the bay. Locals were amazed at his swimming style, floating on his back. They claimed Sensei-San was surely born from the sea. He was happy in the country, out of the city, and suggested they move. But Setsu, in her wisdom, reminded him that in a few more years they would be financially secure and could live anywhere they wanted. Being patient and working hard would give them freedom.

One of Lafcadio's most promising students, a young cadet named Fujisaki, was from Yaizu. He would call on the family in the evenings for games, and songs and stories. By the time they were ready to return to Tokyo, Lafcadio and his student had planned a small holiday of their own. They were going to climb Mount Fuji before the opening of the school year.

Lafcadio described Fuji as "the most beautiful sight in Japan...especially days of spring and autumn, when the greater part of the peak is covered with late or early snows. You can seldom distinguish the snowless base, which remains the same color as the sky; you perceive only the white cone seeming to hang in heaven...the material reality a hundred miles away is grandiose among mountains of the globe. Rising to a height of nearly 12,500 feet, Fuji is visible from thirteen provinces of the Empire. For a thousand years it has been scaled every summer by a multitude of pilgrims. To ascend it at least once in a lifetime is the duty of all who reverence the gods."

"Buddhism loves the grand peak because its form is like the white bud of the Sacred Flower, and because the eight cusps of its top, like the eight petals of the Lotus, symbolize the eight intelligences of Perception, Purpose, Speech, Conduct, Living, Effort, Mindfulness, and Contemplation."

On the day that he started, Mt. Fuji seemed to fill the northern sky. While Lafcadio and Fujisaki made their trek, Setsu and the boys waited at an inn in the town of Gotemba on the north slope of the mountain. To climb Mt. Fujiyama up and back would take at least two days.

Lafcadio dressed in the traditional pilgrim garb---straw cape and sandals, tall walking stick, and mushroom shaped hat. He hired a guide and horses. The hikers made the first part of the pilgrimage across the plains at the foot of the mountain on horseback, but when the slopes became as steep as a stairway, the riding became dangerous and the animals had to be left at a wayside station along the route.

On foot the path he observed, "Fuji has ceased to be blue of any shade. It is black---charcoal black a frightful extinct heap of visible ashes and cinders and slaggy lava. Most of the green has disappeared. Likewise all of the illusion. The tremendous naked black reality, always becoming more sharply, more grimly, more atrociously defined, a nightmare…Above, miles above, the snow patches glare and gleam against the blackness."

The weariness of walking through cinders and sand, like walking over dunes, forced him to watch his step and use the staff constantly. Once they passed through the clouds, the white fog, the wind cut off and he experienced a silence. It was the peace of high places, broken only by the crunch of ashes beneath his feet and the pounding of his heartbeat. Even though it was progressively colder and the air was rarer as they climbed passed 9000 feet, Lafcadio was drenched with perspiration. It was fortunate that he'd built up his stamina swimming because scaling the mountain required strength and persistence. At times his leg muscles and lungs burned. Guides assisted him up the slopes. They stopped periodically to rest at station huts half-buried in the black drifts. The path was littered with discarded straw sandals.

The weary climbers spent the night in a hut near the top. Tired as he was, he limped to the doorway to look out over the clouds miles below, that the Japanese guide call the Sea of Cotton. It turned into a fleece of gold as sun set. Outside was bitter cold, but he couldn't pull himself from the astounding vista. The sky turned blue-black and filled with countless stars. He finally closed and barred the door against the bitter cold. The station-keeper prepared the exhausted trekkers' beds, lit the lamps, and started a small fire. He and Fujisaki pulled three quilts over themselves and slept between their snoring guides.

Lafcadio enjoyed the company of simple, sincere, open-hearted men like his guides. He liked to mingle with laborers, farmers, fishermen, workmen who called a spade a spade. "What splendid, good hearty fellows our guides were, ---and forgive me for saying it, I wish the officials of New Japan could be like them."

The dawn journey to the top of Fuji was the most grueling. Lafcadio crawled on all fours at times and surmounted lava blocks with the help of ladders. He and his student were rewarded for their pain with a sunrise at the huge crater's cusp. Other pilgrims clapped their hands in Shinto prayer to salute the mighty day. A yellow glow ran along the east "like the glare of a wind-blown fire" from the summit supreme of Fuji to the Rising of the Sun. The colossal view and the immense poetry of the moment was seared in his memory.

The descent from the twelve-thousand-foot summit was easier, walking and sliding down snow and ashes into Gotemba. Lafcadio was content with the knowledge that they'd scaled the famous Mount Fuji. He returned with a sense of accomplishment and a pocket full of notes and sacred papers.

When the university reopened, Lafcadio was well organized with his books and subjects outlined. Five hours a week were dedicated to poetry and textual readings, three hours on the history of English literature, and the remaining four hours on individual writers and themes. He still lectured from his own knowledge and made drawings of the chalkboard to clarify difficult concepts. New and old students alike were attentive and eager to attend his classes. Teaching at the university freed him from financial worries so he could pursue his other Japanese writings.

Houghton, Mifflin and Company published his *Gleanings in Buddha-Fields-Studies of Hand and Soul in the Far East* (1897), a collection of stories. Through a series of philosophical essays and sketches he explains the spirit of Buddhism and Japanese life as if he were born into it. The highly individualized charm of the book impressed the reviewers. They noted how sensitive he was to Eastern thought processes and characteristics, his mental metamorphosis. Readers were asking for "more of those touchingly beautiful Japanese tales." But Lafcadio was too busy with his next project *Exotics and Retrospectives*, and other story ideas to pay attention to reviews of work he'd finished. *Exotics'* first half contained his descriptions about the everyday life of the Japanese people and general impressions. The *Reflections'* second half was his personal musings about the almost unknown country.

Shortly after the publication of *Gleanings in Buddha Fields*, Lafcadio wrote to his friend Nobushige Amenomori, "...the Buddhist papers seem to have made an impression. You will be amused at some of the religious notices, regretting my power to debauch the 'minds of my pupils'."

Lafcadio laughed at the criticisms his writing evoked, confident in the final triumph of his ideas. He said, "So far as the success of a man's ideas go, one need never be anxious. Give them to the world, and the world will learn to value them at last, ---even after the writer has ceased to appear on the streets. Time weeds out the errors and stupidities of cheap success and preserves the truth. It takes, like the aloe, a very long time to flower, but the blossom is all the more precious when it appears."

CHAPTER 30

As Lafcadio completed his last chapters for *Exotics and Retrospectives* (1898) he received a large envelope from his American publisher, Houghton Mifflin Company. Believing they could dignify the public's growing interest in his life and personality, they were preparing to publish a short biography of him as an advertisement.

It seemed other literary gossip writers were printing unauthorized anecdotes about his years in America and his idiosyncrasies. The news-mongers' bits barely fell short of libel. Those who criticized his life had no idea the price he paid to get where he was. His very survival had been an act of irreverent revolution. The gossipers' opinions were designed to make them seems important; truth for them was of a secondary consequence.

After all this unsought negative publicity, Houghton Mifflin Company thought they needed to publish an official biographical sketch to ward off the harmful gossip. They sent him a few of the news clippings so he'd get the drift of the objectionable copy the others were circulating. They included their more positive version for Lafcadio to correct and have it published with his approval.

As he read through the clippings and pages of his publisher's proposed biography, he was livid. He felt they had invaded his privacy - an uncalled for expose of his personal weaknesses and eccentricities. How dare anyone else hold the pen when it came to his story! Remarkably for him, he restrained his impulse to write an immediate scathing reply. Instead, he 'corrected' Houghton Mifflin's copy of their biography and then threw the whole package into the flames of his stove. He deferred any other action until he could calm down.

Lafcadio wrote to Captain McDonald about the affront and they conferred on the best course of action. They agreed that what they'd said about him was their reality, not his. He'd developed a strong independence of mind, authority that comes with age, and impatience with the petty.

As a result of the slander and unwanted attention, Lafcadio cancelled the contract with his publisher Houghton, Mifflin and Company. He was relieved to be breaking with the publishers. Additionally, he ceased submitting articles and essays in the *Atlantic Journal* and other magazines until March 1903.

Lafcadio had written a letter in 1899 to William G. Jordan, editor of the *Saturday Evening Post*, on the matter. It was a blistering reply to Jordan's request for more of his articles:

"My Dear Mr. Jordan---Your letter of March 10th is with me. I am afraid my answer to it will not please you; but I have no doubt that you will be able to understand my view of the question, and I propose to be perfectly frank with you. I have stopped writing for magazines, because their editors or perhaps their publishers are the enemies, and, mostly, the irreconcilable enemies of literature. They want work written according to their order. They want only something that is like something which has already pleased the majority of their readers. They do not want anything because it is well done, because it is original, because it contains a new idea,---no, they want only what they think their readers want. And necessarily they desire, as a consequence of this policy, the commonplace, the lifeless, the imitation, the counterfeit, the pinchbeck. Send them an original story---it is too horrible, or too shocking, or too heterodox, or "not likely to please the majority of our readers". Send them an essay; and it is not "exactly suited for the magazine". But write what they want, and you can get your own price for dullness and insipidity. It is no wonder that American writers have to speak for an audience in London! The American magazines are murdering American literature. Under no circumstances and for no remuneration will I ever again write anything to order. I have never done so without regretting it…"

The letter to Jordan contains numerous underlines to give emphasis and a very bold Hearn signature. This insight into Lafcadio's spunky personality demonstrates his commitment to ethical and moral standards for himself as an author and as an intellectual.

All Lafcadio's energies went into writing books. He claimed, "I am thus independent…I am pretty much in the position of a bookkeeper known to have once embezzled, or of a man who has been in prison, or of a prostitute who has been on the street. Talent signifies nothing. Talent starves in the streets and idles in the gin house. Talent helps no one not in some way independent of society."

On and off during the years, when he was in bouts of despondency, Lafcadio would write down fragments of memories he dredged up from his life experiences. He referred to them as "a small scribbler's ups and downs". He tried to disentangle early recollections lost in the fog that surrounded his youth. It had been a rule with him to try to forget disagreeable things, yet in trying to forget them he also lost recall of the agreeable. The past was almost blank for him, as if part of his life had never been lived. He remembered flashes of abandonment, deprivation, and rejection - not much positive except for a few agreeable times in New Orleans and his two years in the West Indies. Was his amnesia due to blocking the dire circumstances throughout his life? Was this selective memory normal?

What was sane, average, regular or normal? Normal changes with time, place, and person. What was acceptable or normal for his mother Rosa in Greece or Aunt Sarah Brenane in Ireland or former slave Mattie Foley in Cincinnati or Elizabeth Bisland in New Orleans or New York City or Setsu Koizumi in Tokyo? Each culture and society had its own rules and expectations. In his life he'd been an integral part of those lives and adapted to all those diverse people and worlds. His open mind allowed him to define and make sense of his personal reality.

He labeled his autobiographical file "Thoughts about Feelings". During his blue devils' periods of mental drought, his mind replayed what his wounded heart couldn't delete. In his depressed state he harshly, outrageously berated himself, "Your ancestors were not religious people; you lack constitutional morality. That's why you are so poor, and unsuccessful, and void of mental balance, and an exile in Japan. You know you cannot be happy in an English moral community. You are a fraud, a vile Latin scalawag, and a liar." Studying Buddhism taught him that his journey would be easier and lighter if he didn't carry his past burdens with him.

So he put the sad chronicle of his unfortunate life away in a drawer. Lafcadio preferred the Japanese idea of *ikigai*, that everyone has a reason to exist. His mission was to write, to transform pain into power. Using colorful stories, he could create word art to lift people out of their sorrows and fears. He felt the highest purpose of his fiction was "the recreation of minds that are weary of the toil and strife of the world". So instead of wallowing in self-pity, he began writing a new volume, *In Ghostly Japan* (1899). It was a collection of well-informed observations of old Japan, parables, and gently spooky fables, with Buddhist overtones. Many stories that started out as ghost stories morphed into anecdotes and thought-provoking meditations on life, death, nature, and the eternal self. He wanted to give his readers a little ghostly pleasure. Assorted essays on Japanese proverbs, incense, spirituality, and haiku are included.

He worked long hard hours on *In Ghostly Japan*. "This book will kill me", he complained to Setsu. "It is no easy matter to write so large a volume in so short a time; there is no one to help me, and I think it very trying to accomplish such a task."

Tense with wanting to finish and edit his book, Lafcadio was becoming more reclusive. To write he needed to be alone and know that no one was going to interrupt or question him. The secret to his success was found in the simplicity of daily routine. He found his highest enjoyments were, after all, intellectual and that progress on his books could only be affected by self-sacrifice to interest and indifference to physical gratification.

When McDonald and Amenomori kept inviting him for outings down in Yokohama, he sent a sharp note:
"I am going to ask you simply not to come and see your friend, and not to ask him to come and see you, for at least three months more. I know this seems horrid---but such are the only conditions upon which literary work is possible, when combined with the duties of a professor of literature. I don't want to see, or hear, or feel anything outside of my work till the book is done, and I therefore have the impudent assurance to ask you to help me stand by my wheel. Of course it would be pleasant to do otherwise; but I can't even think of pleasant things and do decent work at the same time. Please think of a helmsman, offshore, and the ship in rough weather, with breakers in sight. Hate to send you this letter---but think you will sympathize with me in spite of it."

"Poor Hearn!" thought McDonald when he read the letter. He wrote back, "Three months?" He asked if he needed to stay in hiding that long. He compared him to a little crab, backing deeper and deeper into his little hole whenever anyone tried to dig him out. But he agreed not to disturb him until the book was completed and not to write if letters distracted him.

Lafcadio did write back and heartedly admitted that he was like a crab. But added, "There are rich natures that can afford the waste, but I can't, because the best part of my life has been wasted in the wrong direction and I shall have to work like thunder till I die to make up for it."

Lafcadio always held fast to a high artistic standard and his heroic pursuits of an ideal of workmanship. Throughout his life he consistently and resolutely practiced self-discipline when it came to his writing and protecting his privacy. Dr. Gould, who studied him in a scientific way during his developmental years, said that work was "the only religion or ethics he had, and praise God he had it."

As a distinguished professor at Imperial University, Lafcadio received multiple invitations. For anyone else they would have been obligatory, but he was allowed by the administration to decline gracefully. National and international literary travelers and journalists would get his address and send requests for an audience or interview. Since he never allowed a telephone in the house, these written distractions would be tossed in the trash without answer. Occasionally when some caller located his home, he slipped out the back garden and went for a walk. He started using the back entrance when he left or returned home to avoid being seen or bumping into curious intruders.

He shared his feelings about new-found notoriety with McDonald, "You see there are many who come to Japan that want to see me; and you think this is proof of kindly interest. Not a bit of it. It is precisely the same kind of curiosity that impels men to look at strange animals, a six-legged calf, for instance. The interest in the book is in some cases genuine; the interest in the personality is of the *New York Police Gazette* quality. Don't think I am exaggerating."

When he finished *In Ghostly Japan* on schedule, he was pleased. He wrapped the manuscript in boards and paper and sent it to the publisher by registered mail. Then right after in December, he got news that McDonald had suffered a foot injury. He rushed to his friend's side. After three months of separation, the two men talked for ten hours straight. Time vanished like steam from a teacup. Food had to be ordered in. They discussed who the book should be dedicated to - Elizabeth Bisland Wetmore or Alice Behrens who gave him material for the book, and which publisher should get the manuscript. Lafcadio tortured himself over such decisions. In a flurry, he packed it up and sent it eastward to Little, Brown, and Company and dedicated it to Mrs. Behrens.

His greatest satisfaction of the *In Ghostly Japan* book was a story called "A Mountain of Skulls", told to him by Ernest Fenollosa. The Spanish-American professor of philosophy, also a stout advocate of Spencer, became a favorite intellectual companion. Lafcadio spent more hours in the Fenollosa home than any other foreign house in Tokyo. He admired Ernest and his wife for their crusade of rescuing Japanese art works.

Six months later he signed with Little, Brown and Company and they bought and published *Exotics and Retrospectives*. Hasegawa of Tokyo published *The Boy Who Drew Cats* (1898) about a young boy studying for the priesthood who had what is called "the genius of an artist" and could not stop drawing cats everywhere. In a haunted temple one night his realistic cats killed the resident evil goblin rat, so he became a very famous artist.

Lafcadio rescued many stray cats over the years and usually had at least one around his home. In the West Indies he kept two dozen cats to frighten away snakes and insects. He admired cats' absolute emotional honesty. Unlike humans, who for one reason or another, tended to hide their feelings, he felt cats did not pretend or lie about their likes or dislikes.

Year after year, his books would come out with regularity. *In Ghostly Japan* in 1899, *Shadowings* in 1900, and *A Japanese Miscellany* in 1901, all published by Little, Brown. His works were considered an ambling journey of a thoughtful, sensuous traveler through a delightful landscape. In *Shadowings*, his work represents a pioneering effort to circulate Japanese literature internationally. He focused on the uncanny, the exotic, and the relationship between literature and visual and dramatic arts. His creative, rather than strictly literal, translations of old stories shaped the West's cultural understanding and interactions with Japan.

Lafcadio wrote prodigiously, turning out jampacked volumes of studies and reveries on a wide range of topics. There was never any indication that he was running out of subject matter. No subject was beneath or beyond him. With his journalist and novelist eye, he wrote detailed descriptions of Japanese village life, social customs, aesthetics, etiquette, martial arts, schooling of monks, training of geishas, samurai legends, and ghost stories…among many other things. He'd had practically gone native so his insights on the unknown Japan made him a shrewd interpreter who could see into the country's heart.

His essays on subjects such as dragonflies; songs of Japanese children; frogs; and Japanese female names weren't just casual observations; they were fully researched facts. He poured great care into his objective, shorter stories. The impressionistic writings of Lafcadio showed his appreciation for the beauty of nature and the human condition. He was alive to life's mysteries and magic. He praised Japanese civilization as outstanding in its ability to understand the beauty and fascination of the insect kingdom. He too marveled at and loved small creatures.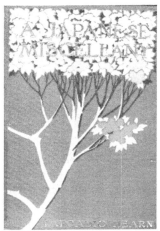
"Kusa-Hibari", a masterpiece about a pet cricket, illuminated his views on fleeting lives and dying.

Originally a *Kaidan* or *Kwaidan* in Hearn's original spelling is a collective term for horror stories or mysteries related to supernatural phenomena. *Yurei* are ghosts or the soul of a dead person that lingers to carry out unfinished business or seek revenge. These apparitions are often pale figures with no legs.

The oppressive 17th century Edo period gave rise to a commoners' culture with distinct art, theater, and storytelling as a mode of entertainment. The *kwaidan* tradition of telling tales of the strange and mysterious ghost stories was to teach life lessons and as a light rebuke of the rigid social and political order. Kwaidan orations were richly infused with cultural motifs of strange, gruesome, and mysterious nature. Tales spun by human fantasy and expressed through symbols. People would gather around a paper lantern filled with one hundred wicked candles. A candle was blown out each time a story was told in hopes of inducing a supernatural event. It was a brave person, who after all the horror tales, could blow out the last candle, casting everyone into darkness.

Stories came from Chinese fiction, Japanese folk tales, and Buddhist teachings. Lafcadio was convinced that a story that had endured a thousand years, renewing its fascination over the centuries, could not help but survive because it contained some deep truth and prove that different areas were rich in history and culture. He voraciously collected these weird tales and ghost stories, often paying his students to translate manuscripts. At times, his lectures and writing assignments seem to be interviewing his students for his own references, which he later used in his writings.

Through the magic of storytelling, he was preserving Japan's ancient myths, legends, and folktales. He understood as well as any writer the universal power of the folk tale and fable. There were also rather autobiographical essays included such as "My Guardian Angel" and "Nightmare Touch". These two works uncovered Lafcadio's early childhood tragedies, like being locked in windowless rooms at night to get over his fear of the dark. In Ireland, where he was raised, the ancient Celtic druid class of priests and teachers studied natural philosophy, astronomy, ancient verse, and religious lore. Their main doctrine was a belief in immortality of the soul and that a soul passed into another being after death. Lafcadio was open to Japanese folk religion, respect for nature, and tales of the supernatural.

Since youth, he'd believed in the existence of spiritual beings, ghosts, and monsters. Lafcadio had a love for the irrational, such as ghosts and superstition. He maintained that the skepticism inherent about science and rationalism of the Enlightenment was because it did not include some important things such as irrational happenings, passion, and instinct. These insights help to understand his indirect motivation for compiling his collection of Japanese ghost stories *Kwaidan*.

CHAPTER 31

Lafcadio's main source for his writing materials and ideas was Setsu. She diligently searched through antiquarian bookshops, estate sales, and libraries for volumes of folklore and ghost stories. Eventually Lafcadio's home library contained hundreds of books of half-forgotten legends. It reinforced his belief in "*littera scripta manet* - the written word survives."

Setsu also loved to read and hear the old-time stories. In her childhood, her grandfather told stories of the glory days of the samurais and other historical figures. Due to financial reasons she had to leave elementary school when she was in the fourth grade. This always gave her a sense of shame and failure. She lamented her lack of education compared to Lafcadio and others.

"Yakumo, I could be of more help to you if I had a college degree," she said to him. He took her hand and walked over to the bookshelf where his works and others were stacked.

"How were these books born? If you were an educated woman, you would laugh at those stories of spirits, ghosts, and former incarnation as ridiculous," he said. "You are the one who helps me by finding and narrating the tales to me. It has to be just your voice, your words, your thoughts."

Lafcadio wanted her to learn folktales by heart and to interpret them and reenact them herself. He instructed her in the method of *omoide no ki* (record of memory), or the art of storytelling. Lafcadio's creative transcriptions of Japanese tales into English was possible through Setsu's performative translation of the oral folklore, ghost stories, and legends.

Setsu was of invaluable assistance to Lafcadio. His Japanese wife was a consummate storyteller, particularly of the supernatural. The narratives took on a life of their own until at times it almost seemed like their house was haunted. He didn't always give her credit or dedicate a book to her, but it was a joint effort to rescue and retell the ancient Japanese stories that made up his book *Kwaidan* and others.

Lafcadio loved a good story. He was fortunate to live with Setsu who would narrate and act out stories to him like his mother Rosa in Greece, Catherine his great aunt's housemaid in Ireland, his first love, ex-slave Mattie Foley in Cincinnati, and Cyrillia a Creole friend in Martinique. Even illiterate Mattie could weave tales of ghostly happenings from her childhood on a farm in Kentucky to entertain and inspire him. She talked of ghosts, of murdered and suicidal slaves, and a haunted house where a "thing" terrified her as she hid under the covers of her bed, very much like Lafcadio's childhood ghost experiences in his locked bedroom.

Folklore that embraced the supernatural melded with the revulsion he felt for his hypocritical great-aunt's strict institutional religion and the cruelties he experienced at the hands of his headmasters at the Roman Catholic boarding schools. Lafcadio seemed to unconsciously seek out elements of horror and morbidity that haunted his youth.

He incorporated his own past experiences, fears, and imagination in his writing. The faceless ghost in "Mujina" was reminiscent of encounters with his frighteningly religious Cousin Jane in Dublin. Various dead lovers haunting live ones were similar to the New Orleans tomb spirits in his early poems. The idea that the dead, whose absences are so painful, are still among us and may want something from the living, is both the seat of horror and fantasy.

"Whoever pretends not to believe in ghosts of any sort, lies to his own heart," he said to doubters.

During Japan's Edo period (1603-1868) the stereotype of a ghost was a female avenger dressed in white with loose ruffled hair. Women in the feudal system were of very low status and completely dependent on men, with no opportunity to demand anything. But the ghost of a dead woman had a strong presence, could stand up for herself, and relentlessly pursue and obtain revenge.

The most famous of the Edo ghosts is O-Owa of Tsuruya Nanboku's kabuki play "Ghost Story of Yotsuya" (1825). In this story, the samurai Iemon plots the murder of his wife O-Iwa so he can marry a rich woman. After the horrific death of O-Iwa, who had been self-sacrificing, loyal and submissive while alive, she directs all her resentment toward her unfaithful husband until her ghost drives him mad.

Characters such as O-Iwa were used to commit acts that were not possible within the laws of the feudal system or its cultural rule norms. Certain streams of Buddhism and Confucianism, which considered women as irrational, sinful, jealous, and impulsive beings, supported the oppression of females. Stories about female monsters and ghosts brought out the supposed worse maligned traits of the gender. The unhappy dead, furious about the repressed, miserable situations they were in, had a tendency to rise up as demons or ghosts because of unaccomplished passion, or return from the dead to care for their family. Women who conformed to the roles society assigned them in life, broke out of restrictive religious and social order and haunted the living.

Lafcadio Hearn adapted and embellished over fifty traditional Japanese ghost stories around 1900. His common motif was a woman returning after death to take revenge or find the love they missed during lifetime. In his nostalgic yearning for an Old Japan, he tended to romanticize Japanese women as ideal wives and mothers from a Western point of view. These transcultural flows influenced the ghost culture in his works.

During the period of modernization in Japan, belief in supernatural beings and ghosts was considered a backward, premodern relic. Yet Lafcadio's dramatic retelling of ancient horror stories were translated to Japanese and appreciated for their versions of past eras and moral lessons. His stories generally ended with a cathartic moral outcome that related to Shinto teachings about the unity of human beings with nature and one's ancestors (the core of Japanese nationalism) or lessons about humility. Some stories feature the Buddhist belief in reincarnation directed by the good and bad actions in a person's past lives.

An unforgettable story that Lafcadio told was about Yuki-Onna, Japanese for Snow Woman. The tale is about an old woodcutter and his young apprentice, Minokichi, who get caught in a blizzard and take shelter in a ferryman's hut. As they wait out the storm, the young man wakes up to see a beautiful woman dressed all in white blowing her cold breath on the older man, killing him. The pretty girl warns that if Minokichi ever spoke of the encounter she would kill him. Later he meets a pretty girl, marries, and they have 10 children. One day the light on his wife reminded him of the visitation by the supernatural woman. He tells her about his haunting experience. She hysterically launches at him, revealing that she was the entity on that fateful night. If their children were not so close by, she would have killed him for telling. Instead she suddenly melted into smoke and disappears forever.

Within Lafcadio's writings over the years and various geographic locations, there are parallels and similarities. Yuki Onna, a female ghost from the Japanese coast covered with white snow, who suddenly appears on a quiet, shivering night is very like his beautiful fatale, she-devil of the Martinique green sugarcane fields who suddenly shows herself in total silence. There is also Oshidori, the sacred duck from the red marshes, and Soukougnan, an enchanted bird from the Martinique green undergrowth.

Lafcadio often wrote with sympathy about humans coming and going to the underworld's afterlife. He was drawn to stories such as Urashima Taro, where Urashima the fisherman rescues a turtle who is really a sea princess, so he is allowed to visit the Dragon Palace at the ocean's bottom. He gets engaged to the dragon god's daughter. When he returns to his village, he finds 348 years have passed. This tale of Urashima is considered the oldest example of a time travel story.

Hearn wrote other folktales about marriages between spirits and humans. He believed that humans would be enriched if they could communicate with the alien world. His retold tales reflect a fundamental universal desire to have communication with others, even conversations between supernatural beings, the dead, and nature personified. People long to reconnect with those who are separated from them.

In Lafcadio's retelling of *Yuki-Onna*, an eternally young snow woman who marries a human man. When he betrays her by confessing that he saw her when he was young, she returns to the underworld. In folk tales it is taboo to ever reveal or mention a sighting of a supernatural. The theme was about the sacred female who is anguished to have lost her love and her home…much like his mother Rosa when she had to leave her young sons and return to Greece. Lafcadio longed for his mother, who had struggled in a foreign country and was abandoned by her husband. Lafcadio's feelings toward his lost mother can be seen throughout his retold tales.

The psychological theory of *amae*, the wish to be completely dependent and loved by a parent, is at play in many of his works. He missed the tenderness a child should receive in early years. Rosa's traumatic abandonment and the lack of maternal *amae* in his life was said to be the reason for his affinity for and fusion of her ancient Greek pagan culture onto Shintoism. His distaste for Christianity and acceptance of nature-based pantheism cultures in Gaelic Ireland, the American South and Caribbean West Indies led him to embrace pre-modern Japanese culture and faiths, and their Chinese origins.

In his reading and writing, Lafcadio liked to contemplate how when one thing faded out and another faded in. He was aware of the intersection of mental states such as that between sleeping and waking or places where fantasy and reality began to merge. Lafcadio had sympathy with stories where humans come and go between worlds or dimensions.

His spooky narratives were not contained by historic eras or national boundaries. They often featured encounters between the living and the dead, in a complex interplay of wish fulfillment and disgust, desire and fear. Interactions between the two worlds were driven by anger, desire for revenge or love. "The Story of Aoyagi", is a love story where a young samurai narrowly escapes the wrath of his lord for marrying without permission, only to discover that his wife is not what she appears to be, but the spirit of a willow tree. Lafcadio sought to give his readers a more intense spiritual and sensual experience.

Lafcadio portrayed spirits as ancient trees. In one legend, a samurai called Tomotada meets a girl and her parents on one of his journeys. He falls in love with the young woman named Aoyagi, which literally means "green willow" and they marry. One day she suffers a tremendous pain and disappears because the tree from which she came was cut down. He visits the place where they met and discovers only three stumps where once stood the family house. The samurai performed ritual suicide *seppuku* where the tree had withered to make it come back to life. This story and others was meant to cause fear of possible consequences of mistreating the environment, especially trees.

Fear and warnings play a major role in many of his stories. In Yuki-Onna, the beautiful snow woman warns of the danger of venturing out in blizzards. The blue monk feeds on children who venture out in the woods alone. A badger takes the form of a human with no face is able to cause mortal scares if encountered late at night. In Japanese fantasy genre, these manifestations were an important element of the peoples' way of thinking and superstitions. Ghost legends encompassed all aspects of the Japanese society, life, and everyday living, from natural phenomena to interpersonal relationships.

The Japanese took the idea of ghosts (*yurei*) visiting the living for granted. They understood that was just how things were. Lafcadio used psychology to create greater horror through the intensity of the human emotions. Such as the excessive hatred and grief that manifested itself in the "Corpse Rider", about a woman who was so angry at being divorced that she died and then haunted the new wife. It begins, "The body was cold as ice; the heart had long ceased to beat; yet there were no signs of death."

In "Of Ghosts and Goblins", a young man is drafted into the army, and his betrothed dies before he can return. He plans to kill himself on her grave, but his love and grief are so powerful that she appears and tells him, 'It was all a mistake…I am not dead. I have seen your heart and that was worth all the waiting and the pain. Let's go away at once to another city, so that people may not know this thing and trouble us; for all still believe me dead." They move to a new home, open a little food shop, and have a son. All is blissful until her parents stumble upon their shop. His wife, who was dead the whole time, vanishes again for good.

In the horrifying story, "Yaburareta Yakusoku - Of a Promise Broken", a man promises his dying wife that he will never remarry. But the widower breaks the deathbed vow and takes a seventeen-year-old bride. The late wife's ghost menaces and eventually beheads the new bride. The theme of unhappy, unfulfilled women betrayed by men may reflect his own mother's sadness, madness, rage, and unrequited love.

In Lafcadio's stories, it is not only the men who get haunted by the returning departed. The vengeance of the dead happens to the women, who are often innocent parties. He believed that the primal fear of ghosts is not based on seeing or hearing them but being touched by them. His fascination with ghost stories that feature the return of the dead, has been analyzed as his waiting for a return visitation of the mother who abandoned him, if only in dreams or tales. Recounting these stories perhaps helped him heal emotional wounds.

So many of the world's tales are projections of traumas and fantasies and have universal themes. Legends, myths, folklore, and fairytales are the expressions of the unconscious and primitive complexes. Whether a spiritual quest or under exotic influence, the common story is a hero's journey and search for home and peace. It was Lafcadio's story as well.

One of Lafcadio's masterpiece stories found within *Kwaidan* was a simple, but creepy story entitled "Mujina". The word *mujina* refers to a badger but is symbolic of shapeshifters in Japanese mythology. In this tale a merchant is walking down a road in Tokyo when he sees a well-dressed woman wailing and sobbing by a moat. He approaches to help because he fears she might drown herself because of her sorrow. He puts his hand on her shoulder, and when she turns toward him, she has no facial features - nothing just a blank. Screaming he runs away as fast as he can until he spots a light in the distance. It belongs to a soba seller. The soba man asks the panicked merchant if he was hurt or robbed. The merchant begins to explain what he saw by the moat. The soba vendor interrupts him, strokes his face and asks if the woman looked like him---and he turns to the man with a face with no nose, eyes or mouth. Right then, the light on his cart goes out.

One night Setsu narrated a story from a half-forgotten book titled *Gayuu Kidan*. She lowered the lamps in their bedroom and began telling him the ghost story of *Mimi-Nashi-Hoichi*, the blind musician.

The story began: "More than seven hundred years ago, at Dan-no-ura, in the Straits of Shimonoseki, was fought the last battle of the long contest between the Heike, or Taira clan, and the Genji, or Minamoto clan. There the Heike perished utterly, with their women and children, and their infant emperor Antoku Tenno. That sea and shore are haunted, and strange crabs are found there, called Heike crabs, have human faces on their backs...on dark nights thousands of ghostly fires hover about the beach...a sound of great shouting comes from the sea, like a clamor of battle."

In summary, there lived a blind man named Hoi-chi, famed for his skill in recitation and playing upon the biwa short-necked wooden lute. When he sang the song of the battle between the Heike and the Genji, two rival clans fighting for control of twelfth century Japan, even the goblins could not refrain from tears. The blind man made the temple his home in exchange for musical performances on certain evenings. One night when Hoi-chi was alone in the temple, a deep voice called the blind man's name, abruptly in the manner of a samurai summoning an inferior.

"Hoichi!"

"Hai!" answered the blind man, frightened by the menacing voice---"I am blind!---I cannot know who calls!"

"There is nothing to fear," the stranger exclaimed, speaking more gently. "My present lord, a person of exceedingly high rank, is now staying in Akamagaseki with many noble attendants...Having heard of your skill in reciting the story of the battle, he now desires to hear your performance; so you will take your biwa and come with me at once to the house where the august assembly is waiting."

Hoichi went with the samurai guide. When they entered, the blind musician heard a great many people assembled and rustling of silk like the sound of leaves in a forest. He played and recited the battle at Dan-no-ura, for the pity of it is most deep. The voices murmured high praise. Then all the listeners uttered together one long shuttering cry of anguish and wept and wailed so loudly the blind man was frightened by the violence of the grief.

The lord demanded that he return and play for them for the next six nights. He commanded that Hoichi speak to no one of his visits. When the blind musician went out the next night, the temple priests were worried for him and sent a servant to follow. He heard Hoichi playing in the cemetery among the tombs of the Heike. The servant pulled him up and hurried him back to the temple telling him that he believed him to be bewitched.

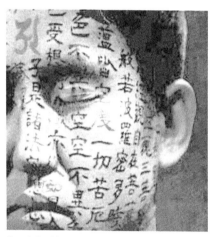

The temple priest heard the story and knew Hoichi was in great danger from ghosts. He was told not to perform any more. They stripped him and painted this entire body, even the soles of his feet, with text of the holy sutra.

Hoichi waited still as a stone and did not answer the samurai's call. He felt his ears gripped by fingers of iron and torn off. Poor Hoichi had text written everywhere but his ears. The wounds healed. The spirits of the dead Heike never troubled Hoichi again. But from the time of his sad adventure, he was known only as Mimi-Nashi-Hoichi---Hoichi the Earless.

As Setsu emphasized the horrific parts of this classic tale, she watched her husband become tearful or tremble. At one point Setsu went into the next room and called out, "Hoichi-ichi! Hoichi-ichi!" Lafcadio enthralled, played his part and answered back, "I am blind. Who are you?"

In writing a legend or ghost story like "Mimi-Nashi-Hoichi", Lafcadio relied on both oral and written versions of the works, and particularly on Setsu's acting out the parts and her interpretations. He would write a tale down, revise, edit, condense, and make each his own. In doing so he left behind his earlier florid prose style in favor of a minimalist style more suitable for the brief yet haunting stories.

The collection and release of fairy tales published by the Brothers Grimm in the 19th century sparked international interest in national folklore. Local myths and tales represented the simplest and purest expression of collective unconscious psychic processes. They contained the basic patterns of human behavior and archetypes.

Lafcadio used Hans Christian Andersen as a literary model. He ordered all his books because he so admired the magical simplicity and the force of his retelling of European fairytales. Like Andersen, while retaining the mystical mood, he modified and retold the dark and macabre Japanese tales to make them more appealing to Western audiences. By shaping the stories for both Western and Eastern audiences, he created his own kind of enlightened art.

In his vast readings and well-traveled life, Lafcadio learned about the gods of Greece, Ireland, and Japan. As he listened to the mysterious stories narrated by Setsu, he began to compare and see parallels. For example, the tale of "Mimi-Nashi-Hoichi", the blind musician has much in common with tales of *Orpheus* in Greek mythology, and the Irish story "Magic Fiddle", and other similar works he knew before coming to Japan.

Lafcadio was struck by the enormous number of parallels and recurrent themes in international collections. Exoticism, the styles or traits considered characteristic of a distant foreign country, was seen by Lafcadio in a broader sense. He found myths from Japan to be less geographically determined and more multi-directional and versatile. Ancient stories represented basic patterns in human behavior through an overlay of cultural material. He discovered that local saga content, when condensed down to universal status of a fairy tale with archetypal experiences, could transcend cultural, racial, and linguistic boundaries. Lafcadio examined the four central components of each tale - time/space, characters, movement, and closing results - so he could begin to amplify the core symbols into language the mind and heart felt deeply. Its emotional value is what gave it life and projected wisdom.

Images in Lafcadio's work came from a deeper center - a life system, not from a concept system. He wrote about myths as symbolic of spiritual powers within a person. Myths were presented as metaphors, coming from where the heart is and where the experience is, even when the mind wondered why folks believed things. His retelling of ghost stories and myths didn't point to facts. They pointed beyond facts and concepts, to the ultimate depths of the psyche.

In *Kokoru* he said that the Japanese had a collective memory that connected them through their ancestors to ancient times. "The strength of Japan, like the strength of her ancient faith, needs little material display: both exist where the deepest power of any people exists, in the 'race ghost'."

Lafcadio would rewrite a story multiple times. If he was unable to settle on the plot or theme that he wanted, he'd put aside his notes until a new concept or companion piece presented itself. From the scattered stories and cross-cultural topics that filled his life, he created a place in the reader's mind where reality and fantasy merged. He wrote for all ages because no one was too old for fairy tales.

He claimed, "The poet or the storyteller who cannot give the reader a little ghostly pleasure at times can be neither a really great writer nor a great thinker."

CHAPTER 32

The one activity that got Lafcadio to take a break from his writing was to spend time on his sons' lessons. He told Japanese parents they should not only discipline their children, but also give them basic education and not be so dependent on schoolteachers. He believed in Herbert Spencer's saying that a father who was able should teach his own children.

"Dare to know! Be curious!" he'd tell the boys and his university students because he knew that curiosity was a certain and permanent characteristic of a vigorous intellect. "Knowledge is food for the soul."

Lafcadio thought it best to teach his sons to read and write Japanese and English at the same time so that one language would not cause a bias or one overtake the other. Japanese would be the practical language and English the language of business and the soul. It was understood that their family's *Herun-san* hybrid dialect was only used at home and never spoken outside.

Daily lessons were varied and inventive to hold the children's attention. Lafcadio would recite poems, rhymes, tell old stories or make up new ones to help them learn letters and words. They would drill on the alphabet for at least an hour a day using large picture books - 'A' is for apple, 'B' is for bear, and so on. Painting and drawing were encouraged to stimulate awareness and imagination. Brushes and pencils were in their hands as soon as they were old enough to sit up at a desk. Writing and artistic beauty were revered.

At times, he let his eldest son Kazuo, nicknamed Kajio, enter his study and work alongside him. A small slant-topped desk was built to allowed Kazuo to stand without bending his head when he wrote or drew pictures. Lafcadio believed that bending the head increased strain on the eyes.

One day Kazuo painted a picture of a soldier on horseback that he was very proud of. He showed it to his mother and father and they praised it. Then Lafcadio mentioned that there was one bad error. Kazuo and his mother couldn't find it. His father pointed out that the soldier's sword was hanging on the right, the improper side. Kazuo's eyes teared up with regret. Setsu began to scold the child, because the eyelids of a samurai are never wet.

Lafcadio stopped her and said, "I can sympathize with his regret. I know it well. In reality I have had many such experiences. I write, thinking that it's all right and give it out to be printed, when those who do not think well of me find something to criticize in my writings. I think, 'There it is'; but it's too late. Kazuo, your critics were father and mother who love you. But in the case of father, being in the book, it was the whole wide world. In such cases I thank my enemies and reproach myself. Thereafter, I try not to make similar mistakes. I write to those who said bad things and thank them. They become my friends. Kazuo, I am sure you will never make like mistakes in such a picture. Oh, I am sure."

Lafcadio wrote about Kazuo's behavior to his editor in New Orleans, Page Baker, "For six years I have been walking up and down over matted floors, just as I used to do in that room you wrote to me from. Curiously, my little boy has the same habit. It is very difficult to keep him still at mealtime. He likes to take a nibble, then walk up and down or run, then another nibble. I hope the gods will save him from adopting other former habits of mine, which are less innocent, when he grows up. For example, if he should take a foolish fancy to every damsel in his path. However, I expect that his mother's strong commonsense, which he seems to inherit, will counterbalance the fantasticalities bequeathed to him by me. It has only been since his entrance into this world that I fully realize what a 'disgraceful person' I used to be."

Lafcadio set up exercise equipment behind the house where the boys would regularly work out with him. His diminished sight kept him from engaging in vigorous sports, but he routinely exercised. He swung twenty-pound dumbbells to strengthen his arms. He admired a robust physique. A walk of five or six miles a day was nothing to him. His walks were more of an excursion than an outing. He and his sons walked long distances in nature in the daytime and marched around the dining room singing national songs after dinner. He was very earnest about whatever he did.

Anxious about his aging father-in-law's need for more exercise, Lafcadio would take him along on his walks. Together they set up an archery range against the temple hill. Grandfather devoted his time to repairing arrows and making targets. He pasted strong Japanese paper on wooden frames, tight like drums. On these he would paint on bull's eyes with ink. When the targets were struck, they produced a resonating, drum-like sound. The old man was an expert with the powerful Japanese bow from his samurai days. With one shoulder bare of sleeve, he would take aim and let his arrow fly. He nearly always hit the center mark. Even Lafcadio, using his telescope to first sight the target, learned to shoot well enough to win the grandfather's praise.

Kazuo loved the simple duty of retrieving arrows from the field. One day he impatiently ran out early just as his grandfather released a razor-sharp arrow at the target. It whizzed right through the boy's hair without cutting his scalp. Lafcadio rushed to hold his son in his arms, crying in relief for several minutes. The old samurai hid his bows and arrows and would never touch them again. There were no more archery sessions after that near miss.

Beyond physical activities and languages, Lafcadio wanted his children to learn ideas, attitudes, and rules of civility. He drilled them on honesty, cleanliness, punctuality, organization, manners, and completing tasks. Their stern father insisted they finish and excel at whatever they had begun. Every student in

Japan was taught the saying, "It matters not what one's work may be, success depends upon perfected skill and earnest purpose." The children had to stand like soldiers - chin up, heels together, toes out, and shoulders straight while being instructed. When Kazuo was not making progress as fast as his father expected, he'd urge him on.

"Please hurry Kajio, Papa-San won't live long enough to teach you everything you should know, so study hard and learn quickly!" There were no days off for holidays and weekends.

Lafcadio did not extend to Iwao, his laughing Japanese-looking son, the nervous regard he had for his firstborn. Kazuo especially received the brunt of Lafcadio's relentless pressure to be the very best. His son was a quick learner and kept a diary in English and notebooks filled with little stories his father dictated for writing practice. Even Lafcadio shared with Setsu that Kazuo was a diligent student and Iwao did his studies very well. "It was simply lovely to see they learn well."

All the exhorting, drilling, and scolding at times drove the first-born child to tears and made him more sensitive and easily hurt. Lafcadio admitted to friends that Kazuo was not as strong as he would wish, and "physical pain he bears well enough; but a mere look, a careless word, a moment of unconscious indifference is fire to his little soul." He worried to see his own emotional, delicate nature in his son. Lafcadio had aways been weighed down by lingering memories of his emotionally disjointed childhood.

The teacher-student role was a harsh one, but the father-son relationship outside the classroom was affectionate. Lafcadio could remember how a few years before they nearly lost Kazuo to an illness. He and Setsu sat up with him night after night for weeks, always dreading that he would be taken from them.

Lafcadio would tell his son, "Don't think me cruel Kajio. It is the world that is cruel and I want you prepared for whatever the future brings."

To put an end to stormy sessions Kazuo would sometimes take advantage of his father and tell him that his eyes hurt, knowing how fearful his dad was of vision troubles. Professing eyestrain, he was at last allowed to go outside to play.

When Kazuo played with his friends, he was a leader among the boys with a big loud voice. But under the angry eye of his father, he would answer questions in barely audible tones. "Are you a mosquito?" Lafcadio would shout and demand repetition. There were cuffs on the ear or stinging slaps during sessions.

Kazuo described his father as very loving and very severe, saying, "I was like the people who live at the foot of a volcano, such as Mount Asama. Each morning and evening is displayed a new and charming aspect of the mountain, but all at once it will send up huge columns of fire and emit voluminous heavy stones from its quiet cone, the sight of which can never be erased from one's memory."

McDonald talked to Lafcadio about making harsh demands on the young boy. "Don't scold so much! He will learn in time. It's good he knows as much as he does. If an American boy knew as much as he did, they would think he was doing fine." The naval officer would praise Kazuo directly, "You are doing very well, young man. Study hard and we'll all be proud of you!" Paymaster McDonald was Kazuo's secret hero.

Setsu would comfort them, "You are lucky boys. Papa is a Tokyo Imperial University professor. Only the brightest young men in the country can study with Papa."

Setsu asked Lafcadio to teach her English also. But he refused to saying, "If you learn English, you will be chattering needless things with foreigners and nothing good would result thereby." She would secretly listen to the lessons from the other side of the room divider. Later she'd study the papers covered with oversized letters to learn the shapes and sounds. But was never quite able to join them together to form the new English words she was learning. She deduced that the capital 'E' started the word 'Elizabeth' in writing exercises, as in 'Elizabeth took an umbrella' or 'Elizabeth likes cats'.

On occasion Lafcadio and Setsu would hire private tutors for the boys. One such teacher was Leonie Gilmour (1873-1933), an American educator, editor, and journalist. She had been the English instructor and editor of Japanese writer Yone Noguchi's book *The American Diary of a Japanese Girl* (1902). Their love affair and possible secret marriage produced Isamu Noguchi, a sculptor. Later Leonie gave birth to accomplished dancer Ailes Gilmour. Leonie moved to Japan with her son at the insistence of Yone only to find him married to a Japanese lady, so she began working at a Yokohama school and privately tutoring the children of Lafcadio and Setsu Hearn. Leonie Gilmour was the subject of a feature film entitled *Leonie* (2010) and a book *Leonie Gilmour: When East Weds West* (2013). Her son Isamu Noguchi (1904-1988) turned out to be one of the twentieth century's most critically acclaimed sculptors. Like Lafcadio, Isamu was the product of two cultures and two countries that added layers to his complex identity.

It was Setsu who tutored the boys in Japanese and the fundamentals of *hiragana* and *katakana* phonetic letters writing systems. It was at her table that Kazuo learned *kanji*, the first of the thousands of characters with their multiple flowing brush strokes. Lafcadio picked up only enough symbols to write Setsu simple childlike letters, peppered with fun drawings. He never mastered Japanese well enough to read a newspaper or book, so relied on Setsu to translate for him. Life around the Hearn household fell into a routine, each person with their role and rules.

CHAPTER 33

One day as Lafcadio and Setsu walked toward the temple across the field from their house on their daily outing, he cried out, "Oh! Oh! Why did they cut down those three trees?" He screamed in pain and anger.

"This temple must be very poor, Yakumo. They must need some money," she replied. But Lafcadio was not consoled.

"Why didn't they tell me? I can easily give money to help them. I should have been happier to give them money and save the trees. Think how long a time was necessary for those trees to grow from little sprouting seeds! I am sorry for Abbot Tatara that he has no money, but I am more sorry for the trees, Mamma-san."

A dead limb from a giant cedar had fallen and damaged one of the tombs under the tree. Three trees were cut down and the wood sold. Lafcadio was depressed by the sight. It hurt his heart to see the destruction. He begged the priests of Kobudera temple not to cut down any more.

About that time, the friendly old abbot was being transferred to Asakusa. When the succeeding younger priests arrived with their small modern suitcases, Tatara asked them in his ironic joking manner, "What have you in that Christian lunchbox?" The more modern priests soon accelerated the program of tree cutting to provide income for the temple. Lafcadio covered his ears so he could not hear the gigantic cedars crashing to the earth. The decimation of the forest made him so wretched, that he and Setsu did not visit the temple hill again.

The parishioners decided to sell the property to developers. All the priests were transferred to another location in Tokyo. Within weeks the hills were bare. Housing lots and tenements were going up in their place. The holy grounds were given over to modern streets and structures. Lafcadio had no more private strolling spot as the hillside was too ugly and public. Additionally, the local jail began to march lines of manacled prisoners past their front door each morning and evening.

Those fallen cedars were the beginning of the end of what Lafcadio called his island of tranquility. Bit by bit his illusion of safety was eroding. When Dr. Toyama died in 1900, Lafcadio attended his sober funeral. The dean was not just a friend, but also a patron of the foreign professors, and his personal advocate. New administrators marked the end of job security at the university. Lafcadio needed a steady income more than ever when his third son, Kiyoshi, was born 1900 in Tokyo.

Lafcadio was worried and talked about moving their growing family back to Matsue or to the Oki Islands. "To be a lighthouse keeper would be wonderful! You've seen everything in Tokyo. Now can we go back to Matsue?" he pleaded with his wife.

Setsu refused to live in the barbaric surroundings of the islands or return to her native province filled with unhappy childhood memories. She knew they needed to save more money from the largest salary he'd ever made. She waited for his temper to cool and suggested instead that they build their own home in Okubo, a rural area in Tokyo known as Gardeners' Quarter. It would be a suitable place to raise children and meet Lafcadio's needs.

The district was known for its azaleas. She found a small, secluded estate with an attractive garden and many fine old trees. She drew up plans for adding rooms and features to make the residence suit their domestic and professional needs. Lafcadio turned the move, remodeling and decorating entirely over to Setsu. All he asked was for a window facing west for his desk and a stove in his study room to ward off the winter cold. If she asked his opinion, he'd answer:

"Do as you please. I know how to write, that is all and you, Mamma-san know much better. I have no time. When that house is ready, you might say, 'Papa-san, please come to our new house in Okubo today'. Then I will say good-bye to this house and go to Okubo just as I would go to the university. That is all."

Lafcadio attended the *tatemae* roof-raising ceremony and watched the proceedings through his telescope. He observed the upward curve of the roof gable ends and ridges that preserved the memory of the nomadic tent. This architectural feature was just one more indication of a nomadic ancestry for the race and characteristics of impermanency. In Shinto tradition the builders chanted and clapped their hands as they raised the roof beam. His name, Koizumi Yakumo, was boldly written in Chinese characters on the main beam.

Even though his father's name was on the placard, eight-year-old Kazuo knew this was his mother's house. She was the one who designed and oversaw the construction of their refined, elegant home in Okubo. Setsu was no ordinary woman. She typified an intelligent, well-bred woman of the old samurai class, inheriting the traditions of duty and courage of the admirable military caste of Old Japan. Setsu also had a very caring nature and loved from the purest place in her heart…so pure and tender that sometimes it ached. But it was important to her that Lafcadio felt loved, supported, and surrounded by a true family in a safe environment.

On March 19, 1902, they moved to the house at 266 Nishi Okubo on the outskirts of town. The rickshaw driver picked Lafcadio up in the morning at the old house and returned him to the new house that evening. He found everything to his liking. The recently built house was in a quiet rural setting, with no Western buildings in sight. It was fashioned in pure Japanese style, with sliding paper doors that he so favored.

After the house was completed, the American paymaster, Mitchell McDonald visited the family. "You have built a fine house, everything included. How much did it cost? he asked.

"Why should I know how much my wife's house cost? I am an adopted son," Lafcadio replied. He was not being sarcastic or secretive. He'd never asked Setsu and honestly didn't know.

The padded floor mats were cream colored, the walls grey, and the sweet scent of early plum blossoms drifted in from the garden. They could hear birds singing in the bamboo groves behind the house. He often retreated into the wilderness of the garden. His spirit needed a place where nature had not been rearranged by the hand of man.

Lafcadio like to write about the consummate refinements of traditional Japanese gardening, commenting on the native concepts of landscape design and nature. He noted that the Japanese garden's artistic purpose was not to convey an ideal landscape, but to affect the viewer with the sensations of peace, joy, or solemnity that nature's scenery affects in one. Gardeners create not just an impression of beauty, but a mood in the soul.

Their gardener, who moved with them to the new property, transplanted the *musa basjoo* plants that reminded Lafcadio of the plantain trees of Martinique. He named that sunny garden corner the 'West Indies' after the small Caribbean island of Martinique and town of St. Pierre, 'Paris of the West Indies', with a rich cultural heritage and birthplace of Empress Josephine, Napoleon's wife. When Lafcadio arrived in 1887, the French painter Paul Gauguin also lived there, desperately trying to capture the unique colors and culture on his canvases.

The new Tokyo home's outdoor sanctuary had not only meticulously placed stones and cultivated plants, but also included many living creatures large and small - a small tortoise left by the previous owners, frogs, crickets, and his pet garden snake. He focused some of his writings on insects and beliefs that the dragonfly, firefly, and butterfly carried the spirits of humans and ancestral souls. The common people loved singing of fleeting, short-lived insects like the cricket. He praised the Japanese custom of enjoying the insect musicians, which was not known in the West, but had commonality with the high culture and literature of the Ancient Greeks.

Lafcadio was content in his new surroundings with his loving wife and family. As a dislocated person most of his life, he had been seeking a home and he found it in Japan. He'd learned something of love and duty that had never been a living reality. His peaceful home environment brought out serenity, replacing his previous survival mode. No one could understand his scars and even less of how he got them. He found a caring, consistent mother-figure in Setsu.

"It hurts my heart. It is too pleasant to last. My home will always have its atmosphere of thousands of years ago. But in the raw light outside, the changings are ugly and sad," he told Setsu. "The world of electricity, steam, and mathematics is blank and cold and void."

CHAPTER 34

Two months after moving to their new home in Okubo, Lafcadio opened his newspaper to tragic news from Martinique. On May 8, 1902, the Mt. Pelee volcano erupted with a catastrophic explosion about 8 am. A cloud of incandescent lava particles and searing hot gases moved at hurricane speed down the steep mountain slopes directly into the flourishing town of St. Pierre at 8:03 am. Escape from the city was virtually impossible. Over thirty thousand people died that day and the following weeks from pyroclastic flows and tsunamis. The Pelee explotion was one of the deadliest eruptions in recorded history.

Setsu found Lafcadio in the West Indies garden corner uncontrollably weeping. "Destroyed. Gone. It's all gone!" he cried.

"What is gone Yakumo?" she asked, thinking the gardener had removed some of his beloved plants.

"Saint Pierre, Sweet Wife. An earthly paradise and all her people have vanished with one searing breath from the volcanic mountain. Wiped off the face of the earth," he answered and collapsed on the pebble gravel path, sobbing.

"Papa, please don't cry. If the boys hear you, they will be frightened," she said as she helped him back to the house. She recalled how fondly her husband spoke of his life on the other side of the world in the city of Saint Pierre, West Indies. No matter how grand the Japanese sunsets, he would claim them inferior to those of Martinique.

Back in his office, Lafcadio sat dazed and only-half believing the shocking news. He opened the last letter he'd received from Saint Pierre. A spray of fern fell out of the envelope, labeled 'From the sunny garden'. Memories of little lemon-colored houses, swaying palms, silver streams, and turquoise seas flooded back. The self-sacrificing, loving friends like Cyrillia, Mimi and little Victoire, and small Jean to whom he'd been sending Oriental stamps---those who kept him alive at one time were all dead in a holocaust. How had it been for Leopold Arnoux, one of his Velvet Souls?

He wrote a few pages about his lost paradise: "But all this was---and is not!...Never again will sun or moon shine upon the streets of that city; never again will its ways be trodden; never again will its gardens bloom---except in dreams."

As he awakened each morning, a jolting bolt of memory of the deadly volcanic eruption attacked him. The loss of friends crept up and tore at his heart over and over. He felt the emptiness fresh each time when he acknowledged that they were truly gone. One doesn't just lose people once, you lose them every day for a lifetime.

It took a few dark days alone for him to emerge from the shock and deep grief of the loss. Such life tragedies could break a man. Nothing can protect one from that, and being alone won't either, because solitude can also break a person with its yearning. One needs to feel, to love. Being strong was the only choice he had. He finally understood that the earthly paradise he'd hope to visit again one day was lost forever.

He recalled from his childhood the Welsh word '*hireath*' that came close to what he was feeling – a deep longing for a place to which you can never return. Realizing that returning to the island had long ago become a shining improbability, he came to accept that the life he now had was enough. For the very first time in his lonely journey, he had a real home and family. He found his paradise in the faces of his loved ones and the local landscape.

His sadness became the kind that did not allow him to shed any more tears. He took the deep pain within him and gave it a place to reside that was not within his body. The body was not a coffin for pain to be buried in. He needed to put it elsewhere. He let it live in his art, in his writing.

Although Captain McDonald's military transfer was delayed two years, he was finally reassigned to San Francisco, California. Lafcadio dreaded the absence of such a great friend. On his last visit to the Okubo house, he roared in with farewell gifts for the children. His smartly uniformed figure filled the study as he sat in his designated rocker for a final chat. The exciting talk of travel got Lafcadio thinking that he should take Kazuo on the same journey across the Pacific to San Francisco or maybe England.

The best way for his son to polish his English language skills would be to live in an English-speaking country for a while. Lafcadio place a gifted photograph of McDonald next to the one of Elizabeth on his study wall.

His world was made lonely by the death, departure, or silence of friends. He began thinking about old friends in America like Ellwood Hendrick and Elizabeth Bisland Wetmore. Elizabeth married Charles W. Wetmore in 1891. Lafcadio heard it was a happy, prosperous marriage that allowed her to write, travel, and do what she pleased. He considered her ensconced in a world of money and fashion, far removed from him in both distance and values, so their communications languished. He was never happy with the letters he composed to her and so they found their way into the fireplace instead of the post.

Finally, he took up the pen to restore his overdue correspondence with both of Elizabeth and Ellwood. All his life he'd been an unsurpassed letter writer. In his correspondence he frankly told of his thoughts, fantasies, disappointments, failures, successes, and describes his inner and outer world. The lucky reader could feel the magic of color artistry and words. In being startlingly unreserved in his writings, he let his correspondent know that he trusted them not to betray his confidences.

Even after the long pause in their correspondence, Lafcadio heard from Elizabeth. He was moved when he got her letter and responded by writing, "Memories of handwriting must have been strong with me; for I recognized the writing before I opened the letter." From then on, they wrote frequently. Lafcadio also exchanged renewed affectionate remonstrance, opinions, and advice with Ellwood Hendrick on a regular basis. He wrote to him about Elizabeth:

"Admirable and wonderful she is; but I certainly cannot think of her as of human kin, altogether. That used to be my feeling in the South; in New York she became wonderfully sweet and bewitched me in a sort of way,--- made me think of the charming side, which with her is one of innumerable facets...
But, while eternally grateful to her, for instance in regard to Major McDonald, I would not like to be at her mercy if I were worth a pawn in her chess-play. I think she looks at men like pawns and has about as much real sense of kinship with them as a supernatural being would have. Then supernatural people are capricious. What would change her, perhaps! would be motherhood. But then again, I can only imagine motherhood for her as a sort of condescension to humanity,---just as one of the ancient goddesses

might have condescended to become incarnate,---just for an elegant recreation."

Lafcadio Hearn frantically wrote stories. In addition to teaching his full load at Tokyo Imperial University, in the time he spent away, he produced one book a year. Living in his own imagination, he provided fascinating vignettes about quaint lore and old customs, about exotic, monstrous, and odd subjects. His finest attribute lay in his retelling folktales in his personal, aesthetically descriptive style.

Writing and teaching were his callings, but also his burden because he had a family and large household to support just on his sole income. For their sake he "went to the treadmill", "the grind", and bore hardships such as he never had when he was single. "I should rather be teaching in a Buddhist or a country school; and the prospects are that I shall be squeezed out in government service. If I didn't belong to other and happier lives than my own, I think I should like to become a monk."

He was becoming oblivious to everything and everyone around him. Seated at his tall desk, he would work away at his manuscript, with his head twisted so his one very near-sighted eye was mere inches from the paper. He would write all night until the lantern sputtered out. When his scratchy pen was moving rapidly over sheet after sheet of paper, he became totally absorbed - seeing, hearing, and feeling nothing else. He was deaf to all sounds, even voices near him.

Setsu came into his study early one morning and exclaimed, "The floor around your desk is covered with blood engorged mosquitoes, rolling fat like little red beans! Your arms are covered in red welts. Don't they itch?"

"I guess I was so focused I never felt the bites."

He was often exhausted and remote even to his own family. Setsu and Kazuo would sometimes find him pacing around the house veranda or garden, weeping or crying out. He couldn't fully explain to them or himself why he was so obsessed or felt such anxiety. They tried to soothe him and bring him back to reality, sometimes without success.

"Don't worry," Setsu consoled her son, "Your father's episode will soon pass. Eventually every storm runs out of rain."

Lafcadio pushed away anything that distracted him from his writings. He did not participate in the practical running of the household, purchases, maintenance or seasonal repairs, and the comings and goings of tradespeople. Occasionally a pilgrim, worker, shopkeeper, or beggar who came to the house for charity or business got his attention long enough to ask them questions---the answers which often turned into stories, anecdotes, or a point of view in his writings. His repeated democratic or folk standard theme was that the real Japan, the true Japan, was found in the common people, not in the rich and powerful. He spoke of his individual pieces as sketches.

At times Lafcadio sent Setsu to browse bookstalls in the Kanda section for old storybooks. She would read the stories and retell them to him. He would take the skeleton of tales and rework them, adding, subtracting, rearranging to largely create his own version from what he had heard. He sent her to Kabuki and other types of theater. When she returned, he wanted her to carefully relate the plots and characters for his research. Some of the tales were very old, known by most Japanese in one form or another. He used the retelling *saiwa* of traditional stories as a vehicle for posing questions about humanity, for exploring the essence of the spirit and soul, and questioning how we should live.

Other stories Lafcadio gleaned from modern sources like current newspaper articles. For example, "The Legend of Yurei-Daki", in which a mother tempted vengeance by stealing the money box from a temple to feed her family. Then ironically the guardian spirit of the shrine took her child's life. He pulled the piercing supernatural into modern times. He believed that every ghost story contained a hidden truth.

The heart of each story was love, hate, jealousy, fear, or pity. Primary terror never existed in a void, nor did he use it just to titillate the nerves like he'd done in his sensational newspaper articles in Cincinnati. Lafcadio's ghost stories demonstrated the core humanity of those unfortunate souls who encountered visitations by spirits. He retold tales of those who'd died and returned in a new reality, often more vibrant, beautiful, and young than they ever were when they were alive in this world. It helped him deal with his own history of hauntings to write about them objectively and at times even humorously.

In the middle of the tale, "The Eternal Haunter", he lets his personal echoes show: "Perhaps---for it happens to some of us---you may have seen this haunter, in dreams of the night, even during childhood. Then, of course, you could know the beautiful shape bending above your rest: possibly you thought her to be an angel...Once that you have seen her, she will never cease to visit you. And this haunting,---ineffably sweet, inexplicably sad,---may fill you with rash desire to wander over the world in search of somebody like her. But however long and far you wander, never will you find that somebody."

He avoided going out of his home or taking trips. Until his friend was reassigned to the States, he would make exceptions to see McDonald in Yokohama. Lafcadio described his "dear Paymaster" as "true as steel" and "no slouch in business" and "one who has more electric energy in him than five average John Bulls." Lafcadio would occasionally visit McDonald at his Grand Hotel.

He wrote thank you notes exclaiming, "That whiskey! Those cigars! That wonderful beefsteak!" But then regret it and refer to his outing as "one more nail in my literary coffin every time I go down."

After visiting open port cities like Yokohama, he complained that "mechanical industrialization and its vices and its ugliness are invading and destroy all things. The plague of machinery is upon the world and is transforming the human mind."

At home Lafcadio was moderate, but particular in his habits. He wore comfortable Japanese clothes when not in public. Other than typical Japanese foods, he relished a thick, well-done beefsteak, and his favorite drink was orange-squash and the best French brand claret, of which he only drank no more than two glasses in an evening. He was an epicure in tobacco, keeping himself supplied with Havana cigars and the best tobaccos. He smoked the latter with fine Japanese pipes. He kept almost a hundred different style pipes of various shapes and workmanship in boxes and cases of his own design.

Lafcadio's reserved seclusion was treated as a mystery and made him an object of curiosity and a growing legend to the public. Stories about his prestige as a university professor, his mastery of Japanese subjects, and admiration for his literary works were printed in magazine articles in America and Europe. He was often misunderstood by the reading public, especially with regard to his character and religious persuasion. He shunned this general interest in his person, whether malicious or friendly. He just wanted to protect his privacy in order to write, support his family, and leave a legacy. If longing to produce quality work was madness, then no serious writer could be considered sane.

At home, he refused visitors and rejected overtures from academic colleagues, admirers who'd read his books, representatives of literary societies, and such. He said, "Attentions numb, paralyze, destroy every vestige of inspiration." His boundaries weren't created to offend anyone. They were created to protect his work.

He wrote a letter to Ernest Fenollosa (American art historian, poet, curator, professor at Tokyo University) that expresses his sentiments on maintaining his privacy to work:

"My Dear Professor, I have been meditating, and after meditation I came to the conclusion not to visit your charming new home again. I suppose I am a beast and an ape; but I nevertheless hope to make you understand.

"The situation makes me think of Beranger's burthen, '*Vive nos amis les ennimis*!' 'My friends are much more dangerous than my enemies'. These latter, with infinite subtlety, spin webs to keep me out of places where I hate to go,---and tell stories of me to people whom it would be vanity and vexation to meet; and they help me so much by their unconscious aid that I almost love them. They help me maintain the isolation indispensable to quiet regularity of work, and the solitude which is absolutely essential to thinking upon such subjects as I am now engaged on. Blessed be my enemies, and forever honored all them that hate me.

"But my friends!---ah! My friends! They speak so beautifully of my work; they believe in it; they say they want more of it, and yet they would destroy it! They do not know what it costs, and they would break the wings and scatter the feather dust, even as a child that only wanted to caress the butterfly. And they speak of communion and converse and sympathy and friendship,---all of which are indeed precious things to others, but mortally deadly to me,---representing the breaking up of habits of industry, and the sin of disobedience.

"And they say, 'Only a day, just an afternoon or evening.' But each of them say this thing. And the sum of days in these holidays, the days inevitable are somewhat more than a week in addition. A week of work dropped forever in the Abyss of what might have been! Therefore, where a visit, and the forced labor of the university, are made by distance even as one and the same thing.

"Alas, I can afford friends only on paper. I can occasionally write,---I can get letters that give me joy, but visiting is out of the possible. I must not even think about other people's kind words and kind faces, but work, work, work...Blessed again I say, are those who don't like me for they do not fill my memory with thoughts and wishes, contrary to the purpose of the eons and eternities!

"When a day passes in which I have not written, much is my torment. Enjoyment is not for me,---excepting in the completion of work. But I have not been the loser by my visits to you both---did I not get that wonderful story? And so I have given you more time than any other person or persons in Tokyo. But now,---through the seasons---I must again disappear. Perhaps *le jeu ne vaudra pas la chandelle*, the game is not worth the candle; nevertheless I have some faith as to ultimate results. Faithfully, with every grateful and kindly sentiment, L. Hearn."

Lafcadio was willing to accept the reputation of being antisocial and ungrateful, if it meant he could have private time to write and better serve his enduring and increasing public audience of readers. It was due to his self-imposed isolation and frenetic writing that the world received his best works. This shy, idiosyncratic little man proved to be one of the world's foremost collectors of exotic impressions and exotic lore. His books became classics in Japan and internationally.

To avoid the haunts of visitors, he isolated himself. He said, "I suppose you must know, or feel, that anyone who wishes and resolves to be purely himself, must be isolated in all countries. The world's fight is to prevent men from being themselves, to mold them into the fashion of the day, deck them with a swallow-tail coat, and educate them to waste life and thought in the cultivation of conventions. Some very clever men are able to make a compromise, at great cost of self-worth but the best men never obey and are therefore left alone." Hearn did not leave the world of his fellow men, he endeavored to leave the world of affectation and conventionalism, and enter into another of simplicity and sincerity.

Lafcadio's insane drive to forgo society and constantly write became more urgent for him in the last weeks of 1902. During an attack of advanced bronchitis, he suffered dangerous hemorrhaging from a burst blood vessel in his throat. His critical condition was problematic. He was bedridden for weeks and forbidden to talk above a whisper.

In Lafcadio's semi conscious delirium, he was tormented by fears of death and lack of security for his family. Would he live until summer when Setsu would give birth to their fourth child? Would that child know its father? What about all the books he had yet to read and write? What about Kazuo's education?

As soon as Lafcadio was strong enough to be propped up in his bed, he had Kazuo bring his schoolbooks into the sickroom for lessons. He stressed how essential reading was for those who sought to rise above the ordinary. They added geography and arithmetic to his English courses. He fretted that too much time had been lost.

He recovered slowly from his general physical collapse and was finally allowed by the doctor to return to his classroom and private study, if he worked at a reduced pace. In spite of his ill health, character flaws, and social awkwardness, Lafcadio continued to write captivating stories to try and preserve Japan's vanishing culture. He loved Japan and was a friend of the people. Making the Japanese world visible gave him a feeling of accomplishment. His folktales can be read as a eulogy for a country that was losing its heritage as it embraced modernism. It seemed to be Lafcadio's pattern to arrive at a place just in time to see what he loved about it disappear

CHAPTER 35

The bronchitis and burst blood vessel in his throat were not the only health issues Lafcadio faced. He experienced reoccurring but mild outbreaks of malaria from his years in New Orleans and Martinique. Examinations during these illnesses revealed that he had a serious case of hardening of the arteries. He forbad Doctor Kizawa from sharing this diagnosis with his wife or family.

Since Lafcadio's voice was failing, a large couch shell was placed on the table in the study so he could signal when he needed tea or wished charcoal fire for his pipe. It pleased him, saying, "What a funny noise! It sounds so well because I still have strong lungs." It was fun for him to make the big "po-wo" noise that vibrated throughout the house. Lafcadio insisted the house be kept totally quiet, no one making a sound when he worked, but then would come the extraordinary roar of his couch shell. There were always three or four rare shells of various shapes and colors on his desk. Looking at the shells and thinking of the sea seemed to calm his restless feelings.

During the last two years Lafcadio had visibly aged. He looked like someone who subsisted on green tea and worry. Even McDonald noticed his friend's frailty to the point that before he left Japan, he came up to Tokyo rather than have Lafcadio make the trip to him.

When McDonald visited, the household could hear them laughing in the office study. Lafcadio had two ways of laughing. One was dainty feminine and the other was powerful uproarious, disregardful of everything. When they heard this excited hearty laugh, the whole family couldn't help but join in. Laughing with those he loved, those he trusted, and who made his world seem brighter, healed him in ways that he didn't know he needed.

In the past when he'd say things like "I need to teach my sons as quickly as I can. Time is running out", Captain McDonald would ridicule the pessimistic remarks and proclaim, 'Have no fear! I am standing by! McDonald is at hand!' Now he saw in his frail friend the reason behind the rush.

Kazuo began accompanying his nearly blind father on outings if he went far from home. After Lafcadio was almost run over by a train, he told his son, "You are my eyes, Kajio. Whenever you see anything unusual, you must tell me so I can look at it too." Young Kazuo watched for anything that might entertain or interest his father - a strange shrine offering; a peculiar species of plant; crabs on the beach; or carved stone Buddha.

"To the child, the world is blue and green; to the old man, grey - both are right," he told Setsu.

His wife and children gave him emotional stability to appreciate the smaller things in life. Setsu laughed when she remembered how she and the boys would report their finding a mound of ants, frogs on hedges, early to bloom cherry blossoms, or how a young bamboo sprout raised its head from the earth. The family didn't worship nature, they honored it. Lafcadio loved to be outdoors.

He admired but pitied the dwarf bonsai plants. He would often free caged birds or insects and replanted potted greenery into open garden soil. Whenever the children would catch birds or insects, he would instruct them, "Be very careful not to injure their delicate wings and legs, and take very good care of them. Before the sun goes down, let them out. These poor creatures otherwise would not know how to find a place to hide from their enemies. Even flies; don't kill them in a cruel way."

One day when Lafcadio was working in his study, a persistence fly walked over his manuscript, buzzed his head, and generally bothered him. He caught it gently between his palms several times, but it always got away. "No one that has such luck in escaping death ought to be killed, not even a fly." He opened the window, saying, "*Sayonara* (goodbye), don't come again," and let it go.

"Matters like these were of great importance in our household. Nature provided a great delight for my husband," said Setsu. "He was pleased innocently. I tried to please him with such topics with all my heart. Perhaps if anyone happened to witness, it would have seemed ridiculous. Frogs, ants, butterflies, bamboo sprouts, morning glory---they were all the best friends to my husband." Apart from completing stories for his books, Lafcadio's greatest joys were watching nature, and his children grow up and develop unique personalities.

He wrote to Elizabeth about Kazuo, "He naturally likes what is delicate, clean, refined, and kindly,---and he naturally shrinks from whatever is course and selfish. I must do all I can to feed the tiny light, and give it a chance to prove what it is worth. It is ME, in another birth, with renewed forces given by a strange and charming blood from the Period of the Gods."

At age fifty-two, Lafcadio found that the hard years on the streets of London, New York, Cincinnati, and New Orleans had taken their toll. He walked slowly, his back stooped making his 5'3" height seem even shorter than usual. He was overweight and winded by the slightest effort. His thick, coarse hair and ragged mustache had turned white. In a note to Watkin he said, "I'm getting down the shady side of the hill, and the horizon before me is already darkening and the winds blowing out of it cold."

Facing anti-foreigner verbal and physical attacks in the streets had become a norm. He could never be Japanese in features or in language. A variant of the sentiment was spreading at Tokyo Imperial University. He was one of the few foreigners left in any educational institution in the whole empire. Ten years before, all the noted schools and university had full staffs of European and American teachers, but since the war with China the Japanese had become so chauvinistic that they turned out all the foreign professors from their schools and foreign officers from their army. Unfriendly forces gathered against him.

His teaching contract was up for renewal in March 1903. He was known as a distinguished man of letters, so while he did not think the university authorities would fire him outright, he dreaded that with a drastic pay cut he'd have to find other employment to supplement his income. If there were problems, he figured he'd worked six and a half years of service, enough to be eligible for a nine-month sabbatical leave with pay. He planned to use that earned break to write full time. Through his position as lecturer in English literature at Tokyo University between 1896 and 1903, he had a crucial influence on an entire generation of Japan's literary elite.

Yet, with his advocate and good friend Dr. Toyama dead, the new administrator was openly antagonistic. With a venomous gaze, he told Lafcadio, "Since you are a Japanese citizen, you should be paid no more than native instructors". Then he threw an ugly remark at him, "If you cannot live upon the reduced salary, you should learn, like any other Japanese, to eat rice."

He came home from the unfriendly and disrespectful Tokyo University encounter and said to Setsu, "Japan does not want me anymore...simplicity, kindness, ghosts, smiles...the old-fashioned individual who loves these things is not wanted."

He feared the new school administrators thought of his literary work as setting down the chronicle of a vanishing world, of him as being a two-bit collector of esoterica, a marginal man of letters with a quirky name and a quarrelsome streak.

In breach of normal rules, an intrusion of a curious English traveler into his classroom during a lecture was permitted by the university administration. Lafcadio's suspicious imagination blew the incident all out of proportion. He saw it as an insult and slight by the school authorities in their drive to get rid of him. His teaching career was often in jeopardy because of intrigues within the Ministry of Education, so that at times he hated and ranted against the Japanese government.

When his teaching contract came up for renewal, as Lafcadio feared, the terms were at the greatly reduced salary. Therefore, he asked for leave under his entitled sabbatical year of vacation. They brusquely announced that his earned paid leave was refused.

"Government, fire, and water know nothing of mercy", he mused aloud to Setsu and friends. The administrators were inflexible. Lafcadio would not beg and refused to yield ground on the issues of salary and sabbatical. He returned their unacceptable contract unsigned.

As soon as he arrived home that afternoon, filled with violent rage, he went to his study and wrote a scathing venomous letter of resignation. It was such that its acceptance was immediate. The university merely announced that Lafcadio Hearn/Koizumi Yakumo was no longer a member of the university faculty.

Lafcadio's dismissal brought indignant protests from his students and colleagues. They bristled over his treatment, "How could the most prestigious university in Japan have severed connections to the most distinguished Western writer of Japan?"

Tokyo newspapers discussed various controversial accounts of the firing incident. The simplest and most blunt answers came down to nationalism and money. His replacement was a Japanese novelist and lecturer, Soseki Natsume, who was hired at a fraction of Lafcadio's salary. While he shied away from the praise and support that rallied around him, he believed the government-run university deserved the rebuke it was receiving.

His students, who loved him, furiously organized agitation among the student body. When he received a delegation of students at his home, he asked them not to press the issue or exert their considerable lever of power in his case. He told them he would never forget their sympathy, and he even cried. He felt the real index of civilization was when people were kinder than they needed to be.

Professor Ume and other friendly instructors visited Lafcadio to console him and inquire if the breach could be mended. He was too distraught and indignant to discuss the incident with them. The loss of his position at Tokyo University was a hammer-blow to the sensitive educator.

He felt Japanese bureaucrats had "no soul…no sentiment of light, of infinity". He found it hard to make peace with the rage in his soul. The world was too rude and too loud for his quiet soul. He was exhausted from fighting the system. Many fears are born of fatigue and frustration. Once alone, the old maddening sense of persecution and mental torture tore at him until he fell ill.

In his earlier renewed correspondence with Elizabeth Bisland Wetmore he'd expressed uneasiness about his position at the university and that he wanted to take Kazuo to the United States to begin his Western education. He asked her to look about for some kind of position for him in America. He'd thought this was how he would use his sabbatical year. Whatever position he accepted must include his boy, because he couldn't be separated from him. "If anything happened to Kajio, the sun would go out." She and Ellwood Hendrick both answered his letters immediately and promised all possible assistance.

He began to think about seeing his old friends Ellwood and Elizabeth in particular. "Only to see you again even for a moment---to hear you speak in some one of the myriad voices, would be such a memory for me. And you would let me walk about gently touching things."

CHAPTER 36

Lafcadio completed his books *Kotto* and *Kwaidan*, using folklore and traditional tales as their basis. They were literature, folktales retold (*saiwa*). *Kwaidan* was first published in America for the stimulation of western fantasies regarding Japan. He had transcribed Japanese medieval and ancient ghost stories into an eclectic hybrid of European, Anglo-Irish, American, French, and Edo tradition ghost stories. He unlocked and shared cultural treasures.

His telling of the *Kwaidan* tales to Western readers was later retranslated back to Japanese. The first anthology of Lafcadio's writings were put into Japanese by Otani Masanobu and Ochiai Teisaburo and published in Tokyo by Daiichi Shobo in 1930-1932. At present those old stories are better known in Japan than the English originals are in the West.

Lafcadio felt the tales were cross-cultural and said, "There is truth in *Kwaidan*." Some of the universal truths he referred to were: Keep your promises; Don't break the laws of nature; A mother's love is stronger than death; and Human curiosity cannot be stopped.

In addition to his collections of stories of the supernatural, Lafcadio was one of the first Westerners to read and appreciate *haiku*. The *haiku* poetic form consists of three lines, with five syllables in the first line, seven in the second and five in the third. One of his favorites was classic *haiku* poet Matsuo Basho's, '*fu-ru-i-ke-ya (5) ka-wa-zu to-bi-ko-mu (7) mi-zu-no-o-to (5)* Translated: old pond, frog leaps in, water's sound.' Another was '*hatsu shigure saru mo komino o hoshige nari* --- the first cold shower even the monkey seems to want a little coat of straw.' Basho was the most famous poet of the Edo period, and the greatest master of the form known as haiku. Verses are a playful game of wit in the form of sublime poetry. Even before Lafcadio discovered *haiku* as a form of poetry, his close awareness of nature and vivid descriptions possessed the *haiku* spirit.

Lafcadio may have been among the first to write about *haiku* as an important literary form that could help the Western world understand something of the soul of the Japanese. He translated *haiku*, that he called *hokku* with understanding and respect. It was a way to stir the imagination without satisfying it, by leaving something unsaid. Lafcadio especially liked that this form of short poem often had an unexpected twist revealed at the end.

He praised the *haiku*'s unique way of connecting people to natural objects or creatures and the simple pleasure of existence. He saw that most *haiku* moments were based on personal experiences and timeless feelings of enlightenment as the environment and the poet's nature are unified.

Japanese poets felt and rejoiced in the beauty of the natural world. With a few well-chosen words, the composers could evoke an image or mood to revive an emotion or sensation. Lafcadio wrote about his magic moments of *ambedo*, which was a kind of melancholic trance in which he became completely absorbed in vivid sensory details, like tall trees leaning in the wind, clouds of cream swirling in his coffee, or raindrops sliding down the window of his office. He could briefly soak in the experience of being alive, an act that was done purely for its own sake. Times and sights like those, combined with a love and facility for language, inspired him to write a number of descriptive passages that demonstrated the sensitive perceptions of a *haiku* poet.

Lafcadio composed *haiku* word-picture poems himself about things that delighted or moved him. It was another way for him to use language as a superb musical instrument. He experimented with it, catching sound combinations, subtle fancies, tricks and turns of phrases. His writings and poems were musically harmonious and sonorous. At times they swelled to a great crescendo, but always clear and resonant to the reader.

He wrote that the best *haiku* are "like a single stroke of a temple-bell, the perfect short poem should set murmuring and undulating, in the mind of the hearer, many a ghostly after-tone of long duration."

In *A Japanese Miscellany* (1901) after he'd translated twenty-eight dragonfly *haiku*, he said, "These compositions help us to understand something of the soul of the elder Japan, the people who could find delight, century after century, in watching the ways of insects, and in making such verses about them, must have comprehended, better than we, the simple pleasure of existence. They could feel the beauty of the world without its sorrow, and rejoice in the beauty, much after the manner of inquisitive and happy children."

Sometimes in Lafcadio's translations he attempted to explain, describe, or add equivalent words suggested by the Japanese writer. He didn't translate poems literally to make sure his English readers would realize the contrast and to elaborate on the musical rhythm of the piece. When he trusted his Western readers and kept translations simple and short, he captured the elusive poetry of the original, as he does in… "*Hiatari no, Dote ya hinemosu, Tombo tobu*….Over the sunlit bank, all day long, the dragonflies flit to and fro." Several of his translations of *haiku* poetry manuscripts were sent to be published.

CHAPTER 37

Lafcadio's tenth Japanese book was the final in a series he'd outlined after he finished *Glimpses*. He was then free to prepare for a working trip to the United States. He received a letter from Elizabeth that she'd interested President Schurman of Cornell University in Lafcadio giving a set of formal lectures about Japan. If he was willing to accept the engagement, he needed to outline a lecture course.

Lafcadio was elated, then struck by moments of inadequacy and doubt. He wrote to Captain McDonald: "I am quite sure that I do not know anything about Japanese art, literature, or ethnology, or politics, or history...At present I have no acquaintance even with the Japanese language. I have held the chair of English Literature here for nearly seven years, by setting all canons at defiance, and attempting to teach only the emotional side of literature, in its relations to modern thought, playing with philosophy, as a child can play with the great sea."

After a while he regained his confidence and wrote, "What I could do would be about thus: I could attempt a series of lectures upon Japanese topics---dealing incidentally with psychology, religious social, and artistic impressions, so as to produce in the minds of my hearers an idea of Japan different from that which is given in books. Something, perhaps, in the manner of Mr. Lowell's *Soul of the Far East* (incomparably the greatest of all books on Japan, and the deepest)---but from a different point of view. What I could not do would to put myself forward as an authority upon Japanese history, or any special Japanese subject. The value of my lectures would depend altogether upon suggestiveness, not upon any crystallizations of fact."

Writing the series of lectures for Cornell University was a new kind of mental exercise for Lafcadio. He researched, read, studied, and organized his notes, coming to new conclusions never thought of before by him. He was planning to leave for America the next summer and wanted all his lectures written out in full. He felt a great responsibility as an interpreter of Japan to the West…a bridge between East and West.

As long as the Japanese government and university were controlled by the religious-political combination, he could no longer hold a position anywhere in Japan. He anxiously waited for Cornell's answer. At last, a letter arrived from Elizabeth. His heart was pounding as he opened it. The news was good. President Schurman was satisfied with the lectures he had proposed and offered him twenty-five hundred US dollars for the series.

He wrote Elizabeth back: "It was a shock to receive your beautiful letter because I had waited so long and anxiously,---fearing that the last gleam of hope in my Eastern horizon had been extinguished. It would be of no use whatever to tell you half my doubts and fears---they made the coming of your letter an almost terrible event."

He told her how being "treated very cruelly by the Japanese government and forced out of the service" had made him ill. His throat might make lecturing impossible, and he might have to find other work. He could come in the fall, but no longer planned to bring Kazuo until it was clear how things would work out. He reassured her that everything was all right and he was recuperating and working on his lectures and other writing.

"You cannot imagine how hungry and thirsty I have become to see you again,---or how much afraid I feel at times that I may not see you," he confided to Elizabeth.

In early 1903 Lafcadio received word from President Schurman of Cornell that the lecture series he had been asked to present would have to be cancelled. All classes, activities, and routine expenditures of Cornell were curtailed because of an outbreak of typhoid fever on campus. University funds would be seriously depleted for some time. The deal folded like a painted fan.

At first Lafcadio was shocked and afraid after his two losses of job and health. He shared with Elizabeth about his deep disappointment and how the devastating news hit him. But when he surveyed his finances, he found that royalty income from his published works had accelerated. Not to waste all the efforts he'd put into the lecture series, he resolved to turn this material into a book.

He wrote to Elizabeth: "I am sorry for my dismal letter of the other day. I feel today much braver and think I can fight it out here in Japan...For the present, I think that I shall simply sit down, and work as hard as Zola...You will hear from me in print."

He assured her that he was safe and sound and asked her not to be disturbed by the Cornell action, even though some called it a breach of contract. She and Hendrick searched for other employment for him, corresponding with Johns Hopkins, Stanford University, Vassar, and Lowell Institute. In any case, he wouldn't be able travel to America until the following spring because he wanted to be home for the birth of his fourth child and its first crucial months of life.

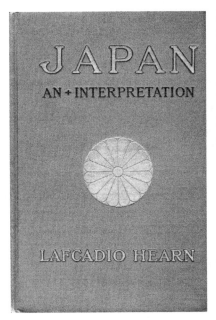

Lafcadio spent the next several months living almost entirely for his work. As he revised and polished his Cornell lecture notes, his confidence in them grew. His completed book was titled *Japan: An Attempt at Interpretation*. He was presenting Japan in a broad outline against the background of her ancient Shinto faith.

"Stated in the simplest possible form, the peculiar element of truth in Shinto is the belief that the world of the living is directly governed by the world of the dead. There is an intimate sense of relationship between the visible and invisible worlds. All the dead become deities of varying power and dignity and every impulse or act of man is influenced by of them." Ancestral memory and karma were accepted without question. He explored the mental history of the Japanese, pointing out that the basis of their mentality exists in their faith in ancestors. The loyalty toward the emperor was closely related to their gratitude and faith for ancestors.

He attempted to decipher the outward strangeness of all things Japanese and place the nation and its people in a larger historical context. He wrote about what he saw, what he heard, and what resonated in his heart. Lafcadio explored the difficulty of comprehending what underlies the surface of Japanese life.

He was one of the first great interpreters of Japanese culture for Western readers. As a romantic folklorist, he recorded Japan's lost buried past that they were loath to expose or recognize until, once safely modernized, they could again take up their bruised nostalgia. His long residence in Japan, personal insight and sympathy, clear writing style, keen intellect, and poetic imagination ensure him a place in his adopted land's literary circle.

The Japan study was in part a reversal of his early conclusions. Rather than portray the Japanese as free and spontaneous, he exhibited them now as disciplined and determined through hundreds of years of the societal organization of habits and instincts. "As a result, the highly civilized man can endure incomparably more than the savage, whether or moral or physical strain. Being better able to control himself under all circumstances, he has a great advantage over the savage."

Even after interactions with the West, the Japanese character and traditions remained fundamentally the same. In his research on international cultures, he found one truth - the truth of a relation subsisting between civilizations and their religions. He had experienced that the Japanese people were generally better than their religion and laws asked them to be. In its modernization movement "Japan must develop her own soul, she cannot borrow another."

Since Lafcadio sprang from diverse cultural parental origins and his life in many countries was full of rich cross-cultural experiences, he developed a rare open-mindedness. His morals and values were not limited by Western-centric ideas or Judeo-Christian religion. He was an iconoclast who challenged conventions and norms. His respect for diversity and philosophy of tolerance influenced readers, students, and others around him at the time and into the future.

His openness allowed him to change his impressions back and forth and contradict himself as necessary. This ambiguous alternately loving and hating his chosen country, was an ingrained characteristic of Lafcadio, no different than his early infatuation to disillusionment with other places in which he lived. His life was ruled by paradoxes. Several times in his life he'd fled from modernization. He was looking for a civilization that could challenge and match Western civilization and yet one that allowed him space to explore his true self.

He never completely altered his first bewitched enchantment with Japan, but his experiences swung him toward realism rather than idealism. He acknowledged his personal feelings when he wrote, "What is there, finally, to love in Japan except what is passing away?" His enchantment with the Japanese gave way on occasion when he contrasted country's newfound machine age prosperity to his idealized vision of a picturesque Japan that embodied simplicity and cultural purity that modernization had laid waste. It was a love-hate relationship.

In *Self Reliance*, Ralph Waldo Emerson said, "A foolish consistency is the hobgoblin of little minds, adored by statesmen and philosophers and divines. With consistency a great soul has simply nothing to do. Speak what you think now in hard words, and tomorrow speak what tomorrow thinks in hard words again, though it contradicts everything you said today. Ah, so you shall be sure to be misunderstood. Is it so bad to be misunderstood? Pythagoras was misunderstood, and Socrates, and Jesus, and Luther, and Copernicus, and Galileo, and Newton, and every pure and wise spirit that ever took flesh. To be great is to be misunderstood."

In Japan, Lafcadio concluded that all good things were not the result of choice, but good came from the propriety of religious and civil practices, subtle adjustments of individual to individual, of people adapting to society, and the delicate beauty of dress, manners, crafts. He showed the great price paid for a great good. It was not an argumentative book; it left it up to the reader to debate the mixture of good and bad in Japanese cultural patterns.

Utamaro, Hiroshige, Korin, Hokusai, and *From the Eastern Sea* author Yone Noguchi described Lafcadio Hearn as a prophet who was no longer bound by the prejudice of Western centrism. As a free thinker, Lafcadio wrote with great insight about the essence of Meiji era Japan. He made proposals for the country's future: National character and natural disasters; Symbiosis with nature; Education of the imagination; Accepting nature as it is; and Truth in tales of the supernatural. He addressed the future of the Far East in a lecture where he said, "Those who can survive are the ones who can coexist with nature and live a simple life." His themes and conclusions are relevant over a hundred years later. In a way, his written words touched people that his physical hands never would---like a ghost.

The one-eyed Hearn couldn't see across the room, but he saw what was happening to his enchanted Japan. "Evil winds from the West are blowing over and the magical atmosphere, alas! Is shrinking away before them…never again to appear save in pictures and poems and dreams…

CHAPTER 38

Setsu gave birth to their fourth child, Suzuko, a healthy little girl in autumn of 1903. Lafcadio felt a sad tenderness when his mother-in-law laid the baby girl in his arms. He knew that at fifty-three, with failing health, he probably wouldn't see her through her childhood. The only security he could provide would be enough money for her care by others. He was determined to provide a buffer between his children and the cruel world that stood ready to devour young victims. "There are love and fear in my heart," he said, looking at her.

"I have to earn all the money I can! There's no time to waste. I can't live many more years," he'd tell Setsu. She didn't let his premonitions of death disturb her outwardly. She chalked it up to another one of his dream world ideas. He got that way when he was overworked.

"Don't say such things!" she scolded. "It only makes your family sad. Be especially careful in front of Kazuo because he grieves deeply when you go on this way. Yakumo, talk of death is foolish. Forget about it, be happy."

Lafcadio felt the protection of money would give them no more problems in life than usual. But he feared that his introspective, mixed-blood, first-born Kazuo, needed more help to face the world. He saw education and usable knowledge as a way to safeguard all his children. From their earliest years his sons had been home-schooled in English, Japanese, and other worldly topics. English lessons consisted of songs, poems, fairy tales, Aesop's Fables, and Grecian gods' stories, plus selections from Macmillan's New Literary Reader Books and eight volumes of Baldwin's Readers.

Lafcadio started Kazuo reading parts of the Old Testament out of a fine, leather-bound Bible, telling him, "It's not necessary to become a Christian, but one should read the Bible at least once." When asked why he made his son read the Bible, Lafcadio smiled and said, "It's the most famous religious book. I am a good friend of Christ's and I am sure Christ would say "Thank you" to me. There are many supposed to be Christians who are only outwardly so, only so in appearance, making a show of the cross and bragging about their pure heart. Such are malicious Christians, and they are all over the world. One like me, though very critical, viewing from a different angle, would be called a heretic by these hypocrites---but He would love me more than all these people, I think." One day he said to his son, "Buddha, Confucius, Christ---all were of their time and place, and though different, were in the same spirit. They were friends."

Lafcadio did not claim to be either a Shintoist or Buddhist. He had no religion. He was an agnostic and firm believer in Herbert Spencer's evolution. As a poet he saw the emotional side of scientific evolution in Buddhism and Shintoism. He found the doctrines quaint, beautiful symbols wherein he could clothe his favorite theories.

Hearn said that in *Kokoru* he wrote "a mingling of Buddhist and Shinto thought with English and French psychology---they do not simply mix well, they absolutely unite, like chemical elements, rush together with a shock." He saw the Western idea of individuality, which lead only to selfishness, as an enemy of human progress. He flanked tenets of Buddhism and Shintoism within strange and weird stories, like medicine taken with sugar, to get Western readers to study beautiful truths and thoughts, and to leave the detestable struggle for profits and material possessions. He knew he had to pass on his love of acquiring knowledge to the world and to his children.

He enrolled Iwao in Okubo elementary school in spring of 1903, but hesitated enrolling the more European looking, sensitive Kazuo. Setsu argued that their first son should have some formal Japanese education. Dr. Kizawa suggested the best private school in Tokyo. But when Lafcadio found out it was a Roman Catholic school, he declared he'd cut off his son's head before he'd send him there.

In April, 1904, ten-year-old Kazuo was finally enrolled in public school with his brother. Socializing with all sorts of children might better prepare him for the future, Setsu and Lafcadio rationalized. His father's teachings were so excellent that Kazuo found the Japanese school lessons easy. He was promoted from fourth to fifth year at the end of his second term.

At home in the afternoons and even on vacation the rigorous English lessons were held on schedule. Education at home was earnest and severe. He would tell MacDonald and others, "It is only necessary for a man to give his sons education enough to start them out in life; after that, they should look after themselves. It is not necessary to leave any fortune. But as for his wife and daughter, it is necessary to make provision for them."

Tension between Lafcadio and Kazuo in the home classroom continued. Being scolded loudly, Kazuo ended up weeping most days. When he appeared with a tear-stained face, the boy's grandmother would always say, "*Yere yare*-poor creature, your lesson was bad again?" She advised him to ask Tenjin-sama, the deified scholar, to make his memory better and improve his studies. This only made him more upset.

Lighthearted Iwao was a different story. He found humor and laughter in most situations, even punishment. He laughed as much as Kazuo wept. He thought English words sounded funny and would repeat them back with his own mocking twist added. "You are a rude boy! A queer little child!" Lafcadio would scold as he swatted the irrepressible youngster. At school Iwao received good grades despite his obvious favoritism toward sports and extra-curricular activities.

Each year Lafcadio took flight from modernity and Westernization to vacation with his family in the small fishing village of Yaizu in Shizuoka Prefecture. He was happiest in such unsophisticated places. He felt a subconscious connection to seaside waterfronts. Perhaps it was his birthplace by the Ionian Sea, summer vacations at his great-aunt's home in Tramore, Waterford, Ireland, or swimming in Louisiana or Martinique. The sounds of the surf and treading mysterious deep waters brought him comfort.

He delighted in the simplicity of daily life and the open-hearted warmth of the local Yaizu people. It was out of the way so no foreigners or city people ever came there, giving Lafcadio the seclusion and privacy he needed. No disagreeable visitors or reporters came there from Tokyo or Yokohama.

The family stayed in Yamaguchi Otokichi's two-storied, board-roof house. It had three rooms upstairs and three downstairs. In front was a fish shop and eaves hung with straw sandals and dried fish. Lafcadio rented the entire upstairs. The low ceiling room walls were pasted with old newspapers or Japanese color prints. The air was full of fish entrail smell and the mats full of fleas. But Lafcadio enjoyed the place without complaint because of the jolly and honest Otokichi whom he admired. He would say "Otokichi is like a god." Also, Lafcadio loved the pebbled covered Yaizu beach and clear water with strong high waves. The fact that fifty feet from the shore the water suddenly dropped off into the deep pleased the avid swimmer.

The compassionate Lafcadio strictly warned his sons not to make fun of the village urchins. He would say, "If a quarrel takes place with these Yaizu children, then the blame is on you. It will be because you have some unkind trait. Yaizu children may be rough, but they are honest, no liars or mean ones. Show your warm heart to them."

In stories like "Otokichi's Daryma" he describes his over-tipping the innkeeper at Yaizu where they lodged, because he ridiculously undercharged him for their summer room and board accommodations. It reminded him of when he tipped one of the women porters in Martinique and she went off on a two hour walk to bring him a fresh mango to express her thanks.

The boys' diverse personalities came out in their swimming lessons when they vacationed by the sea each year. Even as a toddler, Iwao would run straight onto the water and swim out farther than his skill allowed, while Kazuo had been afraid of the water since Lafcadio threw him into the waves when he was very young. But that summer in 1905, Kazuo did well with his swimming lessons, possibly because Captain McDonald told him that no one should take an ocean voyage without being an excellent swimmer. Since he wanted to study abroad where many good things awaited him, he did not want to drown on the way. He didn't realize that death has a perverse habit of making its own appointments.

Without telling anyone, Lafcadio was dismayed that he did not have his former strength or endurance to swim as long and far as before. Once a bold, naked swimmer who ventured far out to sea, he began to fear the abyss and cringed at the innumerable touches, as of groping fingers, of the innumerable fish swirling around him. Still each day at sunrise he would shout out, "Wake up sweet chickens. Down to the beach!" Iwao's energy was boundless and his technique absent. Kazuo persisted until he was a skillful swimmer. The sea calmed his fearful spirit.

To prove himself, one day Kazuo took a long swim with his father beyond the Yaizu harbor out to an anchored fishing vessel. The two swam side by side. He was stung by a jellyfish but continued until they were in the shadow of the boat. They chatted with the impressed fisherman, "For Tokyo visitors, you are great swimmers." They turned and slowly swam back to shore. His success meant more to Lafcadio than it did to Kazuo.

"If you can swim that much, you are quite safe Kajio. Don't ever forget the hard struggle of today!" He praised and warned his son.

Setsu did not accompany her husband and two older sons to Yaizu that summer. She stayed in Tokyo to care for her aging mother and the younger children. Lafcadio would send her regular letters with news of their activities such as catching butterflies, walks, fishing, trying new foods, singing with the locals, and other adventures. He was glad he could take the boys to "live with the fishermen for a month - on fish, rice, and sea water (with sake, of course, for their sire)." He surprised his hosts and children by eating fruits without paring the skin. Every evening the Sensei and his children would sing in the sunset, "*Yu-yake! Ko-yake!*...Evening burning! Little burning! Weather, be fair tomorrow!"

Lafcadio wrote Setsu affectionate letters just for her eyes. Setsu was always his secret rainbow, beautifully drawn upon the gray page of his life where hope and love were found again. She was pleased with the drawings and lettering in childlike attempts at Japanese. They showed his tender side. She kept all those special notes in a box on the top shelf of her wardrobe. She felt his gentle energy wrapped around her heart even when he was far away.

For most of his life, Lafcadio was a physically, emotionally, and morally weak man, It wasn't until he settled in Japan and married Setsu that he found the security of home, family and purpose.

During the winter months of 1903, Lafcadio completed a considerable amount of writing. He concentrated his diminishing energies on work. He used his imaginative writing, not to escape reality, but to create it. His words had power, bringing them together they could bend time and space. He knew he would not live forever, so wanted to write something that would.

Praise for *Kwaidan: Stories and Studies of Strange Things* poured in. The proofs of *Japan: An Attempt at Interpretation* were corrected while the household slept. The book was his faithful transmission of the mind and soul of his beloved Japanese people for the benefit of the Western world. It was a manifestation of his undying attachment to Japan. He sent the book proofs off to America. He wrote to Elizabeth:

"I don't like the work of writing a serious treatise on sociology...I ought to keep to the study of birds and cats and insects and flowers, and queer small things---and leave the subject of the destiny of empires to men with brains. Unfortunately, the men of brains will not state the truth as they see it."

It turned out that the obstacle in his path---the cancellation of the lecture contract with Cornell University, was actually a gift meant to move him in a different direction. Through his book, he was able to promote awareness for Japanese culture around the world. He helped others view Japanese life with his warm, insightful, and understanding perspective. Lafcadio had the gift of transforming the mundane into charming and the ordinary into the mystical.

Elizabeth encouraged him to prepare a collection of his early lesser-known American writings. He considered assembling various articles and essays from the *Times Democrat*, a few poems, revised translations of Gautier, and *Some Chinese Ghosts*.

In a note to Elizabeth he teased, "My Dear Mrs. Wetmore, Perhaps you remember having said, twelve years ago, "I want you to go to Japan, because I want to read the books that you will write about it." As my tenth volume on the subject is now in press, - you ought to be getting satisfied."

By the end of 1903 he'd sold enough stories to build up a sizable savings account for Setsu. The Tokyo publisher Hasegawa was sending him regular royalties from *The Boy Who Drew Cats, The Goblin Spider, The Old Woman Who Lost Her Dumpling*, and *Chin Chin*.

In his later works, he wrote direct and succinct dialogue. His brief stories contained macabre tales of city and country folks, sprinkled with their earthly humor. Lafcadio's heroes came from the realm of paradox and horror: the blind man who made the dead cry; the shark-man who shed rubies instead of tears; the hand of Baku that ate bad dreams; and the painting that lost its color when separated from the owner. He gleaned and conveyed lessons and insights from stories about the invisible, the ghosts.

The stories in *Kotto: Being Japanese Curios, with Sundry Cobwebs* (1902, his ninth Japanese book), *Kwaidan* (1904), and *Japanese Fairy Tales* (1898) were examples of traditional stories rescued and retold. His portraits of tales of the past and the daily world around him are a constant delight. Modern sensibilities may be disturbed on occasion by occasional race-based analysis of cultures, but that just showed how influenced men of his time were by Herbert Spencer's evolutionary psychology.

Some part of himself was woven into each story. He recolored and reshaped the stories and studies of strange things. One of his most sensitive translations was "A Woman's Diary" about an obscure life lived exquisitely and with self-respect amidst the city's most poverty ridden back streets.

In Lafcadio's introduction to *Japan: An Attempt at Interpretation* (1904), he admitted that Japan was so vast and intricate a subject that "the untied labour of a generation of scholars could not exhaust it...This essay of mine can serve only in one direction as a contribution to the Western knowledge of Japan. But this direction is not one of the least important. Hitherto the subject of Japanese religion has been written of chiefly by the sworn enemies of that religion: by others it has been almost entirely ignored. Yet while it continues to be ignored and misrepresented, no real knowledge of Japan is possible.

"Any true comprehension of social conditions requires more than a superficial acquaintance with religious conditions. Even the industrial history of a people cannot be understood without some knowledge of those religious traditions and customs which regulate industrial life...or take the subject of art. Art in Japan is so intimately associated with religion that any attempt to study it without extensive knowledge of the beliefs which it reflects, were mere waste of time. By art I do not mean only painting or sculpture, but every kind of decoration and most kinds of pictorial representation,--the image on a boy's kite or a girl's battledore, design on a lacquered casket, figures on a workman's towel, a paper dog, or the wooden rattle for a baby, not less than the forms of those colossal Ni-o who guard the Buddhist temples.

"And surely there can never be any just estimate made of Japanese literature, until a study shall be made by some scholar, not only able to understand Japanese beliefs, but able also to sympathize with them at least to the same extent that our great humanists can sympathize with the religion of Euripides, of Pindar, and of Theocritus...Even one of Shakespeare's plays must remain incomprehensible to a person knowing nothing either of Christian beliefs or of the beliefs which preceded them.

"Everything is infused with significations unimaginable by any one ignorant of the faith of the people. Nobody knows this better than a man who has passed may years in trying to teach English in Japan, to pupils whose faith is utterly unlike our own, and whose ethics have been shaped by a totally different social experience."

Lafcadio went into depth about the underlying strangeness of Japan - the psychological strangeness, much more startling than the visible and superficial. How expressions of thoughts, emotions, ethics, and such are vastly different from the West. Yet "the outward strangeness of Japan proves to be full of beauty, so the inward strangeness appears to have its charm, ---an ethical charm reflected in the common life of the people."

From the beginning of his own sojourn, Lafcadio was impressed by the apparent kindness of people to each other and himself. Courtesy, at once so artless and so faultless, appeared to spring directly from the heart. He found a constant amenity and tact that elsewhere was only in the friendship of exclusive circles.

He writes of a good-natured cheerfulness no matter what troubles came, laughter, a wish to please, and a common desire to make existence beautiful. He says, "Religion brings no gloom into this sunshine: folk smile before the Buddhas and the Shinto ancestors as they pray; the temple courts are playgrounds for the children; and the enclosure of the great shrines are places of festivity rather than solemnity." He learned that these social conditions had been the same for centuries. He was tempted to believe he'd entered into the domain of a morally superior humanity. Of course, he acknowledged that the conditions of which he spoke were passing away, that the tide of time had turned. That is why he tirelessly wrote in detail about the old traditions, folktales, and a vanished age.

Lafcadio, born on the Greek island of Lafkada, wrote in a similar vein of thought: "Some of us have often wished that it were possible to live for a season in the beautiful, vanished world of Greek culture. Inspired by our first acquaintance with the charm of Greek art and thought, this wish comes to us even before we are capable of imagining the true conditions of the antique civilization. We should certainly find it impossible to accommodate ourselves to those conditions, the greater difficulty of feeling just as people used to feel some thirty centuries ago...unable to understand many aspects of old Greek life no modern mind can really feel. If it were resurrected for us, we could no more become part of it than we could change our mental identities... Japan offers us the living spectacle of conditions older, and psychologically much further away from us, than those of any Greek period with which art and literature have made us closely acquainted."

He reminded his readers that "a civilization less evolved than our own, and intellectually remote from us, is not on that account to be regarded as necessarily inferior in all respects. Hellenic civilization at its best represented an early stage of sociological evolution; yet the arts which it developed still furnish our supreme and unapproachable ideals of beauty. So too, this much more archaic civilization of old Japan attained an aesthetic and moral culture well worthy of our wonder and praise. Only a shallow mind---a very shallow mind---will pronounce the best of that culture inferior."

Lafcadio's book was written to help the world comprehend the Japanese character by studying the nature of the conditions which shaped it, the social and moral experience, layers of culture and history of their national beliefs. A basic character which remained essentially unchanged in spite of exposure to Western influence and modernization.

Little did he know that *Japan: An Attempt at Interpretation* would be one of the crowning achievements of his long effort to interpret and share his adopted country with the world. The year was 1904. He'd lived in Japan for fourteen years and had written numerous books on the country. Lafcadio's writings about Japan went from descriptive to analytical. The Japanese needed a literary spokesman, an interpreter to educate people about the country like Tolstoy did for Russia. His wanderer's curiosity and guileless style chronicles provided the English-speaking world truthful and artful glimpses into the life and culture of his island home.

Chamberlain praised him, "Lafcadio Hearn understands contemporary Japan better, and makes us understand it better, than any other writer, because he loves it better."

CHAPTER 39

During 1904 and 1905, the Empire of Japan and the Russian Empire fought a war over imperial ambitions to establish a sphere of influence in Manchuria and the Korean Empire. The population and students were indoctrinated at school in *bushido*, the way of the warrior, the fierce code of the samurai. People clamored for war and saw diplomacy as weakness.

The nation equipped with advanced Western weapons and Western willpower was deliberately measuring its strength against a powerful enemy. For the Meiji elites the backwardness of Korea was proof of their inferiority, thus giving Japan the right to conquer them. The Japanese then turned their violent storm against the Chinese, in part to show the West what she could do if necessary. Lafcadio was not afraid of the goblins and ghost that he wrote about as much as he was afraid of what real human beings were capable of doing to other real human beings, an immeasurable tragedy. Philosophers said for centuries that war does not determine who is right, only who is left.

Lafcadio was horrified by the New Japan's desire to industrialize and modernize as rapidly as possible, calling it a persecuted nation forced to become strong. Yet Japan demonstrated its capacity to meet all demands made upon it by the new conditions. He expressed hope of someday seeing a strong united Orient alliance against cruel Western civilization.

"If I have been able to do nothing else in my life, I have been able to at least help a little, as a teacher and as a writer, and as an editor, in opposing the growth of what is called society and what is called civilization. It is very little, of course---but the gods ought to love me for it."

As war loomed, he told Setsu, "Japan is coming into her own. Neither the West nor the East can threaten our nation."

He loved the authentic, quaint Japan and loathed the nation casting off the past in favor of a Western defined future. But ironically, he was not immune to the nationalistic fever and patriotic enthusiasm that gripped the nation when it went to war. He attributed victories in war and the moral strength behind this unexpected display of aggressive power to the "long discipline of the past." Saying, "Modern military achievement is a product of Old Japan martial traditions, bushido warrior way chivalry, and spiritually superior to Western material civilization and egotistic individuality."

One summer evening Lafcadio and the boys marched around the dining room mat border singing rousing renditions of *Kimigayo*, the national anthem and other songs. Lafcadio learned most of the songs the children sang so he could join them. But when he sang he also sounded like a young child of four or five in such an innocent baby-like accent that no one would have thought it came from a white-haired old man.

The boys were called bold and brave like their countrymen at war. He did not doubt Japan's strength, but feared that the victorious men of the New Japan empire would eventually bring destruction to all that was left. He called his beloved Old Japan "essentially a fighting race, a nation of the militant type."

He praised Japan's "admirable army and courageous navy," and was known to kiss the picture of Admiral Togo and ask him to please win. Lafcadio disliked it when he heard Admiral Togo compared as the Nelson of the Orient. He told his sons that Nelson did a great thing for Britain, but he indulged in immoral things. He felt to compare Admiral Togo, Rear-Admiral Uryu, or Commander Hirose to Nelson would be lowering the characters of those noble *bushi* or samurai Japanese warriors and disgracing them. He hated those who led hypocritical lives, lied, or took advantage of the weak. Cowardness or wickedness were never overlooked or forgiven. Money or rank could not buy or change his mind.

Lafcadio knew more about Japanese legends, folklore, songs, poetry, and mythology than almost anyone. He tried to avoid debased topics like politics and economics, calling himself an infant in those fields. But about the country's administrative policy and the future of Japan, he was greatly concerned and informed, more so than most people thought.

Kokoro: Hints and Echoes of Japanese Inner Life (1896) essays are filled with diverse observations, including stories about the country's swelling national pride following the First Sino-Japanese War victories.

He also warned that "if they increase their power more, they will one day escape the control of the government." He wrote prophesies of the danger of Japan's arrogance regarding the army and navy wins stating that if the government can't control them, and if "frustrated by the pressure applied by the Powers, they will start a war they cannot win." He feared future internal disorder that might compel suspension of the constitution and lead to a military dictatorship - a resurrected Shogunate in modern uniform.

First Japan was at war with China, the Sino-Japanese War 1894-95. Victory over China established Japan as the predominant power in the Far East. In February of 1904, The Russo-Japanese War (1904-1905) started. The Russians wanted Port Arthur, a warm-water strategic port on the Pacific. They were building railroads in China and had mining and forest concessions in Korea. Japan could not allow such encroachments on territories they planned to conquer. This second great war of the New Order disrupted national life.

During his years living in Japan, Lafcadio's attitude toward nationalism underwent profound change. Before, his writings were attached to purely cultural nationalism,---a nostalgia effort to save or, at least, memorialize dying folk societies such as the American and Caribbean Creoles who were threatened with cultural extinction. Previous ethnographic salvage groundwork and his experiences within Meiji Japan dramatically transformed him into a modern state nationalist who adopted the Japanese cause against China and Russia.

Since the beginning of the Russo-Japanese hostilities, Lafcadio wrote writing articles about the conflict for Western publications. He dedicated his pen to aid his adopted country by drawing the world's sympathies to Japan. It was in his nature to take sides with the weaker underdog. His small, naturalized country was dearer to him than any other country in the world.

He was aware that printed articles had the ability to influence public opinion and turn loyalties one way or the other. He read the foreign papers' reports, checked on battles, ships lost, and territory won. Japan emerged as a world power through their military victories in the Sino-Japanese War, the Russo-Japanese War, and beyond, in Lafcadio's lifetime. The emperor in the Taisho period conferred a posthumous award on Lafcadio for his great support during the Russian-Japanese war. Honors and awards were never the patriotic writer's goals.

Lafcadio wrote nationalistic pieces but knew that war was just organized murder and a symptom of man's failure as a thinking animal. He hoped his sons would never have to fight on battlefields to make tyrants and businessmen rich. One war would just lead to another war. Lafcadio remembered Plato's statement, "Only the dead have seen the end of war."

Several former students, dressed in uniform, came to Lafcadio's door to say farewell before going off to battle. The war even intruded on his traditional Japan summer retreat seaside village of Yaizu. Recruitment of men for the army almost crippled their small fishing fleet.

A favorite pupil, Captain Fujisaki, came to say goodbye. He informed him that he'd be serving on a reception committee for foreign military observers, as an adjunct to Field Marshal Oyama. He gave Lafcadio a picture of himself before he left to be placed on his family shrine if he was killed.

When Lafcadio could regain his voice, he assured his young friend, "Don't worry, you'll come back covered with honors. Remember that in battle, if you make your opponent flinch, you have already won. But the Russians are big fellows, so be careful!"

Fujisaki laughed confidently, "Thank you Sensei-San. But the bigger the target, the easier it is to hit."

He wrote from the battlefield and asked if Sensei-San could send him any interesting novels or plays. "I'll return them if I live. I pray for the health of all of you as I listen to the cannon here in Manchuria."

Lafcadio and Setsu had their sons write to the young officer. Lafcadio sent plays and wrote, "I am still hoping to see you next spring or at latest summer. For this hope, however, I have no foundation beyond the idea that Russia will probably find, before long, that she must think of something else besides fighting with Japan. The commercial powers of the world are disturbed by her aggression; and industrial power, after all, is much more heavy than all the artillery of the Czar. Whatever foreign sympathy really exists is with Japan."

Lafcadio and another gentleman were discussing Eastern countries' economic issues: "If China adopts Western industrial methods, she will be able to underbid us in all the markets of the world", his friend observed.

"Perhaps in cheap production", Lafcadio replied. "But there is no reason why Japan should depend wholly on cheapness of production. I think she may rely more securely on her superiority in art and good taste. The art-genius of a people may have a special value against which all competition by cheap labor is vain. Among Western nations, France offers an example. Her wealth is not due to her ability to underbid her neighbors. Her goods are the dearest in the world; she deals in things of luxury and beauty. But they sell in all civilized countries because they are the best of their kind. Why should not Japan become the France of the Further East?" His words proved to be a benchmark in the future. Producing higher quality goods would prove better for Japan in the long run.

Musings on both the future of wars and how Japan could put its sophistication of craft traditions to good use and undercut European rivals proved original and futuristically prophetic. Lafcadio's fearlessly inquisitive, open mind shocked and impressed readers with its originality. Japanese ideologies were reflected in his timeless themes of simple beauty, life, death, and ever-present spirituality. Beyond writing his cultural-historic analysis, observations, folklore, and travels, Lafcadio transcended to the very heart-inner spirit (*kokoro*) of the mystery of human existence and meaning of life.

CHAPTER 40

Lafcadio's health improved and once again he was in favor within academic circles. Professor Ume and other Japanese friends had been scouting for a position in a private school where Lafcadio could teach without taxing his strength. Waseda University, a private liberal school that attracted more literary students, asked him to teach again. Waseda University was endowed by Count Okuma, whom he greatly admired as a leader of the Meiji generation. The school officials called to discuss his employment contract and he accepted.

"Waseda University, Sweet Wife!" Lafcadio declared happily. "Only four hours a week, two lectures on English literature every Wednesday and Saturday. The Waseda campus is closer to Okubo by rickshaw."

"That is good news Yakumo!" she replied. What pleased her most was that the wavering moth that lived in her husband's throat for months had left his voice.

"Takata, the dean of Waseda looks like Nishida-san. That is a good omen. I will invite him to our home and you can see for yourself, Mama-San. His reception and his wife welcoming me in Japanese greatly pleased me."

Lafcadio's classes and associations at Waseda University made him happier than any he'd known since leaving Matsue. Professor Tsubouchi, a national authority on native drama, introduced him to that aspect of Japanese culture.

When Lafcadio was at home or in bathing resorts he always wore Japanese clothes. But when he went for walks or to school in Tokyo he wore his

Western clothes. His foreign clothes were only two styles. In summer his suits were made of strong white duck cloth like policemen wore, and in winter suits of dull gray wool. He always wore wide-brimmed, good quality hats. Due to wearing what he called "barbarian footwear" that was too tight when he was a boy, Lafcadio's second and third toes overlapped, so he wore broad-toed, soldier-like shoes. He avoided putting the children in shoes and encouraged them to wear clogs or sandals.

Rather than Western suits, the older Waseda professors wore Japanese *haori* hip-length jackets worn over *kimonos* or *hakama* ankle length trousers. Lafcadio felt he was old enough and Japanese enough to do the same. The students and faculty showed open respect for him and a warm desire to please their esteemed professor of English literature.

One day Lafcadio returned from Waseda University very excited. "Today I saw Count Okuma and advised him. It may have been better not to have said what I did, but when I saw him, I couldn't help doing so. It was about those foreign religious people who wear masks of religion, but in reality are offensive politicians. Be careful of them I advised," he said with a mischievous smile.

Lafcadio received an unexpected letter from P. J. Hartog, the Academic Registrar of London University. It read, "I am directed to ask if you will kindly consent to deliver a course of ten lectures for the University of London (under the Martin White Benefaction) on the 'Civilization of Japan' during the coming session, and preferably either in the Lent or Summer terms?"

He was delighted to learn that he could be completely free in his choice and management of topics. Lafcadio wholeheartedly agreed with philosopher Marcus Aurelius when he said, "The educated are not bound by limitations, but instead, they soar freely in the pursuit of truth and self-discovery."

He was hoping that the University of London administration and students would be free thinkers willing to consider things that might clash with their own beliefs, customs, and privileges. He knew his state of mind was not common, but essential for right thinkers who could change the world.

A visiting professorship might be his chance to take Kazuo to the West if this possibility worked out. It was suggested that Oxford University also wished to hear from him. These offers were among the greatest satisfaction he'd known, since Lafcadio had always desired to win recognition from his own country. Little did he know that his books would someday be praised and referred to by such greats as Mark Twain, William Butler Yeats, Albert Einstein, Charles Chaplin, U.S. Presidents, and other world leaders.

Another surprising letter came from Sir William Van Horne, President of the C.P.R.R. Canadian Railroad, generously agreeing to furnish Lafcadio with means of transportation, both ways, to Montreal and back to Japan. He would gladly do some writing for them for such a great offer.

Ever since he shipped corrected and approved proofs off to America, Lafcadio anxiously awaited news on the publication of *Japan: An Attempt at Interpretation*. The publisher only replied with one word---"Good".

"The printers are working on it now, Mama-San," he'd tell Setsu each day. He could imagine the noise of the tick-tack of setting the type.

"My book about Japan is being made, and soon they'll send me copies." It had never seemed so important to him to hold a new book in his hands.

CHAPTER 41

Lafcadio's diminishing energies were concentrated on his writing and his home life. Having a baby girl in the house was a pleasant novelty for him and the rest of the family. Time at the seashore improved his health and outlook. He'd recovered from the earlier illness, but its effects were obvious in his sunken cheeks, sagging shoulders, loss of vigor and vitality.

He began to fear that he didn't have long to live and so he was desperate to provide for his family. Even when the doctor warned him about heart strain, he couldn't stop working to provide an inheritance for his family. "I don't want money for myself, I only want it for my wife and children." He wrote as much as he could, a book a year, in addition to teaching. The double effort took a serious toll on his health.

Taking long walks were part of the past. Warm weather allowed shorter strolls around the neighborhood. When he wished to be alone, he'd visit the Zoshigaya public burial ground nearby. He'd taken Setsu and the boys to see the lovely spot, but they did not share his predilection for graveyards.

Kazuo sometimes went with him to Ochiyai-mura, an area of farms dominated by the tall chimney of a crematorium. His son got upset when Lafcadio would say, "Soon I will turn into smoke and come out of the tall chimney in the trees." When Setsu heard about such talk, she'd reproach her husband.

"You shouldn't say such foolish things. It makes Kazuo sad. Don't you want to live to see your grandchildren? Make up your mind that you are going to live a long time, and you will!"

"*Gomen nasai*, sorry" he would reply. "But I know my own body and it's so. But I'll ask God to fix it your way," he chuckled.

Setsu could see the sorrow behind his humor, the love behind his anger, and the reasons for his silence.

Whiskey and strong cigars were forbidden, only a memory. Rather than his previous angry outbursts, he would sigh, "*Shigata ga nai* - It can't be helped." His writing arm was bothering him the most. Scolding or disciplining the boys made him weak and short of breath.

"Nothing makes me feel more wretched than to punish the children, Mama-San. Each time it shortens my life."

He spent time in his study working, sometimes sighing and staring out the window at the clouds in the late summer sky. One is never too old to yearn. Lafcadio recalled a jagged shard from his childhood and wrote about a day from long ago:

"I have memory of a place and a magical time in which the Sun and the Moon were larger and brighter than now. Whether it was of this life or of some life before I cannot tell. But I know the sky was very much more blue, and nearer to the world,---almost as it seems to become above the masts of a steamer steaming into equatorial summer. The sea was alive, and used to talk,---and the Wind made me cry out for joy when it touched me. Once or twice during other years, in divine days lived among the peaks, I have dreamed just for a moment that the same wind was blowing,---but it was only a remembrance.

"Also in that place the clouds were wonderful, and of colors for which there are no names at all,---colors that used to make me hungry and thirsty. I remember, too, that the days there were new wonders and new pleasures for me. And all the country and time were softly ruled by One who thought only of ways to make me happy. Sometimes I would refuse to be made happy, and that always caused her pain, although she was divine; and I remember that I tried very hard to be sorry. When day was done, and there fell the great hush of the light before moonrise, she would tell me stories that made me tingle from head to foot with pleasure. I have never heard any other stories half so beautiful. And when the pleasure became too great, she would sing a weird little song which always brought sleep. At last there came a parting day; and she wept, and told me of a charm she had given that I must never lose, because it would keep me young, and give me power to return. But I never returned. And the years went; and one day I knew that I had lost the charm and had become ridiculously old."

"Your sentiments remind me of a Japanese word - *yugen* – that speaks of a profound awareness of the universe that triggering feelings too deep and mysterious for words." Setsu responded.

Lafcadio entertained musings on the mysteries of Whither and Whence. In "Revery" he writes about human doubts and fears about the inevitable dissolution-death: "Such doubts disturb us chiefly because of old wrong habits of thought, and the consequent blind fear of knowing that what we have so long called Soul belongs not to Essence, but to form…Forms appear and vanish in perpetual succession; but the Essence alone is Real. Nothing real can be lost, even in the dissipation of a million universes. Utter destruction, everlasting death, --all such terms of fear have no correspondence to any truth but the eternal law of change. Even forms can perish only as waves pass and break; they melt but to swell anew,--nothing can be lost… Transmutation there may be; changes also made by augmentation or diminution of affinities, by subtraction or addition of tendencies; for the dust of us will then have been mingled with the dust of other countless worlds and their peoples. But nothing essential can be lost."

Although Lafcadio still spoke of going to America or England, the plans became vague and mirage-like. Lecture notes he'd prepared for Cornell University had become his latest book *Japan: An Attempt at Interpretation*. It was only one piece of a huge corpus of published work, in the form of books, articles, lectures, and translations, plus an enormous amount of correspondence and other personal writings.

His later writings demonstrated less stylistic exhibitionism, great concentration, control of language, and realism. Lafcadio's authority as an immersed witness gave the assuring sense of being there in person. He shared appreciation for the mysterious and exotic of his new country. He was forthright about the qualities of his life in revolutionary times and the struggles he himself had coming to terms with a foreign culture. By listening to and writing about Japanese life stories, he learned that people are not as different as they are the same.

Reading Hearn was said to rank second only to visiting the country. Henry James said, "For a stranger in a foreign land to cease to be a stranger he must stand ready to pay with his person." That is the price Lafcadio paid.

Books, such as *Exotics and Retrospectives* (1898), *In Ghostly Japan* (1899), *Shadowings* (1900), *A Japanese Miscellany* (1901), *Kwaidan: Stories and Studies of Strange Things* (1904), *Japan: An Attempt at Interpretation* (1904) were translated into Japanese and became as popular in Japan as they did in the United States and other countries. Lafcadio's constant needs were finally met; he had both an appreciative audience of readers and a loving settled homelife.

He was comfortable just staying home, working in his study that was bricked with over two thousand books. Ordinary moments like spending time with his wife and children were no longer distractions or throw away moments, but treasured as portals into the sacred nature of things.

Since the boys were older, they joined their parents at the evening meal. There were times when he was summoned to eat; he'd be so absorbed in his work that the children or Setsu would have to fetch him by the hand. They would have to loudly shout to bring him back to the present.

"Papa-San, this will never do! Supper is ready, and the children will cry!" she would scold him.

"Supper? He would answer vaguely. "Haven't I had supper yet? That's odd. I thought I had already eaten." With an apologetic *"Gomen nasai* or *Sumimasen*---I'm sorry" he would accompany her to the dining room.

Still deeply preoccupied with his work, he'd mistake salt for sugar or eat a slice of meat he'd cut for the boys. "Yakumo, won't you please wake up from your dreaming!" Setsu would jolt him back to reality.

"Kajio, what had Papa-San forgotten this time?" Everyone would laugh at his absentmindedness and supper would continue.

On the nineteenth of September, when he returned from teaching at Waseda, he began tugging at the cloth of his *haori* jacket. Setsu found him pacing in his study clutching his chest.

"Are you ill Yakumo?"

"I have a new kind of sickness. A sickness of the heart, I think."

Setsu sent the household's rickshaw man to fetch Dr. Kizawa. But Lafcadio insisted that a shot of whiskey would make the pain go away. He wouldn't lie down to rest. He went to his desk to write to his friend Ume-San, instructions for arrangements in case he died.

He told Setsu, 'This is a letter to Ume-San. If trouble comes, he will help you. Perhaps if this pain of mine increases, I may die. If I die, do not weep. Buy a little urn; you can find one for three or four sen. Put my bones in it and bury it near a quiet temple in the country. I shall not like it if you cry. Amuse the children and play cards with them---how much better I shall enjoy that! There will be no need of announcing my death. If anyone asks, reply, 'Oh he died some time ago!' That will be quite proper."

Within minutes the pain stopped. He took a cold bath and drank his glass of whiskey. When the doctor arrived later, Lafcadio laughed and told him there was nothing to treat him for. "My illness has vanished. I am well again. I shall not die." Dr. Kizawa knew how he disliked medical attention but insisted on an examination and listened carefully to his chest anyway. He gave instructions for him to rest, halt teaching for a month or two, and eat light meals of tofu and broth.

The doctor looked out the study window and noticed the unseasonal blooming of the cherry tree, with blossoms snowing on the ground below. "*Sakura*", Dr. Kizawa said to Setsu. *Sakura* literally means cherry blossom, but symbolically, he was saying to her, "the fleeting nature of life". Setsu understood the seriousness of the situation. She would send for him immediately if the pain returned.

Outside she heard the song of a cricket like insect *mushi-mushi*, who were usually silent that time of year. Like the out-of-season autumn blossoming of the cherry tree, this mournful music was another bad omen that made Setsu feel weary and sad.

Although Lafcadio insisted that their home life return to its usual patterns, Setsu and the children watched him anxiously. On the morning of

September 26, 1904, the sky was gray and cold. He was sitting up in bed wrapped in thick blankets to ward off the damp chill. The children came in to bid him good morning before heading off to school. Kazuo, enter the room to say goodbye, but somehow said, "Good night, pleasant dreams." Lafcadio replied, "The same to you, darling, good night." Setsu scolded them for such a foolish error. They just looked at each other and laughed. When the boys left for school, Setsu returned to the study to build a fire in his stove. He wanted to tell her about a strange dream.

"It was a most unusual dream," he recalled in a soft tone of voice. "I took a very long journey, and now that I am awake it seems to have been not a real journey in a dream, but a dream journey in a dream! I was traveling in a very strange country, and I was going a long distance, very far away. Not a journey in Europe or Japan. I could smell warm butter cakes, honey, and fragrant crushed thyme." He seemed calm and pleased just to be thinking about sensory images from his infancy.

He wrote: "The light of the mother's smile will survive our sun;--the thrill of her kiss will last beyond the thrilling of stars; --the sweetness of her lullaby will endure in the cradle songs of the worlds yet unevolved; --the tenderness of her faith will quicken the fervor of prayers to be made to the hosts of another heaven,--to the gods of a time beyond Time. And the nectar of her breasts can never fail; that snowy stream will still flow on, to nourish the life of some humanity more perfect than our own, when the Milky Way that spans our night shall have vanished forever out of Space."

During the day Lafcadio worked at his desk. He'd stopped reading newspapers "so that my soul find rest from fury" and he avoided most all social contacts. That morning a letter came from Captain Fujisaki at the front, saying that he was alive and well and praying for the health of the whole Koizumi family. In the afternoon Lafcadio replied at once in a newsy letter to his former student. He told him of seeing his parents while on vacation with the boys in Yaizu. He described how trying the war had been on the village and the country as a whole and hoped for a speedy end to the conflict and a safe return of the country's fighting forces, especially Fujisaki. For Kazuo's writing exercise that afternoon he had him write a letter to Fujisaki-san in English.

At dinner that night, Lafcadio played and laughed with his sons. As the table was cleared, the children started doing writing lessons in their copybooks on the dining room table. Lafcadio went to his library. Setsu checked on her mother who was in bed with stomach trouble and a fever.

About eight o'clock Lafcadio came back into the dining room with a strange drawn look on his face, and went to the cupboard to pour a glass of whiskey. He was shaking and ghostly pale. The children watched in frightened silence. The maid ran to get Setsu. She hurried to his side and found Lafcadio walking on the veranda, his hands clutching at his chest.

"It's that same pain, Mama-San. The sickness of the other day has come back again," he gasped. His expression was sad with apology.

Setsu signaled Kazuo to send a maid for the doctor. She slowly walked Lafcadio down the hall and into his study. He didn't want to get into bed right away. He sat at his desk and took out pen and paper.

"I want to write you a letter, Sweet Wife."

"But Yakumo, I am right here with you. You need to rest and wait for the doctor."

"I'll be quick. I'm better already," he reassured her. "You go check on your mother and the boys," he urged. He pushed aside a partially written manuscript and the natural history book he'd used to Kazuo's lesson that day, and prepared to write his love note.

When she returned moments later, Lafcadio was slumped over his high desk. His breathing was short and sharp. His face twisted in pain. He did not protest this time when she led him to the sleeping mat. As soon as he settled on his futon, he clasped his hands over his chest and in Japanese sighed, "*Ay---byoki no tame*---Ah, on account of the sickness..."

Setsu ran to the door and called the children, "Come at once! All of you!"

In the dim lamplight, Kazuo called out, "Papa-San, Papa-San", but could see that his father's eyes and lips did not move. His spirit had departed. When Dr. Kizawa arrived, there was no heartbeat to listen to.

Setsu leaned on Lafcadio's desk in disbelief and grief. The paper he'd pulled out only minutes ago was still blank, untouched by his pen. She told herself that his last letter was intended for her, that her name 'Setsu' was in the ink on the pen's nib. She took that final blank sheet of paper and locked it away in a silk covered box with all the other love letters he'd written to her.

CHAPTER 42

Lafcadio Hearn had written in *Kwaidan*: "I should like, when my time comes, to be laid away in some Buddhist graveyard of the ancient kind, so that my ghostly company should be ancient, caring nothing for the fashions and the changes and the disintegrations of Meiji."

Although he was deeply knowledgeable of both sophisticated philosophies of Buddhism and Shinto, he was never trapped by the spiritual boundaries of any denomination. His attitude toward all religions of Japan and the world in general was that of the thoughtful observer. He'd told his son and others that upon his death they should just "place his ashes in an ordinary vase and bury him, without any religious ceremony, on a forested site."

In spite of his last written and verbal wishes to slip unnoticed into death, his friends and family decided to hold a funeral. Since historic Zoshigaya cemetery at Kobudera temple was one of his favorite places to visit, and as a public graveyard it was safe from modern encroachments, Setsu arranged for a plot of ground in that cemetery.

His friends and students adamantly insisted that his last rites be formal and public. Within the bounds of what she thought would have pleased Lafcadio, she arranged to hold his funeral at the Kobudera temple in the northern part of Tokyo. The old Abbot, now Archbishop Tatara agreed to return to the temple to officiate at the ceremony.

On September 29th, 1904, the funeral procession left his residence at half past one and wound its way up the now treeless hill to the Kobudera temple. Bearers of Buddhist symbols and great pyramidal bouquets of asters and chrysanthemums, sacred streamers on long poles, and white lanterns led the way. Young boys followed with small bamboo cages filled with birds to be released as symbols of the soul escaping its earthly bonds.

Six men robed in blue carried a portable casket of unpainted wood, trimmed with blue silk tassels and adorned with silver and gold lotus blossoms at the corners. Priests walked behind carrying food for the dead and ringing little bells. Then came white-robed Setsu and their children and close friends, followed by a long line of forty university professors, over a hundred students, and various foreign admirers of his work. Mitchell McDonald was out of the country and unable to attend. Temple bells tolled as the sad party climbed the hill and entered the ancient shrine.

In the dim temple, eight Buddhist priests chanted Kannon dirge sutras from the *Hokkekyo*. The old abbot, in his archbishop gold brocade robes and cap, conducted a ceremony of the Soto school of Zen Buddhism. The eight priests' heads were shaved and they were clothed in white. When the chanting paused, Kazuo walked toward his father's candle-lit coffin. He knelt down, touched his head to the floor, and placed a small incense burner between the candles. A delicate perfume filled the air. Grief and loneliness swept over the ten-year old boy. He looked up through tearing eyes at the serene face of Archbishop Tatara. Having the elderly priest and his father's former student Tanabe beside him gave him strength.

After first son Kazuo withdrew, Setsu and second son Iwao came forward. They wore the ceremonial white robes reserved only for weddings and funerals. She and grave young Iwao prostrated themselves and performed the same ritual of knelling and lighting incense before the coffin. As chanting resumed, the entire congregation knelt with heads bowed to the floor. Lafcadio Hearn aka Koizumi Yakumo was the first westerner to be accorded a full Buddhist funeral.

Students came forward to present a laurel wreath with an inscription---"In memory of Lafcadio Hearn, whose pen was mightier than the sword of the victorious nation which he loved and lived among, and whose highest honor it shall ever be to have given him citizenship and, alas, a grave!"

The poet Yone Noguchi wrote in his tribute, "He was a delicate, easily-broken vase, old as the world, beautiful as a cherry blossom. Alas! That wonderful vase is broken. He is no more with us. Surely we could lose two or three battleships at Port Arthur, rather than Lafcadio Hearn."

Lafcadio would have laughed at the mixed messages of regret and patriotism they expressed. Noguchi also enthusiastically praised him, "We

Japanese have been regenerated by his sudden magic and baptized afresh under his transcendental rapture. Professor Inazo Nitobe described Hearn as, "the most eloquent and truthful interpreter of the Japanese mind."

Among friends, Setsu recalled, "I may name some things that Hearn-san liked extremely---sunsets, summer, the sea, swimming, banana trees, cryptomerias (*sugi*, the Japanese cedar), lonely cemeteries, insects, *Kwaidan* ghost tales, Urashima the rescuer, and *horai* songs. He was fond of beefsteak and plum-pudding and enjoyed smoking. He disliked liars, abuse of the weak, Prince Albert coats, white shirts, the City of New York, and many other things." Lafcadio fondly remembered the islands of Lefkada, Ireland, Martinique, and Japan…but the one island of the world he hated was the island of New York.

Although his life had been marked by abandonment, poverty, misfortunes, scandals, and flaws, his colleagues, friends and family honored him for his personal bravery, virtues, stiff integrity, childlike awe of beauty, and a sympathy for all living creatures.

As Lafcadio wished, his body was cremated and turned into smoke from the tall chimney of Ochiyai-mura, just as he predicted. As soon as Otokichi, his landlord from the seaside town of Yaizu, heard the news that the Sensei died, he came at once by train. After the burning of the body, he was allowed to take part in the ceremony of gathering the bones from the ashes. Otokichi's rough voice recited sutras as he participated.

Ten-year old Kazuo never forgot one incident in the process and later noted, "While muttering Buddhist prayers and picking up father's bones (two people picked up the same bone with unmated chopsticks), Otokichi suddenly remarked, 'Here is something like the cover of *sazae*, top shell round and flat. What is it? He asked the crematory man. 'That is the knee-cap---in common called *hiza kozo*.' When Otokichi heard this, '*He-he-I*, is that so? Then with this, *sensei-sama* moved his leg and swam our sea until just a while ago, eh?' So saying, he wiped his eyes with his blue towel to brush away the tears."

One of Lafcadio's favorite pens, a gift from McDonald, was placed in the funeral urn with his bones. Lafcadio Hearn's remains were buried in Zoshigaya Cemetery in Tokyo, close enough for the family in Okubo to visit often. He was reduced to a handful of dust in a little earthen pot tucked away in a simple Buddhist grave. Conventional gravel paths led to the lush green burial plot under tall trees. The freshly packed earth of his grave was covered with a flat stone whose center was carved out to hold water for his spirit, and on each side a small hole was drilled for incense.

According to Buddhist practice, *kaimyo*, his posthumous name given to the dead was placed over the grave, '*Shogaku In-den Jo-ge Hachi-un Koji*' which means 'Believing man similar to undefiled flower blooming like eight rising clouds, who dwells in mansion of right enlightenment.' These posthumous names, received from the temple, are intentionally long and hard to pronounce as a superstition to prevent the return of the dead person's spirit if their old name is accidently called. In 1915 Koizumi Yakumo was posthumously conferred the Shinto Court rank of Jushii.

A rough stone shaft carved with his name Koizumi Yakumo 1850-1904 was also placed. The memorial marker set up in the town of Yaizu, where he vacationed with his family at the seashore, would have been Lafcadio's favorite. It read: "In commemoration of the place where sang Professor Yakumo Koizumi..." The villagers fondly remembered him singing with his children each evening.

Writer Yone Noguchi , whom Lafcadio called "the finest type of the Japanese man", wrote of him: "Like the lotus the man was in his heart...a poet, thinker, loving husband and father, and sincere friend...Within that man there burned something pure as the vestal fire, and in that flame dwelt a mind that called forth life and poetry out of the dust, and grasped the highest themes of human thought."

At the Hearn home, Setsu built a small Buddhist shrine in Lafcadio's study. It held his commemorative tablet, burning incense, lacquer bowls containing his favorite foods, a lighted lamp, vases of iris shoots, one of his writing pens on a bronze stand, and a portrait of Yakumo/Lafcadio. Until they were grown, all four children would bid him, "Good night, Happy dreams, Papa-san." Each year on September 26th, Setsu would hold an anniversary feast in the study. The children, and eventually grandchildren, attended to honor their ancestor Patrick Lafcadio Hearn-Yakumo Koizumi.

Lafcadio Hearn himself wrote: "I an individual---an individual soul! Nay, I am a population unthinkable for multitude, even by groups of a thousand millions! Generations of generations I am, aeons of aeons! Countless times the concourse now making me has been scattered and mixed with other scatterings. Of what concern then, the next disintegration? Perhaps, after trillions of ages of burning in different dynasties of suns, the very best of me may come together again."

CHAPTER 43

The odyssey of an open mind does not end with one's death, especially for a sage like Lafcadio Hearn/Koizumi Yakumo. The greatness of a man is in his integrity and ability to affect those around him positively. His influence is universal and timeless.

No one in the Meiji Era in late 19th and early 20th century did more to educate and link the East to West. Author and journalist Lafcadio Hearn wrote tirelessly about his images and impressions of Japan's people – their inner thoughts, religions, art, superstition, folklore, and ideals. He received no awards or public recognition at the time. However, as the Japanese say, "*todai moto kurashi* - the foot of the beacon is dark."

Dozens of scholars and intelligent writers, such as Basil Chamberlain, Pierre Loti, Rudyard Kipling, Arthur Waley, Maurice Dekobra, William Plomer John Morris, Fosco Maraini, Ruth Benedict, Edwin Reischauer, and James Kirkup, have attempted to explain the enigmatic nature of the Japanese to Westerners. Yet the Japanese themselves have found Lafcadio Hearn to be the pre-eminent interpreter of their culture and a bridge between the two worlds. His name is well known to Japanese of every class and generation. Hearn/Koizumi books are classics and used in schools to teach English and provide glimpses into their heritage.

In that flame of his being dwelled a mind that called forth life and poetry out of dust and grasped the highest themes of human thought. He is the supreme embodiment of the achievement of an open mind. His example teaches the fact that there is no greater responsibility than holding a mirror up to society, no higher calling than teaching tolerance and diversity, no richer way of life than pursuing the creative truth, and no greater mystery or challenge than merging our dream life to our waking life. In his way of living and teaching, Hearn opened his heart to humanity and hoped to lead others to inner and universal peace in the world.

Lafcadio Hearn-Koizumi Yakumo's life and legacy embody the highest values and the free pursuit of truth in service of the common good. His message is a call to the tolerance, understanding, and peace so deeply needed now.

Following are a few examples of his impact on the world of literature, philosophy, education, government, environment, and arts/cinema:

LAFCADIO HEARN'S LEGACY AND IMPACT

Modern Japanese culture is a kaleidoscope of Eastern and Western cultures. When Japan first opened its borders to foreign contact, ending the Edo period (1603-1852) and entering the Meiji modernization era (1868-1912), this enigmatic civilization began to adapt and assimilate what it needed to avoid colonization by the West and to become a recognized nation state and world power. The adoption or imitation of select reforms and modern ways from Germany, England, France, and United States was a protective veneer. In spite of the fluidity and eclecticism of Meiji Japan, a concurrently strong current of nationalistic purism remained under the surface.

When Lafcadio Hearn arrived in 1890 he observed first-hand the loss of Old Japan and the birth of New Japan in its headlong rush to catch up with the West. He lamented the vanishing of the traditional Japanese life but understood modernization to be both essential and inevitable. He made it his mission to preserve what he could of the peoples' culture, literature, and history before Western influences erased them. Over 135 years later, Lafcadio's heartfelt reflections on the psyche of Japan in its time of transition still captivate readers.

Hearn's books are a treasure trove of folk tales and legends that might otherwise have vanished. His documentary and interpretive essays, novels, folklore, and ghost stories became part of Japan's national cultural treasures. His appeal lies in the glimpses he provides into an older, more mystical Japan that was almost lost during the country's hectic plunge into Western-style industrialization and nation building. It took this foreigner to warn Japan that it was losing its heritage and its heart. Koizumi/Hearn uniquely understood and captured the soul of the Empire of the Rising Sun and shared it with the West. His work was a pioneering effort to circulate

Japanese literature internationally and establish Greek-born Lafcadio as a cultural mediator and the bridge between the East and West.

Although Lafcadio Hearn was abandoned as a child, suffered near blindness, and was on several occasions destitute and homeless, he rose to international prominence as a prolific author, university professor, and living example of global citizenship. The universality of Lafcadio's mind, developed through his multi-national travels and exposure to polytheism in Greece, Ireland, Creole, and Japan. He was a product of genetic and culturally blending and believed in its strength. Through observation and experiences, he was willing to accept new ideas and change. His open heart and mind had equal respect for other cultures, religions, people, and to see through to the essence of life. He was able to see the beauty in all skin color, cultures, and religions. In fact, he cared for all living things---human, feline, canine, fowl, reptile, equine, and even insects. While others separated science and religion, Lafcadio focused on how they were similar and where they overlapped and merged. He saw how they were merely different paths going up the same mountain that led to ultimate truth.

Lafcadio Hearn was one of the first Western writers to adopt karma and meditation into his work. He described Buddhism as a rational, scientific approach to reality, one of simplicity and directness. He avoided belief in a transcendent deity and saw religion as a man-made invention that divided people and nations. To overcome this divisiveness, his writing emphasized connection and became a link between East and West.

Lafcadio Hearn's philosophy, which has left an indelible mark on history, is worthy of continued study. His legacy contains lessons for today.

HEARN ON PROGRESS, POLICY, AND VALUES

Lafcadio Hearn's name and ideas have been used to promote the restoration of Japan's traditions and virtues. In a social climate which views political nationalism as dangerous, cultural nationalism was a considered a safe method of celebrating the old culture of Japan. Immediately after World War II, Hearn's reputation had declined among intellectuals, and he was dismissed as an irrational writer who had extolled a romanticized version of Japan. New Japan had wanted to leave behind Old Japan. However, his reputation started to regain respect as people began to re-examine postwar Japanese culture and its future.

Policymakers used Hearn's words when they warned about American consumerism, saying, 'if they continue to consume so frivolously, human beings will use up all natural resources, and will not be able to coexist with nature." They advised people to heed Hearn's "warnings of little ghosts" and the universal lessons he depicted in his tales. He warned about evils of materialism. Reflection on Hearn's works shows that economic supremacy alone cannot produce richness of the heart. In one of his lectures in Kumamoto about the future of the Far East, he taught, "Assuredly in the future competition between West and East, the races most patient, most economical, most simple in their habits will win. The costly races may totally disappear as the result. Nature is a great economist. She makes no mistakes. The fittest to survive are those best able to live with her, and to be content with a little. Such is the law of the universe."

Many saw Old Japan's culture as a wise path to overcome the inhibitions of Western rationality. Hearn mattered because he understood the limits and the importance of more humane customs. Modernization and rationalism were seen as factors that destroyed many customs and traditions, which in turn caused the spiritual chaos of today. Hearn considered Buddhism and Shintoism, unlike religions in the West, to be ways in which people could come together.

Hearn scholars argued that Japan's Eastern philosophy could overcome the perceived limits of Western philosophy because the Japanese have a civilization of mercy (*jihi no bunmei*) compared to the West's civilization of anger (*ikari no bunmei*). Hearn knew that European society arrogantly assumed itself to be the only true civilization, and his writing empathized the existence of the valuable history and culture of what the West called savage societies. He rejected the dichotomy of a 'civilized' West and a 'non-civilized' East. He sought out and explored cultures that stood out against the advance of standardization under the guise of modernization. He found many honorable values and traditions that serve mankind better.

Novelist Uchida Yasuo notes: "Yakumo, though a foreigner, seems to have understood the proto-scenery of Japan and the subtle parts of the Japanese spiritual structure better than the Japanese. We can indeed learn from Yakumo's works about the 'heart' of the Japanese that modern Japanese have forgotten."

Sekioka Hideyuki, in "Listen to the Voice of Koizumi Yakumo" (2006), warned about the Americanization of Japan which he claims has brought about a moral decline. He starts, "Whenever I want to contact the long-lost nobility of the Japanese soul, I never fail to reach for (the works of) Koizumi Yakumo." He criticized political party suggestions of legislation, saying the nation (*kokuron*) had gone astray. "This is due to the fact that today's Japanese have completely lost the 'moral impluse' (*rinriteki shodo*) and 'moral instinct' (*renreteki hon no*) that Hearn picked up from the behavior of our Meiji ancestors and verbalized. Hearn's works remind us of our loss."

Indeed, Lafcadio Hearn's writings are used as a model to lead Japan in a different direction, and to restore the Japanese 'nobility of the soul'. Lafcadio would be appalled by the prevalence of religious and racial bigotry the world is currently experiencing. The messages in his writing were humanitarian ones. They tried to teach people to be more respectful, tolerant, and empathetic toward others, regardless of their race, religion, or national origin. He stressed the interconnectedness of all humans.

In the symposium inviting the Olympic Games to Tokyo, Hearn was mentioned to remind citizens of the traditional Japanese virtues such as love for nature, family, and all living things. Many feel it is crucial that lost values be restored for the revitalization of Japan.

"It has been wisely observed by the greatest of modern thinkers that mankind has progressed more rapidly in every other respect than in morality." LH

The following statements by Hearn bring into sharp relief several issues that continue in contemporary Japan and identify distinct characteristics of Japanese culture. Reading Hearn is like skimming the latest headlines. Through his global sensibilities and keen observations, he understood the essence of Japanese culture and provided a view of the country's future prospects.

- "I think the future greatness of Japan will depend on the preservation of that Kyushu or Kumamoto spirit, the love of what is plain and good and simple, and the hatred of useless luxury and extravagance."
- "The real religion of Japan, the religion still professed in one form or other, by the entire nation, is that cult which has been the foundation of all civilized religion, and of all civilized society,--- ancestor worship."
- "Japanese education attaches too much importance to rote memorization and does not cultivate the imagination."
- "When one reflects that for thousands of years Japan has suffered natural disasters in precisely the same way, it is difficult not to believe that such extraordinary conditions have had no effect upon national character."

Hearn was ahead of his time when he abandoned Eurocentrism, and discovered the distinctive, ethnic value of non-Western cultures. Hearn specialists today maintain that passion to educate others about his egalitarian spirit, cultural relativity, and open mind.

The contemporary relevance of Lafcadio Hearn/Koizumi Yakumo's insights, analytical perspectives, and predictions are being revisited by scholars, theologians, historians, and policy makers in order to re-examine the direction of Japan and other nations for the future. "We are the ancestors of an age to come."

CHAPTER 44

Examples of Lafcadio Hearn/Koizumi Yakumo's relevance and impact in today's world are outlined and discussed here:

JOURNALISM STYLES

Traditional journalism has always favored a detached style that relies on facts (who, what, when, where, why) and quotations that can be verified by third parties. Lafcadio Hearn was a forerunner in the New Journalism style of the 1960s and 70s in the United States. This method is not the usual neutral narrator recording in the third person what is seen and heard. Participatory journalism is written without claims of objectivity, and often includes a self-referencing narrative of the reporter as part of the story. The reporter is personally involved and writes about what he thinks and feels.

Lafcadio Hearn began injecting himself into his newspaper stories in Cincinnati and New Orleans, referring to himself as "the Dismal Man", "the Ghoul" or "the Enquirer man". His energetic writing style in which the author is a protagonist using first person plural "we" or "this reporter" tells of personal experiences and emotions during the event. His common use of humor, sarcasm, profanity, and exaggeration added personality and involved his readers. A combination of self-satire and social critique gave power to this subjective style of reporting. He sometimes portrayed himself as a curious, mischievous dullard. In mid-story he might switch to a question-and-answer format. He included these irreverent techniques to startle, challenge, and amuse his reading audience. Hearn's use of alliteration, digressions, and nuances of scene created hypnotic stories that transcended the ephemera of daily journalism of this time. He labored to make himself an artist, a wordsmith rather than a mere reporter.

An example of Hearn's participatory, subjective writing was when he accompanied a famous steeplejack named Joseph Rodriguez Weston on a climb to the summit of the Cathedral of St. Peter in Chains, the highest structure in Cincinnati, to repair a lightning rod. His article began, "It is scarcely necessary to observe that the writer, wholly inexperienced in the art of hazardous climbing, did not start out upon such an undertaking without considerable trepidation."

The description of being hauled on Weston's back to the top of the cathedral, and perched terrified on the arm of the cross entertained the newspaper's readers with its high adventure and comic qualities. Hearn described his sense of danger, an agonizing fear of falling, his frantic cries, clenched teeth, and how being strapped to the experienced steeplejack's back gave the appearance of a humpbacked monkey climbing the structure. Part of the joke was that because of his defective vision, he could see nothing after he made his terrifying perilous journey up the steeple.

Hearn's self-referencing journalism style appealed to readers' emotions and senses, making an otherwise dry newspaper report more colorful, palatable, and entertaining. By casting himself as a comic target of mild abuse, he found he could shock, entertain, and educate his readers. There was a serious purpose behind his style. He wanted to expose the powerful and prosperous citizens of Cincinnati to the realities of social evils that they normally tried to ignore. He attempted through journalism to reform society and help needy social outcasts. Stories about common people were used as instruments to articulate dissatisfaction with industrial society. In Cincinnati, his articles on the negro levee quarter are now recognized as trailblazing. The New Orleans and West Indies stories boldly took on issues of race and corruption, and again in Japan, anti-imperialist attitudes separated him out from even his greatest Western contemporaries.

In the New Journalism movement of the twentieth century, Hunter S. Thompson was among the forefathers. He based his new "gonzo" style on Hearn's technique and on William Faulkner's notion that "fiction is often the best fact". Thompson wrote basic truths about people and events, but also included himself in stories and, like Lafcadio, used satirical devices to expose injustices to drive his points home.

"I don't get any satisfaction out of the old traditional journalist's view: I just covered the story. I just gave it a balanced view," Thompson said in an interview regarding subjectivity verses objectivity. He felt that total objectivity in journalism was a myth. "Absolute truth is a very rare and dangerous commodity in the context of professional reporting." Gonzo journalists often blend fact and fiction, use hyperbole and fantasy and dark comedy.

Forerunner Lafcadio Hearn's and then Hunter Thompson's style of subjective, first-person narrative, participatory type reporting is now a bona fide style of writing, a subgenre of New Journalism. Hearn is known as a precursor to Norman Mailer, with work described as "witty, totally detached, and nearly childlike." In the 1960s Tom Wolfe led the stream of consciousness technique in New Journalism. It was also championed by writers such as Terry Southern, Lester Bangs, and John Birmingham. Hearn's influence can be detected in writers like Thompson, Norman Mailer, Joan Didion, Truman Capote, George Plimpton, and others.

PULITZER PRIZE STORY BASED ON HEARN REPORTING

The Pulitzer Prize for History in 2020 was awarded to *"Sweet Taste of Liberty: A True Story of Slavery and Restitution in America"* by W. Caleb McDaniel and published by Oxford University Press. It tells the story of Henrietta Wood, who was born enslaved in Kentucky and then freed in Cincinnati in 1848. She was later kidnapped and re-enslaved for more than a decade. After the Civil War she made her way back to Ohio and sued her kidnapper, Zebulon Ward, in federal court for $20,000 in damages and lost wages. Amazingly, she won, and Ward paid her a sum of $2500, the largest amount awarded in a lawsuit to a former slave.

Although Henrietta Wood could not read or write, she told her story in the 1870s to a young journalist at the *Cincinnati Commercial* newspaper named Lafcadio Hearn. The original printed interview, full of dialogue between Wood and Hearn was used extensively by W. Caleb McDaniel in his award-winning story. Direct quotes in Hearn's sensational journalistic style, written over one hundred and fifty years ago, enabled the tale to ring so true today that it won the Pulitzer Prize.

JAPANESE FOLKLORE STUDIES

Yanagita Kunio (1875-1962) is often called the founder of Japanese native folklore studies (*minzokugaku*) as an academic field. He is best known as the author of *The Legends of Tono* (1910). He began his career as a bureaucrat with the Department of Agriculture but developed an interest in rural Japan and its folk traditions. Yanagita conducted extensive research into local customs, practices, and beliefs in rural areas. From this he established the systematic and scholarly framework and methods for folklore studies in Japan.

Yanagita was a fan of Western literature, especially poetry and ethnologies by anthropologists and was familiar with observations by Lafcadio Hearn. When Yanagita started his folklore studies, Lafcadio's works were widely read. Hearn's fourteen books on Japan and multiple articles were always deeply rooted in folklore as a means of understanding a population. For decades he had recorded the legends, religious customs, and superstitions in New Orleans, Martinique, and Japan.

Although Yanagita established folklore as a new academic field of study, he admired and was inspired by Hearn. In his *Meiji-Taisho shi, seso-hen - History of the Meiji-Taisho Period; Aspects of Social Mores* (1921), Yanagita stated that no foreigner would seldom be able to observe and understand Japan better than Hearn. He also remarked that Hearn's first work, *Glimpses of Unfamiliar Japan*, succeeded in grasping the Japanese mentality. He approved of Hearn's style of combining folklore and travel writing. His *Father of Folklore Studies* repeated mentions Hearn's well-known tales, highlighting the influence and impact that Lafcadio Hearn had on the establishment and character of academic folklore studies in Japan.

HEARN LITERARY LEGACY IN JAPAN

Lafcadio Hearn, an American of Greek-Irish origin, moved to Japan in 1890, became a Japanese citizen called Koizumi Yakumo, and stayed there until his death in 1904. He became famous for studies of Japanese culture and his collection of folklore and ghost stories. He adapted over fifty stories from Japanese sources, which are gathered in six collections: *In Ghostly Japan* (1899), *Shadowings* (1900), *A Japanese Miscellany* (1901), *Kotto* (1902), *Kwaidan: Stories and Studies of Strange Things* (1904), and *The Romance of the Milky Way* (1905). He explored topics as varied as art, architecture, karma, race memory, and Japan's acceptance of impermanence. His books have been called a writer's "love letters to Japan".

Lafcadio played a crucial role in popularizing Japanese folklore. Today's Japanese "ghost culture" has been deeply influenced by his collection of traditional stories about the supernatural. His ghost tales in *Kwaidan*, first written in English and then retranslated and published in a bilingual Japanese-English edition in 1931, are the heart of Japan's folkloric national cultural treasures. The fact that this was written by a foreigner is remarkable.

"A great many things which in times of lesser knowledge we imagined to be superstitious or useless, prove today on examination to have been of immense value to mankind." L.H.

Although Hearn is almost forgotten in the West, every Japanese child reads Koizumi Yakumo's tales in school. The Japanese remain grateful to him for understanding and then teaching the Western world about the soul (*kokoru*) of the Empire of the Rising Sun.

JAPANESE AND GLOBAL HORROR CINEMA BASED ON HEARN'S WORKS

Japanese stories about haunting myths and ghosts were adapted to film as soon as it was technically possible. Filmmaking was first influenced by classical Japanese theater, especially Kabuki and Noh performances. After the Second World War, Japanese cinema showed an interest in copying Western horror films. Soon hybrid works, which combined Japanese motifs and American/European horror elements, began to emerge.

During Japan's Edo period (1603-1868) the classic ghosts were typically women who returned to the world of the living for two reasons: either they are driven by romantic or unaccomplished passion which must be satisfied, or they cannot rest until their family is taken care of. Ancient figures of the female *yurei* ghosts represent both an object of repressed longing and fear.

The stereotypical avenging ghost woman, as written by Lafcadio and others over the centuries, is usually dressed in white with loose hair. One of the most famous female stories is about O-Iwa of Tsuruya Nanboku's play *Tokaido Yotsuya Kaidan*. In this tale, a masterless samurai named Iemon plots the death of his submissive and self-sacrificing wife O-Iwa, so that he can marry a rich woman. After her horrific death the wife's ghost directs all her wrath against her unfaithful husband and drives him insane.

Horror stories of monster female spirits who no longer belonged to human society rose out of cultural frustrations. Women were oppressed by the feudal system culture and certain streams of Buddhism and Confucianism, so in death they broke out of their assigned roles and societal behaviors to undergo transformation into a stronger presence who can stand up for herself and pursue relentless revenge.

A majority of Lafcadio Hearn's ghost stories are based on a combination of ancient tales and Western concepts regarding the spirit world. Their status as cultural revenants make his Japanese female ghosts a model that still haunts cinemas throughout Asia and around the world.

The formation and mythology of female ghost is such a worldwide success because it is so easily adapted, integrated, and transformed to fit various transnational horror films. The constant theme of traditional works is based on a fascination for female passion and women returning after death to find the love they missed during lifetime or the take revenge. Hearn dramatized and romanticized his retellings and embodied the actual fears of people around the world. His ghost stories were and are still highly appreciated in Japan, and today his renditions are the most common versions.

KWAIDAN MOVIE BY KOBAYASHI MASAKI

Hearn's *Kwaidan* ghost tales are the recognized standard for Japan's folklore stories. Japanese director Kobayashi Masaki used a quartet of Hearn's various folktales as the basis for his movie *Kwaidan,* a psychological horror film released in December 1964 at the prestigious Yurakuza Theater in Tokyo. Three quarters into filming the production had exhausted its budget, so Kobayashi, who believed in the story so much, sold his house to complete the movie. *Kwaidan* was reedited to 125 minutes for its theatrical release in the United States in 1965.

In Japan the film won Yoko Mizuki the Kinema Junpo award for Best Screenplay. It also won awards at the Mainichi Film Concours for Best Cinematography and Best Art Direction. *Kwaidan* was given a Special Jury Prize at Cannes in 1965 and received an Academy Award Oscar nomination for Best Foreign Language Film. Reviewers praised the film as "using color to give the stories something of the quality of a legend", "a visually impressive tour-de-force", "almost too beautiful to be scary", and a review that Hearn would have liked, read, "Exquisitely designed and fastidiously ornate, Masaki Kobayashi's ambitious anthology operates less as a frightening example of horror and more as a meditative tribute to Japanese folklore."

Kwaidan is an archaic Japanese word that means "ghost story". The four nightmarish tales adapted by Kobayashi summarized: A man stranded in a blizzard is saved by Yuki the Snow Maiden, but his rescue comes at a cost; A penniless samurai divorces his true love to marry for money with tragic results; A samurai who sees another warrior's reflection in his teacup, one who seeks vengeance; and Blind musician Hoichi is forced to perform for an audience of ghosts.

The common bond that holds the *Kwaidan* tales together is not the typical fear factor characteristic of monster and ghost novels, but rather the basic human emotions of isolation and sadness, beauty, and dread. The fear emanates from stark reality and spiritual power.

True to the nature of Lafcadio's ghost stories that plunge into myth and legend, *Kwaidan* tales are all unforgettable and absolutely haunting. He writes of two kinds of ghosts ---the spirits of the dead and the spirits of the living. Then he invites his readers to take their choice, if they dare.

Shortly after Lafcadio's death, literary critic Edmund Clarence Stedman said, "Hearn will become in time as much of a romantic personality and tradition as Poe is now." The central standing of Lafcadio's literary legacy in Japanese culture, as later reviewed in *American Literature*, "Hearn might, with reference to *Kwaidan*, be called an Orientalized Poe".

In 2000 Masaki Kobeyashi's Ananda spiritual group, dedicated to helping individuals live in joy through meditation, published *Reader's Guide to Lafcadio Hearn*, compiled with the cooperation of more than 50 scholars of his work. In many cities of Japan (Hiroshima, Kobe, Matsue, Kumamoto, Toyama, Yaizu, and others) there are active Yakumo Societies to honor Koizumi Yakumo the renowned writer/professor and his life lessons.

NORGREN KWAIDAN MUSICAL BALLADS

Pehr Hinrik Nordgren (1944-2008) was a Finnish composer who studied musicology at the University of Helsinki and later spent three years at the Tokyo University of the Arts with Yoshi Hasegawa, where he became acquainted with traditional Japanese music. Pehr returned to Finland with his Japanese wife and worked as a freelance composer. In cooperation with the Ostrobothnian Chamber Orchestra, as 'court composer', he created an abundance of orchestral works. His compositions combined elements and instruments of traditional Japanese music with those of Finnish folk ballads.

In 1972 he wrote "Hochi the Earless", the first of 10 ballads for solo piano inspired by the Japanese ghost stories of Lafcadio Hearn. Norgren composed the "Kwaidan Ballads" for piano (1972-1977) based on the book *Kwaidan* by Lafcadio Hearn. It was followed by "Kwaidan II, Three Ballads after Japanese Ghost Stories" for piano left hand, Op. 127 (2004). His music, like the mythical ghost stories, is full of a strong need for expression that seems to well up from the deepest and most tragic abysses of life.

What Lafcadio Hearn's inspirational writing did so well was to present a world whose limits remain unknown, where things happen that we cannot explain. Filled with hushed, hypnotic dread, Hearn stories are full of psychological tension and journey into the dark recesses of the human mind.

KUROSAWA KIYOSHI HORROR FILMS

Kurosawa Kiyoshi is another Japanese film director, screenwriter, film critic, and professor at Tokyo University of the Arts. He has worked in a variety of genres yet is best known for his contributions to the Japanese crime and horror genre. His thrillers have won awards at international film festivals in Cannes, Hong Kong, Rome, Berlin, Locarno, and Venice. He is known as a master of fear and horror who mines real life atrocities. Like Hearn, Kiyoshi is part of a wave of pushing ghost stories into realms of philosophical and existential exploration.

IAN FLEMING'S JAMES BOND BOOK

Another show of influence in the modern creative arts is by the creator of James Bond series, Ian Fleming, and his fascination with and mention of Lafcado Hearn in his book *You Only Live Twice*. He devoted the entire chapter six to Bond and PSIA Chief Tiger Tanaka discussing whether one can truly "become Japanese" and using Lafcadio Hearn as an example.

Tiger had the opinion that people like Hearn can never be ethically or culturally accepted: "...there have from time to time been foreigners who have come to this country and settled here. They have for the most part be cranks and scholars, and the European-born American Lafcadio Hearn, who became a Japanese citizen is a very typical example. In general, they have been tolerated, usually with some amusement."

After discussing how American soldiers in Occupied Japan were ruining Japan, James Bond retorts that a soldier that comes to Japan and lives there for a few years is a very different thing from someone who decides to naturalize: "Presumably your talking of the lower-level G.I.s---second generation Americans---swaggering around a conquered country under the blessed coverlet of the Stars and Stripes with too much money to spend. I daresay they occasionally marry a Japanese girl and settle down here. But surely they pull up stumps pretty quickly. Our Tommies have done the same thing in Germany. But that's quite a different thing from the Lafcadio Hearns of the world."

In the final showdown between James Bond and his nemesis, Blofeld uses the samurai expression "*kirisute gomen*", which loosely means "license to kill", a Bond 007 catchphrase.

"Have you ever heard the Japanese expression "*kirisute gomen?*" asked Blofeld.

"Bond groans and says, "Spare me the Lafcadio Hearn, Blofeld!"

"It dates from the time of the samurai. It means literally "kill and going away". If a low person hindered a samurai's passage along the road or failed to show him proper respect, the samurai was within his rights to lop off the mans' head. I regard myself as a latter-day samurai. My fine sword has not yet been bloodied. Yours will be an admirable head to cut its teeth on."

POPULAR FICTION FEATURING HEARN

In the 1980s and 1990s there was a "Yakumo boom" in fictional literature and film. A notable example of the use of Hearn as a character or reference is in Uchida Yasuo's *Kaidan no michi* (*The Road of Ghost Stories*) 1991. Unlike other detective novels which use Lafcadio as a symbol of a ghostly atmosphere, this detective story has a hero who visits in the footsteps of Hearn and becomes involved with murder cases. The book uses Lafcadio's cultural criticism to make a point. For instance, the hero notes, "Yakumo, though a foreigner, seems to have understood the proto-scenery of Japan and the subtle parts of the Japanese spiritual structure better than the Japanese. We can indeed learn from Yakumo's works about the heart of the Japanese the modern Japanese have forgotten."

Between July 1992 and June 1993, *Kaidan* (Ghost Stories) by Atoda Ko were serialized in newspapers such as *Tokyo shinbun*. The series is a love story in which the hero and heroine become close through their shared interest in the author. They use Lafcadio's observations from the past and present to make comparisons, such as when they contrast the kind and sincere Japanese whom Lafcadio admired with the modern Japanese who have become *kosukarai shonin* (mean shopkeepers). His descriptions are used as symbols to restore "True Japan" - the innocent and simple pre-modern Japan they found in Hearn's *Kwaidan* and the country which was lost in the process of modernization.

A best-selling book *Before the coffee gets cold* by Toshikazu Kawaguchi is a series of chilling images about a small café in Tokyo that offers carefully brewed coffee and a chance to travel back in time. The main rule for visiting a meaningful person not of the present is that the time travel trip can only last as long as it takes for the coffee to get cold. Each of the four book characters manage to sit in the special café chair and go back. Reminiscent of Koizumi/Hearn's mysterious, quirky stories, Kawaguchi explores the age-old question of who you would visit. Knowing you couldn't change anything would you still return to the past? It seems likely that Kawaguchi sat in the chair and had a chat with Lafcadio Hearn about people's desire to hold on to or change their life experiences and how to find happiness despite the past.

TV DRAMA SERIES WITH GEORGE CHAKIRIS AS HEARN/KOIZUMI

A number of films and dramatizations of Hearn's life or work have been produced. A stage play, *Nihon no omokage* (*Vestiges of Japan*) by playwright Yamada Taichi was made into a 1984 TV drama mini-series by the same title. George Chakiris, also a Greek-American, played Yakumo Koizumi/Lafcadio Hearn in the TV series.

It tracks Hearn's 1890 arrival in Japan, teaching career, marriage, collecting folktales and writing numerous articles and books on Japan, especially retelling old ghost stories. The series illustrates the rapid modernization changes taking place in Japan that take away the magic of his beloved traditional Japanese life and the resulting spiritual poverty. The story was later re-adapted to theatrical productions.

PING CHONG PUPPET THEATER

Additionally, Ping Chong is an American playwright and theater director whose multimedia productions examine cultural and ethical differences and pressing social issues. He is best known for his ongoing series *Undesirable Elements* about the experiences of outsiders. Chong, in collaboration with set designer Mirsuru Ishii and puppet maker Jon Ludwig, adapted several of

Koizumi Yakumo/Lafcadio Hearn's stories into his puppet theater, including the 1999 *Kwaidan* and the 2002 *OBON: Tales of Moonlight and Rain*. Hearn created the art of literature and theater out of the art of oral story telling. The way he wrote his ghost stories helped revive the methods used in ancient tales being performed onstage. Just like when Hearn's wife Setsu would act out the various parts of a story, their performative transaction style became the creative theatrical interaction dynamic between the actor and audience.

TOUHOU PROJECT COMPUTER GAMES

In recent years the *Touhou Project* computer games and audio music CDs developed by Jun'ya Ota, under the pseudonym ZUN, named main characters Yukari Yakumo and Maribel Hearn after Koizumi Yakumo-Lafcadio Hearn. The plots of ZUN's *Touhou Project* game revolve around strange phenomenon that occur in the fictional realm of Gensokyo (literally Fantasy Land), which was near a human village in a remote Japanese mountain range separated from our world with a magical barrier.

The basic plot is that long ago many non-humans *yokai* ghosts, like those in Lafcadio's stories, lived in the area. The humans decided to eliminate the *yokai* spirits, so the *yokai* sage named Yukari Yakumo, developed a barrier between the two worlds, the "boundary of phantasm and substance" to separate them and protect the balance. Maribel Hearn is a college student who lives in Kyoto and can see Gensokyo in her dreams. The project games focus on events called supernatural incidents that occur when the barrier is breeched. Gamers use characters, spells, and weapons at various levels of difficulty to collect points. The *Touhou Project* has been a prominent source of Japanese *dojin* content and it has spawned a vast amount of fan-made artwork, music prints, video games, and internet memes. The popular game series has gained a cult following both inside and outside Japan. Maribel also appears in a series of music albums in ZUN collections.

Two manga graphic cartoon book versions of Hearn's Japanese stories have been produced by Sean Michael Wilson, who is also half Irish like Hearn and lives in Kumamoto as Hearn did. These are *The Faceless Ghost* manga book (2015) with Japanese artist Michiru Morikawa and *Manga Yokai Stories* (2020) with artist Ai Takita.

PHYSIC DETECTIVE YAKUMO SAITO: Additionally, *Psychic Detective Yakumo Saitou* is the title character of an anime and manga series. Yakumo is an attractive young college student who lives in the filming club room at the university. He is exceptionally guarded with his feelings. He acts like a

stranger and is not good with other people. He is sarcastic, blunt, and comes off as condescending and cold. Yet he has a kind heart and will go to great lengths to help others, even risking his life to save them. Yakumo was born with heterochromia, a difference in eye colors. With his red eye he can see ghosts. He believes that spirits and ghosts are bound to earth because of a certain "cause", and eliminating that cause allows the spirits to rest in peace. Any strong emotion, such as extreme hatred or sadness, ties a human soul to the earth, a thing, or person until they are released. Being intelligent, logical, and observant Yakumo can solve mysterious crimes before the police. Detective Yakumo has a sad personal past, but changes a little once he meets Haruka, a kind and honest girl.

There are so many parallels between the Yakumo Saitou character and Yakumo Koizumi that there is no doubt the series had its foundation in the life and writings of Lafcadio Hearn, the master of *yokai* ghost stories.

FRANK LLOYD WRIGHT

The famous architect Wright was a passionate Japanophile. He proclaimed Japan to be "the most romantic, artistic, nature-inspired country on earth." Throughout his life Japanese art, literature and architecture influenced his work. He spent much of his free time collecting and selling *ukiyo-e* woodblock prints and books about Japan. He found inspiration in Japanese art as organic wholeness because of its understated, harmonic, and pure aesthetics. His ideas about art and the culture of Japan were drawn greatly from Lafcadio Hearn's books and the activities of Ernest Fenollosa, a close friend of Hearn's in Tokyo. Wright always acknowledged his indebtedness to Japanese principles and style.

Other well-known people like Mark Twain, William Butler Yeats, Albert Einstein, Charlie Chaplin, General Douglas MacArthur, Several US Presidents like Ronald Reagan, writers such as Ben Hecht, John Erskine, Malcolm Cowley, and Jorge Luis Borges lauded Hearn's literary genius and found it inspirational.

WORLD WAR II LIBERTY SHIP, THE LAFCADIO HEARN

"Liberty Ship" was the name given to the 2,711 EC2-type ships designed for "emergency construction" by the United States Maritime Commission during World War II. President Franklin Delano Roosevelt nicknamed the ships "ugly ducklings".

The first Liberty ship was launched on September 27, 1941, built to a mass produced, standard design. The 250,000 parts were pre-fabricated in sections and welded together in about seventy days, at the cost of $2,000,000 dollars. The Liberty was 441 feet long and 56 feet wide. Oil burning boilers fed her three-cylinder reciprocating steam engine up to a speed of 11 knots. Her hold could carry over 9,000 tons of cargo and passengers.

Liberty Ships were named after prominent (deceased) Americans, starting with the Patrick Henry and the signers of the Declaration of Independence. Any group that raised $2 million dollars in War Bonds could suggest a name for a Liberty Ship.

The Delta Shipbuilding Co. of New Orleans, Louisiana launched the Lafcadio Hearn Liberty Ship, Identification Number 1740, Ship design Z-ET1-S-C3, on July 31, 1943. It was a 7176-ton tanker with a 17.34 beam and 8.41 draft. Since the ship was constructed in New Orleans it is likely that Lafcadio's friends such as Dr. Matas from his days as a reporter in the Crescent City, raised War Bond money to place his name on the Liberty Ship.

After her war service, the Lafcadio Hearn was transferred to the reserve fleet in Brunswick, Georgia, then Wilmington, North Carolina. In 1948 she was sold to the private Polarus Steamship Company, New York and renamed Polarusoil. In 1955 it was converted to dry cargo vessel, lengthened, and served in Greece until scrapped at Kaohsiung in 1969.

GENERAL BONNER FELLERS:

Brigadier General Bonner Fellers (1896-1973) was a United States Army officer who served during War World II as a military attache and director of psychological warfare. Before the war he'd visited Japan several times and wrote his graduate thesis on "Psychology of the Japanese Soldier". Fellers is often credited with saving the life of the Japanese emperor after World War II.

LAFCADIO'S LEGACY

During the Pacific war and afterwards during the occupation of Japan, Fellers advised General Douglas MacArthur about the psyche of the Japanese people, among other things. When the Western world and United States politicians were demanding that the invading US forces "hang Hirohito" as a war criminal, General MacArthur, Supreme Commander for the Allied Powers in the occupation of Japan, read Bonner Fellers' several influential memoranda on why it would be advantageous for the reconstruction of Japan to exonerate Emperor Hirohito and all members of his family of war crimes. On Fellers' sage advice, there was no criminal prosecution of the Emperor. MacArthur agreed that it would be in long-term US interest to restore the imperial legacy and preserve the symbolic imperialism, rather than execute the Emperor. Fellers' counsel was followed because he was "a person who is well versed in Japanese culture."

MacArthur served as the de facto absolute ruler for six years (1945-1951) and was nicknamed *Gaijin Shogun* (foreign Shogun). He worked with Bonner Fellers regarding management of the war end, occupation, and re-inventing of Japan. This included observing the traditional politeness, generosity, a face saving by not prosecuting or debasing the Emperor in any way. In post-war discussions, Fellers was one of the few Americans who truly understood the Emperor's place in the heart of the people.

Whenever asked, Fellers claimed that the basis of his deep understanding of the issues were the writings of Lafcadio Hearn. He'd read all of Hearn's books and articles to learn about Japan's people and culture. He told an interviewer who asked if he read any authors other than Hearn, "No, he alone is enough. Never needed anyone else." After studying Hearn, Fellers learned to hate war, despise racism, love travel, and maintain an open mind and curiosity about life. Upon MacArthur's death, seven books by Lafcadio Hearn were found in the famous general's personal library.

In 1971 Hirohito conferred on Bonner Fellers the Second Order of the Sacred Treasure "in recognition of your long-standing contribution to promoting friendship between Japan and the United States." Fellers became friends with the Koizumi family. In fact, Lafcadio's great-grandson Bon Koizumi was named after Bonner.

NEW ORLEANS RESTORATION INSPIRATION

Although Lafcadio Hearn is known primarily for his books about Japanese culture at the turn of the twentieth century, he also lived in New Orleans, Louisiana from 1877 to 1887. He worked for two newspapers, *The Item* and the *Times Democrat*, where he fully immersed himself in the city's unique way of life and wrote extensively about the Crescent City at the bend in the Mississippi River. "I find much to gratify an Artist's eye in this quaint, curious, crooked French Quarter," Hearn wrote. In addition to his observations of the history, architecture, and exotic culture--- he tackled contentious issues such as racial tensions, police and political corruption, religious issues, and sanitation problems.

Lafcadio was enamored with the mixed cultures he encountered there and made the old Creole town the inspiration for his literary creations. He wrote stirring accounts of the city's cuisine, voodoo practices, rich heritage, and indiscretions for national publications such as *Harper's Weekly* and *Scribner's Magazine*. His romanticized versions of New Orleans as being unlike any other American city persist today. It is said that he "invented New Orleans". In explaining the city to the world, he essentially created its brand - the image of music, sex, and sorcery that continues to beckon people from marketing campaigns and tourist brochures.

Hearn wrote of New Orleans as a woman, a treasured lover. "There are few who can visit her for the first time without delight; and few who can ever leave her without regret; and none who can forget her strange charm when they have once felt its influence."

When New Orleans, especially the Vieux Carre French Quarter, fell into disrepair at the end of the nineteenth century, most locals were indifferent or outright opposed to its preservation. However, Lafcadio's national audience of notable creative figures, because of his romantic stories, decided to take up residence in the Vieux Carre and restore the area to its former glory. The ensuing cultural renaissance of the 1920s made New Orleans fashionable again and ultimately played a key role in its preservation. Lafcadio's conjuring of a mythic aura about the Crescent City attracted creative minds and fueled a cultural revival that saved the heart of New Orleans and made it a favorite international destination.

NEW ORLEANS MARDI GRAS KREWE OF LAFCADIO

During New Orleans' annual Mardi Gras festivities, a Krewe of Lafcadio honors their icon, the great 19th century journalist and writer Lafcadio Hearn. They parade in the French Quarter celebrating and satirizing New Orleans culture. The main theme of the Krewe is the world-famous culinary arts of New Orleans, because Hearn was the author of the first Creole cookbook, *La Cuisine Creole* (1885). A mule-drawn float carries a top local chef as their King and a chosen waiter as a Duke.

The Krewe of Lafcadio coat of arms features a crossed spoon and spatula. They hand out wooden cooking spoons and other food/cooking related items. Excess parade funds are donated to support a program that sends top local chefs to cook New Orleans-style meals for sailors on the *USS New Orleans* and the *USS Louisiana*.

In 2024 the theme of Mardi Gras was "The Two Worlds of Lafcadio Hearn". A poster by Patti Adams featured him as Rex, King of the New Orleans Carnival.

POSTAGE STAMP

Yet another reminder as to what a major figure Lafcadio Hearn/Koizumi Yakumo (1850-1904) still is in Japan, a colorful commemorative postal stamp was issued in 2004 for the 100th anniversary of his death. The striking 'Men of Culture' series (28 x 39 mm) postage stamp (JP 2907) references *Kwaidan* (1904) his legendary book of ghost stories.

The honor was in memory of this culturally eminent man's remarkable achievement of writing numerous books explaining Japan culture and legends to the West, particularly the United States of America.

CHAPTER 45

LIBRARIES, MUSEUMS, COLLECTIONS, AND EXHIBITS

Museum collections and exhibits featuring Lafcadio Hearn/Koizumi Yakumo history and materials can be found in worldwide locations that include, but are not limited to: Lafkada, Corfu, and Athens, Greece; Matsue, Tokyo, Toyama, and Oki, Japan; Dublin and Tramore, Ireland; Martinique, West Indies; New Orleans, New York Metropolitan Museum, Columbia University, Morgan Pierpont Library and Museum; plus Cincinnati and Cleveland, Ohio in the United States of America.

University of Toyama Library: Lafcadio Hearn, the Irish-Greek-born author known in Japan as Koizumi Yakumo, died in Tokyo on September 26, 1904 at age fifty-four. In 1924, twenty years after his death and soon after the great 1923 earthquake disaster in Tokyo, his wife, Setsu Koizumi was seriously concerned over the possible destruction of her late husband's book collection. When it became known that she was looking for a safe location, there were many offers to buy the collection.

Mr. Nannichi Tsunetaro, the first principal of Toyama High school, heard from his brother Tanabe Ryuji, a former student of Lafcadio's at Tokyo Imperial University, that the family planned to distribute and sell most of Hearn's library. He suggested that Lafcadio's personal library should go to a new school in Toyama which was founded in 1924 by a generous benefactor, Madame Haruko Baba. Lafcadio Hearn's personal library was secured by her for the Toyama Kotogakko High School.

Rather than donate the collection to universities in Tokyo, Setsu allowed Mrs. Haruko Baba, the widow of Baba Masajaru, a successful ship merchant in Higashi Iwase-machi, Toyama-shi to purchase the Hearn Library to present to the school during the opening ceremony held June 10, 1924. The campus and library were moved after World War II and became today's Toyama University. For her public benefactions, the Japanese Government awarded Mrs. Haruko Baba the Dark Blue-Ribbon Decoration.

The Hearn private collection of books in four languages consisted of 2069 foreign books, 364 Japanese books, and Hearn's handwritten manuscript of *Japan: An Attempt at Interpretation* composed of two manuscripts and 1,200 leaves. The Japanese books included ghost stories by Takizawa Bakin, Santo Kyoden, and Juppensha Ikku. There were 38 books by Teikoku Bunko. Most of the volumes are Japanese style woodprint books. In addition to the original collection materials, the library contains about 2,600 pieces of research literature related to Lafcadio Hearn. The knowledgeable caretaker of the "sacred books" for years was librarian Mrs. Kuribayashi.

Because the Lafcadio Hearn Library in Toyama is a collection of such rare and valuable books, one must fill out an application and receive advance permission in order to have access to the materials. The Hearn Library is currently open to the public on the second, third and fourth Wednesday of every month.

In honor of the 120th anniversary of Hearn's death and in celebration of his life and work, Toyama University is planning to conduct a series of seminars and events in 2024. Many programs are in conjunction and with the support of the Embassy of Japan and the Museum of Literature in Ireland.

Lafkada, Greece: The first Lafcadio Hearn museum in Europe, the Lafcadio Hearn Historical Center in Lafkada, Greece, the city of his birth, was opened July 2014. Rare books, 1st editions, painted art works,

serigraphs, and Japanese collectibles make up the exhibits housed in the Cultural Center of Lefkada Municipality next to the Archaeological Museum. The Cultural Center organizes two-day events dedicated to Japanese culture and language classes. Hearn has a statue in the Garden of Poets, next to other significant writers of Lefkada, and a street with his name.

The principal collection for the creation of the historic center to honor Hearn was donated by Greek-American Takis Efstathiou, a fine arts dealer-advisor. In addition to numerous rare books, he contributed an array of large Japanese artists' works, including a Wanda S. Masaki Nonta hand-painted shirt, numerous serigraphs, one co-created with Stamos, and serigraphs created by the Greek sculptor Theo, silkscreens, art works by Hearn, and movie posters. The hall and rooms housing the museum bear the Efstathiou name. By combining literature and art, he conveys Hearn's spirit through artistic expressions. The success of the exhibits has built people's empathy for Hearn's philosophy of tolerance.

Great-grandson of Lafcadio Hearn, Bon and his wife Shoko Koizumi offered personal items, letters, and photographs to complete the exhibits. Additionally, the municipalities of Kuamoto, Matsue, Shinjuku, Yaizu, Toyoma University, and others contributed to the establishment of the Lafcadio Hearn Historical Center.

Through photographs, documents, displays, and interactive audio-visual applications, a visitor to the Hearn Historical Center can observe the important milestones of the extraordinary life of Lafcadio Hearn in Europe, America, and Japan. The first room contains the life of Lafcadio from his 1850 birth in Lafkada, Greece until his 1890 departure to Japan. Panels along the walls describe his connections with Kythira, Lafkada, Ireland, England, Cincinnati, New Orleans, and Martinique.

The second room chronicles Hearn's life in Japan. His legendary literary works are featured in showcases filled with original books, articles, letters, postcards of the era, and personal memorabilia. The images and objects give visitors the opportunity to learn about the legendary life and works of the man who bridged the two cultures of Greece and Japan. Students regularly travel to the museum for tours, demonstrations, and talks about the man who defined the personality of Japan to the West and who serves as an example of a person with an open mind and open heart to humanity and world peace.

In 2014 an international symposium, "The Open Mind of Lafcadio Hearn: His Spirit from West to East" marked the 160th anniversary of the writer's birth in Lefkada. Over two days, performances, papers, and presentations by scholars, artists, writers, and dignitaries from Japan, Greece, Martinique, USA, and Ireland educated and entertained more than 1,000 people. The series of events, civic, artistic, and academic were mainly organized and funded by Hearn's great-grandson Bon Koizumi and his wife Shoko, Greek art dealer Takis Efstathiou, and the American College of Greece in Athens. The key symposium event for locals was opening of the Lafcadio Hearn Historical Center. The city where Hearn was born now stands with museums in Athens, New Orleans, New York, Tokyo, Matsue, Durham, Dublin, and Tramore.

Athens, Greece---American College of Greece: The American College of Greece (ACG) is the oldest American-accredited college in Europe and the largest private college in Greece. The ACG 64-acre campus is located at 6 Gravias Street, Agia Paraskevi, Athens. The college hosts a vibrant international student community.

In 2009, the American College of Greece hosted an art exhibit and symposium, "The Open Mind of Lafcadio Hearn", exploring his life, concepts, values, and spirit. The multifaceted events featured international

speakers who aimed to promote interest and attention to Greek-born Hearn and his work. Bon Koizumi, great-grandson of Hearn, started with a memorial speech "A Spiritual Odyssey from Greece to Japan'. The opening attracted over forty artists and five hundred visitors. The symposium's success inspired similar events to be held later in Lafkada, Greece; New Orleans, Louisiana; Manhattan, New York; and Matsue, Japan.

In *Insects and Greek Poetry*, he wrote, "Those old Greeks, though happy as children and as kindly; were very great philosophers, to whom we go for instructions even this day. What the world needs now most feels in need of is the return of that old Greek spirit of happiness and kindness." Therefore, it was appropriate to first conduct international symposiums around Greece to reinforce Hearn's love of a kind, tolerant, humanistic spirit. Public interest and sensitivity to Lafcadio are consistently rising and spreading.

The tribute to Hearn (1850-1904) was held on the 110th anniversary of friendship between Greece and Japan. The Greek-born extraordinary international man of letters was celebrated as the embodiment of an open mind. His example teaches that there is no higher calling than cultivating tolerance, no greater responsibility that holding a mirror up to the injustices of society, no richer way of life than one spent pursuing truth, and no greater challenge or mystery than merging creative energy into our daily life. By expanding his mind Lafcadio opened his heart to humanity, an action which can lead to peace within oneself and ultimately the world.

The Open Mind Concept is the creation of Takis Efstathiou to help people understand Hearn's love of humanity. He also donated a large collection of rare Hearn books and artifacts to the American College of Greece for permanent display to promote the author and literary tourism. Japanese actor Shiro Sano contributed the 16-volume first edition of *The Writings of Lafcadio Hearn* (1922) with an autograph by Setsu Koizumi, Hearn's wife.

The American College of Greece in Athens commissioned Japanese-American artist Masaaki Noda, a graduate from the Osaka University of Arts, to create a monumental sculpture entitled "The Open Mind of Lafcadio Hearn". The finished piece is a flow of metallic wings twisting toward the sky. One wing points Westward, the other East to represent Hearn being a bridge between nations and his multi-cultural mindset. Viewed from the right angle, the sculpture forms an open heart. The sculpture greets visitors to the ACG campus in the Office of Admissions Plaza. It serves as a symbol of the college's emphasis on attracting and serving a culturally diverse student population. Success of the Greek monument led to a sister

sculpture by Noda on the shores of Lake Shinji in Matsue, Japan where Hearn lived and taught (1890-1891).

In 2010 an art exhibit, curated by Megakles Rogakos, featured artworks from the American College of Greece Art collection and dozens of commissioned international award-winning artists. The exhibition covered all art forms (painting, sculpture, photography, etc.) and types from conceptual art to naturalism inspired by Lafcadio Hearn. The exhibit, marking the 160th anniversary of Hearn's birth, later opened at the Lafcadio Hearn Memorial Museum in Matsue, Japan.

Corfu Museum of Asian Arts, Kerkyra, Greece: In 2016, an exhibition entitled "Lafcadio Hearn-The Unfamiliar Japan" was set up in the Corfu Museum of Asian Arts in Kerkira, Corfu, Greece. The museum is housed in a Greek Revival style neoclassic palace built between 1819 and 1824 to serve as the residence of the British Lord High Commissioner of the Ionian Islands. It was also the home of the Ionian Senate and the Order of St. Michael and St. George. Since 1927, the palace has housed the Museum of Asian Art.

The Museum of Asiatic Art is unique, the only museum of its kind in Greece dedicated exclusively to the arts and culture of Asian countries. It contains over fifteen thousand works, spanning ten centuries from a variety of eastern countries. The museum collections have grown through private donations.

"Lafcadio Hearn - The Unfamiliar Japan" exhibition was made up of rare first editions, selected essays (translated in French German and Japanese), and original writings---all donated by fine art dealer Takis Efstathiou of Athens and New York. Efstathiou is known as the man who brought Hearn back to his birthplace and owns one of

the largest collections of Hearn's works (first editions, rare books, and Japanese collectibles.) Thanks to him the Corfu Museum of Asian Art (CMAA) now has one of the best Hearn book collections in Europe.

Greek-born Hearn frequently referred to Japanese artists like Hiroshige (1797-1858), Kunisada (1786-1864), and Hokusai (1760-1849). The Corfu Museum exhibit is enriched by woodblock prints of these major ukiyo-e artists, artworks of unique value from the collection of the museum's founder Gregorious Manos.

The Corfu Museum of Asian Art has produced several other exhibitions on Lafcadio Hearn, such as 2019-2020 shows at the Athens Municipal Gallery and the Greek Consulate in New York City as part of events celebrating the Greece-Japan connection. The exhibit in Athens was titled "Japan and Literature" and included a section on the Japanese engraver Katsushika Hokusai (1760-1849). The New York show focused entirely on Greek-born Hearn (1850-1904), who, before moving to Japan, spent over twenty years in the United States as a journalist and author.

In 2014 the Corfu Museum of Asian Art held workshops, readings, and a Japanese Tea Ceremony to commemorate the 110th anniversary of Lafcadio Hearn's death. The event was entitled "The Open Mind of Lafcadio Hearn---His Spirit from the West to the East." Corfu Museum director Despina Zernioti co-organized with the Municipality of Matsue, Japan, the Lefkada, Greece Cultural Center, and the Embassy of Japan in Greece.

Additionally, "Nostalgia: The Eternal Home of the Spirit" based on *Kwaidan* themed recitations by Shiro Sano accompanied by guitar master Kyoji Yamamoto performances brought readings to the realm of art. Members of Lafcadio Hearn International Societies will gather in Corfu in 2024 to celebrate the life and continued impact of Hearn.

Japanese Embassy, Athens, Greece: Embassy of Japan in Athens, Greece is a strong bond of communication between Japan's government and Greece. It conducts a range of consular services to local, Japanese, and international citizens. The Embassy contains a fine collection of books written by and about Lafcadio Hearn (1850-1904). When Hearn became a Japanese citizen, took the name Koizumi Yakumo, and lived in Japan until his death.

Matsue, Japan: The Lafcadio Hearn Memorial Museum, a landmark and historical site, is located at 322 Okudanicho, Matsue-shi, Shimane, Japan. The original museum was established in 1933, on a site adjoining Hearn's old residence with a fund of $3000 contributed by admirers and pupils of Hearn. Through the efforts of Hearn disciples Seiichi Kishi and Teizaburo Ochiai, manuscripts donated by the Koizumi family, and 350 books from the commemorative society, the museum opened to house collection displays. The Hearn Memorial Museum and Hearn's former residence 10 meters from the museum are located in Shiomi Nawate, where samurai homes and gardens line the moat of Matsue Castle.

The museum looks like a traditional Japanese building, the kind he would have loved. The city of Matsue was the foundation of experiences and knowledge that became immortalized in his famous *Glimpses of Unfamiliar Japan*, and the *Kwaidan* collection of ghost stories, and others.

The current museum facility was renovated and expanded in 2016. It now contains approximately 1,500 items, including Hearn's personal belongings such as the battered suitcases he arrived in Japan with, personal letters/drawings, furnishings from his home, family photographs, long-stemmed pipes, pens, reading monocle, and of course books. His books, manuscripts, related materials, and valuable relics gifted by his wife Setsu make up the core collection. Hearn's great-grandson Bon Koizumi and his wife Shoko serve as directors and cultural ambassadors. Over 50,000 visitors visit the museum annually.

The museum's displays are filled with memorabilia that trace the writer's life from Greece to Ireland to England to the United States of America to Japan with the use of photographs and descriptive texts in English and Japanese. Wherever possible, exhibits are accompanied with relevant excerpts from Hearn's works.

As you enter the historical center hall, you will see a statue called 'Odyssey of an Open Mind'. This monument shows wings that blend in the middle and create the shape of a heart. There are separate exhibition rooms that house various changing displays about Hearn, his legacy, and contributions. Don't miss the sculptures, art, or regular lectures, concerts, readings, and impressive library. The Takis Efstathiou Library is one of the largest and most important collections of original Hearn literary materials in the world.

Matsue, Japan - Hearn Residence and Literary Tourism

Matsue, Japan, the capital city of Shimane Prefecture and ancient Izumo Province, has a population of approximately 200,000 residents. It is known for the beautiful Lake Shinji, Tokugawa era Matsue Castle, and Izumo Taisha, one of the oldest and most important Shinto shrines in Japan. Matsue is where Lafcadio Hearn first lived, taught, married, and wrote his famous *Glimpses of Unfamiliar Japan* between 1890-1891. Hearn residence:

Matsue appears so often in Hearn's books that most Japanese associate him with the city, even though he spent the majority of his 14 years in Japan in other provinces. Hearn sites draw millions of tourists, mostly Japanese, to Matsue to find the original essence of Japan in his writings. Matsue passed an ordinance in 2021 to include Yakumo Koizumi as one of Matsue's seven key elements of cultural power. The city aims to be "a town where everyone recognizes various values through an open mind that respects diversity."

The Hearn Society of Matsue invites scholars, artists and musicians to conferences and exhibitions. The city holds a national speech contest each year for high school students to read Hearn's stories in English. Bon Koizumi, Hearn's great-grandson has become Matsue's steward of his ancestor's memory. Bon and his wife Shoko are directors of the Memorial Museum, lead symposiums and tours, and run a summer camp for children to learn about Lafcadio Hearn's life, literature, and philosophy.

The city celebrates its most famous adopted son with museums, exhibits, lectures, art, murals, sculptures, portraits, and street signs. Hearn-themed souvenirs feature sake, beer, and even instant coffee with his face on the labels.

In 1994 Matsue became a sister city with New Orleans, Louisiana, USA, where Hearn was a journalist for ten years. The two cities are united by the life and writings of Lafcadio Hearn (1850-1904), known in Japan as Koizumi Yakumo. The Japanese Society of New Orleans and the Koizumi Yakumo Society continue to bond the two city's ties and cultural appreciation with shared passion for jazz music, a New Orleans style brass band, gumbo among other Creole cuisine, and Krewe of Japan celebrations of Mardi Gras.

Although not an official friendship city of Matsue, there is an ongoing exchange with Dublin, Ireland where Patrick Lafcadio Hearn lived as a child. The city promotes the Hearn legacy with Irish cooking festivals and classes in Gaelic. The Irish pub festively celebrates St. Patrick's Day with Hearn related events. Matsue's Irish parade is the biggest in Japan.

In October, 2010, "The Open Mind of Lafcadio Hearn" Japanese symposium, similar to the 2009 version at the American College of Greece in Athens, was organized by the City of Matsue and the Koizumi family and held inside Matsue Castle. The art exhibit commemorated both the 120th anniversary of Hearn's arrival in Japan and the 160th anniversary of his birth. By holding the exhibition, Mayor Matsuura shared his appreciation of Hearn's open mind, his unbiased approach to such things as race and cultural background - and recognized the importance of passing this mindset on to future generations. He expressed hope for a new sense of destiny that will continue to grow and prosper.

The themed exhibits and presentations about Hearn's life and values attracted thousands of people. Diverse themes were at play - Hearn as free-spirited man, nomadic traveler (the other Odysseus), storyteller, sage teacher, preserver of cultural history, symbol of multiculturalism and tolerance, and even figure of myth and legend. The Hellenic and Japanese bonding further reinforced Lafcadio's quest for an open-minded world.

Tokyo Gravesite: The ashes of Lafcadio Hearn/Koizumi Yakumo, his wife Setsu, and son Kazuo now rest in the quiet Zoshigaya Cemetery, near Ikebukuro in Tokyo, Japan. His humble tombstone bears this inscription: "*Shogaku in den jo ge hachi un koji* - Like an Undefiled Flower Blooming like Eight Rising Clouds who dwells in Mansion of Right Enlightenment". The gravesite is nestled under trees and in good condition. Visitors often decorate the tombstone with flowers and other tokens of affection. Hearn's gravesite is a well-known spiritual pilgrimage place for Japanese to this day.

Tokyo - Koizumi Yakumo Memorial Park: In the heart of Japan's capital Tokyo, in Shinjuku at 7-30, Tomihisacho, there is a little-known treasure. The Koizumi Yakumo Commemorative Park is set in a walled flower garden framed with towering Greek columns. The centerpiece is a bust of the famed writer on a pedestal. English inscriptions of his quotes

are engraved in stone and Japanese honorifics by Dr. Miki Ishikawa. Takashi Onoha, Mayor of Shinjuku City. His dedication of the park monument says: "Lafcadio Hearn (in Japanese Yakumo Koizumi), a literary figure of the Meiji Era, was born on the Greek island of Lefkas, and died in Shinjuku. Owing to this relationship, bonds of friendship were established between the municipalities of Shinjuku and Lefkas in October, 1989. The Lafcadio Hearn Memorial Park features characteristic elements of Greece, Yakumo's country of birth. I hope that this park will remind visitors of Lafcadio Hearn, who through his literary works greatly contributed in introducing Japan to the world, and that the friendship between Shinjuku and Lafkas will further deepen in the future." This message is carved in Greek also. Another plaque titled "The

Place Where Yakumo Koizumi Died" was installed by the city of Shinjuku in 1986 and says, "…His great love for the nature and culture of our country and his efforts in introducing their true aspects is valued highly."

Yaizu Hearn Museum: Yaizu, in Shizuoka prefecture, Japan was Hearn's favorite vacation beach town. The Yaizu Hearn Museum was opened on June 27th (Lafcadio's birthday) in 2007. It is dedicated to the contemporary relevance of Hearn. "Yakumo literature shows us the power of a nation that we inherit from our ancestors and are now forgetting. We hope the museum will function to encourage people to look back on what we have lost…"

Omi, Japan: One summer Lafcadio went to Ishiyama in the province of Omi, where the ancient poetess Murasaki Shikibu composed her well-known novel *Genji-Monogatari*. He liked the place immensely and wrote to a friend, "Ishiyama is not of this world. It is paradise. Just to live here one summer, ---what happiness." The city erected a sculpture of a bench with seated Lafcadio, Setsu and a raven all looking out to sea.

Kumamoto, Japan: Hearn taught at Kumamoto's Fifth High School for three years until 1894. He first lived at 34 Tetorihoncho, but in the 1960s the Lafcadio Hearn's Former Residence Preservation Society relocated his home to 2-6 Ansei-machi, Chuo Ward and opened it the public.

Dublin Writers' Museum, Ireland: The Dublin Writers Museum featured famous poets and writers such as James Joyce, George Bernard Shaw, Seamus Heaney, William Butler Yeats, Patrick Pearse, and Lafcadio Hearn, all who exerted an unparalleled influence on the literary world.

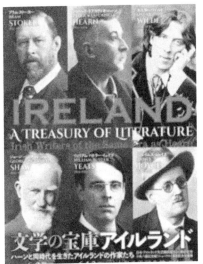

The museum opened in November 1991 at No 18, Parnell Square N, Rotunda, Dublin in an original 18th century townhouse. It is next door to the Irish Writers' Centre and offices of the Irish Writers' Union and other literary associations. It was established to promote interest, through its collections, displays and activities, in Irish literature as a whole and in the lives and works of individual Irish writers.

The Dublin Writers' Museum at one time featured a series of books from the Takis Efstathiou collection with additional materials provided by the Koizumi family and Paul Murray, author of *A Fantastic Journey: The Life and Literature of Lafcadio Hearn*. The Japanese Embassy supported the exhibit to mark sixty years of diplomatic relations between Ireland and Japan.

The Dublin Writers Museum closed in March 2020 due to Covid-19 lockdown. The facility never reopened and has been permanently closed over concerns that the landmark is 'too old-fashioned' and does not meet contemporary visitors' expectations in terms of presentation accessibility, and interpretation.

Select collections were transferred to the Museum of Literature Ireland (MoLI) in the historic UCD Naughton Joyce Centre, Newman House at 86 St. Stephen's Green in the heart of Dublin. MoLI is a partnership between University College of Dublin and the National Library of Ireland. Exhibits and immersive experiences are available Tuesday-Sunday 10-6. There is a bookshop filled with literature and local hand-made gifts and a café at the garden level.

The **Little Museum of Dublin** on St. Stephen's Green hosted a three-month long "Coming Home – The Open Mind of Lafcadio Hearn" series of lectures, cultural events, and music. The writer is at last being honored in his hometown. Exhibitions at the Little Museum drew a large delegation from Japan, including Professor Bon Koizumi, Hearn's great-grandson and his wife Shoko.

The celebration party was greeted by the President of Ireland to commemorate the Little Museum and the opening of Tramore Gardens. "The Dublin Haunting of Lafcadio Hearn" play by Paul Murray and "Maraudo Voices from the World Beyond" readings by Japanese actor Shiro Sani accompanied by Kyoji Yamamoto on electric guitar have been performed at the Little Museum. Dublin City University periodically gives talks about "Hearn and Japan". An exhibition featuring works by twenty leading artists from Ireland and twenty artists from Japan inspired by a story of their choice from Hearn's *Kwaidan* premiered at the SO Fine Arts Editions Gallery in the Powerscourt Townhouse Centre in Dublin. The art exhibits will be staged in six venues in Ireland and six venues in Japan through 2025. An Ireland-Japan Society meets regularly in Dublin.

In 1984 an International Association for the Study of Irish Literature (IASIL) was established in Japan. Their purpose was to encourage and act as a forum for Irish studies in Japan through teaching and research. They held a founding Conference at Waseda University, the last place Lafcadio Hearn taught, and have held a conference every year since. In 1984 IASIL Japan also began publication of a bulletin, "The Harp", whose title changed to "The Journal of Irish Studies" in 2000.

Lafcadio Hearn Japanese Gardens in Tramore, Ireland: The 2.5-acre Lafcadio Hearn Japanese Gardens in Tramore, County Waterford, Ireland, are set on a hillside overlooking the dramatic sweep of Tramore Bay. Young Patrick Lafcadio Hearn spent childhood summers with his guardian great-aunt Sarah Brenane in the seaside town of Tramore in the 1850 and 60s.

Tramore Japanese Gardens officially opened June, 2015. The grounds started as a walled Victorian garden by the villa of his aunt. Between 2017 and 2019 an American garden and a Greek garden were added, in addition to an authentic Japanese Tea House, a series of Japanese inspired landscapes, a Summer Pavilion viewing the lily pond, a Stream Garden leading to ponds and a waterfall and an extensive woodland area. The gardens attempt to tell the intriguing and unique story of Hearn's life journey from West to East, by reflecting the countries and cultures traversed by him during his varied life. Visitors are introduced to aspects of Japanese folklore that Hearn wrote about, including "The Cave of the Children's Ghosts" and the "The Legend of Urashima Taro".

A major source of inspiration for the Tramore Gardens was Hearn's essay "In a Japanese Garden", published in 1892. It details elements of his own garden in Matsue, Japan and interpretations of the ancient and revered Japanese philosophy of gardening. Ideas about a memorial garden were further awakened when Professor Bon Koizumi the great-grandson of Hearn, with his wife Shoko, visited Tramore to retrace the steps of his famous ancestor. Dublin-based photographer Motoko Fujita initiated events honoring Hearn, hosted the Koizumis, and worked on plans for Tramore Gardens in his name.

The Lafcadio Hearn Gardens combines the western idea of biography with the spiritual symbolism and traditional architecture of the East. To enhance visitors' experiences, Takis Efstathiou of Greece and New York gifted the Tramore Development Trust several books by Hearn, biographies, photographs, and first day envelopes of the 2004 special issue postage stamp by the Japanese government, to commemorate the 100th anniversary of his death. His most outstanding donation was a rare antiquarian book by Hearn, containing five Japanese Folk Stories, hand-painted on crepe paper, with magical, delicate color illustrations, to enhance the exhibit collections. Donations were made in Memory of Sarah Brenane, Lafcadio's great aunt.

The Lafcadio Hearn Tramore gardens are a Non-For-Profit Social/Community Enterprise open to the public open almost every day, except Christmas and St. Patrick's Day of course.

Saint Cuthbert's College and the University of Durham, England:

Patrick Lafcadio Hearn attended St. Cuthbert College at Ushaw in the Yorkshire Hills near Durham, England from September 1863 to October 1867. St. Cuthbert was rich in liturgical celebrations and produced a number of notable churchmen, including bishops and a Catholic cardinal. Although Hearn's family had given up hopes of the priesthood for Patrick, they believed that a rigorous religious school would at least protect him from bad influences. St. Cuthbert seminary was where Lafcadio suffered a schoolyard mishap and lost his left eye. Due to reduced family financial circumstances, he was withdrawn from St. Cuthbert College, later renamed Ushaw College.

Although independent, Ushaw College had a close working relationship with Durham University. The University of Durham in England was founded by an Act of Parliament in 1832, making it the third oldest

university in England, after Oxford and Cambridge. In 1990 Teikyo University (TUID) of Japan in Durham became an active branch. TUID plays a key role in embodying the university's three educational policies based on Lafcadio Hearn philosophies of teaching: Practical Learning, Developing International Perspectives, and Nurturing Open-Mindedness. Each April and September a group of about thirty Japanese students join the study-abroad program for language and cultural exchange. Having Teikyo University students is meaningful for both the Japanese students, for Durham University, as well as locals.

Durham University has three buildings for the Teikyo program. The main building is called "Lafcadio Hearn Cultural Centre", after the Greek-born Irish writer who spent his teen years studying at Ushaw College in Durham. TUID hosts various outreach activities such as an annual Japanese Festival and readings of Hearn's works.

"The Open Mind of Lafcadio Hearn" tours, sponsored by Greek (or Hellenic as he prefers to be called), New York-based art dealer Takis Efstatiou, were held in Durham, England, Ireland, Japan, Greece, and the USA. In 2022 Durham University held a conference about writer and translator Lafcadio Hearn/Koizumi Yakumo and his significance for conceptions of global and transnational cultural exchange, both in the late-nineteenth and early-twentieth centuries and in his legacy today. Topics explored all aspects of his multicultural heritage, life and writing, including, but not limited to his literary style, international reception and translations, engagement with science and medicine, disabilities, journalistic works, global aesthetics, lopsided fame, neo-Buddhism visions, ghost stories, worldliness and otherworldliness, and continuously growing legacies.

Cincinnati, Ohio: During his years as a journalist for the *Cincinnati Enquirer* and the *Cincinnati Commercial* newspapers (1869-1877), Patrick Lafcadio Hearn contributed hundreds of articles and developed a sensationalist, personal narrative style of reporting. He briefly served as a secretary to Thomas Vickers a director at the Public Library of Cincinnati and Hamilton County. Hearn wrote that he "wandered the streets and nourished his dreams in the public library."

Currently, the Cincinnati Public Library houses an exhibit of more than 600 volumes by and about Hearn in English, Japanese, and other European languages. The library also owns the only known complete set "Ye Giglampz: A Weekly Illustrated Journal Devoted to Art, Literature, and Satire", Hearn's short-lived journal in collaboration with artist Henry Farny. The Vickers' personal collection of Hearn materials was donated to the library in the 1950s. These special collections are available in the Joseph S. Stern, Jr. Cincinnati Room at the Downtown Main Library.

In September 2019 a "Coming Home – The Open Mind of Patrick Lafcadio Hearn" symposium was held by the Hearn Society International in celebration of Lafcadio Hearn's 150th anniversary of his arrival in the USA. The symposium featured five Hearn scholars and aficionados speaking about his works and his impact. Speakers at the gathering included Kinji Tanaka, chairman of the Japan Research Center of Greater Cincinnati; Kevin Grace, head of the Archives and Rare Books Library at the University of Cincinnati; Hidenobu Paul Tanaka; Dr. Mary Gallagher; Steve Kemme; and Dr. Noriko Tsunoda Reider, Japanese professor at Miami University. Bon Koizumi, Hearn's great-grandson and curator with his wife Shoko of the museum in Matsue, Japan, provided welcoming remarks and introductions. Several grants allowed lectures and entertainment to be free to full houses at the Huenefeld Tower Room at the Downtown Main Library and the Cincinnati Art Museum.

In their symposium article, *The Cincinnati Enquirer* newspaper, where Hearn began his writing career in the 1870s, referred to him as "perhaps Cincinnati's most famous writer you've never heard of." He left Cincinnati to live in New Orleans, Martinique, and then Japan where he became a cultural icon for his interpretations of Japanese culture and recording of their folklore.

Steve Kemme, a retired *Enquirer* reporter, president of the Lafcadio Hearn Society/USA (founded 1989), and author of *The Outsider*, a 2023 Hearn biography, said, "To me, it's one of the many examples of Hearn finding the truth in beauty in places where most people wouldn't even look."

New Orleans, Louisiana, Tulane University: Tulane University has hosted several exhibitions featuring first edition books and art works by Lafcadio Hearn, whose writings promoted the mystique of New Orleans to the nation. Hearn lived in the Crescent City for ten years before moving to Japan. The Tulane Special Collections Division of Howard-Tilton Memorial Library and the Research Collection, located in Jones Hall, Room 205, includes *La Cuisine Creole, A Collection of Culinary Recipes, Gombo Zhebes*, and *Two Years in the French West Indies*, unpublished photographs, original newspaper/magazine articles, correspondence, and numerous Hearn works.

In 2019, The Newcomb Art Museum of Tulane and the Japan Society of New Orleans, Tulane Asian Studies and Tulane English Department sponsored *Kwaidan – Call of Salvation Heard from the Depths of Fear*, based on Hearn's books. After an introduction by Bon Koizumi, Hearn's great-grandson from Matsue, Japan, actor Shiro Sano and guitarist Kyoji Yamamoto conducted a musical reading performance.

"The Open Mind of Lafcadio Hearn" world tour symposium in 2012 celebrated Hearn's cooperative mindset and tolerance with art from Greece and Japan and the Hearn Collection at Tulane. The book and art exposition, sponsored by Tulane's Asian Studies Program, Louisiana Research Collection, and Matsue City, Japan, offered an opportunity to view many of Hearn's personal items and gain insight into how he has influenced Japan and the world regarding contact and fusion of cultures.

Loyola University New Orleans: Loyola University New Orleans is a private, co-educational Jesuit university located at 6363 Charles Avenue, New Orleans. The Special Collections and Archives, J. Edgar & Louise S. Monroe Library, consists almost entirely of fifty-nine letters, mostly written between 1884 and 1905. Of the fifty-nine letters, forty-five are written by Hearn to Page Baker, his editor at the *Times Democrat* newspaper. Hearn wrote from various places - New Orleans, Grand Isle, New York, West Indies, and Japan. One is a draft of a letter Baker wrote to Elizabeth Bisland-Wetmore, an early biographer of Hearn, his thought about Hearn. The remaining correspondence and telegraphs are between Baker and *McClure's Magazine*. There are twenty-five envelopes addressed by Hearn to Baker, one contains a poem written in Hearn's hand. The Loyola University Collections has digitized Lafcadio Hearn's correspondences.

Additionally, the **Lafcadio Hearn House** in New Orleans was designated a Historic Landmark by the City Council of New Orleans in 2004, and in 2006 listed in the National Register of Historic Places. The metal plaque on the building reads: "This transitional Greek Revival-Italianate double townhouse of ca. 1860 was the residence of the Greek Anglo-Irish writer/journalist Lafcadio Hearn (1850-1904), known in Japan as Koizumi Yakumo. While living here, between 1882 and 1887, Hearn wrote *Chita, A Memory of Last Island* and published *La Cuisine Creole* and *Gombo Zhebes*."

New York, USA: "The Open Mind of Lafcadio Hearn" (2011) was presented in the Nippon Gallery at the Nippon Club. The book and art exposition displayed twenty-five pieces from Matsue, Japan, two pieces from the American College of Greece, two pieces of Hearn's cherished personal items from the Lafcadio Hearn Memorial Museum Matsue, and over twenty bound first editions of Hearn books (Efstathiou Family Collection… recent editions obtained from the private library of Jenkin

Lloyd Jones, whose sister was Frank Lloyd Wright's mother and Hearn books from the private collection of President and Mrs. Ronald Reagan.). The idea of the open mind tribute symposiums originated from Takis Efstathiou, a Greek-American art dealer who has long-term friendships with the Koizumi family and other descendants of Lafcadio. He organizes events around the globe to celebrate international relations and peace. The open-mindedness concept comes from Lafcadio's multi-cultural origins and cross-cultural experiences that gave him values, not limited by religion or Western-centric thinking.

Metropolitan Museum and Morgan Library & Museum, New York:

Manhattan museums, Metropolitan Museum at 1000 Fifth Avenue, Central Park, and the Morgan Library & Museum at 225 Madison Avenue feature collections of Lafcadio Hearn's rare volumes. These include children's fairy tale books published by Hasewawa Takejiro of Tokyo (1885), *Chita, Two Years in the West Indies, Sketches of New Orleans,* Hearn autographed letters (notably his 'Don't disgust me' rejection letter to a Cincinnati socialite), and archival items. Takis Efstathiou who has been collecting Lafcadio Hearn books and objects for more than 30 years has made significant donations to the Met Museum and the Morgan Library & Museum.

The New York Public Library:
New York Public Library is located at Fifth Avenue and 42nd Street, New York City. The Henry W. and Albert A Berg Collection of English and American Literature contains a collection of papers, manuscripts, and correspondence by and about Lafcadio Hearn dating from 1896 to 1904. The manuscripts include stories,

translations, a reading list, and fragments of stories. The bulk of the collection consists of correspondence by Hearn dating from 1883 to 1904 to Ellwood Hendrick, William O'Connor, Elizabeth Bisland-Wetmore, and literary agent T. Fisher Unwin. Other letters are relating to the author between H.M. Alden, G.M. Gould, Albert Mordell and others.

Columbia University: Columbia University in the City of New York is a private Ivy League research university. Their Rare Book and Manuscript Library Repository contains a group of fifteen letters from Hearn to Basil Hall Chamberlain (1850-1935), professor of Japanese and Philology at the Imperial University in Tokyo and one of Hearn's closest Western friends in Japan. The letters cover a wide range of topics including Hearn's methods of work and use of language; his opinion of his own writing; his discontent as a teacher at the government college at Kumamoto; his views on philosophy, religion, and music; Japanese customs, mythology, art, and language; the Oriental character vs. the Occidental; and opinions of Paul Boerget and Lewis Carroll. The letters are bound in six Japanese bindings of wrappers and cloth. To gain access to the collection, one must make an appointment in advance through the Special Collections Research Account.

Harvard University, Cambridge, Massachusetts: The Houghton Library, Harvard College's principal repository for rare books and manuscripts, and archives has a collection, chiefly letters of the writer Hearn from 1885-1893, several written to H. Adzukizawa. It also includes two signed photographs, notes, a manuscript, and various signed envelopes.

University of Virginia: The Albert and Shirley Small Collections Library at the University of Virginia holds one of the finest Hearn collections ever assembled, including nearly 300 letters, 25 groups of manuscripts, 30 notebooks, and innumerable periodical appearances and translations, all donated by avid book collector Clifton Waller Barrett as a part of a comprehensive collection of American literature. The pieces were on display in "Lafcadio Hearn: Glimpses of Invisible Worlds", showcasing Hearn's life and the invisible worlds that inspired him. One of the exhibits features *Kwaidan: Stories and Studies of Strange Things* original manuscript and unpublished watercolor illustrations by Hearn's son Kazuo Koizumi.

Samford University Library: Samford University is a private Baptist university in Homewood, Alabama, a suburb of Birmingham. A collection of Hearn items is found in Samford's Library Special Collection.

Ohio University, Athens, Ohio: The Ohio University Rare Book Collection contains more than 140 volumes by Lafcadio Hearn in their Robert E. and Jean R. Mahn Center for Archives and Special Collections.

West Virginia University Library: Among the many books by Lafcadio Hearn in the West Virginia University Rare Books Collection, there are three notable books he wrote on Japan: *Glimpses of Unfamiliar Japan, Kwaidan, and Shadowings*.

Harry Ransom Center, The University of Texas at Austin: At the University of Texas in Austin there is a collection dated from 1879 which contains manuscripts and letters written by Lafcadio Hearn. The bulk of the manuscripts concern Japan, including two notebooks recording Hearn's thoughts impressions readings and understanding of Japan. The materials are in both English and Japanese.

Iowa State University-Parks Library: The Iowa State University Special Collections and University Archives houses a five-volume set of *Japanese Fairy Tales* written in English by Lafcadio Hearn. The collection was hand-printed on crepe paper and bound with silk ties in Tokyo by T. Hasegawa Publishers c. 1930s. Titles in the set included *The Boy Who Drew Cats; The Fountain of Youth; The Goblin Spider; The Old Woman Who Lost Her Dumplings;* and *Chin Chin Kobakama.*

Martinique, West Indies: Lafcadio Hearn spent two years (1887-1889) in Martinique, West Indies. He acted as a correspondent for *Harper's* and produced two books, *Youma, The Story of a West Indian Slave* and *Two Years in the French West Indies*, both published in 1890. His quasi-ethnography of Martinique was a valuable contribution to Caribbean folklore studies. In Port-de- France the city has designated a treed corner lot as the Lafcadio Hearn Park. It is the home to an outdoor fresh foods market that he would have enjoyed. There is also a parking garage at 1505 Rue du pave named Lafcadio Hearn in Port-de-France close to the bus station Gare Nardal and the church Christ-Roi.

CHAPTER 46

TAKIS EFSTATHIOU: A name that continuously appears in association with Lafcadio Hearn/Koizumi Yakumo is Takis Efstathiou, an international fine art advisor based in Athens and New York City. Generous contributions from his vast private collection of Hearn rare books and items have been donated to: The Lafcadio Hearn Memorial Museum Matsue, Japan; American College of Greece, Athens; Corfu Museum of Asian Art; Lafcadio Hearn Historical Center, Lafkada Greece; Metropolitan Museum Manhattan; Morgan Library and Museum Manhattan; Lafcadio Hearn Japanese Gardens Tramore, Ireland; Irish Writers' Museum Dublin; Japanese Embassy, Athens; and more. He was the originator and sponsor of the "Open Mind of Lafcadio Hearn" worldwide series of symposiums. Efstathiou has done his utmost to repatriate the Greek writer to places around the world where he lived and to create cultural spaces and enrich museums with works related to Hearn. Takis' story is an important element in Lafcadio's continuing legacy and impact.

In the spring of 2023, the Ministry of Foreign Affairs announced that Takis Efstathiou would receive the Badge of the Empire of Japan with the Medal of the Order of the Rising Sun, Silver Rays from the Emperor of Japan. On July 5, 2023, Japan's Ambassador Yasunori Nakayama presented Efstathiou with his certificate and medal in recognition of his many years of service to broadening the understanding of Japanese culture in Greece and strengthening the bilateral relationships of friendship. The distinguished award worthily reflects Efstathiou's long-standing contributions to the development of relations between the people and cultures of Greece and Japan.

The basis for this great honor from Japan arose from Takis Efstathiou's decades of research and collecting Lafcadio Hearn books and artifacts, his worldwide donations of hundreds of items to establish and promote exhibits, museums, and libraries, and the originator and producer of "Open Mind of Lafcadio Hearn" lectures and symposiums in six countries. He serves as the International Cultural Coordinator for Hearn Society and several organizations.

Takis' own rags to riches story often parallels that of Lafcadio's wandering the world in search of beauty and truths. Young Takis Efstathiou arrived in New York by ship in 1963 with his family, refugees from Greece. Starting with nothing and being self-educated, he engaged in various art-related fields like theater, painting, photography, and assisting artist Nikos Icaris. Art dealer Alexander Iolas recognized rare talent and encouraged him to enter the art market, a field in which Efstathiou excelled. He became a renown international fine art advisor, dealer, collector, and benefactor.

Takis Efstathiou (b. 1944) has been associated with the largest public and private collections in the world's art capitals and received acknowledgement in many museum and galleries' exhibition catalogs. He successively operated Tchernov Gallery in Manhattan next to Carnegie Hall; Ericson Gallery on Madison Avenue: and PTE Fine Arts. Additionally, he served as advisor to the Hans Hinterreiter Foundation in Zurich and managing de-accession of artworks for the Guggeheim Foundation. At various times during his career, he supported The Metropolitan Museum of Art, Brooklyn Museum, Herbert Johnson Museum, Brooklyn Museum, and other major American Institutions with significant gifts and collections.

While collaborating on an exhibit in Tokyo, Japan, Greek abstract painter Theo Stamos introduced Efstathiou to the literary works of Lafcadio Hearn aka Koizumi Yakumo, the Greek-born writer who had become a legend/national poet in Japan. Since then, for over thirty years Takis

Efstathiou collected books and objects. His library consists of over a thousand books by and about Hearn. Significant rare and important items have been gifted to collections, libraries, and museums internationally.

It was through Efstathiou's concept and donations that the Lafcadio Hearn Historical Center in Lefkada, the first museum in Europe for Hearn, was established in 1996. The Takis Efstathiou Wing is filled with rare books, early editions, serigraphs, posters, sculptures, photographs, art, and Japanese collectibles. He brought together the municipalities of Kumamoto, Matsue, Shinjuku, Yaizu, Toyama University, Hearn decedents Bon and Shoko Koizumi, and others from Japan and Greece to contribute to the opening of the Historical Center in the Cultural Center of Lafkada. Efstathiou was awarded Honorary citizenship in Lafkada. The Voice of Greece program 'The Land of My Soul' applauded him as "the man who brought Lafcadio Hearn back home to his birthplace".

In 1996 Efstathiou visited the Koizumi family in Matsue, Japan and invited great-grandson Bon and his wife Shoko to Hellas-Greece. It was the beginning of a productive partnership to reintroduce the world to Lafcadio Hearn. Together they refurbished the museum in Matsue with generous donations of Efstathiou's extensive rare books and art collection. He escorted the Koizumis to Greece, Ireland, France and England, New York, Cincinnati, New Orleans, and around Japan to retrace the extraordinary lifetime journey of Lafcadio.

Efstathiou's inspirational, original idea of "The Open Mind of Lafcadio Hearn" first evolved into a "Tribute to Lafcadio Hearn" exhibition by the Cultural Affairs Office at the American College of Greece in October 2009. In addition to Efstathiou's and others' generously given Japanese artworks, rare books, and artifacts to the ACG Art Collection, through Efstathiou's efforts sculptor Masaaki Noda was commissioned for his monumental metal work in honor of Hearn's open mind as a symbol of cultural diversity.

Later an International Symposium, entitled "The Open Mind of Lafcadio Hearn – His Spirit from the West to the East", took place July 5th and 6th, 2014 in Lafkada. This celebrated the 110th anniversary of his death and friendship between Greece and Japan. Presenters, government officials, organizations, and artists from around the world gathered to revisit and promote Hearn's literary contributions and legacy.

Over the years, "Coming Home-The Open Mind of Lafcadio Hearn" literary tourism traveling exhibitions were produced by the Hearn Society, with Efstathiou and Bon & Shoko Koizumi as Cultural Coordinators, at the

Nippon Club in New York, Cincinnati, Tulane University-New Orleans, USA and Matsue Castle, Japan.

Efstathiou continues to donate his promotional talents, money, and substantial gifts of rare Hearn-related items to numerous universities, libraries, and museums. Takis Efstathiou allowed the author of *Lafcadio's Legacy* access to his vast library collection, resources, personal knowledge, and collaborated on this historical novel about Koizumi Yakumo's years in Japan and his ongoing impact and legacy.

Anyone can see why Japan's Minister of Foreign Affairs chose to confer the Order of the Rising sun, Silver Rays to Takis Efstathiou for his valuable contributions to the introduction of Japanese culture in Greece and the promotion of mutual understanding between Japan and Greece. Takis Efstathiou's biography is to be published in 2024.

CHAPTER 47

KOIZUMI CLAN FAMILY TREE - ACHIEVEMENTS

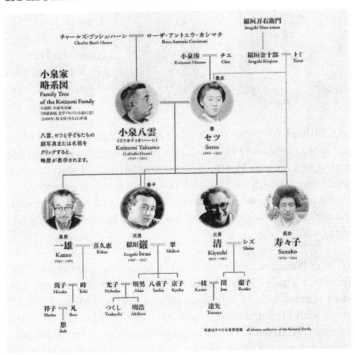

Like Koizumi Yakumo/Lafcadio Hearn, several of his immediate family members were relatively well known and achieved much with their lives. Yakumo's wife Setsu Koizumi (1868-1932) published her 88 pages of memoirs in *Reminiscences of Lafcadio Hearn* (1918, Houghton Mifflin Co.) with the assistance of writer Yone Noguchi (1875-1947), Frontispiece by Shoshu

Saito, and sketches by Genjiro Kataoka and Lafcadio Hearn. Setsu's stories of her young life in a deposed, impoverished samurai family before meeting Hearn and later their almost fourteen years of married life together. Setsu wrote simple and affectionate recollections of her years with Hearn. The sometimes tragic, sometimes humorous insights into herself, Hearn, their family, and his writings about Old Japan fill the pages, along with profuse illustrations, rare black and white photographs, and letters from her private collection.

Hayato Tokugawa, who edited, illustrated, and annotated *Reminiscences of Lafcadio Hearn*, was a San Francisco police officer and instructor of Japanese martial arts turned journalist and author. He was an avid student of Japanese art andl culture who lived part time in Japan. Setsu's book was translated from the Japanese by Paul Kiyoshi Hisada and Fredrick Johnson.

Elizabeth Bisland Wetmore wrote *The Life and Letters of Lafcadio Hearn (1906)*. *Lafcadio in Japan* (1911) by Yone Noguchi featured his appreciation and defense of Lafcadio Hearn, stories from Setsu, and materials regarding his lectures and farewell address at Tokyo University. It contained illustrated end papers and was printed on one side of double leaves in Japanese style. Since his death many books have been written about his life and contributions.

In 1997, Yoji Hasegawa wrote *A Walk in Kumamoto: The Life and Times of Setsu Koizumi, Lafcadio Hearn's Japanese Wife*. It covers Setsu's early life and the end of samurai culture following Japan's decision to modernize, her first encounters with Hearn, marriage, and her children's later lives. It also includes a new translation of her memoir *Reminiscences*. In Monique Truong's novel *Sweetest Fruits*, she focuses on the women in Hearn's life: his mother Rosa Cassimati Hearn; Alethea Foley, an African American cook/first annulled wife; and especially Setsu Koizumi, his Japanese wife and mother of his four children.

Everyone agrees that Setsu Koizumi was a vital resource and inspiration for Hearn. She maintained his peaceful home base, provided resources and enactments of the ancient stories.

Setsu bore four children with Lafcadio: Kazuo, Iwao, Kiyoshi, and Suzuko who continued in their father's footsteps.

Leopold Kazuo Koizumi (November 1, 1893-1965), was born while Hearn was teaching in Kumamoto, Kyushu. Kazuo's Japanese name means 'first son' or 'harmonious man'. His father gave him the nickname Kajio. Lafcadio Hearn's motivation for taking Setsu's family name of Koizumi was connected to the preservation of this first son's Japanese nationality and inheritance rights. Kazuo was only ten years old when his father Lafcadio died in 1904.

Kazuo majored in English literature at Waseda University and after graduation earned his living by editing his father's letters and writing books about his reminiscences of life with Hearn. Kazuo wrote *Father and I: Memories of Lafcadio Hearn* (1893, Houghton Mifflin Co.) and *Father Koizumi Yakumo* (1950, Koyama Shoten) and *Re-Echo*, a volume of mystic thoughts and memories of Lafcadio Hearn on Japan, edited by Nancy Jane Fellers. It was illustrated with photographs and original pen and watercolor sketches by Lafcadio.

Five hundred limited and numbered editions of *Japanese Goblin Poetry: Rendered into English by Lafcadio Hearn and Illustrated*, was compiled by Kazuo as a special tribute to his father's 30th death anniversary and published in 1934 in Tokyo. The stories were collected from Hearn's own draft notebook containing Japanese comic poems about goblins and monsters. The text is in both Hearns published English translations of "Goblin

Poetry", and the original Japanese text of the *Kyoka hyaku monogatari*. Hearn's grandson wrote the book title slip and the design of the cover cloth was inspired by Hearn's favorite bedcover.

All of Kazuo's works offer insights to a daily home life full of both discipline and human warmth, and peeks into Hearn's writing habits. Kazuo had a tall desk like his father and they took walks and long swims together. The first son being rather sensitive and appearing more European than Japanese, Kazuo was homeschooled by Lafcadio in English and other subjects and in Japanese by his mother. He also had private tutors such as writer Leonie Gilmour Noguchi, who was the mother of sculptor Isamu Noguchi, and after Hearn's death, by a former student Aizu Yaichi, to make sure his sons did not stray from their true course.

Kazuo married Kikue and had one child Toki who married Hisako and had a son, Bon Koizumi. Bon married Shoko and fathered Soh.

Second son, **Iwao** was born with Hearn's Japanese name Koizumi in 1897. He was adopted into the Inagaki family in 1901. His mother Setsu had been married into the Inagaki clan in her youth. Although the marriage was annulled, she stayed close to the family. When Katsumo and Haruyo Inagaki had no children, they looked for a male successor. Setsu and Lafcadio allowed their second son to take on the Inagaki family name. This practice was common among Japanese families when there are no male heirs, the woman's family name has high status, or the man's name has low status or is tainted by scandal.

Iwao entered Kyoto Imperial University in 1920 and majored in engineering, but later transferred to the English literature department. He wrote a thesis titled "Hidden Meanings in Lord Dunsany's Five Plays" and graduated in 1927. He had a twelve-year career teaching English at Momoyama Junior High School in Fushimi Ward in Kyoto. It is estimated that approximately 2000 students studied English from him using textbooks like Charles Dicken's *David Copperfield* and *Aesopica*.

Iwao married Midori and had three children – Akio, Yaeko and Kyoko. Akio married Nobuko and gave birth to Tsukushi and Akihiro.

On an interesting personal note, Iwao had a phobia about frogs and a great enthusiasm for baseball. He went to Tokyo's Mejii Jingu Stadium in 1931 to watch Lou Gehrig and Lefty Grove play in a game between the Japanese team and the U.S. counterpart.

Often reporters and literary scholar admirers of his father would bagger Iwao at his school or at home for information about Lafcadio Hearn. He never mentioned to his students that he was descended from the legendary man of letters. Yet in 1934, he did a radio interview "Chichi Herun wo Kataru", telling personal stories of home life with the renown writer.

From 1926 to 1927, Iwao Inagaki helped complete a translation of his father's works for *Koizumi Yakumo Zenshu - Collected Works of Koizumi Yakumo*. In 1928 he published *Lectures on Shakespeare* and edited records of Lafcadio's classroom lectures.

In September 1934 the violent Muroto typhoon battered many parts of Japan, including Kyoto, claiming over 3000 lives. He and his students at Momoyama Junior High School survived the life-or-death crisis without death or injury. On the other hand, soon after he was stricken with cancer and had successful surgery. In his fortieth year he suffered a relapse. He was admitted to Keio University Hospital in Tokyo, where on August 15, 1937 he died. His colleagues and students mourned his early death and continued to honor his achievements and good reputation for a great many years.

Third-born son, **Kiyoshi Koizumi** (1899-1962), had the English first name Paul. Kiyoshi, like his father, used his middle name. He was a poet and artist. Kiyoshi was educated at Waseda Junior High School. He went to art school and became an artist of renown. His works hang in the Matsue Lafcadio Hearn Museum. He married Hiizu and had two children, Jun and Ranko. Jun married Kazue and had Tatsuya.

Setsu and Lafcadio's daughter, **Suzuko Koizumi** (1903-1944) was sickly and never married. Suzuko was just one year old when Hearn died.

Many of Lafcadio's family members and descendants were well known writers, artists, educators, and achieved much with their lives.

Bon and Shoko Koizumi: Bon Koizumi is the son of Toki Koizumi, grandson of Kazuo Koizumi, and great-grandson of Yakumo Koizumi aka Lafcadio Hearn. Bon and his wife Shoko have taken up the baton of preserving and promoting the legacy of Lafcadio Hearn around the world. They serve as cultural ambassadors and messengers of hope and open-minded thinking.

Bon studied Folklore at Seijo University and graduate school. He and Shoko moved from Tokyo to Matsue in 1987. He is a professor at the University of Shimane Junior College. Bon serves as Director at the Lafcadio Hearn Memorial Museum, and Honorary Director of the Yaizu Lafcadio Hearn Museum. He researches and writes about Japanese folklore and the supernatural, which is used in cultural events and tourism. He has published works including *Minzoku Gakusha---Koizumi Yakumo* (Kobunsho 1995) and *Kwaidan yondaiki---Yakumo no itazura* (Kodansho, 1996).

Bon has been a keynote speaker at "The Open Mind of Lafcadio Hearn" symposiums in Lafkada, Greece; New York City; New Orleans; Dublin and Tramore, Ireland; and throughout Japan. In July 2017, he and Shoko were the recipients of the Foreign Minister's Commendation for outstanding contribution to the cultural exchange and mutual understanding between Japan and Ireland. Recently Bon participated in Lafcadio Hearn reading performances along with the actor Shiro Sano and musician Kyoji Yamamoto. Telling stories based on Koizumi Yakumo's themes plus mystic guitar music has successfully elevated the recitation to the realm of art. Shoko Koizumi is a Hearn Memorial Museum Founder and Director, photographer, and coordinator of Lafcadio Hearn events around the world. She not only publicizes Bon's great-grandfather, but has introduced Greek and Irish culture to Japan.

Thanks to her efforts, Matuse City, where Lafcadio Hearn used to live, has a strong relationship with Dublin and often exchanges reciprocal visits. She is a driving force behind the renewed interest in Hearn in the present day as a multi-faceted figure relevant to the needs of contemporary society.

Soh, the son of Shoko and Bon Koizumi is an artist following in the footsteps of his great-great-grandfather.

CHAPTER 48

HEARN LITERATURE AND BIBLIOGRAPHY

The life of a literary man like Lafcadio Hearn is of interest and value to the world because of the literature he has created. Lafcadio was one of the nineteenth century's best-known writers. In America his name was celebrated alongside those of Mark Twain and Robert Lewis Stevenson. But he left that fame all behind in 1890 and moved to Japan, where he is considered a national treasure for his classic reports on the culture and for saving Japanese folklore and ghost stories. American critic, poet, essayist, and scientist Edmund C. Stedman (1833-1903) claimed that "Hearn will in time be as much of a romantic personality and tradition as Poe now is."

BIBLIOGRAPHY of major works Hearn created or compiled for publication:

- *One of Cleopatra's Nights and Other Fantastic Romances*, by Theophile Gautier; Lafcadio Hearn, translator. New York: R. Worthington, 1882.
- *Stray Leaves from Strange Literature*. Boston; J.R. Osgood and Co. 1884.
- *La Cuisine Creole: A Collection of Culinary Recipes*. New York: Will H. Coleman, 1885.
- *Gombo Zhebes: A Little Dictionary of Creole Proverbs, Selected from Six Creole Dialects*. New York: W.H. Coleman, 1885.

- *Historical Sketch Book and Guide to New Orleans.* (edited and compiled by several leading writers of the New Orleans press). New York: Will H. Coleman, 1885.
- *Some Chinese Ghosts.* Boston: Roberts Brothers, 1887.
- *Chita: A Memory of Last Island.* New York: Harper & Brothers, 1889.
- *The Crime of Sylvestre Bonnard.* (by Anatole France; Lafcadio Hearn, translator). New York: Harper & Brothers, 1890.
- *Two Years in the French West Indies.* New York: Harpers & Brothers, 1890.
- *Youma: The Story of a West Indian Slave.* New York: Harper & Brothers, 1890.
- *Glimpses of Unfamiliar Japan* (two volumes). Boston: Houghton Mifflin Co., 1894.
- *Out of the East: Reveries and Studies in the New Japan.* Boston: Houghton Mifflin Co., 1895.
- *Kokoro: Hints and Echoes of Japanese Inner Life.* Boston: Houghton Mifflin Co., 1895.
- *Gleanings in Buddha-Fields: Studies of Hand and Soul in the Far East.* Boston: Houghton Mifflin Co., 1897.
- *Exotics and Retrospectives.* Boston: Little, Brown and Co., 1898.
- *Japanese Fairy Tales* (five volumes). Tokyo. T. Hasegawa, 1898-1903.
- *In Ghostly Japan.* Boston: Little, Brown and Co., 1899.
- *Shadowings.* Boston: Little, Brown and Co., 1900.
- *A Japanese Miscellany.* Boston: Little, Brown and Co., 1901.
- *Kotto: Being Japanese Curios, With Sundry Cobwebs.* New York: The Macmillan Co., 1902.
- *Kwaidan: Stories and Studies of Strange Things.* New York: The Macmillan Co., 1904.
- *Japan: An Attempt at Interpretation.* New York: The Macmillan Co., 1904.

BIBLIOGRAPHY of magazine articles and papers published by Lafcadio Hearn in chronological order. (If later published in book form, the title of the book is given.)

- "The Scenes of Cable's Romances", *The Century Magazine*, November 1883, vol 27 (N.S. Vol 5), p. 40.
- "Quaint New Orleans and its Inhabitants", *Harper's Weekly*, December 6, 1884, vol. 28, p. 812.

- "New Orleans Exposition", *Harper's Weekly*, January 3, 1885, vol. 29, p. 14.
- "The Creole Patois", *Harper's Weekly*, January 10, 1885, vol. 29, p. 27.
- "The Creole Patois", *Harper's Weekly*, January 17, 1885, vol. 29, p. 43.
- "New Orleans Exposition", *Harper's Weekly*, January 31, 1885, vol. 29 p. 71.
- "The East at New Orleans", *Harper's Weekly*, March 7, 1885, vol. 29, p. 155.
- "Mexico at New Orleans", *Harper's Weekly*, March 14, 1885, vol. 29, p. 167.
- "The New Orleans Exposition. Some Oriental Curiosities", *Harper's Bazaar*, March 28, 1885, vol. 18, p. 201.
- "The New Orleans Exposition. Notes of a Curiosity Hunter.", *Harper's Bazaar*, April 4, 1885, vol. 18, p. 218.
- "The Government Exhibit at New Orleans", *Harper's Weekly*, April 11, 1885, vol. 29, p. 234.
- "The Legend of Tchi-Nui. A Chinese Story of Filial Piety", *Harper's Bazaar*, October 31, 1885, vol 18, p. 703. *Some Chinese Ghosts* (1887).
- "The Last of the Voudoos", *Harper's Weekly*, November 7, 1885, vol. 29, p. 726.
- "New Orleans Superstitions", *Harper's Weekly*, December 25, 1886, vol. 30, p. 843.
- "Rabyah's Last Ride. A Tradition of Pre-Islamic Arabia", *Harper's Bazaar*, April 2, 1887, vol. 20, p. 239.
- "Chita", *Harper's Monthly*, April 1888, vol. 76, p. 733. *Chita* (1890).
- "A Midsummer Trip to the West Indies", *Harper's Monthly*, July-September, 1888, vol 77, pp. 209, 327, 614. *Two Years in the French West Indies* (1890).
- "La Verette and the Carnival in St. Pierre, Martinique", *Harper's Monthly*, October, 1888, vol 77, p. 737. *Two Years in the French West Indies* (1890).
- "Les Porteuses", *Harper's Monthly*, July, 1889, vol. 79, p. 299. *Two Years in the French West Indies* (1890).
- "At Grand Anse", *Harper's Monthly*, November, 1889, vol. 79, p. 844. *Two Years in the French West Indies* (1890).
- "A Ghost", *Harper's Monthly*, December, 1889, vol. 80, p. 116.

- "Youma", *Harper's Monthly*, January-February, 1890, vol. 80, pp. 218, 408. *Youma* (1890).
- "Karma", *Lippincott's Magazine*, May, 1890, vol. 45, p. 667.
- "A Study of Half-Breed Races in the West Indies", *The Cosmopolitan* June, 1890, vol. 9, p. 167.
- "West Indian Society of Many Colourings", *The Cosmopolitan*, July, 1890, vol. 9, p. 337.
- "A Winter Journey to Japan", *Harper's Monthly*, November, 1890, vol. 81, p. 860.
- "At the Market of the Dead", *Atlantic Monthly*, September, 1891, vol. 68, p. 382. *Glimpses of Unfamiliar Japan* (1894).
- "The Chief City of the Province of the gods", *Atlantic Monthly*, November, 1891, vol. 68, p. 621. *Glimpses of Unfamiliar Japan* (1894).
- "The Most Ancient Shrine in Japan", *Atlantic Monthly*, December, 1891, vol. 68, p. 780. *Glimpses of Unfamiliar Japan* (1894).
- "In a Japanese Garden", *Atlantic Monthly*, July, 1892, vol. 70, p. 14. *Glimpses of Unfamiliar Japan* (1894).
- "Of a Dancing Girl", *Atlantic Monthly*, March, 1983, vol 71, p. 332. *Glimpses of Unfamiliar Japan* (1894).
- "The Japanese Smile", <u>Atlantic Monthly</u>, May, 1893, vol. 71, p. 634. *Glimpses of Unfamiliar Japan* (1894).
- "Of the Eternal Feminine", Atlantic Monthly, December, 1893, vol 72, p. 761. *Out of the East* (1895).
- "The Red Bridal", *Atlantic Monthly*, July, 1894, vol. 74, p. 74. *Out of the East* (1895).
- "At Hakata", *Atlantic Monthly*, October, 1894, vol. 74, p. 510. *Out of the East* (1895).
- "From My Japanese Diary", *Atlantic Monthly*, November, 1894, vol. 74, p. 609.
- "A Wish Fulfilled", *Atlantic Monthly*, January, 1895, vol. 75, p. 90. *Out of the East* (1895).
- "In the Twilight of the Gods", *Atlantic Monthly*, June, 1895, vol. 75, p. 791. *Kokoro* (1896).
- "The Genius of Japanese Civilization", *Atlantic Monthly*, October, 1895, vol. 76, p. 449. *Kokoro* (1896).
- "After the War", *Atlantic Monthly*, November, 1895, vol, 76, p. 599. *Kokoro* (1896).
- "Notes from a Traveling Diary", *Atlantic Monthly*, December, 1895, vol. 76, p. 815. *Kokoro* (1896).

- "China and the Western World", *Atlantic Monthly*, April, 1896, vol. 77, p. 450.
- "A Trip to Kyoto", *Atlantic Monthly*, May, 1896, vol. 77, p. 613. *Gleanings in Buddha-Fields* (1897).
- "About Faces in Japanese Art", *Atlantic Monthly*, August, 1896, vol. 78, p. 219. *Gleanings in Buddha-Fields* (1897).
- "Out of the Street: Japanee Folk-Songs", *Atlantic Monthly*, September, 1896, vol. 78, p. 3437. *Gleanings in Buddha-Fields* (1897).
- "Dust", *Atlantic Monthly*, November, 1896, vol. 78, p. 642. *Gleanings in Buddha-Fields* (1897).
- "A Living God", *Atlantic Monthly*, December, 1896, vol. 78, p. 833. *Gleanings in Buddha-Fields* (1897).
- "Notes of a Trip to Izumo", *Atlantic Monthly*, May, 1897, vol. 79, p. 678.
- "The Story of Mimi-Nashi-Hoichi", *Atlantic Monthly*, August, 1903, vol. 92, p. 237. *Kwaidan* (1904).
- "The Dream of Akinosuke", *Atlantic Monthly*, March, 1904, vol. 93, p. 340. *Kwaidan* (1904).
- "A Letter from Japan", *Atlantic Monthly*, November, 1904, vol 94, p. 625. *The Romance of the Milky Way* (1905).
- "The Story of Ito Norisuke", *Atlantic Monthly*, January, 1905, vol. 95, p. 98. *The Romance of the Milky Way* (1905).
- "Stranger than Fiction", *Atlantic Monthly*, April, 1905, vol 95, p. 494. *The Romance of the Milky Way* (1905).
- "The Romance of the Milky Way", *Atlantic Monthly*, August, 1905, vol. 96, p. 238. *The Romance of the Milky Way* (1905).
- "Ultimate Questions", *Atlantic Monthly*, September, 1905, vol. 96, p. 391. *The Romance of the Milky Way* (1905).
- "Two Memories of a Childhood", *Atlantic Monthly*, October, 1906, vol. 98, p. 445.

ABOUT THE AUTHOR

After careers in both archaeology and law, Linda Lindholm began writing historical fiction and biographies. In-depth research for *Lafcadio's Legacy* took her around the world to seek out interesting facts & photographs, consult Lafcadio's family and other authorities, and visit locations relative to Lafcadio Hearn aka Koizumi Yakumo's history in Japan, and realize his international impact. Linda divides her time between book-lined homes in Mexico and the USA.

Acknowledgments

With heartfelt appreciation to:

Max Marbles, Takis Efstathiou, Marianne Kehoe, Andrew Brown, Kathleen Werner, Margie Alexy, and Beckam's Bookshop NOLA

Made in the USA
Middletown, DE
03 February 2024

48471349R00195